BUNTER SAHIB

BUNTER SAHIB

DANIEL GREEN

HODDER AND STOUGHTON
LONDON SYDNEY AUCKLAND TORONTO

British Library Cataloguing in Publication Data
Green, Daniel
    Bunter sahib.
    I. Title
    823'.914[F]   PR6057.R33/

ISBN 0 340 36429 7

Hodder and Stoughton Editorial Office: 47 Bedford Square, London WC1B 3DP.

This work is dedicated *sans permission*
but with all due apologies to

William Wilberforce, Lord Byron, the Grand Old Duke of York,
Charles Lamb, Omar Khayyam, Harriette Wilson, Mary Anne
Clarke, Bishop Heber

and to
the late Frank Richards

CONTENTS

8   Contents

PROLOGUE

I owe the public an explanation of how this extract from my youthful writings comes to be published. I recently received an ill-written letter from a certain great-grandson of mine who I didn't even know existed, although he is my namesake and wrote from the same boarding school as I had attended full seventy-five years earlier.

It was, of course, a begging letter, but a different sort of begging letter from the majority I receive and it encouraged me to believe that one at least of my many descendants has inherited something of my spirit and enterprise. The boy, who cannot be much more than ten, had struck a bargain with the woman who runs the school tuck-shop—an establishment unheard of in my day—by which he would purchase all her stale stock at half-price. All he lacked was the capital with which to embark on his venture. That was why he wrote asking whether I could advance him the sum of ten shillings, or a sovereign if I was feeling flush. Either sum would be sufficient to launch him into that second-hand, carry-away food business in which I have made my own fortune.

I did not, of course, send him any money. That would have been to stifle enterprise and make business too easy. But many years ago in India, during a period of hardship and enforced idleness, I wrote something about my own childhood experiences at that self-same school. Thinking it might be instructive, I recovered the piece from among my papers and sent it to him by reply.

Then the worst happened. The wretched boy, perhaps in order to finance his schemes, sold the manuscript to a publisher who makes a living out of the sale of moral and uplifting literature. That same publisher has begged me to write this brief explanation, and as I have never turned down an opportunity to make even a small amount of money, I have agreed to his special pleading.

Whether the tale this tells is a moral or instructive one I shall now leave to the reader. All I would add is that it is a plain and unvarnished account of some of the youthful adventures of one who now signs himself

BUNTINGFORD

Buntingford Towers
1 April 1890

1 *Solvitur Scribendo*

I was rising fifteen when, for decency's sake, they pushed me into the Upper School at Christ's Hospital where the Reverend Boyer held sway. He, as petty and grinding a tyrant as you could come across in any conventicle of ushers, once found me reading *Bell's London Life* when I should have been turning into English verse whatever it was that the pious Aeneas had done to Dido of Carthage.

'Bunter,' said he, snatching the paper from me and fetching me a resounding thump on the ear: 'Bunter,' said he, 'if I ever caught you reading anything but trash and writing anything but drivel, I'm sure I'd expire from astonishment.'

The sarcastic beast was, as usual, being less than fair. I've never been what you might call a scholar, but that don't mean that I'm an out-and-out ignoramus. And that's why, now I've had to take to the pen, I intend to show I have read more books than old Boyer ever imagined and that, though I shall deal only in facts, I can scribble away as fast as Walter Scott once I'm put to it.

And the fact is, I am very much put to it, for two reasons. The first is funk. I arrived in Sumroo in a funk; I've been in a funk, on and off, ever since: and what passed between the Begum and myself in the early hours of this morning has so added to that funk that when I finally got back to my quarters my jowls and paunch were still quivering like one of dear old Bessy's jellies.

The second reason is that I cannot, for the life of me, work out how I managed to end up in this scrape. Ever since my schooldays, I've been described as a cunning sort of cove; but though I may be quick-witted enough to think up some bright wheeze or other for getting myself out of trouble, that don't mean those wheezes always succeed. Most of them in fact have ended in disaster, though never before in the sort of ultimate disaster that threatens me at this moment.

So what I most need now is to unmuddle my mind, and the best way I can do this is by putting everything down on paper, as it happened. That's why I said to myself early this morning, as I left the Begum's bed: 'Bunter, my boy, *solvitur scribendo*. That's your answer! Work it out by writing.'

The Begum had been all hospitality and friendliness when the Bishop and I visited her in 1825. But how was I to know that, being half Nepalese, she practised her own form of polyandry? Or that my fleeing from the Maharajah to her was a perfect case of climbing out of the frying pan and into the fire?

At the time of that first visit to Sumroo, three years ago now, I was still Bishop Heber's secretary; so I had to accompany him on his Grand Tour of most of the Indian States, he being the first Anglican bishop to have been given All-India as his see. That didn't just mean he'd been given a devilish large diocese to look after. It meant also that, once we'd left British territory, no one exactly knew who or what he was since, although obviously a Nob, he was not one of the civil or military sort Indians were used to.

Rumours, in native India, always out-travel the traveller. So, by the time we had made our painful way to a State capital, whether it had been by bhotia, pony, elephant, gharee or palanquin, we always found that its ruler had developed quite exaggerated ideas concerning the Bishop's power, position and importance. This was not just another fakir or peripatetic and foolish Feringhi missionary attempting to bring the Gospels to the heathen. No! This was an entirely new sort of holy man: a true Burra Sahib who had been sent to Hind by King Georgey himself with full powers to tell the Governor General what he should do to India and the Indians. The consequence was, each local potentate was determined to impress the Bishop, and not one of them was willing to lose face by impressing him less than his neighbours had done.

So, just as soon as we got close to his capital the local Raja or Nawab would see to it that we were received by as impressive an escort as his revenues could provide. There would be elephants for us to ride—decorated with gold leaf if the ruler was prosperous, and with whitewash if he wasn't. Mace bearers and musicians would march in front of us and a guard of honour would flank us, this consisting of anything from half a dozen aged and shabbily-dressed spearmen to a whole squadron of prancing cavalrymen resplendent in helmets, plumes, breastplates and gold brocades. They were supposed to keep the crowds at a distance though these would fall in behind us until we had half the town's population at our heels.

But the best part of the tomasha came after we arrived at the ruler's palace. The guard would present arms. The Vizier would present us to the ruler. The ruler and the Bishop would exchange presents. It was not an equal exchange since the Bishop's nuzzur was invariably a copy of the Gospels translated into either Persian or Sanskrit depending on the ruler's religion; and if he was an especially important ruler Heber would add a velvet-bound copy, in its native English, of his epic poem *Jerusalem* which had won him the Craven when he was at Oxford.

In return, each of us would be given a richly-brocaded Kellut, or robe of honour, together with other varyingly valuable gifts such as purses of gold mohurs, rich shawls and kincobs, pearl necklaces, jewelled aigrettes and tulwars and, on occasion, a caparisoned horse or even an elephant. Even though there was barely a Briton in India who had not come out to the country for the sole purpose of, as they put it, shaking the gold mohur tree, it had been laid down by the Governor General that all such gifts had to be returned when we departed. I thought this improvident; but, since the Bishop insisted that a Bishop's secretary must on such occasions behave as though he too were a Bishop, I found much to object to.

Later there would be banquets, military parades, dancing girls, wild animal fights, visits to local temples and suchlike. But since one Indian dancing girl or one Indian temple is very like another, these soon became very suchlike indeed. The worst of it, however, was that no sooner had one potentate got down to all this nuzzuring and entertaining business, than all his neighbours would insist on doing the same; and any local Raja, Nawab or even Zemindar who failed to receive a visit from this new species of Burra Sahib would have felt as snubbed as a London lady of fashion who failed to receive her ticket to Almack's.

This was how, while we were at Lucknow, a small, travel-weary delegation arrived from the Begum of Sumroo, bearing a letter from their mistress written in quite tolerable French. She had learnt, she wrote, that we were about to travel to Lahore as the guests of the Maharajah Runjeet Singh. Since Sumroo was not many leagues distant from that city she hoped the Bishop would find the time to honour her with a visit. She had heard of his great fame as a divine, a philosopher and a poet and, since she herself had always taken a great interest in such matters, she hoped to enjoy the company of the most eminent writer and scholar ever to come from Bilatee to the land of the five rivers.

To my mind it was the reference to his poetry that did it. Runjeet Singh had let it be known that he had prepared a whole series of entertainments for us when we reached Lahore but the Bishop by now longed for some intellectual company. So he decided that we might, without insulting the Maharajah, claim a couple of rest days from his entertainments and journey to Sumroo before returning to do honour to the rest of the tomasha. He was encouraged in this by Mr Ricketts, who had done much to arouse his curiosity about the Begum.

This Mr Ricketts, who had acquired a yellow complexion and a somewhat languid manner as a result of the years he had spent in India, was, at that time, the British Resident Agent in Oudh and something of an authority on the history and politics of even the smallest Indian States. He had also been a contemporary of the Bishop's at Brasenose and so was probably the only man in India apart from myself who addressed him as Reggy. The Bishop, for his part, called him Shaky in private, which I took to be a typically weak under-graduate pun on Mr Ricketts' surname.

'Sumroo,' he said, 'ain't really large enough to be classed as a State. It was a jaidad of about twenty-seven villages when Mahadaji Sindhia gave it to Colonel Sommers in return for past services and for allowing the Begum to marry him. It's called Sumroo because the natives found it difficult to get their tongues around Sommers. But the only object of interest in the whole miserable place is the Begum herself.'

'To judge from her letter,' said the Bishop, 'and its unusual references to religious and cultural matters, she don't sound at all like one of your usual zenana women.'

'Unusual ain't the word for it. As for zenanas, it's t'other way round with her. But you'll get on famously with her, Reggy. She'll quote you Firdausi, and Sa'adi, and the Puranas, and the Ramayana just as soon as look at you. Or if you prefer it, she'll discuss the Vedas, the Tripitaka, the Qu'ran, the Gospels, Transubstantiation, Metempsychosis, Predestination, Reincarnation, or anything else in that line you may fancy.'

'A truly remarkable lady, and certainly devout.'

'The second don't necessarily follow on the first.'

'Come now. If she is as you describe her, a student of religions, there has to be one of them she adheres to.'

'If you leave the Parsees and the Jews out of it, she's adhered to most of 'em in her time and for a time. It wasn't ever a question of belief. It was always a question of family and the men she was married to.'

'That is a most cynical remark, and I refuse to believe that the lady shares your obvious scepticism.'

'She don't. She's practical rather than sceptical. You see, Reggy, her Ma was a Mahratta and her Pa a Gurkha, which meant no one could decide whether she'd been born a Hindoo or a Buddhist. That sort of cross-breeding and confusion weren't uncommon when the Gurkhas were hammering at the gates of Delhi. But she was related on her Ma's side to Sindhia who soon took charge of her and married her off when she was twelve to a sickly boy who was grandson to Ahmad Shah of Kabool. The Afghans were squatting in Lahore at that time and Sindhia thought it politic to be on good terms with 'em, even if it meant his niece converting to Islam.'

'A sad, sad story, only to be heard in this tormented and bloody land. Here's a poor girl who, by the time she's twelve, doesn't even know whether she's Hindoo, Buddhist or Muslim.'

'Lord bless you, she never minded. None of her conversions lasted long enough to trouble her. She's always been a high-spirited filly and, just as soon as she'd been widowed for the first time, she went back to Sindhia. Led some of his Mahratta cavalry for him, they say. That's how she met Sommers and became a Catholic for a while.'

'Alas, Shaky, no one becomes a Catholic just for a while—unless, of course, they've seen no more than half the light and will, in due course, find a more permanent refuge in the bosom of the Church of England.'

'I don't think she ever got as far as that, not even for ex-Private Jones. It was a different business with Sommers who was a Colonel, and one of De Boigne's right-hand men, you know; and like him he was a Savoyard and devout, even though he was a soldier of fortune. That's why he wouldn't marry her unless she turned Catholic. But when poor Sommers had his head taken off by a cannon ball, she married Udham Singh, who was Runjeet Singh's nephew. So she became a Sikh, until Udham got killed when a gatehouse fell down on him.'

'And this ex-Private Jones you mention. When did she marry him?'

'She couldn't marry a private, Reggy, however much she may have valued his parts. After all, he was a deserter from the British Army who got himself a job as drill sergeant to her sepoys when she finally retired to Sumroo. How could she marry such a fellow, even though he was a great strapping chap with shoulders on him like an ox? She just made him one of her concubines.'

'A male concubine? Surely not!'

'I don't know what else you would call him. She had four or five of 'em in her zenana at one time.'

'But the zenana is for women.'

'The Begum's wasn't.'

'I am, I hope, a philosopher as well as a Bishop. But I won't conceal from you, Shaky, the horror I still feel for the sexual depravities of the Indian ruling classes—for their polygamy, their concubines, their harems and their zenanas. But that an Indian woman should actually reverse these practices and keep members of our sex in concubinage seems to me monstrous.'

'Custom of the country, Reggy.'

'That it is not. Runjeet Singh and other Indian sybarites may keep male concubines in order to indulge their unnatural and deplorable appetites, but I have never, in all my travels in this country, come across a woman who did the same thing.'

'I wasn't referring to India. You've got to remember that the Begum's father came from the far north of Nepal.'

'And what, pray, has that got to do with it?'

'They've some damned queer customs up in those mountainy places, including polyandry. So I suppose once the Begum had grown weary of being widowed she began to follow inherited instincts and took to keeping her own private stud. You can't really call it polyandry because she's never actually married any of 'em, but the intention's much the same.'

'And yet you suggest, Shaky, that this is the sort of woman a Bishop of All-India ought to visit?'

'God bless you, Reggy; you'll be quite safe. Your cloth will protect you, quite apart from your position and the fact that you'll be talking about poetry and religion all the time. Even your plump young secretary will be safe, unless he's got hidden depths or certain secret assets or something of that sort.'

I am sure that the Bishop, who was a man of insatiable curiosity, was more curious than horrified at this description and so decided he must make the Begum's acquaintance whether she was a multiple apostate and practised polyandry or not. That was why we took time off from the tomasha in Lahore to pay a brief visit to Sumroo.

The Begum, as I've already mentioned, was all hospitality and friendliness and never once thought it necessary to make us visit temples or watch dancing girls. Instead she and the Bishop spent two pleasant days testing each other's knowledge of the poets and Holy Books of several different countries. She seemed to take little notice of me, but that may only have been because I wasn't in their class when it came to that kind of intellectual catch-as-catch-can.

I remember feeling slightly huffed at being so conspicuously overlooked, especially as I was wearing an outfit my Calcutta dhurzi had created to my instructions. It could be that I owe my interest in dress, uniforms, decorations and suchlike to the Guelph blood that may or may not run in my veins, but I have an eye for such things and have frequently been complimented on my impeccable taste. On this occasion I wore skin-tight buckskin unmentionables which did attract a glance or two from the Begum, a heavily-frilled shirt under a flowered silk waistcoat, a bird's-eye neckcloth which came near choking me and was held in place by a large cameo brooch my mother had given me, and a double-breasted, brass-buttoned, swallow-tailed coat of military cut but suitably subdued grey clerical hue. These, together with a pair of tasselled Hessian boots, a large-brimmed, low-crowned straw hat tied around with a green veil and the red flannel cummerbund I wore as a specific against the cholera completed what I considered to be both a tasteful and suitable get-up for the place and the occasion.

But the Begum, as I've said, looked only at my unmentionables. Thereafter she concentrated all her attention on the Bishop and seemed to have dismissed me entirely from her thoughts. But now that I put these things down, more than three years later, I wonder whether she had.

How differently was I dressed when I next turned up at the Begum's gates little more than a couple of months ago, though it now seems an age. This time there was no tomasha and I had to argue with the guards before they would let me in to see the Begum. This was not, perhaps, to be wondered at, for I was wearing the dirty dhoti, striped cotton vest and dingy white skullcap of a Bengalee baboo. Moreover the walnut stain with which I had darkened my skin was beginning to wear off, so I was looking as mottled as though I had leprosy.

The Begum, however, recognised me at once. It's true that she laughed heartily at my appearance, but her reception of me was a deal warmer than I had dared to expect.

'Welcome, welcome, Bunter Sahib,' said she. 'Your arrival comes like a cup of cool water to slake the thirst of our curiosity. For even here in the mofussil we have heard of your exploits and have wondered at them.'

'Kind of you, Ma'am,' said I, 'but I'm in particular need of your help at the moment.'

'That also we have heard.'

'You have?'

'Rumours travel swiftly in Hind. Those which concern your

seduction of the wives of a certain bunniah called Hurree Ram
Thukoor have been discussed in every zenana between here
and Calcutta for such things are always of interest to women.'

I wondered what Hurree would have thought of being
referred to as a mere bunniah and of having his other two
wives lumped in with Mahtab who was merely the oldest of
'em. But before I could say anything the Begum continued:

'They also tell us that the widow of the late Bishop Heber,
may his soul rest in peace, gave birth to a girl child who, if she
also wore spectacles, would greatly resemble Bunter Sahib. It
is also well known that no less a person than Runjeet Singh
was so impressed by your . . . endowments, when these were
brought to his notice during a certain tiger hunt, that he has
entertained a passion for you ever since.'

'That at least, Ma'am, is true, and is why I'm here asking
for sanctuary.'

'And that you shall have, Bunter Sahib, even though the
Maharajah's agents and the bunniah Thukoor are even now
scouring the countryside for you, not to mention another, one
Coker Sahib, though what it was you did to his wives I do not
know.'

'Nothing at all, I assure you,' said I, 'and I'm mighty
grateful to you for your offer.'

'I, too, am a woman,' she said, 'and so curious. You shall
stay with me until the hunt for you dies down. It would be
best never to venture outside this palace unless you are
accompanied by three or four of my most trusted sowars. And
in the meantime we shall'—and here she grinned at me in a
meaningful manner— 'entertain one another.'

That was when I should have realised what I had achieved
by climbing out of the frying pan. But I had been in such a
funk during my flight from Lahore, and so relieved to be
recognised and given sanctuary, that I was paying no attention to the morrow.

'Meanwhile,' said the Begum, 'it's not fitting either to
myself or to you that a Feringhi sahib should go around
looking like a piebald Bengalee baboo. I cannot give you
Feringhi clothes, but I shall see to it that you are more
suitably dressed and that your beautiful pink complexion is
restored to you. Gurmakh Singh!'

A plump, white-bearded Sikh who'd been squatting with other retainers behind the Begum rose to his feet and salaamed.

'Gurmakh Singh,' said she, 'it will be your task to attend on Bunter Sahib for so long as he is our guest. He shall have the little pavilion in the Shalimar as his quarters, and you will see to it that, in matters of food, clothing, attendance and overall comfort, all that I wish for him shall be carried out.'

'On my head be it,' said Gurmakh Singh, bowing first to her and subsequently to me.

'He is,' said the Begum to me, not bothering to lower her voice and discussing him as though she were offering me a horse, 'a dishonest rogue. But he is well used to Feringhis for he served many years in the forces of John Company, and even speaks some English . . .'

'Tenth Native Infantry,' said Gurmakh Singh, springing smartly to attention and grinning at this opportunity to show off his command of my language. 'I serve under Macgregor Sahib and O'Hara Sahib and many other English Sahibs. I know loading-and-firing drill, brandy-panee, trouser-pressings, mulligatawny soupses, treacle puddings, and all other Feringhi customs such as drunk-in-mess, church-paradings . . .'

'That,' said the Begum, who could never endure interruptions, 'is quite enough. You have our Rukhsat.'

This, I knew, was the dismissal demanded by court etiquette. Without it one could not politely withdraw from a durbar. After it one could no longer safely stay. So I bowed to the Begum as courteously as my dhoti would allow. As I was unaccustomed to such things I had to clutch at it to prevent it from falling apart. Gurmakh Singh also bowed, though with a deal more grace, and I followed him out of the durbar.

When my new wardrobe arrived, Gurmakh Singh, using a good deal of hot water, soap, rubbing oil, and a loofah, succeeded in ridding me of the walnut stain. Then, having dried and massaged me, he helped me put on the costume ordained for me by the Begum, and I looked into one of the many mirrors decorating the walls of my quarters.

I found it difficult, at first, to recognise myself. What I was now wearing, Gurmakh Singh assured me, was what a dashing young Sikh blood, a khub jewan, even a chabuk sowar or gay cavalier would wear. My pajamas, or voluminous trousers, were in blue, heavily brocaded in gold and were tucked into red leather riding boots equipped with a most unwieldy set of long-spiked spurs. The pajamas were held up by a draw-string, although this was concealed by a great scarlet cummerbund into which was tucked a whole variety of daggers and pistols, all of them more ornamental than otherwise.

Over this I wore a white muslin shirt, a scarlet silk waistcoat and a blue shawl chogha or pelisse, which last was also heavily embroidered in gold. After he had, with a good deal of encouraging chatter, got me into all of these, Gurmakh Singh wound a towering scarlet turban round my head, taking as many pains over its folds as Mr Brummell takes over his neckcloth. A gold-hilted tulwar hanging from a red leather baldric completed the ensemble. Much as I have always appreciated a well-designed turn-out, it is little wonder that I failed to recognise the colourful, imposing, and portly figure looking back at me from the mirror.

'Not the spectacles, Sahib,' said Gurmakh Singh, as I put those essential aids on in order to study myself better. 'Spectacles is for baboos.'

'In my country,' I said firmly, 'even our greatest men wear spectacles.'

'Yours is indeed a strange and wonderful country.'

'And,' I continued, 'now that I can see myself more clearly, it seems to me, O Gurmakh Singh, that these fine clothes must have been made for a man taller than myself, although it is helpful that I take up in girth most of what the original wearer took up in height. Who,' I added, sticking one hand on my hip and turning round to see whether pajamas were more flattering to my figure than skin-tight unmentionables . . . 'who was that man?'

'Aiee, Bunter Sahib, he is best not mentioned.'

'Why so?'

'The Begum has commanded that he should be forgotten. It is dangerous even to mention his name.'

'Come now,' said I, feeling a deal cockier now that I was

out of that confounded dhoti. 'We're between four walls and did not the Begum order you to serve me in all things? Would you have me send you back to her with a request for a more obedient attendant?'

'My head would pay for it.'

'Then answer what I asked.'

Gurmakh Singh looked fearfully around as though he suspected that even the mirrors were listening. Then he bent towards me and whispered in my ear: 'Jones Sahib.'

The name reminded me of something Mr Ricketts had said three years earlier and, although I couldn't properly remember what it was, I sensed it could be important.

'Why is it that such a name, which is a very ordinary one in my country, may only be whispered? And what is it that the Begum must not be reminded of?'

He took me into the centre of the room, sat me down on one of the uncomfortable little French chairs with which it was furnished, and crouched at my feet before he began his whispered reply, much of which was given in his version of English.

'The Begum, Sahib, very, very randy woman. Very much like jigajig with many, o many mans.'

'So I once heard. But we have a saying that you can take a horse to water but you can't make him drink. So what if a man politely declines to "jigajig" with the Begum?'

Gurmakh Singh shuddered, drew a finger across his throat, and made the sort of noise one makes when attempting to spit hearty.

'He dead. When she say jigajig is necessary to jigajig. If jigajig often enough and good enough then, when Begum gets tired of the mans, maybe he get sent away; maybe he get present.'

'And if not?' I asked, beginning to feel a deal less cocky.

'Aiee, Sahib. Then it is very, very dangerous for the man. If Begum is ever thinking he is – how you say in Army? – Idle on Parade, then . . .' His forefinger and the spitting noise came into action once more. 'Or maybe worse.'

'Worse?' I quavered.

'There can be starvings to death. There can be whippings to death. There can be boilings in oil.'

'Just for being idle on parade?'

Suddenly, as though he had just remembered events best forgotten, an expression of bitter and vengeful anger crossed his face, and this time he really did spit.

'My own sister's son, Bunter Sahib,' he said, abandoning his pidgin English so as to be able to do justice to his feelings in his own language. 'My own sister's son was a Jemadar in the Begum's guard regiment. A brave fighting man and a fine, strong, handsome fellow, a true khub jewan. But he had two young, lusty, and demanding wives . . .'

'So?'

'So, when the Begum ordered him to her bed he was vain-glorious enough to think he could satisfy all three of 'em. But even a Sikh khub jewan is no more than a man, and men are not gods. So she had him boiled in oil, may her soul rot in the hereafter.'

'But he doesn't sound an idle fellow. That was the very opposite of idle on parade.'

'Nor was he idle. But weariness overtook him in the end, and he fell asleep on the Begum in the middle of a jigajig.'

'And Jones Sahib, did he also weary?'

Gurmakh Singh shuddered at the sound of that forbidden name.

'I beg my Lord to place the bit of discretion between his imprudent jaws so that no mention of that person comes slipping off his tongue when he is, as he assuredly will be, closeted with the Begum.'

Everything he said added to my growing suspicion that Bunter had landed himself in yet another scrape. My funk was mounting, but so, also, was my determination to get to the bottom of this.

'We speak, here, between ourselves, Gurmakh Singh. If, which Heaven forbid, dangers threaten me in Sumroo, it is your duty to reveal them to me. It is a matter of Izzut.'

That brought him up since, unlike us, honour or face or whatever you care to call it is a matter of some importance to Indians. He swallowed hard before replying.

'Jones Sahib was not at all like you, my Lord. He was not even like my sister's son. For he was such a bull of a man that even the Begum could not weary him or do anything to diminish his randiness. One morning, when she had dismissed him from her bed, he went straight off and performed jigajig with a nautch girl half the Begum's age and almost her equal in her tirelessness. Ah, Bunter Sahib, she was such a dancing girl as would arouse the passion of dotards and lend added vigour to vigorous young men – agile as a serpent and more beautiful than a lotus flower. But . . .' here he spread his hands in a gesture suggesting disaster.

'But what?'

'Jones Sahib was caught when he was mounting her yet once more. Before he was hanged the Begum ordered that those of his members which had most delighted both the nautch girl and herself should be cut off and placed in his mouth.'

'Good God! But what of the nautch girl?'

'She, my Lord, was lowered into a pit dug out from under the Begum's bed. This was then bricked up, the bed was replaced, and the Begum never left it until the girl's last moans had died away.'

'And all this is true? You are not, for some reason of the Begum's, attempting to frighten me?'

'I have bared my soul to you, as Izzut demands. And judge, Bunter Sahib, whether I, a true Sikh, would, when he can avoid it, do anything to assist one who has the blood of my sister's son on her head.'

'But what of me? What dangers await Bunter in Sumroo? Am I to follow your sister's son and Jones Sahib in the Begum's bed? Speak truly, O Gurmakh Singh.'

He shook his head sadly.

'The truth, my Lord, is a savage whip, yet must I use it. The Begum was plain with me about you. She ordered that, when I washed and massaged you, I should take careful notice of your endowments, for the rumour said that they were truly noble. And so, in truth, they are.'

'Yet you need not report this.'

His hands fluttered in agitated protest.

'Already have I put my head at risk by telling you of these things. But it will avail you nothing if I report falsely to the Begum. For, if I say you are not well equipped, she will hand you over to the Maharajah and then if report comes back that I was wrong, my head will fall. Therefore it is better for both of us that I report truthfully. Thus you may at least hope that, having lived up to your promise, she will when she has wearied of you send you away unharmed and with gifts suitable for one who has satisfied an expert.'

'And if I don't live up to my promise?'

His hands fluttered once more.

2 *Well-Hung's Nigh Well-Hanged*

Dawn in India is a damned impulsive affair. It didn't do any tiptoeing on the mountain tops a few hours ago but fairly rushed through the bedroom windows just as I rolled off the Begum panting, sweating, and feeling as if I had gone ten rounds with Tom Cribb. At that moment there wasn't a scrap of impulsiveness left in Bunter.

However the Begum, who is not given to post-coital languors, was sitting up in the bed as naked as the day she was born and looking as fresh as a daisy and as cool as a cucumber. She gave my panting, sweating body one of those long, businesslike, appraising looks which always make me smell danger. It was the sort of look a Newmarket trainer might give a horse he'd just put through a sharpish trial gallop on the Heath. I hoped she would decide that I might, with time and further training, turn out to be a Derby winner. But she could, for all I knew, have been thinking that I wasn't worth training on and ought to be sent to the knackers. I shuddered, and remembered what Gurmakh Singh had told me.

It's strange, however, how the human mind works at such moments. Even though my uneasiness increased with every second of that examination I still couldn't help examining her in return. She was, I had to tell myself, a fine figure of a woman and confoundedly well preserved for her age. Or that, at least, was how it seemed to my inexpert eye. I've always preferred food to fornication, which makes me a better judge of a beefsteak-and-oyster pie than of a woman in her birthday suit.

Nevertheless I do believe that the most hardened and experienced womaniser would have approved of her. She has one of those wide-cheeked, fine-boned, almond-eyed, almost Mongolian faces you often come across in Northern India, and I'll swear that there ain't a line or a wrinkle on it. She's a deal lighter-skinned than most Indian women, and her complexion makes you think of ripening apricots rather than old saddle leather. Her legs might be a mite on the short side and slightly bandy and there may be just a suspicion of shrinkage and saggage about her still outstanding boobs but, take it all in all, she has retained the sort of figure one of old Boyer's Greek nymphs would have envied.

She has a mass of glossy, ink-black hair, although she has to rely on the dye-pot if it's not to show white at the roots. Her hands, which become deucedly active as soon as we get down to it, are just beginning to show a few liver spots. But white hair-roots and brown liver spots ain't really surprising in a woman who, by her own account, is old enough to be my mother or even, at a pinch, my grandmother. What is surprising about her though is that she's still so remarkably spry and so tirelessly randy. That randiness has kept me in more than half a funk ever since my first day in Sumroo. But it was only after we had concluded our conversation this morning that I began to realise how much more of a funk I needed to be in.

'It's a great pity,' she said, using the Urdu in which we normally conversed, 'that a young man as well-hung as you should be so lacking in staying power.'

It was the first time she'd raised the subject. She always sets the pace for our feather-bed jigs, but she'd never before suggested that I'd failed to keep up with it. Which, seeing that, as usual, I'd just been urged on into mounting her for the fifth or sixth time in a night, I thought beastly ungrateful of her.

But it was when she went on to add a few remarks in her bad French and even worse English that I began to get really worried. She only does this when she's trying to come to a decision she doesn't want to share with her advisers. She got her French from Sommers who, being a Savoyard, spoke it atrociously. Her English she had picked up from the few Britons she'd come across, and most of them, like the late Private Jones, were deserters from the British forces who'd taken service with one or other of the local rulers. So it's a rough, barrack-room sort of English that she speaks.

'*Je crois que c'est à cause de ta corpulence. Tu es fort bien fourni, mon pauvre* Bunter, but bugger me if you ain't bleedin' feeble. Big belly spoils big cock is old Gurkha saying. Is great pity you just one fattee boy.'

'Not really a fatty,' said I, sticking to the Urdu which I thought safer. 'Just stoutly built, as you might say.'

I'd forgotten how dangerous it was to contradict her, even over trifles, for she loses her temper quicker than a Bedlamite. I've seen one of her oldest and most dignified Sirdars taken out and bastinadoed just because when she had idly remarked that it was a fine day he'd been imprudent enough to point out that it was raining. She wasn't quite so drastic with me: you need to have your clothes on before you can be really drastic. But she lost her temper, right enough, and screamed 'Fattee boy' at me four or five times before deciding that she could do better in Urdu.

'Do you dare argue with me in my own bed, you corpulent Feringhi dog? Let me remind you that there are still those in Lahore and Calcutta who would love to argue with you, even if I sent you back to them with your tongue torn out.'

I'm not such a fool as not to know when I'm on the wrong tack, so I decided to try her in Farsi. It's a more flowery language than Urdu and just made for buttering-up a woman.

'Queen amongst Women and Dispenser of all Delights,' said I. 'Would Bunter, the humblest and most adoring of all your slaves, have argued with you if he were sober? It's only because he's drunk . . .'

At which point she became even angrier.

'Drunk! It is not permitted to you to get drunk. Alcohol is fattening. I've given the strictest orders that you should be allowed nothing but doodh panee.'

'And I swear to you that nothing but milk-and-water *has* crossed my lips ever since you were gracious enough to turn the Face of Favour towards your unworthy slave. Let not the Cloud of Anger now cloud that loveliness. If I have argued,

it is because I am drunk. And if I am drunk, it is not on
wine. No! It is not even on Bhang or on Toddy. I am drunk,
O Pearl among Women, on the power of your beauty and the
amplitude of your bounty.'

I thought this wasn't half bad, seeing that it had been got
up impromptu, though I couldn't really tell whether it was the
buttering-up or the Farsi that calmed her down. She sometimes drops into Farsi herself on those rare occasions when
she's had enough of jigajig and comes as close to feeling
romantic as a woman of her practical and basically simple
nature ever can be.

'Billee,' she said, dropping her voice at least half an octave.
'My great, fat, soft Bunterjee. It may possibly be wrong of me
to blame you for being a barn owl rather than an eagle. We
are all what the gods made us, and only few of us did they
make perfect. In your case they jested over your making. They
gave you a pizzle a temple bull could envy. But they also gave
you a belly larger than the biggest watermelon ever grown in
any of the kingdoms of Hind.'

I thought this sounded a bit more hopeful, even though she
was being so beastly personal.

'The pizzle without the belly would have made you such a
hero in bed that I could have delighted in you for thrice one
thousand and one nights. The belly without the pizzle could
have turned you into such a very tolerable eunuch that I could
have traded you off to the Nawab-Vizier at Lucknow as part
of the dustoor I must render him each year. But, as it is,
you're something between a well-furnished cockerel and a
well-fatted capon, and I truly don't know what to do with
you.'

I hadn't wanted her to do anything with me except put me
on my way to some distant port from which I could safely take
ship for England. The suggestion that she might have other
things in mind was therefore unsettling. It might even be
better, thought I, to settle for the status quo.

'We can't all be eagles,' I said. 'But if I'm an owl, it means
that I'm well suited to night work. And if I'm a cockerel,
you'll have to admit that I'm one who crows loud enough at
night.'

She refused to be either impressed or amused.

'At night, but not all night,' she said, 'and that's the trouble.'

This brought the conversation back to its starting point and left me flummoxed. The fact is I don't really know where the truth of the matter lies. I'm too inexperienced to be able to tell whether she's over-demanding or I'm under-performing. Mahtab, who is Hurree's senior wife, had frequently seduced me whilst I was living with them in Calcutta and she had been at least half enthusiastic. The Bishop's wife and Mistress MacPherson had contrived to rape me on the voyage over but had both refrained from comment. These brief experiences apart, that was all the fornicating I had done in the whole of my twenty-odd years prior to ending up in Sumroo and the Begum's bed.

'Just look at you,' she grumbled on. 'You're panting like a wild dog and sweating like a horse. Yet I've done my best to slim you down and build up your stamina. My sowars have gone riding with you. My sepoys have wrestled with you. And when they all told me that you had no skill in such things, I had you instructed in yoga.'

'I ain't the right build for yoga,' I said, but she ignored such interruptions.

'Then there's the matter of your correct feeding. My cooks have had the strictest instructions concerning your diet. You have been given only those foods that are known to reduce fat and increase vigour. Yet what has happened? After almost two months of exercise and diet you're fatter and feebler than before. I don't know how this has happened, and I must tell you, Bunterjee, that it makes me suspicious.'

It was bad enough being reminded of the riding, the wrestling and the yoga, but it was even worse to be reminded of the disgusting diet she'd put me on. Indians are convinced that it's possible to put extra lead in a chap's pencil through his mouth. It is, in the truest sense of the word, just so much poppycock. Nevertheless ever since I came to Sumroo I've been fed very largely on vegetables.

There are the heating vegetables, which are served to me raw. They consist of such things as garlics, strong spring onions, radishes, and infernally hot chillies, all lavishly garnished with strong pickles and cayenne pepper. The heats these engender are supposed to melt the fat off me.

Then there are the strengthening vegetables. These, at least, are served to me cooked. But since they are always either spinach or horse beans, that don't make them much more palatable. Spinach, they keep telling me, builds muscle and strengthens the sinews. The horse beans, as their name suggests, form part of the diet recommended for working stallions.

The only flesh food I'm allowed is a large helping each day of what dear old Bessy used to call Lamb's Fry. She used to give it as often as she dared to her husband, Trotter, although it seemed to me that he stood in no need of it. For, if you discount the herbs and the sauce and the tails, Lamb's Fry has as its operative ingredient those bits of the tup-lamb that have been sacrificed to the shepherd's castrating knife. They make rubbery morsels however they're cooked, and eating them benefits a civilised man no more than eating his enemy's brains benefits a cannibal.

I'll go further. I am convinced that there is not a scrap of benefit to either the Begum or myself in the whole of this mumbo-jumbo diet. The spinach makes me scour, which is weakening. The beans make me costive, which is fattening. The raw vegetables make me so thirsty that I have to drink vast quantities of doodh panee, which puts back all and more of the liquids sweated out of me by the chillies and the cayenne pepper. In short, it's a diet that would have left me weaker, fatter, and infinitely hungrier than any I've suffered from since my schooldays.

This can't be what the Begum wants. And this, I discovered, is what's making her so infernally testy and suspicious.

'They tell me,' she said, 'that large dishes of chicken and mutton pilau and whole trays of meetai have been disappearing night after night from the kitchens. Many of us are fond of pilaus and sweetmeats. But if I thought, Bunterjee, that one of my cooks had been suborned and was smuggling such things in to you, I'd have him boiled in sugar-syrup and pegged out as meetai for the vultures. What's more, if I thought you had done the suborning, and that you were stuffing yourself to satisfy your own needs instead of strengthening yourself to satisfy mine, things would go far worse for you, Bunterjee, than for the cook.'

I couldn't really tell whether she had actually rumbled me or was merely at the suspicious stage. Her Gurkha blood generally allowed her to look somewhat jollier than the majority of Indians, but it also allowed her to look uncommonly cruel. Then, noticing the state I'd been thrown into by her last remarks, she grinned at me and said:

'*C'est tout que je veux dire à ce moment.* Dismiss to your quarters and bleedin' stay there till I send for you. And when I do, my great, fat *hibou, ça t'avantagera d'être plus mince, plus fort, et plus en training.*'

'And then?' I stammered.

'And then . . . *on verra.*'

My quarters, as she calls them, in the little pavilion at one end of the large courtyard at the back of the palace, must have been intended for Feringhis since they are furnished, very vulgarly, in the ornate French style which did so much to lead to the Revolution. It has gilt mirrors and prints of shepherds fondling shepherdesses' tits hanging on almost every inch of wall space. I was in such a state of physical and nervous exhaustion when I got there that I almost failed to notice Gurmakh Singh.

He was, as usual, squatting on his hunkers on the steps awaiting my return. He rose to his feet with the slow dignity befitting his white beard and his position as Bunter's khansaman, khitmutgar, confidant, and fellow-conspirator rolled into one. His teeth flashed in his customary grin which, I have to say, is at least half a leer and half the dental equivalent of a knowing nudge in the ribs. It became even more of a leer as soon as he had noticed my condition.

'She has asked too much of you yet again, Sahib?'

'I'm too weary for idle chatter, Gurmakh Singh. I need rest.'

'But first your servant will bring you hot water so that you may wash away the sweats of this night. Then shall he rub you with sweet oils to ease the stiffness of your muscles.'

'No bath, no oils, no massage. I'm for bed.'

'At least let my Lord restore his forces with food. See, I have secured you a particularly fine pilau, which I took from the kitchens ere the cooks were awake.'

I grabbed him by the shoulder and, to his amazement, shook him heartily to emphasise that Bunter was serious.

'No more pilaus, do you hear? And no more smuggling out of meetai and halva.'

'But how else, Huzoor, can you build up the energy you need for all your exhausting labours?'

'Gurmakh Singh,' said I, releasing his shoulder, 'have you ever seen a man boiled alive in sugar-syrup?'

He looked at me in horror, his eyes rolling upwards to the heavens.

'Only once, Bunter Sahib.'

'Tell me about it.'

'It is to talk of horrors.'

'Nevertheless talk.'

'He was the Begum's head hulwai, and in charge of all cakes and sweetmeats served to the Begum. She, as you know, places great store on such things and will have only the finest that can be made.'

'So?'

'So it came out that her hulwai had been cheating her. He had charged for the best-quality sugars, ghee and rose water but had been using the unrefined sugars and low-quality ghees such as are sold in the bazaars to the poor. Worst of all, he substituted common lavender water for the rose water.'

'Surely the Begum would have discovered this as soon as she'd tasted even a single sweetmeat?'

'It was the fact that she didn't that so enraged her. She only learnt about it in the end from the bunniah who supplied the palace. She was examining him over a small matter of his taxes.'

'And so she had the hulwai boiled in sugar-syrup?'

'Naturally. She had a great fire built in this very courtyard and over it they hung the largest cauldron in the kitchens. This was then half-filled with water into which all the hulwai's sugar sacks were emptied. The hulwai himself followed and the fire was lit. Then the Begum, to give him, as she said, a fragrant ending, had a phial of the very best rose water added. Aiee! How that hulwai screamed and begged for mercy before he himself turned to candy.'

'Can a man be turned to candy?'

'Only very slowly, my Lord. He shrank a good deal in the boiling, but he was so well-preserved by the time it was done that he was kept in the kitchen for a good many years as a warning to others. And thus it happened that what was a sweet revenge for the Begum involved a bitter ending for the hulwai.'

'And how, O Gurmakh Singh, would you enjoy such an ending?'

He turned as pale as his complexion would allow.

'Am I to be candied?'

'If you are ever caught smuggling pilaus and meetai in to me. And what even worse fate awaits me for eating 'em she has only hinted at.'

'Then, Bunter Sahib, you and I must flee at once.'

'How may I do that, with people watching me inside the palace and my enemies waiting for me outside?'

'It would be better to be caught by them than to be candied by her.'

'Come, man, all is not lost, and we don't know that we have to suffer either fate. Nothing has been proven. These are still but suspicions in the Begum's mind . . .'

Gurmakh Singh collapsed on the floor and wailed.

'You still do not know the Begum,' he sobbed, wiping his eyes with his turban end and then blowing his nose into it. 'With her suspecting is to act. Remember the fate of Jones Sahib.'

I could very easily have sat down on the floor and wailed with him, but that would have done no good and Bunter's not one to give up too easily. So I said as firmly as my growing funk would allow: 'Go now and get rid, privily, of the pilau. On your head be it that there are no witnesses. Meanwhile I shall sleep, and in sleep, perhaps, my cunning will return, and I shall think of a way in which we may save ourselves.'

Now that I have read what I have written so far I realise that I may have sorted out one problem without even beginning to tackle the others. In short, although I have worked out *how* I got into this dreadful scrape, I still haven't worked out *why* I was ever in the position to get into it.

As I look back I see such a multitude of reasons for my

eventual arrival in Sumroo that it seems almost impossible that I should ever sort them all out into a single chain, where one link follows another in an inevitable order of events. Yet the questions I have to ask myself are simple ones.

Query: Why am I in Sumroo?

Answer: Because I had to escape from the East India Company, Runjeet Singh, Hurree Ram Thukoor and Coker.

Query: Why did I have to escape from the East India Company?

Answer: Because of Hurree and the opium.

Query: Why did I have to escape from Runjeet Singh?

Answer: Because of the tiger hunt.

Query: Why was I on the tiger hunt?

Answer: Because of the Bishop's Grand Tour.

Query: How did I get involved with the Bishop?

Answer: Through Mr Wilberforce.

Query: Why did I have to escape from Hurree and Coker?

Answer: Because I went to school with them.

Query: How was it that I came to go to school with them?

Answer: Because of Mr Wilberforce.

Query: Then it all actually started with Mr Wilberforce?

Answer: Not exactly. Mr Wilberforce only got involved because of my mother.

Query: Then the First Cause is my mother?

Answer: Not precisely. She would never have known Mr Wilberforce had it not been for my grandfather.

So there it is. If I am really to unmuddle my mind in the fearful days that face me as I await the next summons from the Begum, I must start at the beginning and go back to my grandfather who was, like Mr Wilberforce, a House of Commons man, and to those far-off days before either my mother or myself had been born.

3 The Bunter Name

My mother, who is an immensely practical woman, and full of common sense, always used to laugh with me when I was a child about the prolonged investigations into her ancestors the Duke of York commissioned just as soon as I was on the way to being born.

The College of Heralds agreed that Bunter was a later corruption of an old Norman name, but they differed about whether it had belonged to a certain Guillaume de Bonne Terre, who had been a market gardener on the outskirts of Falaise prior to landing with the Conqueror at Pevensey, or to Jehan le Bonnetier, who had been the Conqueror's hatter and hosier, but had not arrived in England until well after the Conquest. But in either case, Garter King at Arms assured the Duke, anyone called Bunter was certainly of Norman and therefore noble descent.

Whenever my mother spoke about it she would end by doing something quite unusual for her. She would wink at me, and I would wink back. For we both knew that my maternal grandfather had even less hereditary right to the name of Bunter than I have.

What his rightful name was no one ever discovered on account of his having been one of Captain Coram's foundlings. But that is not to say he had no legal right to the name which Captain Coram quite haphazardly gave him. Registration can make almost anything legal, and that was why my mother had every right in the world to call herself Dorothea Bunter right up to the day she married her first husband. My own right to the name of Bunter is, on the other hand, less securely established.

All that I know about my maternal grandmother is that she was so self-effacing that she decided, once she had given birth to my mother, to go into a decline. That decline was so unobtrusively conducted that, when she finally passed away, only Bessy noticed what had happened.

Bessy, I should explain, was a bold, cheerful, loquacious, pink-cheeked, fat-rumped, full-breasted, wholesome sort of girl of about fifteen whom my grandfather had engaged to act as sick nurse to my grandmother and, following her decease, as nursemaid to my mother. She was, in fact, all the playmate, companion, teacher and parent my mother had during the early years of her life.

It may have been because of her attachment to my mother, or it may merely have been because she wanted to rise in the world, that Bessy, once my grandmother had been buried, started to think that it would be no bad thing if she became Mrs William Bunter the Second. She accordingly laid siege to my grandfather, and goodness knows what lengths she went to over the next six or seven years without ever once admitting to herself that she might just as well have been laying siege to the Egyptian pyramids. Indeed she might have continued besieging him for another six years if she had not been run down by a carriage in the Haymarket when she was on her way to the cheesemonger's in Jermyn Street for a few pounds of the Suffolk cheese my grandfather liked for his rarebit.

Bessy was not much hurt by the collision, although her skirt was ripped off her by the nearside wheel around whose hub it got wound, and she was left sprawling in the gutter with her petticoats around her ears. The carriage, which was an elegant one, drew up pretty sharply, and an equally elegant lady got out of it and came across to Bessy followed by a worried-looking coachman.

'Are you all right, girl?' she asked.

'Give or take an inch or two of skin,' said Bessy, struggling to her feet, 'I believe that I am. But my skirt ain't, nor never will be.'

'In that case,' said the lady, taking a little gold sovereign case from her reticule and clicking it until three gold coins lay in her outstretched palm, 'in that case, you must let me pay for a new one.'

Bessy, who had been brought up poor and economical, had never before been offered three whole sovereigns at once.

'Gawd bless you, Ma'am,' said she, 'my skirts 'ave never

cost that much. Two 'alf-crowns will pay for a skirt, and an 'aporth of arnica will cover the rest.'

'You are,' said the lady, 'an unusually honest girl. Trotter, give her two half-crowns and a ha'penny.'

The coachman, a large, burly man with a broken nose and scar tissue over his eyes, dug into his breeches pocket, took out a fistful of coins, and gave Bessy the three that had been mentioned.

'And now,' said the lady, 'we must drive you home.'

And that was how Bessy found herself in a carriage, sharing a pint flask of brandy with the lady as a precaution against shock, and telling her, in her own artless way, the story of her life and of her fruitless siege of my grandfather.

'I can't understand it,' said the lady. 'But if that is the case, you must give him an ultimatum.'

'Give 'im a what?'

'Give him a choice, my dear. Either he stops this nonsense and proves it in a practical manner, or else you leave him and come to work for me. It so happens I need a lady's maid, and with a little training and polishing I think you'd make exactly the sort of lady's maid I'm looking for.'

'So your Grandpa,' Bessy would tell me, '"ad 'is hultimatum almost immediate an' in pretty plain language at that. But confound the man! 'E didn't even know what a hultimatum meant, let alone begin to understand what I were a-hultimatuming 'im about. So I just 'ad to leave 'im an' your Ma an' transfer to York Place as 'Arriette's lady's maid. Female pride would hallow of no less.'

Bessy's ''Arriette' turned out to be no less a celebrity than Harriette Wilson who was by far the most fashionable of all the fashionable Grand Horizontals of that day. In short, her new mistress was mistress also to just about every man of rank, wit, or wealth in London, from the Marquis of Lorne to Mr George Brummell, from my Lord Byron to the later Duke of Wellington, and from old Meyler, the wealthy and randy sugar-boiler, to old Coutts, the even wealthier and randier banker. But although Harriette was just about as intimate as a woman could be with these pillars and ornaments of Society, there never was any side or snobbishness about her, and she and Bessy got on famously.

My mother was inconsolable, however. After Bessy departed, my grandfather hired one woman after another in an effort to provide a satisfactory Bessy-substitute but not one of them was to my mother's liking, nor would they stay to endure that infant hellion's displeasure. In the end my grandfather decided there was nothing for it but to send my mother away to boarding school.

Since he knew nothing about such establishments, he consulted someone at the House of Commons who did. That is, he took advice from Mr Wilberforce, so initiating that gentleman's long and close connection with the Bunters.

Mr Wilberforce was the leader of that forceful group of Evangelicals collectively known as The Clapham Saints. These Saints, being for the most part reformed rakes, repentant slave traders and lapsed pirates, were determined that the next generation of Englishmen should be more godly than they had been. So they had, to this purpose, opened a good many village and Sunday schools, and had recently added to these a boarding school in the rural seclusion of Kensington where respectable females between the ages of nine and nineteen could be educated in a manner calculated to inoculate them against worldliness, and to prepare them for their future tasks as Evangelical wives and mothers.

Mr Wilberforce's recommendation secured my mother a place there, and so she spent the rest of her days until she was seventeen very unhappily at Kensington. For, having placed her there, my grandfather came very close to forgetting her existence, and so she never went home even for the holidays, and the only person who visited her regularly, and to whom she could complain, was Bessy.

Bessy, who by now was Bessy Trotter and married to Harriette Wilson's coachman, an old soldier in every sense of the term, used to gossip endlessly to me in later years about my mother and how she behaved, but her favourite story concerned how my mother finally arranged to get away from Kensington and out into the world.

'Do you realise,' my mother said to Bessy during the last but one of the latter's visits to Kensington, 'that I'm now seventeen and have been shut up in this establishment for spayed tabby-cats for nine whole years?'

' 'As it been that long? Bugger me if it don't seem only a
year or two ago that I left you and your Pa and went to look
after 'Arriette.'

'And do you know,' continued my mother, 'how often my
father has come here to see me in all those years?'

' 'E always were wrapped up in 'is work.'

'And he still is. So wrapped up that I do believe he'll forget
to take me away from here, even when I'm nineteen. So do
you know what I'm going to do, Bessy?'

'Something pretty 'ellish if I know my Dotty,' said Bessy,
who was the only person to reduce such a stately name as
Dorothea to such a diminutive as Dotty.

'I'm going to run away. And I'll probably do it next
Sunday.'

'It ain't the least bit of good,' said Bessy authoritatively and
sounding rather like Solon must have sounded when he gave
his laws to the Athenians. 'It ain't the least bit of good
running away from anywhere if you ain't got some other
where worth running to.'

'Oh, but I have.'

'And where might that be?'

'I propose,' said my mother, clapping one hand to her
rapidly burgeoning bosom, 'to try my luck on the stage.'

'And you might just as well say that you propose to try your
luck with the pox and a passel of bastards.'

'Bessy!'

'Don't you get missish with me, my gal. You're a sight too
green an' a lot too heducated to go as a hactress.'

'You know nothing at all about actresses.'

'An' you know nothing at all about Drury Lane an' Covent
Garden, not to mention the provinces. Hinnocence and hedu-
cation are clean wasted in such places.'

'Well, if I mustn't run away as an actress, what must I run
away as?'

'Well, my pet, now that you're a-hasking me rather than
a-telling me, I think you should run away as a lady's companion or, at a pinch, as a governess.'

'And where, pray, would that lead?'

Bessy looked at my mother carefully before giving an
answer.

'You've got an 'andsome face, a good pair of legs, an' your boobs is coming along fine. So it could lead, if you does it proper, to an 'ouse'old where there's a young Hearl what's a bachelor or an old Nabob what's a widower, or anything else in between what's rich, unattached, and still hinclined towards matrimony.'

'With all my heart, if it's possible,' said my mother, who already had a sound bottom of common sense underlying all her girlish nonsense. 'But where can such a household, such a post, and such a match be found?'

'That,' said Bessy, 'is something I'll 'ave to consult my 'Arriette about.'

And that, in essence, was how Harriette Wilson came to arrange for my mother to go to Gloucester Place as companion to Mrs Mary Anne Clarke. That lady was an old friend of Harriette's, the two having started at more or less the same time in more or less the same line of business. What's more they had remained friends in spite of the fact that Mary Anne had done even better for herself than Harriette. That is to say, Mrs Clarke moved in the same circles as Mrs Jordan and Mrs Fitzherbert, even though she was not a talented actress like the one or a pious and respectable woman like the other. But she was like the both of them in that she was being officially kept by one of the King's sons: in her case the Duke of York who was also, at that time, the Commander-in-Chief.

It was already rumoured, however, that the Duke was no more successful at keeping Mary Anne than he was at commanding the Army. It was certainly true that he had got sixty thousand British soldiers and officers killed in Flanders with nothing to show for it, but it was also true that he had promised Mary Anne a thousand pounds a month when he first set her up in Gloucester Place and never paid her the half of it. The consequence of the first was that he was mighty popular in the Army where, as nobody ever minds the butcher's bill, he was known as the Soldier's Friend. The consequence of the other was that he and Mary Anne had frequent and often violent quarrels over money.

Both my mother and the Honourable George FitzThistlethwaite, who was the Duke's ADC, did their best to avert or soften these quarrels but some of them became very violent indeed. After the worst of them, Mary Anne was liable to flounce upstairs, lock her bedroom door, and leave the Duke to spend his night on the wrong side of it. This did not suit him. Since he was just as randy and just as sentimental as his brother, the Regent, he would stand outside the door in his nightgown and in tears, pleading to be let in, although all he'd get from the other side of the door would be more accusations of meanness.

Such scenes seemed, at first, quite shocking to my mother. She was still, at that time, a Royalist, and so she expected something more in the way of majesty from a Royal Prince as well as something more in the way of manliness from a Commander-in-Chief.

Later, however, she came to the conclusion that it was her plain duty as a woman and a subject to support and comfort the Duke when he was in one of these tantrums. So she got into the habit of taking him by the hand and leading him upstairs to the second floor and her own little boudoir. There a coal fire would still be burning in the grate, and there she could feed him brandy and sympathy until she had succeeded in calming him down.

This could, however, take several hours and the best part of a bottle or two of brandy for, just when the sympathy was beginning to soothe him, the alcohol would, once again, excite him. Like the rest of the Guelphs, he would get maudlin in his cups and was almost incapable of drinking like a gentleman. Consequently, just when it seemed to my mother that he was quietening down, he would start blubbing again. Then, when my mother had mopped up his tears with her handkerchief, he would take some more brandy, seize her by the hand and declare in his throaty German accent that 'his dearest, dearest liddle Miss Bunter'—my mother was only two inches short of five foot ten—'was der best, der truest, der most understanding friend any Prince ever had'.

But when Mary Anne and the Duke were not quarrelling over money they would be very friendly and loving with one another. And at such times there was nothing—money apart—that he would refuse her. A great many Army men took advantage of this, as they also did of Mary Anne's good-heartedness. They used to flock to Gloucester Place to beg Mary Anne to use her influence with the Duke to procure them some promotion, command, or office of profit they were not entitled to on grounds of seniority or merit. Since she could never say 'No' to them, and the Duke could never say 'No' to her, these suitors generally got whatever they begged for.

My mother soon saw the folly of Mary Anne's quarrelling with the Duke over money.

'What you must do,' she told Mrs Clarke with her characteristic and direct common sense, 'is to charge for the favours you now give away for nothing.'

'I never give my favours for nothing,' said Mary Anne haughtily. 'That would be most unprofessional.'

'I refer to when you act outside your profession, Ma'am. For I assume, Ma'am, that none of the military gentlemen who come to see you does so professionally.'

'Of course they don't! Even the most thick-headed soldier knows that when you're whore to a Royal Duke you have to be *hors de combat* to everyone else.'

'In that case there's no professional reason why you shouldn't charge a man for persuading the Duke to give him a company, or a regiment, or even a post as a Barrack Master.'

'There may be something in what you suggest,' said Mary Anne.

I have little doubt that it was at that precise moment that my mother, all unwittingly, started that chain of events which culminated in the famous Parliamentary Committee of Enquiry into Corruption in the Army, and the eventual summoning of Mrs Clarke to the Bar of the House. But that scandal still lay some time into the future, and well before then my mother had left Gloucester Place. This was because the Duke had suddenly announced that it was his firm opinion that she ought to marry the Hon. Fitz instanter. The Hon. Fitz, who was an obliging little man well accustomed, as the younger son of a penniless Irish peer, to doing what he was told, concurred.

And so the two of them were married at Windsor the very next week. The Duke himself acted as groomsman, and his wedding presents were a portrait of himself and a pension of two hundred pounds for the bride, charged to his Privy Purse.

When my mother married, the Hon. Fitz had no more than her pension and his own pay and allowances to live on. So the two of them set up house in three rooms over a shoe shop in Bond Street, where I was born not six months later.

The three of us lived there, I'm told, very happily until two things happened. The first was that the Duke turned Mary Anne out of Gloucester Place and took up with a certain Mrs Carey who was reputed to have the longest legs of any of the Covent Garden corps de ballet. This happened because the Duke had discovered that Mrs Clarke was not, as she had always said she was, a widow. Mr Clarke, in fact, was still very much alive, a circumstance that was made painfully clear to the Duke when a seedy, drunken fellow forced his way into the house shouting that he had come to claim his conjugal rights, and swearing that he would start a suit for crim. con. 'For,' said he, 'I'd be no true Englishman if I didn't.'

The Duke soon had his lawyers buy and bully Mr Clarke into silence, but the damage had been done. 'The lying slut,' he said in his bluff, straightforward way. 'She could at least have warned me about crim. con.'

So out of the door went Mary Anne, and it was as a direct consequence of that that the scandal about corruption in the Army was first brought to the attention of Parliament where the Whigs made a great uproar in the hope of bringing the Duke down and, with him, the Tory administration. Mary Anne cheerfully gave evidence against the Duke but, since the Committee was packed with Tories, this failed to produce a verdict that the Duke had been guilty of corruption. None the less the evidence she gave, which was widely reported, set the whole of England laughing. The cartoonists had a holiday with their pictures of a Royal Duke scratching at Mary Anne's door which had been locked against him because of his mean-ness. It was the meanness, and not the corruption, that did for him. He had to resign as Commander-in-Chief, even though the General's Club brought out a manifesto declaring him to have been the best Commander-in-Chief the British had had since Harold Godwinson.

All of this caused the Duke so much chagrin that he swore he would be revenged against Mary Anne and everyone ever connected with her. Mary Anne he eventually had thrown into prison for criminal libel. The poor woman had thought to recoup her fortunes by writing the story of her life with the Duke and selling it to a publisher. But long before that the Duke had stopped my mother's pension and dismissed the Hon. Fitz from his staff. This last act of spite meant that poor Fitz had to rejoin his regiment which was on active service in the Peninsula.

He got no nearer a battlefield, however, than Lisbon. That city was full of staff officers who were very ready to commiserate with him on his recent fall from grace. They took him off to dine, native fashion, at the best inn in Lisbon, where they all drank and ate very heartily. But since Fitz was the only one of the company who came fresh to Portuguese cooking, he was the only one to suffer from the olive oil, which gave him a bloody flux. He died of it a bare forty-eight hours after first setting foot on Portuguese soil.

And so my mother found herself, for the first time, a widow, and an impoverished one at that, some weeks before her twentieth birthday. The Hon. Fitz had left her nothing but mess bills and tailors' bills. Worse than that, the Horse Guards cut down by half the pension she was entitled to as the widow of a field officer who had died on active service, arguing that the only active part of that service had been an unsuccessful engagement with Portuguese cooks. Not unnaturally, my mother saw the Duke's hand in this, for he still had great influence at the Horse Guards; but she then had scarcely enough money to keep the two of us in food and with a roof over our heads. It was at this moment, however, that Mr Wilberforce, who had followed her career with increasing interest ever since she had begun to grow up, came forward with his proposal that she should return to her old school as its headmistress, a post that had become vacant because its former occupant had suddenly run off to America with the father of one of her pupils.

The fact that there was one man prepared to come to her assistance did little, I fear, to restore my mother's respect for the male sex. The Duke, her father and her father-in-law had all, in their various ways, let her down. Even the Hon. Fitz, by neglecting to die from a French bullet, had been less helpful than he might have been. It was from that moment that my mother became a militant feminist.

I have never met a woman, mark you, who has less need to feel inferior to men or discriminated against by them. Nevertheless it was around this time that she came across Mary Wollstonecraft's *Vindication of the Rights of Woman*, since reading which she has always been mighty scornful of the rights of men; and it was in order to demonstrate her growing disrespect for men that she now reverted to her maiden name. Since I was a babe at the time, that was the name I bore too, and have borne ever since.

It was only just before I left England, incidentally, that I discovered I had been entered in the parish register as a FitzThistlethwaite. But it is a name I have no desire to use. It refuses to come easily off the tongue. It belongs to a family of bog-hoppers with scarcely a shilling to share between them. And it has never done an Englishman anything but harm to have Irish connections.

Finally, there is the matter of likenesses. These, for what they are worth, suggest that I may have less right to FitzThistle-thwaite than I have to Bunter. For the position is this: I am not very much like my mother, even less like my grandfather, and not at all like the Hon. Fitz who was a little, black, skinny, lantern-jawed Irishman of the sort you can come across almost anywhere between Cork and Dublin.

I have always fancied, on the other hand, that certain elements of likeness exist between myself and the person who looks out of the portrait the Duke gave my mother as a wedding present. That fat, fair, greedy-looking, prematurely bald gentleman with protuberant, very pale blue eyes and a series of receding chins is typically, of course, a Guelph. But some, if not all, of those features are also typically Bunter.

4 *Temporary Reprieve*

Gurmakh Singh has just left me. He had brought me my usual mess of spinach, horse beans and other garbage and, seeing that I was scribbling away as fast as I could, said, 'It is a pious act that surely will be recorded in Heaven.'

'What is?' said I.

'The Sahib's desire to commit his last thoughts to paper.'

'I sincerely hope that they ain't my last thoughts, and you're a gallows-bird sort of comforter to suggest that they could be.'

He brushed the rebuke aside and actually grinned at me.

'There is now no need to hurry with your writing. It will be some time before the Begum sends for you. It may even be that she will forget all about you.'

'What makes you say that?'

'The Sahib would not know Ismail Khan?'

'No.'

'He is a famous Afridi horse coper and a fine-looking, swaggering sort of fellow. He came to Sumroo three or four days ago with a string of horses he was hoping to sell to the Begum as remounts for her sowars.'

'And?'

'And now, Bunter Sahib, he is having to do a great deal of mounting and remounting himself, for the Begum won't let him get far away from her bedroom. He seems strong enough to me to last her for several moons, and while she's in that mood you will have all the time you need for writing.'

5 *Tragedy Enters my Young Life*

If my mother's return as headmistress to her old school at Kensington was one of the more bizarre things she has done in her picaresque career, it was probably no more bizarre than her idea of setting up a sort of sister establishment just around the corner.

This arose almost by chance. The Trotters suddenly became unemployed because Harriette Wilson, who was ageing, had been forced to retrench to meet a marked falling-off in her trade. Thereupon Bessy turned to my mother for help and she, of course, turned to Mr Wilberforce.

'You, Sir,' she said to him, 'are President of the Society for the Suppression of Vice.'

'I am, Ma'am, and I have to admit that it's a losing battle we fight.'

'It has often seemed to me,' said my mother, with the air of one who had thought of nothing else for the past twelvemonth, 'that the vice your Society is most eager to suppress could best be suppressed by opening an Asylum for *younger* Fallen Women.'

'It's an interesting thought, Ma'am, but why would you have it confined to the younger ones?'

'I'm no expert in such matters, but I have often been told that the older ones are well past both the suppressing and the reforming.'

'That, sadly, is too often true. Gin and the gutter is all those unfortunate creatures can look forward to.'

'Now it so happens,' said my mother firmly, 'that there is a large old house just round the corner from here that is up for sale at a reasonable price. It could hold as many as thirty Younger Fallen Women, and has grounds large enough for them to exercise in when they are not stitching shirts, embroidering hassocks, and engaging in other rehabilitative works.'

'What's the price?' said Mr Wilberforce who, coming of commercial stock, could be sharp enough in such matters.

'A mere three hundred guineas. Moreover I know of a couple, good, honest, hard-working people with some experience of fallen women, who would run it very nicely for your Society.'

'I shall recommend your plan and them to the Society, Ma'am, immediately.'

It would be wrong to say that my mother led Mr Wilberforce by the nose, for the two have always had a good deal of respect for each other. My mother's a remarkably handsome woman and Mr Wilberforce, in spite of having known her since she was in pinafores, has always admired her quite as much as a man of his years and a Claphamite should. But one of the endearing qualities of their relationship is its old-fashioned formality. She might at times play Egeria to his Numa, and he, in a quite innocent manner, Antony to her Cleopatra, but they still 'Sir' and 'Ma'am' one another as though they were characters out of Addison's *Spectator*.

Bessy had doted on my mother ever since it had been her duty to keep my mother's infant nose and bottom clean. So now that they were neighbours Bessy thought that day wasted when she had not spent an hour or two of it gossiping to her Dotty; and how could my mother, masterful woman though she is, restrain, let alone Bowdlerise, a bawdy-tongued woman who had once trained her to the chamber-pot?

This visiting, however, was not wholly one-sided. Ever since my fat little legs could carry me there I would, when my mother wasn't looking, trot around the corner to the Asylum to spend the pleasantest part of my day in the company of the Trotters. I do believe I have never been half as fond of any woman as I am of Bessy. Whenever I arrived at the Asylum there would always be a fine selection of pies, lardy cakes, tarts, syllabubs, custards and cordials waiting for me, and these were all things forbidden me at home. My mother always insisted that such foods could only add to my already outstanding stoutness.

But one fateful day when Bessy came over, she was all unknowingly to play the ominous role of Greek Herald in my tragedy. I was not part of the audience then for I was not yet nine and my mother thought me too young for Bessy's cheerful bawdiness. But Bessy used to tell me about it often enough in later years, and seldom varied a sentence in the telling.

'We was talking about you, my pet,' she would say, pressing me to take another lardy cake, 'or, to be more haccurate, I were talking about you and your Ma were polishing 'er nails an' nodding 'er 'ead from time to time. Then do you know what?'

'No,' I would say, having by then been well trained in my responses.

'I suddenly realised your Ma weren't more nor 'alf listening. So to waken 'er up, and seeing as 'ow we was supposed to be talking woman to woman, I hobserved that, 'owever fast the rest of you might be growing, that rest weren't growing 'alf as fast as your pecker was.

'"Whatever are you a-talking about?" said your Ma, looking up at last from 'er nails.

'"Come off the grass, Dotty," said I. "You know just as well as what I do what I was halluding to. I was halluding to Master Willy's Little Willy."

'"Was you hindeed!" said your Ma. "An' what, pray, is so interesting about Master William's Little Willy?"

'"Only that it's not 'alf as little as it ought to be for 'is age," said I. "That's something you must 'ave noticed, Dotty, an' been thankful for. If the poor little wretch won't ever 'ave anything else in the way of features,'e'll always 'ave that."

'"You've never 'ad children, Bessy," said your Ma 'aughtily, 'an she only ever 'aving 'ad no more than you so that she's 'ad no other infant peckers to judge by. "You don't know, therefore, that small boys always develop unevenly. The rest of Master William will catch up with his pecker soon enough. I'm sure I don't know why you take such an interest in the matter."

'"What female worth 'er salt wouldn't be hinterested in such a whopper? I know that I am an' ever shall be. An' the same goes for my hinmates."

'"Your hinmates?" said your mother, even more 'aughtily.

'"Them far more than you an' me. They're more hexpert,

you might say. When it comes to peckers they're as much at 'ome as a pork butcher is with 'is sossidges."'

Bessy's 'hinmates' were, of course, the Younger Fallen Women. Young though I then was, I already realised that my mother, even though she was the prime reason for their congregating in Kensington, was as much opposed to their taking that sort of interest in me as she would have been had I taken a similar sort of interest in them.

'"And 'ow, Bessy, did your hinmates come to be hinterested in Master William's tickler?"' asked my mother, in a voice Bessy always described as 'Cold enough to freeze a Heskimo's balls'.

'"Ain't that just what I've been a-trying to tell you the past quarter of an hour?"'

'"Then do you get on with it."'

'"Well you know 'ow the little pet makes an 'abit of running over to the 'Sylum to see me an' Trotter."'

'"I'm haware," said your Ma, "that 'e's fond of you, but I suspect that it's cupboard love. You stuff 'im up with the things I won't let 'im 'ave at 'ome because they are fattening."'

'"Some think they are and some think they ain't,"' said I.

'"'Owsomever, an' to get on with it, it were last week—No! I tell a lie—it were the week afore that when I sent Master Willy out to play in the yard when the hinmates were hexercising. 'E'd just took some refreshment. Nothing, mark you, that weren't entirely 'olesome an' strength-building. It were a warm day, as you may well recall, an' the little lamb might 'ave 'ad a glass or two too much lemonade, what I make special for 'im. Mighty partial to my lemonade 'e is, which is no wonder, seeing as 'ow I always put in a hextra dose of the double-refined with the lemon . . ."'

'"If you don't come to the point," said your Ma, "I'll 'ave a hapoplexy."'

'"The point?" said I. "Ain't I just been telling you that the point is Master Willy's pecker, the which would be stamped Triple X at Whitbread's Brewery if so be they could brew an' barrel such things, which they can't? For which we ought to be thankful that all such peckers are in the gift of the Lord, who's far from generous when it comes to giving away hextra-specials such as Master Willy's . . ."'

' "Come to the point!" ' shouted my mother, who ought to have known that it was the one thing Bessy never came to.

' "Well, as I was a-telling you, Dotty," ' said Bessy, who wouldn't have shortened her stride for the Archbishop of Canterbury himself, ' "the poor little angel must 'ave 'ad a drop too much of my lemonade in 'is poor little bladder. So what did 'e do?"

' "What?" ' screamed my mother.

' "Just what little boys do all the world over. 'E dropped 'is little breeches, got a 'old of 'is pecker, an' started to piss."

' "Was that all?"

' "Not hexactly. There were them hinmates what I've been a-referring to."

' "Even fallen women who, as everyone knows, destroy their offspring at birth, must 'ave seen little boys drop their breeches before."

' "Not one so remarkable well-'ung as our Willy they 'aven't. I tell you what. It were a real blessing the little innocent were too young to 'ave got an 'orn on, or I'd not 'ave answered for the hinmates. It's my firm opinion that, Society or no Society, 'Sylum or no 'Sylum, you ain't ever going to suppress that pertiklar vice in the likes of them, if vice it be, an' I often wonders about that. Anyways, an' to cut a short story shorter, there were our little lamb with 'is hextra-special pecker in 'is 'and an' do you know, Dotty, what the hinmates did?"

' "What?"

' "They gave 'im a right British cheer, that's what. A regular three times three an' one more for luck." '

My mother is not easily ruffled, but at this stage, according to Bessy, she became 'as ruffled as an 'en in a thunder storm'.

' "This is quite outrageous, Bessy. The Society would never countenance such behaviour, and nor will I."

' "Continence or no continence," ' said Bessy, who was plainly confused but still enjoying herself. ' "All I can tell you is that my hinmates were mightily himpressed, an' if there are any women what ain't easily himpressed it's them. Ever since then I 'ardly dare let Master Willy go out by 'imself in the yard, they're all that eager to 'ug an' fondle 'im. That one they call Randy Ruby is forever asking 'im what 'e's got hinside of 'is breeches.''

'An' then,' Bessy would conclude , 'damn me eyes if your Ma didn't stand up a-looking just like the Hangel of Judgment might 'ave looked if so be it 'e'd been a female. Then she told me, sharper than she's ever spoken to me before, that I was to go 'ome immediate an' send Trotter round to 'er, for she'd a pertikler himportant errand 'e 'ad to run.'

That errand was to carry a note to the House of Commons. It required Mr Wilberforce to wait on my mother as near to immediately as was possible. It was late that afternoon, however, when my mother and I found ourselves facing Mr Wilberforce, the dust and the smell of Westminster still on him, in our front parlour.

'Sir,' said my mother, just as soon as Mr Wilberforce had come through the door. 'Sir,' said she, placing a firm hand on my head, which was a most unusual thing for her to do unless it was a preliminary to a cuff on the ear, 'this boy must be sent away immediately to boarding school.'

If I was surprised at this announcement, so was Mr Wilberforce.

'It must be as you say, Ma'am, but I thought you entertained somewhat opposite opinions. I'm sure you've told me often enough that Eton had come close to being the ruin of your late husband.'

'Circumstances,' said my mother, 'alter cases, and circumstances have.'

'I'm sorry to hear it, Ma'am, upon my soul I am. However, I shall give the subject much thought in the weeks to come. "Horses for courses" we used to say in my unregenerate days when, I'm sorry to say, I gambled and drank and whor . . . horsed around with the best of 'em . . . I mean, of course, the worst of 'em. We'll have to make a most careful study of every boarding school in the land before we decide on the particular course our young colt here should run on.'

'Mr Wilberforce,' said my mother, bringing him up sharp. 'We have no time for lengthy considerations and even less time for talk about courses and colts and your former unregenerate days.'

Mr Wilberforce was taken aback. For all his later Evangelicalism, he had quite enjoyed lapsing into the sporting and horsy language of his youth.

'If that's the case, Ma'am,' said he, 'what is it that William Wilberforce can do for you? He is, as always, yours to command.' At which point he gave her a look which, if he'd been an aged buck instead of a latter-day Saint, would have been described as an ogle.

My mother ignored it.

'You are,' she said, 'a Governor of Christ's Hospital.'

'I am, Ma'am,' he said uneasily.

'And as a Governor, you can always nominate a boy for that school?'

'I can, Ma'am, just so long as I observe the statutes and regulations. Christ's Hospital is one of our most ancient charitable foundations, and its rules are not easily changed.'

'I'm sorry to hear it. Yet if you cannot or will not bend those rules to William, then William, I am sure, can be bent to your rules. You talk, Sir, as though there could be insurmountable difficulties over such a nomination. May I ask what they are?'

Now Mr Wilberforce may have been a leading Evangelical, a Clapham Saint, and my mother's most persistent admirer, but he was also a High Tory. This meant that he abhorred anything that threatened departure from ancient traditions or the establishment of a precedent.

'In the first instance, Ma'am, there is the question of age. No boy over the age of nine can be accepted into Christ's Hospital.'

'In that case, you must stir your stumps. William is still ten weeks from being ineligible.'

'But then, Ma'am, there is also the matter of his parentage.'

'What,' said my mother menacingly, 'have you or anyone else to object to in his parentage?'

'I beg you not to misunderstand me, Ma'am. It's a question of liveries and not of lineages.'

This was no more than a preliminary line of defence which my mother was very willing to breach.

'Liveries, Sir! What should William have to do with liveries?'

'Nothing, Ma'am, and there's the rub of it. Now if only he'd been the son of a London liveryman . . .'

'The Hon. Fitz,' said my mother haughtily, 'was a soldier and a hero, not a Cheapside grocer.'

'Yet for this purpose, Ma'am, it would have been more convenient if he had been a liveryman. The sons of such have the first call on the charitable funds by which the Hospital is supported.'

'Do we talk now of charitable funds, Mr Wilberforce? Do you presume to talk to a hero's widow who has been left by an ungrateful government with no more by way of a pension than would keep a beggar woman in matches about charitable funds? Does William, here'—at this stage she dabbed with her handkerchief at a pair of remarkably dry and flashing eyes—'deserve less from the inhabitants of a city Major FitzThistlethwaite died defending than the orphan brat of some obese, turtle-gobbling, stay-at-home liveryman?'

Mr Wilberforce looked alarmed.

'Before we follow that line of argument, Ma'am, ought we not to remember that your late husband died, or so I've been told, of a surfeit of greasy Portuguese food, and not of a French bullet?'

'Quibble me no quibbles, Sir! We're not in the House of Commons now. Whatever my late husband may have died of, he died of it in the process of defending the City of London.'

Mr Wilberforce, having seen his skirmishers and piquets driven back, retreated behind his main line of defence.

'I have never doubted, Ma'am, that you and your William fully deserve both the nation's and the City of London's charity. But will that charity produce what is desirable? Have you considered, Ma'am, that a place such as Christ's Hospital could be a harsh, harsh home for a child as lovingly and as gently nurtured as your William? It is not for me to tell you what can happen at boarding schools. But would you have his innocence corrupted?'

'If he's going to be corrupted,' said my mother, 'I'd rather he was corrupted at school, and by the boys and ushers of Christ's Hospital than at home, and by the Younger Fallen Women.'

Mr Wilberforce, who had now seen his glacis stormed, his fosse occupied, and the attacker streaming on towards his escarp, still tried, however feebly, to defend his position.

'But are you certain, Ma'am,' he said, 'that your William can survive all the Greek and the Latin—yes, and all the birching and the bullying which will fall to his lot as a Bluecoat?'

My mother drew herself up to her full height and came close to shaking her truly impressive bust at him.

'Are you suggesting, Sir, that my son, *my son*, Sir, is either a dullard or a weakling?'

'By no means, Ma'am, I assure you. I know him to be a remarkably . . . stout and cunning . . . that is to say intelligent little boy.'

'Then I can only conclude, Sir,' said my mother, who already had the scent of victory in her nostrils, 'that all these shiftings and wrigglings on your part amount to but one thing.'

'And what might that be, Ma'am?' bleated Mr Wilberforce, who had the odour of defeat in his.

'Why, Sir, that you believe that a poor widow who has always thought of herself as your friend, and who has striven to act as your confidante and adviser, and her unloved, friendless, orphaned son'—here she made a second dab with her handkerchief—'lack so much of merit in your eyes as to have no claim to your sympathy.'

Napoleon in his prime could have done no better. Mr Wilberforce, who was after all only a politician, didn't even attempt a fighting withdrawal but surrendered immediately, foot, horse and baggage train.

'I swear, Ma'am, you wrong me! Upon my soul you do! No one holds you in higher regard than myself. And, though it may not be quite so apparent, I have some regard for your William who is, after all, my godson.'

'Then, Sir,' said my mother, 'you will do something about Christ's Hospital?'

'My name's not William Wilberforce else.'

My mother put her handkerchief away and became all smiles. Once she gets her way she knows well how a victor should behave.

'I am, as always,' she said, sweeping him a curtsy fit, as she well knew, for a duke, 'Mr Wilberforce's most humble, most faithful, and most grateful friend.'

'And I yours, Ma'am.' He made a leg and a bow after the manner of the last century, clapped on his hat, and departed.

And that, largely because of Bessy, was how tragedy entered my childhood and I entered Christ's Hospital.

6   *Fine Portraits and Pinched Bellies*

Everyone knows, or ought to know, that Christ's Hospital is an ancient foundation occupying the site in the Newgate where, in pre-Reformation days, the Greyfriars' Monastery once stood. I've sometimes thought that if only Henry VIII hadn't been so uxorious, it might have been called the Greyfriars' School—but that's neither here nor there. I was all but nine in 1815 when I first entered the place and just past seventeen when I left it, rather unexpectedly, in 1823. Those may have been formative years, but I'll be damned if they were enjoyable ones.

The school is a magnificent place to look at but a miserable one for a small boy to live in. It was no more consolation to me that Sir Christopher Wren had designed the new buildings, or that Antonio Verrio had painted so many of the portraits hung in the Great Hall than it was that we were so conspicuously set apart from all other boys by the medieval blue gowns and caps and bright yellow breeches and stockings we had to wear.

They may not have looked quite so ridiculous in Verrio's day. Several of the pictures in the Great Hall had boys wearing that dress looking up from the bottom corners of the picture at some long-dead benefactor, who occupied most of the rest of it, with quite improbable expressions of happiness, gratitude and general well-being. In that respect they were nothing like us, their distant descendants, for such well-fed,

smug little buggers couldn't possibly have had bums to be
birched and bellies to be starved. We had both.

I found it easier to deal with the birching than the starvation for I soon learnt what to do whenever I was threatened
with physical violence. School buffoons, I discovered, are
allowed certain privileges. So, making the most of my fat and
somewhat simple appearance and the fact that I had to wear
spectacles, I burbled and clowned and played the fool and was
very willing to be everyone's butt. By inviting ridicule I was
less frequently subjected to anything crueller than ridicule,
and that I never have minded.

But if ever it seemed that being ridiculous wasn't going
to save me from violence, I would fall back on cowardice.
Whether it was the threat of a ceremonial birching which
would have placed me on the beadle's back with my breeches
down, or of a caning by some puffed-up, out-of-humour usher,
or of merely being bullied and knocked about by my school
fellows, my tactics were very much the same. I would fall to
my knees and beg for mercy before ever my breeches had been
taken down or the first stroke or blow had been offered. If this
didn't work, I would be howling and yowling and yarooing
louder than any half-dozen Irishwomen at an Irish wake long
before the second. If such tactics didn't always prevent the
assault, they could generally mitigate it. Strong men are silly
enough to believe that they should remain silent on such
occasions, and they suffer accordingly. Cowards, especially fat
ones, are expected to be cowards.

Starvation was a different matter. God knows that I've
been hungry enough here in Sumroo, dieting for the Begum's
pleasure. But never have I been so hungry as I was during my
first year at Christ's Hospital.

I was then little more than an infant and in proportion to
my stature, quite as fat as I am now, although how I remained
so still puzzles me. I had great exercise because I had to
engage, however reluctantly, in a good deal of physical and
mental activity. I was growing fast, not just in respect of that
which had attracted the Younger Fallen Women, but in every
direction in which a small boy might grow. These things
were the cause of my ever-growing hunger; for their method
of feeding us at Christ's Hospital left us, according to their

calculations, just this side of starvation, and according to mine, well on t'other side.

We broke our morning fast with what was called our 'crug'. This consisted of no more than one quarter of a dry penny loaf which we were allowed to wash down with a limited quantity of well-watered small beer. This was poured into our little wooden piggins from great leather jacks, and it tasted and smelt so vilely of the leather that I've never been able to pass a saddler's or a cobbler's shop since without remembering Christ's Hospital. And this was supposed to line our bellies and stay our appetites until we came to our dinners.

That dinner—our only hot meal of the day—was, for three days of the week, of an entirely cereal nature. Even then, it was a poor brew that they gave us. For, whether it was burgoo, barley or millet, it was ladled out to us as something slightly thicker than a Frenchman's *soupe maigre* but considerably thinner than a Scotsman's porridge. Nor were we allowed a stoup of milk or a knob of butter to give it some richness. No! Not even a few grains of salt or a spoonful of Demerara, let alone a grating of nutmeg or a root of ginger which could have given those bland and watery messes the smack of something.

Yet if our grain foods suffered from a deficiency of richness, our flesh foods suffered from an excess of it. Whether it was cow-beef, fresh-boiled on the Thursdays and half-pickled on the Sundays, or ewe-mutton seethed on the Fridays and rotten-roasted on the Tuesdays, the most of what we saw on our platters was fat.

These gobbets of fat, which we called 'gags', were not things to be eaten in any quantity. So, starving though so many of us in the Lower School were, more gags were left on our plates than found their way into our bellies. It weren't that every poor old knacker's-yard beast that had died for us had been wholly deficient in lean. It was rather that the best part of whatever lean they had had on their bones had been cut off beforehand and carried away by our 'nurses'. These creatures, who were supposed to attend to our needs and to stand to us, in some ways, as mothers, served us on meat days in much the same way as the Harpies had served blind Phineus before the Argonauts came to his rescue.

Nor, so far as we smaller boys were concerned, were these

the only Harpies to be found in Christ's Hospital. For if, by some mischance, a slice of lean did end up on our platters, you could depend on it that some older and stronger boy would appropriate it to himself.

I still remember vividly how, as a very new boy, I had the justification for this tyranny explained to me by one of our tyrants. He was a much older boy with whom, later, I would be on quite friendly terms. He had the reputation of being a very sporting sort of fellow and was much revered as a consequence.

I was sitting in the Great Hall looking at the pile of gags on my plate when he approached me, which he did by turning over everything on that plate in an attempt to uncover something lean enough to tempt the terrier he kept, quite illegally, in an attic under the leads. He was said to be organising a rat-pit in those same attics, and he needed to keep his terrier fit if he was to make any money out of him.

'You're a new boy, ain't you?' said he, examining one of the more promising gags which actually had veins of meat and gristle running through it.

'Yes, if you please, Sir,' said I.

'Seeing that you're so new, it could be that you're wondering why I should make so free with your vittles.'

'Certainly not, Sir. I wouldn't dream of wondering. And as for making free, pray make as free as you wish.'

He looked at me suspiciously.

'You ain't, by any chance, young-'un, trying to come the old soldier with me, are you?'

'The old soldier, Sir? The only old soldier I know is Trotter, and he left the Hussars years and years ago.'

'I thought so,' said he, grasping me by the ear and giving it such a twist that it brought me up off my seat hallooing and yarooing and whimpering 'Leggo'. 'You're being sarcy. It's always very dangerous, young-'un, being sarcy with the Upper School.'

'I don't rightly know what sarcy is,' said I, twisting my head so as to give my ear a bit of leeway. 'But whatever it is, I swear I meant no offence by it.'

I must have convinced him, for he let go of my ear and looked at me with some astonishment.

''Pon my soul, I do believe that you didn't. You're just

green, that's what it is. The fattest and greenest new boy we've had here for years. Ain't I right?'

'If you say so, Sir.'

'I do say so, and I don't want to hear you contradicting me.'

'Indeed I won't.'

'I tell you what, young-'un. Seeing as how you're so new and so green, I'll try to explain things to you. Ask yourself why your pater sent you to school.'

'I haven't got a pater, Sir,' said I, playing for sympathy.

'You must have had one at some time, and he would have known that this school is nothing more nor less than a preparation for the great school of life. And what will be your experience in that great school of life, young-'un?'

'I'm sure I don't know.'

'Why, you fat little shaver, it's as certain as death or the pox that there'll be politicians to make your life miserable and taxmen to make it poor. That's why it's our duty, as your elders and betters, to keep bullying you and taxing you as a preparation for what's to come. You've got to look on me as your trainer, and if you ever think I ain't training you enough, just let me know.'

With that he speared what I had thought of as the only edible piece of beef on my plate and walked away with it muttering that he didn't rightly know what his terrier would think of it. I was left eyeing the yellow, congealing gags in front of me, and crying with hunger and the injustice of it all.

And yet, looking back on it, I don't know that there weren't a good deal of sense in what he had said.

7   *My First Venture in Trade*

Approximately once a month there arrived at Christ's Hospital something that was known as a 'leave-day'. On such a day we were all of us turned out of the school to make

what use we might of twelve hours of idleness. Those boys
who had their homes close by would be entertained and fed
by their families. But a boy like myself, who lived in far-off
Kensington, and who had no circle of relations or friends
with carriages at their disposal, found little to enjoy in such a
holiday. So far as I was concerned, a day of idleness meant
a day of even greater hunger since, except for our crugs, we
were turned out into the world with nothing in our bellies and
nothing certain in the way of food for the next twenty-four
hours.

If, which was not always the case, I was turned out with a
few pence in my pocket, the most of these would very soon be
spent with the hot-pie man and the polony-and-baked-potato
man outside the school gates. After this there was nothing for
it but to pass the time peering into the windows of cookshops,
eating houses and bakeries, slavering over what was inside
them and envying those rich enough to make use of them.
Such exercise, tantalising enough in summer, was torment
itself in winter.

I was most frequently attracted to the window of a certain
pastry-cook's shop in Pudding Lane, which aptly-named
thoroughfare was no more than five minutes' stroll from
Newgate. I doubt whether, even on my Sumroo diet, I would
now be captivated by the greasy-looking mutton pies, the
fly-blown cakes and the faded jam tarts displayed in that
Pudding Lane window. In those days, however, I lusted after
them more fiercely than randy Turk ever lusted after the
houris of Paradise. Many was the hour I spent with my nose
flattened against that window wondering whether, if I still
had three ha'pence in my pocket, that would entitle me to
enter Paradise and taste of its delights.

My constitutional timidity and the fact that I seldom had
the three ha'pence prevented me for most of that first year
from doing anything but wonder. But on one of the leave-days
towards the end of that year I happened to notice a ragged
urchin walk boldly into the shop with a basket over his
arm. That basket contained objects that were familiar to me:
namely, a good many scraps of fat, and none of them over-
clean.

The sight of such a cargo made me curious. By applying

my nose once more to the window I could follow, albeit in dumb crambo, what happened inside. The boy, having put his basket down on the counter, which was unattended, appeared to halloo for someone. A swag-bellied man in a greasy apron and dirty nightcap who must have been both proprietor and cook emerged from the back premises. He nodded to the boy and then poked a finger into the basket, turning the scraps over in what seemed to me to be a disparaging sort of way. The two then appeared to argue for a while before swag-belly tipped the contents of the basket into a wooden tub that sat on the far end of his counter. After a bit more argument the pastry-cook, expostulating all the while, put a quantity of stale-looking rolls, half of a decaying mutton pie, about a dozen crumbling jam tarts, and a thick wedge of plum cake into the boy's basket. The two, who had been haggling so fiercely, then shook hands in a friendly way and the lad departed.

It was the plum cake, more than anything else, that attracted me. Moreover, it was one of those rare days when I still had three ha'pence in my pocket. Now, thought I, displaying an understanding of commerce surprising in one of my age, that lad has clearly been engaging in the wholesale trade which he has entered by way of barter. I, having nothing to barter with and no more than three ha'pence by way of cash, cannot hope to do as he has done. But that same three ha'pence might tempt the lad into the retail trade. More particularly, three ha'pence could tempt him to part with the plum cake.

The boy was already stuffing a jam tart into his mouth when he emerged. He must, I imagine, have been surprised to find a small, fat, bespectacled boy wearing a blue, medieval gown, waiting for him with three ha'pence lying in his outstretched palm. It may have been the unexpectedness of this that made it difficult, at first, for us to come to any meeting of minds. He refused, initially, to have anything to do with me and turned down Pudding Lane with me trotting at his heels and begging him to listen. It took some time before he realised what I would be at, and even then there followed a period of haggling as difficult as any I later experienced in the bazaars of India.

The plum cake he would not part with. 'No, not for three times three ha'pence.' In the end we settled, quite amicably, for half a dozen of the most decrepit of the jam tarts and walked together down Pudding Lane, our two sets of jaws busily at work. In between our chewing and swallowing and licking of our fingers he told me something about himself and his trade with the pastry-cook.

He was employed, it seems, as a sweeper-up in nearby Smithfield. The butchers there paid him little enough in cash, but they did allow him to recover and keep all the pieces of fat and offal he could find in the heaps of sawdust he had to collect and cart away. The sawdust went to a nearby publican who paid for it with a tankard of ale. The offal went, under a long-standing agreement, to a cat's-meat man who paid cash on the nail.

The lad, however, never wanted to have too much cash on him since his mother took every penny of it off him just as soon as he got home. So, on the principle that no one could confiscate what was already in his belly, all his scraps of fat went to the Pudding Lane pastry-cook who rendered them down to use in his bakings. This gave me an insight into the underlying realities of the food trade which I have never forgotten.

By the time we parted I already had it firmly in my mind that I, too, would enter into a barter trade with the pastry-cook. And so, from that moment on, I began to put into my pocket all the gags I had formerly left on my plate. Moreover, by lingering when the others had left table, I could generally manage to pocket all the gags left on plates within reasonable reach of me. Once I had smuggled these back to my dormitory, I would conceal them in the carpet bag I had brought with me from home.

The consequence was that when the next leave-day came round the carpet bag, which was a capacious one, was better than half full of gags, and not smelling over-sweet, even though it was a cold winter. I picked out all the scraps that were not too obviously tainted and bundled them up in a large, red-chequered handkerchief which Trotter had given me when I was packed off to school. The other, more gamey gags I took up to the attic and fed to the ratting terrier. Since he had already had the benefit of the lean, thought I, it was no more than right that he should have the burden of the fat.

As for the bundle in the red-chequered handkerchief, I jumped on it until it seemed flat enough to conceal under my gown. Then, as leave-day dawned, and with plum cake in mind and terror in my heart, I smuggled the bundle through the gates. The terror was solely because of Gosling, the gate porter. He was thought to be sharper-eyed than Cerberus, even though he had but two eyes, and they seeming to look in opposite directions.

There was good justification for terror. All Lower School boys were suspected, not unreasonably, of wanting to run away. As leave-days were clearly the best running-away days it was then that Gosling looked most closely at each Lower School boy going through his gates. If any one of them was discovered to be concealing a packet, parcel or bundle, that would be taken as prima-facie proof of an intention to abscond, and the boy would be seized and taken off to judgment, for running away was just about the most serious crime a Bluecoat could commit.

If he was a first offender, the boy would be publicly birched before being confined for a week on bread and water in one of the old underground cells in which, before the Pope was chased out of England, peccant Franciscans were left to repent of their sins. A second attempt always involved a ceremonial expulsion. After the criminal had been birched before the whole school in the Great Hall assembled, he would be stripped of his blue gown and yellow breeches and thrust out of the gates in his underclothes. There he would be taken in charge by the beadle of his native parish, summoned there for that purpose. Except that they actually shot the absconder before posting his name on the door of his parish church, this came close to copying the manner with which the Army dealt with its deserters.

That, in short, was why I was terrified as I passed Gosling on my first gag-smuggling foray. All went well, however. I was noted for my corpulence, that being an uncommon condition amongst Lower School boys, and Gosling must simply have attributed the bulge under my gown to that. But there was no dawdling once I'd got through the gates. The hot-pie man and the polony man were both passed at a trot and in no time at all I was asking a somewhat startled Pudding Lane pastry-cook what his current rates on the Fat Exchange might be. He tried, at first, to adopt a high-and-mighty manner.

'I don't,' said he, after I had shown him what was inside my bundle, 'hengage in trade with hinfants, 'owever fat they may be in themselves, an' 'owever revolting the fats they brings me might be.'

I hadn't braved Gosling to be talked down by such a greasy citizen as this.

'Not much more of an infant,' said I, 'than the one you deal with from Smithfield. And I'll have you notice, fellow, that my fats aren't nearly so revolting as his.'

He looked at me, then, quite sharply and, seeing that I was not quite the simpleton I seemed, he switched, as any trades-man would, to trying to talk down my wares.

'Why,' said he, delicately holding out one of my gags to an imaginary audience of fat experts. 'Here's some fine stuff for you. Here's tallow as yellow as any cow what died of old age could ever 'ave produced, an' what's more, it's already more than 'alf-cooked.'

'That doesn't mean that you can't still make use of it.'

'Make use of it? Sweeney Todd 'imself couldn't make use of it, an' we all know what 'e put into 'is mutton pies. No, young Sir, fats such as these ain't to be used by a cook such as me. I've my reputation to consider. I'm known throughout the City as one what uses only the very finest suets and lards in 'is bakings.'

I sensed that he wasn't serious since, all the time he was speaking, he kept turning the heap of gags over with his forefinger. But I also sensed that it was now or never. I had to let him know the sort of boy he was dealing with. And so I blinked at him very innocently through my spectacles and said:

'I wonder whether your customers know that those same finest lards and suets are recovered, for the most part, from the sawdust and dirt of the floors of Smithfield Market?'

That set him a-spluttering. I let him call me a blackmailing young varmint and other such names before I cut across his protests with certain well-reasoned arguments.

'You'll have noticed,' said I, 'that my fats are considerably cleaner than those you get from your Smithfield accomplice. As to their yellowness, why that could be pure gain to you. It could persuade your customers that you use nothing but the richest and yellowest country butters in your bakings.'

At this he began to look at me with considerably more respect.

'Oo taught you the secrets of the trade? An 'ow do you know they don't already think that I use butter? But be that as it may, you still can't get away from the fact that these fats of yours 'ave already seen the fire an' are better nor 'alf cooked.'

'In that case,' said I, 'just think of what you'll be saving in the way of fuel when you come to the rendering of 'em down. Half done is well done in that respect.'

I had surprised myself by the fluency and cogency of my arguments, which must have impressed the pastry-cook for we then got down to the actual haggling. He refused to do a deal over the plum cake—'That would be trading right out of your class, young Sir.' Nevertheless I eventually left his shop with a bulkier bundle than I had brought into it, and with more than enough time-expired rolls, tarts and lardy cakes to keep my jaws working, on and off, for the rest of the morning.

What I enjoyed almost as much was being accepted as an equal by the pastry-cook. For the first time in my life an adult recognised in me what I like to think of as a fund of commercial sagacity, though it has since been described by some as criminal cunning. The pastry-cook, perhaps, lay half-way between these two.

'I'll take your fats,' he had said, 'whenever you can bring 'em, an' the more you bring the better I'll like it. But I'll tell you this now an' I'll tell it you straight. I'd rather do business with a 'ole synagogue of Jews than with such an innocent-seeming, fat, sharp little bugger as yourself.'

I returned to Christ's Hospital that night dreaming of a greatly enlarged gag trade, and of a future so full of plum cake and jam tarts that I would never need to go hungry from one leave-day to another. And that, I suppose, is why I fell into the trap so many successful speculators fall into before they end up in Carey Street. For I was determined to establish what commodity men call 'a corner' in gags.

In order to do this I had to form a small consortium, which I did by getting together all the boys small enough and weak enough for me to bully, together with a few stronger ones whom I had to bribe with promises of a share in the profits. They got to work with such effect that our 'nurses' were soon unable to find even one gag left abandoned on a platter. This worried them. Until then they had been able to justify the tribute they exacted from every joint by claiming that we were over-fed and by pointing to what we had previously left on our plates as proof of it. Whether or not they suspected anything I cannot say.

But although I had succeeded in organising my supplies, and that on a rising scale, I could not safely claim to have done the same when it came to their marketing. The contraband still had to be smuggled past Gosling, and there lay my dilemma. The more boys I involved in the smuggling the greater the risk of detection. Moreover some showed signs of wanting to set up in trade on their own account. So, although I allowed one or two of 'em to smuggle for me on occasion, I assumed the main burden myself. The larger my trade with the pastry-cook grew the more my gown had to expand to meet it.

And so, almost inevitably, the pitcher went once too oft to the well. In short, instead of being content to smuggle out a mere bundle of gags, I decided to try a whole carpet bag full. Proud Coriolanus spoke of 'mountainous error too highly heaped', and so it was with Bunter.

As I approached the gates on that fateful day even the most casual observer would have wondered how one so young could suffer from such a monstrous dropsy. Gosling took but one look before he grabbed hold of me, and it didn't take him many minutes to discover the carpet bag strapped to my middle.

He immediately sent for the beadle, the beadle sent for the steward, and the steward dragged me before the Upper Master without even one of them bothering to look inside the carpet bag. Nor would any of 'em heed my appeals for mercy and my loud denials of any intention to abscond. A carpet bag meant a runagate, and so a runagate I had to be.

8   *Cowardice and Cockiness*

No boy could have been more terrified than I was of the Reverend James Boyer; nor was there, in the whole of Christ's Hospital, anyone better qualified to inspire terror. Even the oldest boys were scared of him, for he had the reputation of being at once the most pedantic and the most tyrannical of all the ushers.

He was never seen without his wig, and there were those who claimed that his ferocity varied according to which of 'em he wore. If it was his best one, which was a well-tended bob-tail affair, he could be almost lenient. But if it was his workaday scratch wig, the worst had to be expected. My heart sank when I saw that this was one of the scratch-wig days.

Boyer listened in silence to all that Gosling, the beadle, the steward, and Bunter had to say. Then he bade Gosling open the carpet bag. He looked with distaste at the gags and then turned to the steward, a monstrously dignified man called Jones.

'Mr Jones,' said he, 'the boy tells no more than the truth. No one in his senses would run away with nothing more to sustain him in his flight than decaying gobbets of fat. Ergo, Mr Jones, here is no intention to abscond.'

If I looked delighted by this and Mr Jones disappointed, these roles were reversed as Boyer continued his judgment.

'Yet, even if we accept that these disgusting fragments were no more than scraps that had been left on the boys' plates, leftovers, and things of little or no value—a *res nullius* as the lawyers would have it—that *res nullius* is still the school's *res nullius*, is it not? And so we have here, not a running away, but a theft of school property, which is almost as serious an offence.'

'I could not have hoped to put it better myself,' said Mr Jones, at which the Reverend Boyer looked pretty sharply at him before focusing his attention on me.

'Sir!' he thundered, leaning over to survey my four-foot-ten from his imposing six-foot-two. 'Sir,' said he. 'I have accepted that here was an intent to steal rather than one to abscond. But what I have not yet decided, boy, is whether the greater turpitude resides in the theft or the gluttony that inspired it.'

'Sir,' said I, quite simply, for by now my wits had wholly deserted me, 'I was hungry.'

'Hungry, Sir! Hungry! Only a glutton could want for more than the ample and wholesome diet supplied in this ancient and most charitable establishment.'

'Yet I was hungry.'

'And therefore, boy, you're a glutton.'

'If you say so, Sir.'

'I do say so, Sir. And do you know, Sir, what Aulius Persius Flaccus had to say about gluttons?'

'I ain't up to him yet, Sir. We're still on Caesar.'

'The slow progress of learning in the Lower School never fails to dismay me. So you know nothing of Flaccus?'

'I'm afraid so, Sir.'

'Then I'm afraid, Sir, that you'll have to learn about him, even if you have to acquire that knowledge through your bum rather than through a book.'

Thereupon he reached up to a shelf, took down a copy of the Six Satires of Aulius Persius Flaccus, and began to read aloud that one of 'em which deals with gluttony. And, to drive the point home, he fetched me a shrewd swipe with his cane at the end of every line. Persius, I discovered later, had never written very much and none of what he wrote was very long. Nevertheless I could have wished that he had written far less, and that more epigrammatically, before Boyer had finished with me. And long before he had finished, I had near lost my voice with howling.

But the more I howled the louder he read, and the louder he had to read the more he made me smart. Nor did my usual trick of sinking to my knees and begging for mercy serve in this case. Boyer merely pulled up a chair and sat on it, the better to be at a level from which he read and beat to greater effect.

No one could have been more cowed than the snivelling wretch who was finally released from Boyer's study. But both the beating I'd received and the reasons for it soon became the talk of the school, and that talk would have it that I was, if anything, something of a hero. And just as soon as that was accepted, I started to grow cocky. I have never doubted that I am a coward. But I also know that when things go well with me I can act cockier than any Duke has dared to act since the Frogs stormed the Tuileries and thereby let it be known that, if anyone was to be cocky, all had to be cocky.

The punishment I had received from Boyer, which had been sharp enough, grew no less sharp in the telling. And as boys are perpetually at war with their ushers, those whom the ushers have scourged, schoolboys will always make much of and cherish. And that's how, for the first time in my school career, I became popular and acquired more friends than I really needed.

But it wasn't merely the beating that made me popular. The Bluecoats all seemed to think that I had displayed ingenuity in embarking on my trade in gags and daring in seeking to expand it. There wasn't a boy in the Lower School who didn't wish that he had thought of something similar. And in the Upper School they were saying that they'd been wrong to think of young Bunter as just a fat buffoon. He was, in fact, a deep-'un, and as full of spunk and wily stratagems as Ulysses himself.

The idea that I was full of spunk was arrived at by mistake. I had not been at my best when I was dragged in front of Boyer. In fact, I had quite lost the use of my wits and wasn't far off from soiling my breeches. Consequently I never even considered the possibility of mitigating my offence by spreading the blame for it. In short, I never blabbed on my accomplices, and the fact that I hadn't blabbed was accepted as additional proof of my staunchness.

Schoolboys' memories are short, and my new popularity might soon have worn off but for an event which earned me a good deal of misplaced pity from my fellows. This occurred whilst I still had a few weals and bruises to show my new-found friends, and it occurred in the shape of a small boy who came panting up to tell me that I was required, once more, in the Reverend Boyer's study.

God knows I've been frightened often enough here in Sumroo, but scarcely more so than I was at having to face Boyer again. Yet, when I crept most apprehensively into that room off the Great Hall where Boyer lurked, like some tiger waiting to rush out of its den to savage anything that passed, I found that same tiger had turned into a lamb or, to judge by the noises he was making, a turtle dove. What's more, I found my mother closeted with him and looking handsomer than ever, possibly because she was wearing black, which has always suited her.

'Ah, there you are, Bunter,' cooed Boyer in this strange new voice of his. 'Come in, my dear boy, come in.'

'How are you, William?' asked my mother.

I was so surprised that I failed to answer her and remained frozen in the doorway. This brought a more familiar Boyer into action.

'Don't stand there gaping like an idiot, boy. Your mother—your quite delightful mother, if I may so put it, along with Catullus, and you know how sweet-tongued Catullus put it, don't you?'

'Not really, Sir.'

'Of course you do, Bunter. "*Et quantum est hominum venustiorum*" is how he put it, as we all know. And how would you construe that, Bunter?'

'I'm sure I don't know, Sir. We ain't up to Catullus yet.'

'Don't glory in your ignorance, boy. It means, of course, "How greatly charming to men". Now where was I?'

'You was, Sir, with sweet-tongued Catullus.'

He gave me a hard stare.

'No I wasn't, boy. I was with your mother.'

'Was you, Sir?'

'Come out of that doorway, Bunter, and take a seat. You must brace yourself and play the man today, for your mother has sad things to tell you. "*Sunt lacrimae rerum*," as the great Mantuan had it, "*Et mentem mortalis tangunt*". And now, dear lady, I shall leave you with your no less dear son so that the two of you may share this sorrow in private.'

Although the pedantic old humbug gave me what I'm sure he thought was a comforting smile before he sidled out of the room, he had been acting and cooing so out of character that it was not until after he left that it dawned on me that my mother was in mourning. When it did, I blurted out the worst of my fears.

'I hope, Mamma, that it ain't Bessy who's dead.'

'Bessy,' said my mother coldly, 'is quite as well as can be expected of anyone who has to deal, day in and day out, with thirty Younger Fallen Women. No, William, it's your grandfather Bunter who's dead.'

'Oh,' said I, 'is that all?'

'Isn't it enough?'

'Not for you to go into mourning and for old Boyer to be carrying on about *lacrimae rerum*.'

'You must show more respect for the Reverend Boyer, William—and for the dead. He was, after all, my father and your grandfather.'

'And we neither of us ever saw anything of him or cared anything for him.'

'Nevertheless he was, in his way, a very great man, and he's going to be given a rather grand funeral. What's more, I've come to take you to it since you are, after all, his only other descendant.'

'Does that mean,' said I eagerly, 'that I'll be able to skip afternoon school?'

'You'll miss more than that. On Friday Mr Speaker has to make a formal announcement of your grandfather's death to the House of Commons, following on which there will be what they call "Tributes from the Members". Mr Wilberforce has arranged for us to have seats in the Ambassadors' Gallery for that, and so your Mr Boyer has agreed that you may be away until the following Monday.'

This was such pleasant news to me that I had to use a recently acquired word which I greatly treasured. 'I can't,' said I, dancing a sort of Irish jig around Boyer's study, 'think of anything more serendipitous.'

So I went off to the funeral, to a good blow-out at Bellamy's, and to five blissful days away from school. The funeral itself was enjoyable. It was quite well-attended considering what a self-centred, single-minded, reclusive sort of cove my grandfather had been. Speeches the day after in the Commons were a different kettle of fish. There ain't ever many Members present on a Friday so there weren't all that many Tributes. But that merely meant that those who did speak could be longer-winded than ever, even though they all said much the same thing. After going on for a while about how much Parliament and the nation owed my grandfather, they all, in their different ways, suggested that, had it not been for him, there'd have been no refinements in life, England would have been as uncivilised as the Sandwich Islands, and a Parliamentary sitting would have been as tedious and uncouth as an Indian pow-wow.

The only good thing about that part of the day was that, once the speechifying was over, we all went upstairs to Bellamy's, where I enjoyed an even better tuck-in than Bessy could provide. The only drawback was that everyone from Mr Speaker to Lord Liverpool and from Mr Wilberforce to Mr Bellamy insisted on telling me more and more tales about my grandfather. And when I finally got back to Kensington, my mother and Bessy carried on doing the same.

And damned boring tales they were. But, remembering them now, I feel there is perhaps something more in heredity than I, in my ancestorless state, used to think. For with him, too, cockiness brought disaster, and recovery brought cockiness.

9   *Tales of my Grandfather*

My grandfather Bunter was, everybody acknowledged, first, last and always an Artist. But since even his greatest masterpieces were not of the sort that endure and carry a signature for later generations to marvel at, his was an emphemeral Art. Yet Art it was, as is proved by the title chosen for his world-famous work by the Master he was apprenticed to. Mr John Farley called that work 'The London ART of Cookery'.

That same Mr Farley was head cook at the London Tavern. This was then commonly accepted as the best eating house in London, just as it was accepted that Mr Farley was quite as valuable an artist as Sir Joshua Reynolds or Mr Handel. How my grandfather got from the Foundling Hospital to the London Tavern no one ever knew and he would never say. Sufficient it is that he started there as a ragged-arsed boy of twelve or thirteen whose sole duty it was to keep the spits a-turning, and that by the time he was twenty he had risen to the position of second in command to Mr Farley himself.

That great man had early seen the seeds of an even greater genius in my grandfather who quickly became his favourite pupil, and one to whom Mr Farley assiduously taught every principle of his Art. But in the end, and because they were men of different generations, Mr Farley's principles were not enough for my grandfather.

As Mr Bellamy told it to me after the funeral, the situation was thus: Mr Farley, who was a Tory of the old school, had failed to keep up with the times. He still believed that every dish had to be cloaked in a traditional sauce which was generally an elaborate affair seldom containing less than twenty different ingredients. My grandfather, on the other hand, had become attracted to the notions then coming over from France, where M. Rousseau was beginning to sing the praises of the natural life and French chefs were evolving what they referred to as *la cuisine simple*.

The matter came to a head over the subject of Pulled Chicken. A customer—it was Mr Richard Sheridan, the theatre man and Whig politician—had sent his order of Pulled Chicken back complaining that the sauce was lacking in lovage. Now Mr Farley knew that lovage had no need to get within a mile of a Pulled Chicken, but since it was my grandfather who had prepared the dish, he thought it a good opportunity to read him a lecture on his new, Frenchified, and revolutionary ideas.

'It's the sauce again, Bunter,' said Mr Farley. 'How many times have I told you that the Unities must be preserved? For the sauce, mark you, is to the dish as the rhyme is to the verse, the melody to the music, the pigments to the painting. Take these away and there are only words, noises and squiggles; take your correct sauce away and there are only dead animals and decaying vegetation.'

'I agree with you about the Unities with all my heart,' said my grandfather. 'But your Unities are those of Mr Dryden, whereas mine are those of Mr Wordsworth. I would follow Nature and bring simplicity back into our Art.'

'You've read too much Rousseau and Wordsworth,' said Mr Farley, 'and what they've got to do with cooking I'm damned if I know.'

This irritated my grandfather: 'They have this to do with it, Mr Farley. They have discovered that only the natural is truly beautiful, and I have applied that discovery to our own Art. No true cook will, in the future, rely on the richness of the sauce to cloak the poverty of the cooking. Food, like Nature, must go unadorned, and a sauce, if sauce there has to be, should be as plain and as simple as a Quaker prayer meeting.'

'So you're a Quaker now, as well as a Frog,' scoffed Mr Farley, who was naturally angered by the suggestion that he was behind the times. 'Why, my boy, you're as much off course with your sauces as a whore in a convent.'

This, in its turn, angered my grandfather.

'If it's whores and not sauces that we're discussing,' said he, 'I shall gladly bow to your greater experience.'

Mr Farley turned puce with suppressed rage. Great and good man though he was he had a fondness for the Cyprians from nearby Covent Garden and was only then recovering from a dose of the clap.

'With your permission, Mr Bunter,' he said sarcastically, 'I shall indeed take a whore as the text for this sermon.'

'A whore in a sermon?' said my grandfather, trading sarcasm for sarcasm.

'Even so, since nothing could be more to the point. For your plain sauce, look you, is as much use to a dish as a dirty shift is to a London drab. Neither of 'em does anything to make more appetising what it covers. But put your drab into a clean shift with some lace and a few ribbons to it, and you've a different dish altogether.'

'And yet, Sir, since there's still a clap at the end of it, it's a recipe cooked up by a pox-doctor.'

This touched Mr Farley too near home.

'Damn your impudence,' he roared. 'Would you dare call me a pox-doctor?'

At that point the argument degenerated into a brawl which ended with my grandfather walking out of the London Tavern swearing never to return. It was, with him, a matter of artistic pride, although I would call it little more than cockiness. Either way, there he was out of a place, and all because he was as puffed up about his Art as Sir Joshua Reynolds was about his.

Yet he was not out of a place for long. Luck, in the ample shape of Mr Charles James Fox, came to his rescue. This was the great Whig man, son of my Lord Holland and political adviser and boozing companion to the Prince Regent. He was also a man with a great liking for food and as fine a belly to put it in as ever a man could wish. That, by the by, is a matter of the greatest importance. For what, beyond a choice between chronic dyspepsia and the torments of Tantalus awaits a man who has been born with a good appetite and a discerning palate but without a stomach robust enough to digest what the palate craves and a gut capacious enough to contain all that stomach can deal with?

Mr Fox, not to put too fine a point to it, was then at one of those recurring moments in his career when he was in money but out of a cook. He had quarrelled with his last one over the proper devilling of marrow bones. So hearing, as almost everyone in London had, of the quarrel at the Tavern, he straightway sent for my grandfather, who had, by then, cooled down and reverted to his natural timidity, which was now heightened by his having to appear before such a magnifico as Mr Fox. He was, therefore, all bows and scrapes and diffidence as he listened to what Mr Fox had to offer. And what Mr Fox offered was this: a post as head cook; complete control of the kitchens; a salary that doubled what he had been paid at the Tavern; a free hand with the bills; and a prearranged concordat with the butler. All of this subject, however, to one over-riding condition.

'For lookee here, Bunter,' said Mr Fox. 'I've heard about your Frenchified, revolutionary notions for sauces, and I won't have 'em. I know that I came out for the Frogs when they made their confounded Revolution, but that was merely in the way of politics. I may be one of the most enlightened and forward-looking Whigs in this Kingdom, but my belly's always been High Tory. I'll have no Jean-Jacques Rousseaus in my kitchens. No, not even a Billy Wordsworth. Dishes that were good enough for my father are good enough for me. I trust you understand me.'

My grandfather understood him very well indeed, and assured him of the fact with stuttering sincerity. Mr Fox engaged him on the spot and the consequence was that my grandfather never again cooked a dish that failed to be accompanied by its traditional sauce, even though that sauce might have to contain fifty different ingredients. So far as avant-garde ideas were concerned, he had been out-Foxed.

That, then, was how my grandfather first entered the world of politics. And a very political world it was too. Mr Fox gave almost daily dinner parties for his political friends and followers, and it was his amiable custom, at the end of such dinners, to send for my grandfather so that he might receive his employer's congratulations and the applause of his guests. Since few politicians are reluctant to sing for their suppers, these were given with all the warmth an artist could desire.

All of which did a good deal to restore my grandfather's confidence or, as I would put it, cockiness. He'd been used to a lot of unappreciative munching at the London Tavern and found this recognition of his talents gratifying. He had all the normal Englishman's fondness for the gentry, and he now developed an additional weakness for politicians. Whig or Tory, in government or out of it, they all seemed equally estimable to him so long as they were gentlemen and politicians. It never entered his uncomplicated mind that such a combination has always been unusual.

The fact was that serving these Whig grandees and their hangers-on had given him romantic ideas about politics, and he had come to believe that all politicians had to be gentlemen and that politicking and fine eating had to go together as inevitably as Punch goes with Judy, Gog with Magog, and tripe with onions.

These beliefs, together with his burgeoning self-esteem, seemed likely to be disturbed when Mr Fox had to dismiss him. This Mr Fox only did because of his inability to remain solvent for much longer than a couple of years at a time. He was a man who loved good living, high play, fast horses and pretty actresses, a combination which has seldom failed to put a man into the hands of the Jews.

'I'm damned if I want you to go, Bunter,' said Mr Fox, 'but I'll be dunned even more if you don't. But if I can do anything about it, I won't see your talents wasted on some Indian Nabob who knows nothing but curries, or on some City Alderman who'll want his turtle soup, whitebait and roast saddle of mutton every day of the week. You've got to go somewhere where your Pigeon Fricando, your Goose-à-la-Mode, your Cutlets-à-la-Maintenon and your Tarte de Moi will be properly appreciated.'

My grandfather, who was stuttering once again, asked Mr Fox what sort of household he had in mind.

'That,' said Mr Fox, 'largely depends on what sort of master you prefer to serve.'

'Someone as like yourself as possible,' said my grandfather.

Mr Fox looked puzzled and asked him what he meant.

'Whilst I have had the honour of serving you, Sir,' said my grandfather, 'I have greatly enjoyed my duties cooking for political gentlemen and I would greatly like to continue serving such.'

'Why then,' said Mr Fox, 'I shall recommend you to John Bellamy, for I swear there's nowhere else in Europe where you'd have so many political gentlemen to cook for.'

Mr Fox was as good as his word, and my grandfather soon discovered that Mr Bellamy owned and ran the coffee-house that was situated upstairs from the Commons Chamber and was as much a part of the Palace of Westminster as the Palace of Westminster was part of Bellamy's.

This Mr Bellamy was what the French would call an entrepreneur. He had made a fortune out of his coffee-house and his position as sole caterer and vintner to the Commons.

Some of that fortune he had invested in the newspaper business, having been persuaded by Mr Perry, the newspaper man, to take a share, along with such as 'Jockey' Howard, the Radical Duke of Norfolk, in the *Morning Chronicle*. Now that the lower classes were beginning to read, Radical newspapers such as the *Chronicle* were becoming profitable.

But Mr Bellamy, being a true business man, would never allow the revolutionary views expressed in the *Chronicle* to subtract by even one bow or compliment from the deep respect he felt and showed for such of his Parliamentary patrons as were Tories. He remained, as a consequence, in the happy position of being able to feed them meals, drink and courtesies at one end of his business and insults at the other. And the whole joy of it to him was that he made both activities pay.

Yet if Mr Bellamy was a shrewd business man he was an equally shrewd judge of an artist. And so, in no time at all, my grandfather rose to become Clerk of the Kitchens, Head Cook, and Piemaker-in-Chief. This last title was the most important one. We are, as a race, great lovers of pies and puddings, and politicians love 'em more than any of us. It was my grandfather's hand with a pie-crust and a pie-filling that made Bellamy's so particularly attractive to politicians of every persuasion.

But what finally established my grandfather as a true House of Commons man was the wish that the dying William Pitt expressed for a veal pie. I know that his actual words were 'I think I could eat one of *Bellamy's* veal pies' but everyone knew that these were prepared by my grandfather.

However timid and diffident he may have been when he was away from Westminster, my grandfather's pride in his Art, and consequently his cockiness, increased with every year he spent in Bellamy's kitchens. In the end he came to believe that his Art was more important to the proper government of our Empire than anything else provided by the Constitution.

'Eating and debating ain't the same thing,' he once said to Mr Bellamy, 'though I'll agree that each provides a different way of bringing a man around to your point of view. But of the two, you and I know which works the best. You can speechify a man almost to death, either in the Lords or the Commons, and it will be odds against your shifting his opinions by even a thumb's-breadth. But get him with his legs under a table, feed him a half-reasonable meal, and before he's even dealt with the second remove and the third bottle he'll be starting to agree with you. It's my belief that there's no more persuasive an introduction to a political argument than a dish of broiled lobsters, and no better way of clinching it than with my Almond Cheesecake.'

I don't know that my grandfather ever put it into so many words, but it was clearly his belief that without Bellamy's, and without the support his artistry gave to Bellamy's, laws would never have been passed, taxes would never have been paid, Boney would never have been thrashed, and the whole of the British Empire would have crumbled away. It's jolly difficult to get cockier than that.

This increasing cockiness of my grandfather's was never, in fact, better exemplified than when the news first came of the great victory the Duke of Wellington had won in Belgium. Everyone was quoting his remark that 'The Battle of Waterloo had been won on the playing fields of Eton', but my grandfather insisted that this had to be a misquotation.

'I know Arthur Wellesley,' he said, 'and he's always been more of a politician than a soldier. That's why I'm convinced that what he actually said was that Waterloo had been won because of what the politicians had eaten.' I don't know that it isn't the better version since with respect to grub I thoroughly agree with that Radical villain, Will Cobbett. He always argued that it is what men eat that's important, and not where they go to school. And when the Yankee frigates licked ours in 1812, he pointed out that this was because Yankee seamen were bigger and stronger than our own Jack Tars. 'Why,' said he, 'every Yankee infant, whilst still at the breast, is given a piece of beefsteak as long as your thumb to suck as a supplement to his mother's milk. From which derives the Yankee phrase "hard tit", this being used when one is faced with alternatives and makes the wrong choice.'

When the news of Waterloo came to London, it was decided by the Commons that a great banquet should be held to celebrate it, and that it should be held at Bellamy's with Wellesley, who'd won the battle, as one guest of honour, and the Prince Regent, who had persuaded himself that it was he who had led the troops on that bloody day as another.

Mr Bellamy and my grandfather did a great deal of planning for that banquet. And when all other details had been decided, Mr Bellamy charged my grandfather with the task of planning and cooking the grandest and noblest pie ever devised by a Briton.

'For,' said he, 'pies are what all true Britons like best and pies are what Bellamy's and Bunter are most famous for. So now that the flower of our nation is about to dine at Bellamy's, do you give them a pie of such excellence and grandeur as will demonstrate to the entire world the superiority, invincibility and ingenuity of our race. Not to mention showing that one English cook is worth as many Frog chefs as you care to put together, not forgetting that Monsewer Carême.'

My grandfather must have felt that he was being challenged in much the same way as Michelangelo was when given the commission to paint *The Last Judgment* on the ceiling of the Sistine Chapel. I don't know that he did any praying, but I do know that he went to great lengths whilst planning his Pie. He wasn't the sort of man to leave much in the way of family archives, but my mother probably still has the Notes and the Chart which he worked with.

He had, according to those Notes, decided that it must be a Venison Pie, for Venison is Royal Meat and the Prince Regent was to be there to eat it. Therefore there could be no ordinary filling—no beef, veal, pork, ham, cow's cheek, calf's head, goose, game, giblets, alone or in combination, with or without the addition of oysters or mushrooms, would suffice.

It was strange that my grandfather, then coming to the end of a long and successful career, and cockier than ever, should have turned for the basic concept to the man who had taught him the rudiments of his art forty years earlier. Yet pinned to those Notes are pages 200 and 201 of Mr Farley's *London Art of Cookery*, which pages contain his receipt for a Venison Pasty.

But my grandfather's was not to be just a larger version of that Pasty, which was nothing more than the sort a nobleman might serve his tenants at an Audit Supper. No! This had to be a pie that would astonish the world and establish its creator as the artist he was.

The first Note, therefore, ran: 'These quantities to be multiplied fourfold.' Accepting that this was what he did, I have calculated that the old man must have boned out four haunches, each taken from nothing smaller than a six-pointer, and have added to these the breasts of half a dozen hoggets, every one fat enough to provide the unction the dryness of the venison required. Where Mr Farley had decreed that the meats should be marinated in half a bottle of red wine my grandfather had noted, 'Let this be three bottles of the Haut Brion such as is favoured by the Prince Regent.'

Mr Farley had recommended no more than salt, pepper and mace for the seasoning. My grandfather added 'A quart of mushroom ketchup and a cupful of the finest lemon pickle.' Where Mr Farley had used a pound of butter for the thickening of the gravy my grandfather had multiplied this by four and had added 'Two quarts of well-scalded cream and a paste made from the yolks of a dozen hard-boiled eggs.'

Yet thus far my grandfather had done little more than any master cook might have done by way of enlarging and enriching another man's receipt. It was when he came to the casing of the Pie, and, more particularly, to the decorating of that casing, that he truly showed what an Artist and a Patriot was capable of.

He followed Mr Farley to the extent of having two bakings for his Pie. The first, designed to bring about a true marriage of the different elements in the filling, was done under an ordinary sort of crust which was then discarded. A second crust was then prepared of the finest puff pastry such as can only be arrived at by forcing as much butter into the flour as repeated rollings could bring about. The resulting paste was then divided into two equal halves: one to be used for the crust itself; the other for the decorating of that crust.

Mr Farley had laid it down that these decorations should take the form of pretty little flower and leaf shapes cut out of the paste, but for a Pie such as my grandfather planned, flowers and leaves would have been no more appropriate than thumb marks. For the Pie, according to his calculations, would have a crust area in excess of twelve square feet and he had ordered a special pie dish made to accommodate it. He would have to plan boldly if he was to decorate such a surface well enough to justify his fame as the greatest Pie artist in Europe.

That was where the Chart came in. He had stuck several sheets of paper together to produce a single sheet as large as the proposed crust. On this Chart he had most carefully marked out all the physical features of the Waterloo battlefield together with the positions originally occupied by every Army, Corps, Division and Brigade engaged or held in reserve on that fateful and bloody day. All of these he had carefully copied from the plan published in the *London Gazette* shortly after the battle.

There, then, was the great forest of Soignies to the rear of the Allied position. And there were the Allied deployments stretching from Frischermont and the farmhouse at La Haye Sainte through Hougomont to Braine Merbes. There also was the ridge from which the Frogs, with their centre at La Belle Alliance, launched so many bold, bloody and futile attacks. The only manner in which my grandfather departed from historical accuracy was by showing Bülow's 4th Prussian Corps already emerging from in front of St Lambert, something which did not in fact happen until much later in the day.

And now, after the first baking, and after the making and placing of the second crust, my grandfather translated every marking on the Chart into puff pastry, and these were then positioned, with the utmost accuracy, on that crust. Yes! Each single ridge, hollow, ditch, hedge and building was cut out in paste and added to the lid, as were all the different units of the different armies engaged. Infantry he represented, aptly enough, by squares, cavalry by oblongs, and artillery by cones. He must, at one time, have contemplated colouring these according to their nationalities, for there was a Note which ran, 'Cochineal for our brave lads? Indigo for the Frogs? But green for the Hollanders and black for the Brunswickers too difficult. Best leave alone.'

It took three whole days to prepare the Pie for its final baking, and by then it took four of his assistants to lift it into the oven, for it weighed the best part of twenty stone. It had to be done carefully, moreover, so as not to disturb any of the superincumbent topography and puff-pastry armies. But when it came to the testing, to see whether Pie and battlefield were properly cooked, my grandfather would trust no one but himself. Thereby he met his own Waterloo. Thinking to do no more than slide enough of that great dish out of the oven as would allow him to appraise the whole, he stumbled, and by so doing allowed the whole massive structure to slide and to engulf him. He died as a consequence, but whether it was through crushing, scalding, or drowning in the gravy, the coroner found it impossible to decide. His verdict was that he had been killed in the execution of his duty. Mine would have been that he had died through being a mite too cocky.

They said that, when they finally got the dish off him, they found his face buried in that farmhouse at La Haye Sainte that had been so gallantly defended by our fellows and only taken by Ney at a heavy cost. Mr Bellamy waxed lyrical to me about this for he had, by his association with the newspaper world, fallen into the bad habit of talking like a *Globe* editorial.

'La Haye Sainte,' said he, 'became the grave of many of our brave lads and of even more Frogs. Your grandfather hated all Frogs and Monsewer Carême in particular. Ain't it fitting, therefore, that his paste farmhouse should have constituted the final resting place of another who had the same right to be described as a true Briton and a true patriot?'

I didn't rightly know what he was talking about, but I blinked at him through my spectacles and said, 'What happened to the Waterloo Pie?'

'Once we'd picked your grandfather out of it,' said Mr Bellamy, 'we pieced it together as best we could and it was greatly enjoyed by the Prince and all the other notables who tucked into it later in the day.'

10   *My First School Chums*

The first boy I spoke to when I got back to Christ's Hospital after my grandfather's funeral was Sam Merry. He was, and still is, one of the kindest and friendliest of chaps, but he's mis-matched to his name. For in appearance he looks as glum and ungregarious as an undertaker at a pauper's funeral.

It may, with us, have been a case of the attraction of opposites—he looking so dismal and I seeming such a carefree buffoon. But, whatever the reason Sam, although a year in front of me, went out of his way to help me, to instruct me in the arcane conventions of Christ's Hospital, and to let me know what others were saying about me. Few of my attachments can be described as disinterested ones and most of my later school friendships had something to do with the swapping of grub. But Sam who, like myself, was an orphan—his father, who had commanded the 22nd Bengal Native Infantry, having been killed in a skirmish with the Pindaris—was not in the least interested in food. I like to think, however, that the Bunters are sufficiently broad-minded to be able, on occasion, to separate friendship from interest.

'Did you have a good time?' said Sam.

'Five days away from here must always be a good time, and I had a top-hole blow-out at Bellamy's and the funeral wasn't half bad.'

'That funeral has done you no harm here.'

'How so?'

He then recounted to me, by way of example, a conversation he had overheard when three Upper School boys had been discussing my grandfather's death.

'Have you heard about young Bunter?' said the first.

'Called away to his grandfather's funeral,' said the second.

'That's right,' said the third, who had a reputation for knowing everyone's business. 'Sad affair. Only male relative poor little beggar had.'

'Is that so?' said the first.

'Gospel truth,' said the knowing one. 'Poor little chap's an orphan. Father killed in the Peninsula.'

'Where in the Peninsula?' asked the second, who was considered an expert on military affairs on account of his father being a clerk at the Horse Guards.

'Badajoz,' said the knowing one.

'Ah, Badajoz. Now that *was* a bloody business.'

'I had it straight from the horse's mouth,' said the knowing one, 'that Wellesley himself said he'd never have taken Badajoz if it hadn't been for Bunter's Pa.'

'Is that a fact?' said the first who, coming from a civilian family, knew nothing of Army matters.

'Common knowledge. Beaky swore he'd have made Bunter's Pa a General if he hadn't got himself killed. Fell at the head of his men, you know, just after they'd stormed the breach. They say he'd skewered thirteen Frogs by then, and I dare say he'd have made it a score if the fourteenth hadn't smashed his head in with a musket butt. Everyone in the Peninsula was talking about it. Regular out-and-out hero.'

'So that's where young Bunter got his spunk from,' said the second. 'I'm told he stood up to old Scratch-Wig like a well-plucked 'un t'other day. Clenched his fists at him and told him he could beat the lights and liver out of him before he'd blab on his mates.'

'Blood will out,' said the first who, if he knew nothing about the military, did know something about breeding, his late father having been a Court Tailor.

'Aye, breeding always tells,' said the second. 'All the same, poor little beggar must be properly cut up at losing his Grandpa.'

'He is,' said the knowing one. 'I know for certain that he blubbed fit to bust when his Ma broke the news to him. Poor little blighter don't really deserve any more punishment. Not after what that bloodthirsty old blackguard Boyer dished out to him t'other week.'

'Talking about breeding,' said the second, 'who *was* his Grandpa?'

'Big-wig in Parliament,' said the third. 'Commons have all gone into mourning. That's why they invited Bunter and his Ma to a slap-up do at Bellamy's once they had dealt with the corpse.'

That, according to Sam, was the sort of thing the whole school had been saying about me, and that was why I was paid so much attention when I got back. As a consequence I not only became cockier than ever: I also felt that, as the grandson of a Parliamentary hero and the son of a military one I had hardly needed to be thrashed by Boyer in order to earn my popularity.

But if Sam was the first true friend I had made amongst my lowly contemporaries, J.J. was the first in the Upper School to strike up a friendship with me. Yet this friendship undoubtedly had its origins in our common interest in grub.

John Jewkes, which was his full name, was that older boy who, in my first days at Christ's Hospital, had fed his terrier at my expense and then lectured me on the value of schooling as a preparation for life.

What he then called my greenness must have appealed to him, for thereafter he would always nod to me as we passed, and I would politely nod back. Eventually he began to stop me and ask me how I was getting on. I, being still in the timid stage, would say, 'Tolerably well, thank you, Sir,' and scuttle away.

But eventually the grub came into it. I had begun to notice that some of the boys, and J.J. pre-eminently, were considerably better fed than the starvelings of the Lower School and most of the heroes of the Upper. This was because they had extra food carried to them every now and again by relatives or servants who brought it to the school gates. In J.J.'s case this happened two or three times a week.

This aroused in me almost as much of curiosity as of envy. How often did I, choking over my crug in the early morning, look across at the Upper School tables where he would be breaking his fast on a great dish of buttered eggs, or on a thick slab of fresh-boiled ham surrounded by sausages? Or again, at dinner time, when the rest of us were queasily picking at our congealing gags, he could be seen tucking into some such dish as the best part of a well-roasted and stuffed leg of veal nestling on a sward of green peas and surrounded by a positive thicket of floury boiled potatoes, the whole revealing by its ascending steam that it had not long left the heat of the oven.

Eventually, as we passed one another in the corridors, I plucked up the courage to stop him and to ask how his extra supplies were arranged.

'Why, young-'un,' he said, looking at me in an amused but quite friendly way, 'my family lives close by in Coram Street, and my Pa, who's a grocer and wholesale tea merchant, has his shop in St Botolph's Lane, which ain't very distant either.'

'But what does that mean?'

'It means that the raw materials ain't ever very far away from the family oven, and that the family oven ain't ever very far away from Christ's Hospital.'

'So it's your family who feed you?'

'Of course. We're a family what's particular attached to its vittles, so it would be an odd thing if my Ma and Pa didn't see to it that their only son was provided with a deal more prog than gets dished out to him in this particular establishment. My little sister, Maria, nips over with the cooked article from Coram Street, and I've so trained the lot of 'em that, just as soon as they hear I might be in need of sustenance, they get it to me before it's had time to get cold.'

'But, Sir . . .' said I.

'You've got more "buts" in you than a billy-goat. "But" what?'

'But how do you get the food through the gates? I'm sure Gosling has orders to stop that sort of traffic.'

'Not him. He's the one who tips the wink to my Pa whenever I'm in any danger of going short. He gets a bottle of porter for doing so.'

'But, Sir . . .'

'How long have you been a Bluecoat, young-'un?'

'Best part of a year, Sir.'

'Then you ought to have learnt by now that 'most everyone here calls me J.J. And if you're going to keep firing your "buts" at me, you'd best do the same.'

'Thanks most awfully, Sir . . . I mean J.J. . . . . But . . .'

'There you go again. What's your "but" this time?'

'How,' said I, quivering with impatience, 'do you square the beaks? I'm sure they don't drink porter.'

'You're still spinach-green, ain't you? It's just a matter of influence.'

'Influence with whom, J.J.?'

'With your Governor, of course.'

'But I've only got a Ma.'

'I don't mean that sort of Governor, you ignorant toad. I mean the Governor who first nominated you to Christ's Hospital.'

'That was Mr Wilberforce.'

'Then it ain't so good. He's one of those Clapham square-toes, ain't he?'

'They say he's a Saint.'

'That's what I mean. Your Saints are seldom interested in the fleshpots, so they ain't likely to worry about a growing boy who is. I can't see your Mr Wilberforce telling his fellow-Governors that young Bunter's so delicate that he's got to have extra grub. It would be a lie, and Saints don't lie.'

'But you're allowed it, and you don't seem delicate.'

'Don't get personal with me, young-'un.'

'I didn't mean to, J.J. Honestly I didn't.'

'That's all right. It's different with me, you see. My Governor ain't a Saint. He's Alderman Wilkins.'

Seeing, to his surprise, that the name meant nothing to me, he went on to explain who Alderman Wilkins was.

'Number One: He's Chairman of the Governors here. Number Two: He's also Worshipful Master of the Grocers' Guild and as good a turtle soup, roast sirloin of beef and batter-pudding man as you'll ever find. Number Three: He's known me since I was a tiddler, for he's in the same line of business as my Pa, and the two of 'em go shooting on Wimbledon Common and hack out together when they hunt with the Surrey Staghounds. Number Four: Old Wilkins was once a Bluecoat boy himself, and so he knows what's what in this place. So, young-'un, if he says I'm delicate then delicate I am, and everyone has to agree with him from Gosling upwards.'

'I don't suppose Mr Wilberforce knows what's what,' said I, 'but at least I'll try him.'

'Do you do that,' said he encouragingly, and went on his way.

So when the summer holiday came and I returned to Kensington, I raised this matter of extra food supplies with my mother who was not, at first, helpful.

'It will do you no harm,' said she, 'to continue on short commons, for I see no signs that doing so has made you any the less stout.'

It was only Bessy, in the end, who bullied her into changing her mind. 'It stands to reason,' Bessy argued, 'that the poor little lamb 'as to 'ave 'is strength kep' up, what 'e won't 'ave on what 'e tells me they feed 'im at that 'Ospital. 'Ospital, hindeed. They feeds better in the 'ulks.'

'He seems none the worse for it,' said my mother.

'You can never tell,' said Bessy darkly, 'what it's a-doing to 'is vital forces.'

'His vital forces, such as they are, seem much as usual.'

'Come off it, Dotty. 'E tells me that 'e's 'aving to learn Greek an' Lating till they spout out of 'is pore little ears. Now what can be more strength-sapping than that? It's my hopinion that 'e could waste right away atween now and Christmas if you don't speak about 'im to that Mr Wilberforce. So you just harrange Mr Wilberforce an' I'll harrange the keeping up of the pore little wretch's strength.'

'And how,' asked my mother, 'will you manage that?'

'Same way as I managed all those years when you kept Master William so wonderful short that 'e'd 'ave starved if 'e 'adn't always been able to slip round the corner to Bessy.'

'But he can't slip round the corner now. He'll be away over in Newgate.'

'What use is Trotter if that great 'ulk can't carry a basket of nourishing food to Newgate whenever 'e ain't needed at the 'Sylum?'

My mother never has won an argument with Bessy, and so she finally agreed to speak to Mr Wilberforce. Once she'd done that he readily agreed that I was delicate enough to qualify for supplementary nourishment, and raised the matter at the next Governors' meeting. And so, in a very short while, Trotter became a familiar figure outside the school gates and I ceased to starve.

Although some of those who had supplies from outside became misers of food and so kept more and more to a solitary way of life, Bessy's estimate of what I needed from day to day in the way of extra grub actually added to my circle of acquaintances. Not even I could consume all that she had Trotter bring me, and so I always had a surplus to trade with, either by way of barter or sale. The food trade has always attracted me, and I was soon at its centre. But I did most of my trade with just two or three boys who, being as well supplied as myself, could provide the best swaps.

Until he left school, which he did the following year, I traded a good deal with J.J. This so strengthened our friendship that he invited me, on several occasions, to spend a leave-day with his family in Coram Street, where, as he put it, 'you can generally count on a hearty tuck-in and a not half-bad drop of port'.

I've never met a family that tucked in more heartily than J.J.'s. His Ma was clearly of the Bessy Trotter school when it came to the question of diet, and his Pa bore witness to that fact. He had a belly on him like a beer barrel, a prodigious capacity for food and drink, and a carbuncled nose. But for all that he was the most amiable of grocers and, like his son, he was a most ardent sportsman. He was as devoted to hunting, shooting and other country pastimes as a man who'd never travelled farther than twenty miles from the sound of Bow Bells could be.

And then there was Maria. What shall I say of her at that time except that she was a small, friendly, extremely plump child inordinately fond of food and with a capacity for putting it away that a Smithfield porter would have envied?

Those Coram Street tuck-ins strained even my digestion, and so, afterwards, J.J. and I would go for a walk to settle things down. It was only after we'd done that for the first time that I realised why J.J. was always described as the sportingest boy ever to have passed through Christ's Hospital.

'Take that quadruped out of its shafts,' he said, pointing to a ewe-necked, sway-backed, goose-rumped, spavined old screw on a cab rank that even I could see must be soon for the knacker's yard. 'Take him out and put him on a stone of oats a day and a couple of good linseed mashes a week; give him plenty of strapping and a bit of schooling over jumps, and what have you got?'

'I'm sure I don't know,' said I.

'Why, young-'un, you've got just the sort of hunter you'll need when you and I go out with the Surrey Staghounds.'

'But I don't hunt, J.J.'

'You'll want to hunt soon enough once you've got an extra-special-double-patent-safety mount such as that nag can be turned into between your legs. Fly any ditch you put him to, I'll be bound, not to mention popping backwards and forwards over five-barred and finches quicker than the stag itself.'

'I'll think about it,' said I, and did so until a mongrel dog put a cat up in front of us and chased it into a holly bush.

J.J. watched this with a knowing eye and then proceeded to lecture me on gundogs.

'I hope you noticed how that dog froze when he first caught that cat's scent. That proves he's got pointer blood in him. And I'm sure you marked the way in which he followed Puss up once he'd flushed her out of the holly bush That shows a strong retrieving instinct.'

'Is that a good thing?'

'A good thing, young-'un? Why, there's nothing more valuable to a shooting man than a dog that can both point and retrieve. That's just the sort of animal I'm going to get for myself as soon as I've left school. My terrier's all right for ratting, but he's nothing of a gundog, and it's a gundog like that I'll need when I go shooting with Alderman Wilkins and my Pa on Wimbledon Common.'

'It will be a cat shoot, I take it,' said I, for I was wearying of all this sporting lecturing. This silenced J.J. for a while, but then a crow flew low overhead and he swung an imaginary fowling piece at it and grunted with satisfaction as he marked its imaginary fall.

'There, Billy,' said he, 'that's how you deal with your crossing bird. Swing through it from tail to tit and keep swinging to give yourself a lead before you pepper him.'

J.J. joined his father in the grocery business when he left school, and I've no doubt that he's replaced his Pa, who must be past it by now, on Wimbledon Common and with the Surrey Staghounds. If there is anywhere in England a sporting author who wants a Cockney sportsman for his hero, he should take J.J. as his model.

One of my later, grub-centred friendships was struck up with
a chap you'd never expect to find in an English boarding
school. Hurree Ram Thukoor, who was naturally known as
Harry, may well have been the first Indian ever to end up in
Christ's Hospital in spite of the close connections that school
had with the Honourable East India Company. He was very
nearly twice my age, had to shave every day, and had, he
proudly told us, left two wives and half a dozen children
behind him before he sailed to England in order to complete
his education.

We were inclined to be proud of him even though, in his
blue gown and yellow breeches, he did not always seem as
exotic as we liked to make out. But what, more than anything
else, made him interesting, were his food supplies. Once every
week or so a smart barouche drawn by a spanking pair of
matched bays and driven by a coachman in India House
livery would pull up in front of the school gates. A porter, also
in India House livery, would descend from it carrying a basket
crammed with all the different sorts of foods schoolboys dream
of, together with some that were so different that they could
only wonder at them. These last consisted of strange, rich,
sticky Indian cakes and sweetmeats and hitherto legendary
Indian fruits such as pineapples, bananas, durians and
mangoes.

Harry's food-trading instincts were even stronger than
mine. He never, except with myself, engaged in swaps. What
he traded for was service. That's to say he'd give away quite
large quantities of grub in return for help with his Greek
exercises and for pieces of Latin verse he could then pass off
as his own.

I was never enough of a scholar to be included in this trade.
But I did have, thanks to Bessy, some of the best pork pies
and beef patties you ever set eyes on, and Harry became

inordinately fond of these, as I did of Indian sweetmeats and mangoes. It became natural, therefore, for us to engage in straight-forward barter, and this we did to such an extent that a strong friendship developed between us based, as the best of friendships must be, on mutuality of interests.

It was because of that friendship that Harry eventually revealed to me the reason for his presence in Christ's Hospital and for the smart barouche, the India House porter, and the bulging hampers. I remember we were behind the fives court sharing a pineapple when the subject arose and, as his belly must have already been full of Bessy's pork pie and the sun was shining warmly enough to remind him of India, he must have been ripe for confidences.

'Bunter, dearest friend,' said he, in his rather flowery way. 'Have I told you about my father?'

'No,' said I. 'What about him?'

'He comes of a most fearfully rich, very, very respectable family. That family, naturally, being a Brahmin one.'

I knew next to nothing about India in those days, and so I asked him what being a Brahmin meant.

'It means being absolutely top-notch in Indian society. Being the sort of Brahmin my father was is even more top-notch than belonging to your House of Lords. But it also means, just like your House of Lords peoples, that you must not have any intimate intercourses with other castes, which is what we call the lower classes in India.'

I let him chatter on because I knew that he had a couple of mangoes on him and was in high hopes he would pass me one.

'But alack, dear friend,' he continued, reaching out a sticky hand and taking hold of mine, 'my father, whilst still young, had many intimate intercourses with Englishmen in Calcutta, and that was his updoing.'

No one can be long at an English boarding school and not learn to be suspicious about such things as hand-holding and talk of intimate intercourses. I pulled my hand away and said:

'You must mean his undoing.'

'Not at all. I mean it was then all up with him as a Brahmin.'

'I suppose it was the intimate intercourses that did it.'

'Right. And such intercourses! He not only visited English-men in their homes, my dear. He actually dined with them. Yes, he even ate their roast beef off their English plates and with their English knives and forks!'

'What on earth was wrong with that?'

'Such excessively intimate intercourses with the lower castes are for ever defiling for a Brahmin. That's why he lost his cord.'

'Lost his what?' said I. 'And whilst you're about it, Harry, you might pass over one of those mangoes.'

He was so eager to continue with his confidences that he passed the mango over and didn't even make me promise him another pork pie.

'All Brahmins, my dear, have a cord put around their necks at birth to show that they are heaven-born. But if they mix with low-class peoples like Englishmen, and most especially if they eat their low-class food off their low-class plates they immediately lose caste and their cords are taken away. And that's what happened to my father. His family, you see, was very, very particular—much more particular than your Lords are with dancing girls and suchlike.'

'Did your father mind losing his cord?'

'Quite the contrary. He started to enjoy himself.'

'I don't see why he shouldn't have done. Our Lords, as you call 'em, generally enjoy themselves with their dancing girls.'

'You fail to understand me. My father was not having carnal enjoyments. Not at all. His enjoyment was quite intellectual. He is a very scholarly man and quite empirical in his tastes. You see, he had studied the English for a long time, and had found them very interesting. And now he could mix with them and with all the other low castes as much as he liked.'

I didn't greatly enjoy this repeated reference to the low-caste English, but I was busy getting into the mango and so contented myself with asking Harry what his father had done then.

'He became a banker and lent a lot, a lot of money to his English friends, which helped him in his studies of the English because, as you know, dear friend, there is absolutely no better way of getting to the bottoms of people than by having them owe you money.'

'I don't know about that,' said I, 'I've tried to borrow often enough, but no one's ever lent me anything. But what you've told me still don't explain why you're here in Christ's Hospital when you're well over twenty and have got at least a couple of wives.'

'Wives are not material to the situation, being peoples of little importance. But if you are enquiring why I am here, then I must tell you, dear friend, it is because of the most estimable Barings.'

'Barings? Oh, you mean those German banker fellows.'

'Not at all and not in the least German now, my dear, but veritable blossoms of British aristocracy. They have all become knights, baronets, lords and suchlikes even though they are bankers and moneylenders, which is the opposite of what would have happened to them in India. My high-class father could never have become a banker and moneylender until he had ceased being a Brahmin and had lost all his respectability. But, although the Barings have become high-class in England and my father has become low-class in India they are both bankers and moneylenders, which is why the Barings so much needed help from my father.'

'How on earth could your father help the Barings?'

'It was all a matter of gold bullion. My father, as an Indian banker, had a great, great deal of it. The Barings, because of the war and Mr Pitt had very, very little of it. So my father lent them much gold, at very good interest, because of former Imperial Majesty, viz. one-time Emperor Napoleon.'

I was getting very muddled by this time, but at least we had got away from a boring lecture on the Brahmins.

'Can you tell me, Harry, what Boney had to do with it?'

'I am not up-to-the-dating with all the details, my dear, but essentially it was because of the damn-smart Yankees.'

'Harry,' said I, 'take a deep breath and then tell me, as plainly as you can, how the Yankees had anything to do with your father lending gold bullion to the Barings. You can leave Boney out of it. He'll only muddle the issue.'

'No, no, no, my friend, the Emperor must not be being left out of it, though he was, I think, only First Consort at the time. But he started the whole business by selling Louisiana, which really belonged to the King of Spain, to the Yankees, who were going to take it anyway.'

'Go on.'

'Well Napoleon offered it to the Yankees very cheaply, but the Yankees, being smart traders, paid him in paper, which was no good to Napoleon because, as everyone knows, the French like to have gold to hide under their beds. So Napoleon gave the bills to the Barings to discount, which they could have done very, very profitably, if Mr Pitt had let them have any gold. But Mr Pitt was paying for the war by making all Englishmen take bank notes instead of sovereigns, so the Barings had to turn to my revered pater for the gold they needed to discount the bills Napoleon had taken for the sale of Louisiana to the Yankees. It was what they call international finance.'

'And did your father give them the gold?'

'Not at first. You see he wasn't realising then that the Barings were high-class Englishmen. He thought they were just low-class moneylenders like he had become. But then some of his English friends told him that the House of Lords was full of Barings and so he thought that if he lent them the gold the Barings could help him in his studies of England and the English. So, my dear, he discounted the bills, at a heavy discount of course, even though they were signed by Mr Thomas Jefferson who was President, and the smartest Yankee of them all.'

'It still don't make sense to me.'

'Oh, you are being stupid today, my dear. My pater did a favouring to the Barings because they promised to advise him about the English.'

'It don't add up, Harry, honestly it don't.'

'But it is all being so simple. I shall explain it to you all over again. Since my pater was no longer able to be heaven-born I, his only son, also was not able to be heaven-born. Since he had made deep study of the English, I must make even deeper study and so be following in his foot paces. Since he helped Barings, Barings had to help him. First they send out English nanny for me from Scotland. Then English tutor, the Reverend Timothy O'Connor, former Fellow of Balliol College

Cantab. He was teaching me Shakespeare and Latin and cricket and birchings and so on for many years. But at last he is telling my father that I can only learn more of these things if I am going to an English boarding school. So my father is writing to Sir Thomas Baring, and that is how I come to this school.'

'You mean Baring nominated you?'

'Sir Thomas, my dear friend, is a Governor of Christ's Hospital.'

'But that still don't explain why you get all that grub from India House.'

'Sir Thomas is also Governor of the Court of Directors of the Honourable East India Company. *Verbum sap.?*'

'*Verbum sap*, as you say, and if you really don't want that other mango, chuck it over.'

I missed Harry considerably when, the following term, Sir Thomas himself drove up to the school and told Harry that his father was dead, and that he must return to Calcutta at once to take control of the Bank. Harry didn't seem to mind his father's death overmuch but wept when he took his leave of me. He then departed in the custody of a wizened, serious-looking fellow who, I was told, was a clerk from Barings' Bank lent to Harry to advise him on banking matters. My own opinion was that if Harry was half as good at banking as he was at food-trading, the clerk would have very little to do.

Horace Augustus Coker was, so far as I am concerned, a very different sort of Bluecoat. He has, for who knows what reason, always hated me. And at that time, since he's a born bully, he would go out of his way to persecute me. I've never been able to understand why anyone should dislike, let alone hate me. I ain't a quarrelsome sort of chap and in those days there was no question of trouble over wives and business dealings. Yet hate me Coker did. It seemed an unworthy sentiment for a boy whose parents had been entirely worthy missionaries in India, where he had been born. Nor did the fact that they had both died of the cholera morbus, leaving him an orphan to be brought up by a great-aunt in Edmonton who believed herself to be a reincarnation of Queen Elizabeth, constitute an excuse.

The only reason I can imagine for his quite irrational hatred of me is jealousy. He was the least-liked boy in the school whereas I had steadily progressed from being something of a buffoon to being something of a hero. This he never understood for he was as handsome, intelligent and athletic as any boy in the school and I was his opposite. He never seemed to realise that his bullying, blustering, overbearing ways, coupled with his too-obvious longing to be liked, appealed less to schoolboys than Bunter's buffoonery.

Be that as it may, he increasingly went out of his way to demonstrate his hatred of me and, since he was a good deal stronger than I was, those demonstrations were generally physical ones. I did my best to keep out of his way if I was alone, but if he could catch me when I wasn't with friends, he would give vent to his feelings in various humiliating ways, such as booting me round the court, holding me up by my ears, or forcing me to kneel in front of him and lick his boots.

He had once forced me to engage in this last degrading exercise when the Head Grecian and most godlike of all Bluecoats, Percival Wharton, happened to come upon us. He could not have known who I was, but he did know something about Coker. And so, in a matter of seconds, the situations were reversed. Coker was in the dust licking my boots and Wharton was encouraging him in that task with a number of hearty kicks.

Coker never again lifted a finger against me for so long as the two of us were at the school. But nor did he ever pass me without a glare of undisguised hatred. As for Wharton, I went so far as to give him the whole of one of Bessy's tipsy cakes which I had intended for myself. He was good enough to accept, and I hope he enjoyed it. He left soon afterwards and, after a brilliant career at Oxford, he entered the Church. I'm not much given to hero-worship, but if they don't make him a Bishop before very long, there won't be any understanding of the need for muscular Christianity in either Buckingham or Lambeth Palace.

During all the years I spent at Christ's Hospital I was never happier, nor, I'm sorry to say, cockier than I was at this time. I had become increasingly popular; Bessy and Trotter between them kept me well this side of hunger; and I was experimenting with exotic foods through my barter trade with Harry. But above all, I was not then old enough to appreciate what I now suspect to be true, which is that whenever a Bunter starts feeling happy and confident he is no more than a short time away from disaster.

Trotter contributed considerably to my popularity and, therefore, to my happiness by becoming even more popular with the Bluecoats than myself. Whenever that broken-nosed and somewhat bloated giant turned up at the school gates with my grub it soon transpired that I would not be the only boy waiting for him there. I would be surrounded by friends, and these not just food-trading ones eager to see what Bessy would have put in Trotter's basket. They would be boys panting to listen to another of Trotter's yarns, and we would stand round the gates listening to one until fat little Gosling plucked up enough courage to tell Trotter, who could have eaten him in a single mouthful, that he had to move on.

At that stage in our lives we were ardent readers of such sorts of literature as our ushers deplored. We enjoyed Pierce Egan's *Boxiana* when it was not a matter of fiction, and *The Adventures of the Hon. Captain Robert Boyle—The Fortunate Bluecoat Boy* when it was. But nothing that the Captain was supposed to have done was half as interesting as the tales of Army life Trotter told us, nor was any one of the prize fights recorded by Egan half as exciting or as bloody as those that Trotter swore he had engaged in.

But of all the yarns he told us about Army life, the prize ring, single-stick matches, soldiers' drunks and brawls, and four-in-hand races to Brighton, coachmen against Corinthians, our favourite was his highly-coloured, not to say fanciful account of the single-stick match he had once fought against the champion of all-Middlesex for a prize of ten guineas and a gold-laced hat. He would take us through this, blow by blow, always demonstrating some of his subtler strokes with the blackthorn cudgel he carried. The tale invariably ended with his opening his jaws to show us the gap in his teeth, the Middlesex man having knocked three of 'em out in the first three minutes.

'But,' he would say, 'none of you young sportsmen would 'ave hexpected me to let 'im see what he'd done, seein' as 'ow the man what draws the first blood 'as to be given the match. No, cullies, I swallowed them there teeth—bone, spit, blood an' all—without so much as a gulp. There wasn't even a speck of blood to be seen anywhere 'til I brought me back-stroke into haction an' split that Middlesex bugger's skull for 'im. An' as that just couldn't be 'id, I was hawarded the match. Wouldn't each one of you young sparks 'ave done the same for ten guineas an' a gold-laced 'at?'

If the Bluecoats enjoyed Trotter, Trotter, for his part, enjoyed the Bluecoats. He always had been fond of children, the more so, perhaps, because Bessy's only valid grumble against him was that he had never, as she put it, 'managed to put a bun in her oven'. This she attributed to the vast amounts of porter he drank, for, as she often said to me, 'Porter makes 'em randy but hinfertile. It hinspires 'em to reckless an' hindiscriminate depositing of seed what's already been drownded.'

So, deprived of sons of his own, Trotter gradually took upon himself the task of accompanying a whole group of us on our leave-days, partly to keep us out of trouble, and partly to pass on to us some of his skills as a pug and all-round master-at-arms.

Whilst it was still summer time he would take us down to the New River for swimming instruction, and it wasn't too long before he had all of them except me going through the water as merrily as tadpoles. With me, however, he got nowhere. Try as he might to teach me to float, I would sink like a stone just as soon as I got beyond wading depth. This, I've since discovered, was because it was river water. Once I get into the sea I can bob around bolt upright just like a well-corked bottle. Mr McGregor, who's the naval architect at the Calcutta shipyard, has assured me that it's all a question of weight, displacement, and the specific gravity of the circumambient waters.

When it got to winter time Trotter would take us to some open place, such as Newington Green, where he would make us mark out a ring with our gowns. He would then divide us into pairs and set us to sparring, wrestling and single-stick playing. Yet here again I was the only member quite incapable of absorbing even one of the several arts of self-defence.

'No! No! Master Willum,' he would shout, as I stood blinking my tears away after one of my friends had pranced round me in true Trotter style, giving me every now and again what Trotter called a 'facer'. 'You've got to stand up to 'im with your maulers 'eld like I showed you. That way 'e can't go on tapping your claret the way 'e is a-tapping it. If you can't do the same to 'im, then at least you can block 'im.'

I would try the blocking but, just as soon as my claret was tapped once more, I would start backing away as quick as my legs could carry me. That would bring another agonised cry from Trotter.

'Don't you hever start goin' backwards, Master Willum, unless you've got it in mind to bring 'im on to a cross-buttock. An' that, seeing as 'ow 'e's a sight more hagile than what you are, I wouldn't recommend you to hattempt. So stand up to him now, even though you are getting a bit of a milling. Show us as 'ow you've got *some* bottom to you.'

But bottom in that metaphysical sense is something I've never been able to show and, indeed, have never wanted to. So just as soon as my opponent had danced around me two or three more times and had tapped another half-pint of my claret I would retire from the ring. At which point Trotter would always throw his hat on the ground and jump on it. On one occasion he got so exasperated that he said, 'What the 'ell does you do at school if another boy sets about you in earnest?'

'I generally run away.'

'Run away hindeed! An' what 'appens if you can't run away?'

'I get one of my friends to protect me,' said I, telling no more than the truth and gratefully remembering Wharton.

'An' what would 'appen to you if you 'ad no friend close
by?'

'Why,' said I, puzzled by all these hypothetical questions,
'I'd beg for mercy.'

'God damn me missing gnashers! That's no way to go about
things, an' never will be. Even if you ain't one for giving or
taking a leveller, you'll 'ave to learn 'ow to defend yourself, or
you won't be long for this world.'

'I'm afraid, Trotter,' said I, 'that I'm not very good at
levellers.'

'That, Master Willum, is what they calls stating the
hobvious. 'Owever, if you can't learn 'ow to defend yourself
fair an' square, I'll 'ave to larn you 'ow to do it crooked an'
dirty.'

And so he tried, for some considerable time, to teach me a
few of the tricks pugs use in the ring when they think no one is
looking, such as sticking a finger in your opponent's eye, or
putting a knee into his testicles. But I was so slow and clumsy
at these that even a short-sighted pigmy would have seen what
I was trying for and would have laughed at it.

And that was why Trotter finally came to the conclusion
that the only way I could ever hope to defend myself would be
with a weapon.

'It can't be a sword,' he declared, 'on account of your being
so clumsy that you're likely to do more damage to yourself
than to your hopponent. I'd never trust you to last even two
minutes with a sword of any description. So, Master Willum,
it'll just 'ave to be pistols.'

'But they don't let us have pistols at school, Trotter.'

'So far as school's concerned I've already give you up.
You'll just 'ave to do what you say you do, what is either run
away or hask for mercy. But I'm a-thinkin' forrard to the time
when you'll 'ave left school.'

'You're thinking of duels, Trotter, ain't you? You don't
need to. I'm sure I'll never want to engage in a duel however
old I am.'

'You don't 'ave to go looking for a duel in horder to be in
one. 'Owever, since it's most unlikely that it'll be you what's
doin' the looking, you'll at least 'ave the hadvantage of doin'
the choosing.'

'I don't follow you, Trotter.'

'Why it's as plain as the nose on your face that you'll always be the challenged party, the which means that you'll always be the party what chooses the weapons. An' so you'll always 'ave to choose pistols, the which, once I've taught you 'ow to 'andle one, does at least give you some chance of surviving.'

So, during what turned out to be the last summer holiday Trotter and I would spend in Kensington, Trotter set about teaching me how to handle a duelling pistol. He produced a very neat pair of Joe Mantons for that purpose, although how he came by them I never cared to ask. Day after day we would stand back to back at the bottom of the Asylum yard, march our ten paces, turn, and snap our locks at each other in what Trotter always described as a 'dry run'. But even here I failed to satisfy Trotter.

'No! No! Master Willum,' he would cry as I turned and snapped for the twentieth time. ' 'Ow often 'ave I got to tell you that it ain't safe or traditional to stand to your hopponent foursquare as you does? Sideways hon it 'as to be if you want to do things in style an' to hoffer the smallest possible target. Though I don't rightly know that, hunless you grow hout of that belly of yourn, you won't hoffer as much of a target the one way as t'other.'

Even when I remembered to turn at the end of my ten paces in such a manner as to offer myself sideways on Trotter still found a great deal to criticise in the way I handled my weapon.

'Don't you ever, Master Willum, let me see you 'olding your weapon up in the air again afore you turn, when you turn, or ever. You're not a 'igh-class 'ore waving to a customer from 'er box at Drury Lane. You're a duellist, that's what you are, an' it's your hobjective to drop your hopponent afore 'e gets a chance to drop you. So just you keep 'olding that pistol at harm's length an' pointing downwards until you start to turn. Then bring it up slow an' when you think you might be pointing at 'is knees, you can start to squeeze the trigger. But gentle-like, mark you, just as though you was squeezin' your sweet'eart's tit. Then, always supposing 'e 'asn't got there first, if you don't 'it 'im in the belly, even you can't always fail to 'it 'im 'igher up.'

I gave him enough to worry about even when we were doing

nothing more than this snapping of unprimed locks at one another. But then Trotter decided that I had to get used to the sound and smell of powder, and so we began to practise with pistols that had been primed and charged with everything but shot. This always made me shut my eyes for several seconds before and after I had fired, which made it impossible to know the direction in which the wads flew. I don't know whether Trotter was trying to reassure me or himself when he finally remarked that he'd no doubt I would be so staring-eyed when it came to the real thing that I wouldn't be able to close my eyes if I wanted to.

It was even worse when Trotter decided that the time had come to make some practical test of my aim. He rammed a candle-end in on top of the charge and a wad on top of the candle-end and had me aim at a large white spot he'd painted on the trunk of a big elm some twenty paces away. The first candle-end buried itself in the ground not five yards from my feet. The second hit a branch some forty feet up.

'I can only 'ope,' said Trotter despairingly, 'that if your wits ain't always sharp enough to keep you out of trouble, your legs'll always be fast enough to get you clear away from it. For atween you an' me, Master Willum, you'd 'ave about as much chance as a rat in a rat-pit once the dawgs 'ave been put in, if you'd no more to rely on than your dooks or your pistol.'

As I was then in the push-me, pull-me stage between childhood and adolescence, I took more pride in all these manly pursuits than my prowess at them warranted. The consequence was that I swaggered not a little to my mother and talked a good deal to her about facers, flying mares, and winging my man. This, to my surprise, seemed to distress her, even though she had until then always deplored what she referred to as my plumpness and softness. There was no denying the fact that my mother was in a deuced odd frame of mind that summer.

'I've noticed,' she said on one occasion after I'd been showing her how a cross-buttock worked, 'an increasing roughness and coarseness in you, William. I had hoped that school would make you more civilised and more cultured as well as more learned.' And with that she pointed at me with the book she'd been reading which was, I remember, the most recently published of the *Childe Harold* cantos.

'Just look at you,' she went on. 'You're fatter than ever and dirtier and more untidy than ever. All that you can think about these holidays is gobbling pies and tarts with Bessy and training to be a ruffian with Trotter. Not once have I seen you studying a book of even the most ordinary description, let alone one containing verse as refined and elevating as this.'

'You weren't ever much of a one for refined and elevating verse before this summer,' said I angrily. And indeed I'd rarely seen my mother read anything but the *London Gazette* and *Bell's London Life* before in her idle moments.

'You don't know what you're talking about, William. I am, as you well know, a great artist's daughter. How could his *only* child fail to worship great Art whenever she comes across it?'

'That ain't great Art,' said I, pointing to *Childe Harold*, 'that's just some more of that satirical, erotic stuff turned out by that notorious womaniser and sodomite, Byron. Old Boyer thinks nothing of him. He says he's a degenerate.'

'Lord Byron a degenerate!' exclaimed my mother, coming as near to screeching as a woman of her disposition could.

'He writes dirty, and he's a rotten poet. Leastways that's what old Scratch-Wig says.'

'And what, pray, can your Mr Boyer know about poets?'

'Not much unless they're Greek or Roman ones. But he does say that Byron's verse is full of false quantities and Cockney rhymes. Very hot on false quantities is Boyer: a deal hotter than he is against sodomy.'

'How,' enquired my mother, 'can such vile words issue from such innocent lips?'

'Come off it, Mama. You went to boarding school, didn't you?'

'I can only assume,' said my mother, 'that you have acquired your coarseness from your school and have inherited your vulgarity from your father's family. Apart from the fact that they were all of them fond of Mr Handel's very commonplace music, there's never been one of them possessed of an ounce of sensibility.'

'As you've told me next to nothing about my father and his family I can't tell whether they are noted for anything.'

My mother looked at me rather oddly, and then put an end to our conversation by leaving the room, taking *Childe Harold* with her. And that, now I come to think of it, was to be almost the last word I would have with her for the next five years. For this summer I'd spent quibbling with my mother, gobbling with Bessy, and duelling with Trotter was to be our last summer together. Before winter had come all these, whom I thought of as my only family, were flushed from Kensington like a covey of partridges. But, unlike partridges, the covey hasn't come together again from that day to this.

13   'Eat and Grow Strong'

When Gurmakh Singh brought me my spinach, horse beans and other garbage at noon today he seemed to me to be both windier and cockier than usual. Just as soon as he had deposited his tray he put his finger to his lips, went to the door, opened it, looked out and closed it before he began to unwind his lofty and elaborately arranged turban. Once two or three folds had been removed I could see, balancing on his skull, a fairly sizeable bundle done up in half a banana leaf. He put this down in front of me, rewound his turban, and then unwrapped the parcel to reveal as fine and as fat a cold roast fowl as anyone could hope to find in India, which is a country where the moorgies are notoriously small and skinny.

'Eat and grow strong, Bunter Sahib,' said he.

It was now my turn to look at the door and wonder whether anyone was lurking behind it.

'Is this wisely done, O Gurmakh Singh?' I whispered.

'Wisely and prudently,' he whispered back, looking as pleased with himself as Little Jack Horner.

Hunger, so far as I'm concerned, is the only thing that can supersede funk. My gastric juices were already running and so, although I didn't half like the risk, I tore off a drumstick and said, between munchings, 'What if the Begum should learn of this?'

'My Lord must not allow the hot breath of fear to dry up the rich juices of appetite. Take now this wing, Sahib. Never fear it, for it comes from a bird the Begum's cooks never saw.'

I accepted the wing whilst still reserving my position.

'From your head it comes and on your head lies the blame for its coming, O soon-to-be-candied one.'

'Do not mention such things, Huzoor, even in jest.'

'I jest not, Gurmakh Singh. I do no more than establish that it was not at my prompting that you brought me this excellent fowl. Whence comes it?'

'From my sister's kitchen. Her daughters-in-law, they who were first deprived of their conjugal rights and then of their husband by the Begum, may she rot in Hell, basted this bird with their tears and larded it with their sweat for revenge.'

'Highly poetical, Gurmakh Singh, but let us be plain with one another. This fowl calls for caution, not quatrains.'

'And caution there has been, my Lord, as well as cunning in full measure.'

'And whose cunning was it that induced the bird to wrap itself in a banana leaf and then nest inside your turban?'

'My sister's daughters-in-law, Lord, would not have your strength drained away by your scribbling, than which there is nothing more enfeebling. And doubly so when you have naught but spinach and other camel fodder to restore you. They are still young and lusty enough to remember what men need if they are to retain their vigour, and that is what they beg you to do, for they are cooking up more than a fowl for your deliverance. They bid me tell you that you will need more strength than spinach can bring you when this other dish of theirs comes to the eating.'

'Have they plans, then, for my escape?'

'Doors may not have eyes, Bunter Sahib, but walls may have ears. The dish you mention is still in the cooking.'

'Then tell your sister's daughters-in-law not to stay too long at the stove. Any hour now, as you know, the Begum may send for me, and what happens then, O Gurmakh Singh?'

'That hour is not yet. Ismail Khan is not the sort of stallion to be easily worn down by any mare. All court, kitchen and bazaar gossip tells how he still goes lustily and swaggeringly about his servicing. So long as he continues thus the Begum will rest content and will come close to forgetting Your Excellency's very existence.'

'That is as well, for I have, as you know, grown neither thinner nor stronger on spinach and scribbling.'

'Men such as you, Bunter Sahib, never grow thinner. As to your strength'—and here he looked sly and patted his turban—'on my head be it.'

'And the scribbling?'

'You may continue to scribble without fear, Lord, for just so long as Ismail Khan continues thus . . .' He then clapped his right hand to his left bicep and jerked his left forearm upwards, fist clenched, in a gesture much used by Indian men when they discuss the intercourse of the sexes.

14   *The Kensington Catastrophes*

It saddens me even now to write about all that must have happened that winter in Kensington. I put down 'must have happened' because I knew nothing of it at the time and would have been too young to understand what was happening even if I had not been away at school. Since then I have learnt a good deal more about human nature and so can piece the sorry course of events together from what Mr Wilberforce let slip from time to time, and all that Bessy wrote me from France. Even then, the answer to the ultimate riddle came to me much later, when I saw my mother for the last time.

The first signs of trouble apparently developed at the Asylum for Younger Fallen Women, where the Inmates had begun to grow discontented and restless. Bessy, unfortunately, took little notice of this. She was too busy in her kitchen or gossiping with my mother. As for Trotter, he had been instructed by Mr Wilberforce that Fallen Women must be forbidden fruit so far as he was concerned. So he had as little to do with the

Inmates as possible, being afraid he might, with a little too much porter inside him, revert to his old Army ways.

Neither of them, therefore, knew what the Inmates were thinking, which was that there must be something very wrong with their working and social lives, since the first brought them no money, and the other no pleasure. Randy Ruby was the first to give voice to this sentiment, as she was the first to begin creeping out of the Asylum at night. Then one or two of the others began to accompany her, and the habit spread until in the end there were quite large bands of 'em roaming the streets and lanes of Kensington. When they got weary of wandering they would end up at one or other of the ale-houses.

But even ale-house drink costs money, and that none of them had, so they had to hang around waiting to be treated. When they were treated, they felt as any other honest woman would have felt, which was that they had to give something in return, even though it meant returning to that which they had been rescued from. This was easily enough arranged during the warm summer nights when the surrounding gardens, hayfields and corn ricks provided agreeable venues for the transacting of business and the settling of debts. But it was quite otherwise when winter came and a black frost gripped the land. Then the best they could do as debtors was to smuggle their boozing companions into the Asylum and up to their dormitories.

It was inevitable that a certain amount of whispering, giggling, shushing and gin-drinking should follow the smuggling and precede the actual settling of debts. But when the gin began to flow too freely the shushing would be replaced by singing, swearing, quarrelling and general blackguarding.

That the Trotters never heard this has to be blamed on the porter. Trotter rarely went to bed without his full ration of it and this caused him to lie on his back, once he had done his duty by Bessy, and snore like a bull. Bessy, as a consequence, had to put tow in her ears if she was to sleep. And so, what between the porter and the tow, the Last Trump could have been sounded without disturbing them.

But if the Trotters could not hear what was going on, there were those among the local housewives, who put overmuch value on their own virtue and too little trust in that of their husbands, who could.

Eventually one of these laid an information with the magistrates. From then on the law had to take its course. That is to say that those same magistrates, whether they wished to or not, had to start criminal proceedings against Bessy. Since she knew nothing of what had been going on, the serving on her of a summons came as a considerable shock, and she went rushing round to my mother for counsel and help.

'Dotty! Dotty!' she cried, bursting in on her in the front parlour. ''Ere's 'ores an' 'orrors! 'Ere's brothels an' Bridewells! 'Ere's summonses an' magistrates an' ruin for us all!'

With that she burst into tears. It was not until she realised that her sobs were fading away into a most unreceptive and unsympathetic silence that she looked around her and saw that my mother was not alone. Facing her from the other side of the table was a stern, not to say sour-looking Committee of the Clapham Saints. Not even the King's Bench could have produced a likelier-looking set of hanging judges.

They were, indeed, sitting in judgment on my mother, and that because they had received an anonymous letter which had almost certainly been written by the same outraged Kensington housewife as had informed against Bessy. It was well known, the letter said, that my mother had been responsible for the setting up of the Asylum. It was impossible, therefore, that she should be ignorant of what it was now being used for. Moreover, one of the certain consequences of what had been going on at the Asylum was that my mother, who'd been widowed now for many years, was big with child, as the Claphamites could easily establish by sending observers to Kensington to take one look at her waistline.

Self-confessed saints, in my experience, are frequently the first to believe the worst of anyone. That was why the Committee of Claphamites had come hotfoot to Kensington where one sight of my mother's waistline had convinced them of the truth of at least one half of that anonymous letter. Then Bessy had burst in babbling of brothels, and Bridewells, and God knows what besides, to convince 'em of the truth of the other half. This immediately persuaded them that they had, under Mr Wilberforce's original urging, taken the very Whore of

Babylon to their bosoms in the shape of my mother. If they blamed Mr Wilberforce for this, they did so in private. He was too close to true saintliness to be blamed for anything to his face.

It was quite otherwise, however, in the case of my mother. She, sensible woman, realised from the start that it was not the least good defending herself or arguing with them in any way. She accepted that her dismissal from Kensington was inevitable. But what she would not accept was that she was under any necessity to reveal to the Committee the name of her seducer.

She did not even, so far as I know, reveal it to Mr Wilberforce. Flabbergasted though he was by what he thought of as his angel's primal fall, he none the less placed himself unhesitatingly at her disposal. She, however, insisted that the Trotters stood in even greater need of help than herself, whereupon Mr Wilberforce grudgingly agreed to include them in his rescue plan. This, to put it briefly, was that all three of them should leave for France before the Kensington magistrates started to issue warrants.

A man of Mr Wilberforce's standing and reputation is never without influence in the right places. So within a day or two my mother and the Trotters were able to slip over to France with no questions asked and no answers given. They then, on Mr Wilberforce's advice, headed for the small town of Nonant. He, casting his mind back to his own unregenerate days when he and the young William Pitt were making the Grand Tour, had remembered a certain Mme Duplessis of that town who seemed to him, from past experience, to be likely to attend to my mother's affair for her.

So the three of them, according to Bessy's letters, spent the next four months quietly in Nonant before proceeding to Paris. They left behind them an infant girl, whom Mme Duplessis undertook to adopt, and almost all that was left of the money Mr Wilberforce had given my mother at her departure.

It was fortunate for them that, just as soon as they arrived in Paris, they met up with Harriette Wilson. That lady's business affairs had so continued to deteriorate that she had had to go into exile to escape her creditors and imprisonment in the Fleet. As Paris was then full of Englishmen Harriette had thought it might be profitable to set up—in this alien city—something so like her old York Place establishment that former clients would feel that here was a home from home. And re-engaging the Trotters would, she thought, add to that sense of homecoming.

But things at York-Place-in-Paris never went as well as Harriette had hoped. It was not just that she was past her first flush of youth. She had also been imprudent enough to ally herself, even though only by a Fleet marriage, to an Irish adventurer who called himself Colonel Rochfort. Whatever income she had left after he had drunk and gambled a large part of it away he further reduced by his blackguarding, blustering, blackmailing ways with her clients. This, in the end, caused Harriette to turn to my mother for advice, the two of them having been close friends ever since Harriette had been the means of introducing my mother to Mrs Mary Anne Clarke.

My mother, according to Bessy, soon found a way in which Harriette could increase her income. 'You must,' she told her, 'write your Memoirs, and continue to write them until you have filled as many volumes as you can with the names of as many of your former clients as you can remember. You're well-enough remembered in London to ensure that a great many readers will willingly part with their guineas in order to read about their friends, and those same friends will willingly part with a great many more guineas not to be read about.'

'It would be a sound idea,' said Harriette, 'if I were capable of writing anything longer than a billet-doux.'

'In that case,' said my mother, 'I'll write your Memoirs for you, so long as I get thirty per cent of what you're paid for them.'

'Twenty-five per cent,' said Harriette.

'Thirty per cent,' repeated my mother, 'and for another five per cent, I'll act as your literary agent.'

'Thirty per cent,' said Harriette, 'and you'll live with me here with no charge made for lodgings and the use of your teeth.'

'One third,' said my mother, 'and it's done.'

'And that, my pet,' Bessy wrote to me a few months later, 'is 'ow all three of us 'ave settled down 'ere with 'Arriette just as snug as four bugs in a rug.'

15 *Hard Work and Hard Commons*

Mr Wilberforce was the first person to tell me about the disasters at Kensington.

'You must not,' he said after giving me a Bowdlerised version of events, 'feel entirely deserted. Your mother and I prayed together, yesterday, before she left, and it was then that I promised her that I would stand to you as guardian as well as godfather. You shall come to me for your holidays, and I shall always be at hand to supervise your education, look to your welfare and plan for your future.'

These kind words did so little to console me that I burst into tears. I have always been able to blub easily. Mr Wilberforce lent me his handkerchief and begged me not to take the loss of my mother so much to heart.

'It ain't her that I'm blubbing over, it's the Trotters. Who's going to cook my extra grub and bring it to me now that they're gone?'

This took something of the edge off Mr Wilberforce's kindliness, and he told me, pretty sharply, to fix my mind on more important things.

'There is nothing more important,' said I.

'Nonsense, boy. Think of what your future and your mission could be.'

'What mission is that?'

'You must learn, William, to see the Lord's hand in everything. For myself, I am convinced that all that happened at Kensington and your present abandonment to my tutelage are but parts of the Divine Purpose. And my name isn't William Wilberforce if I don't see that Purpose carried out.'

He was so emphatic in this that I stopped snivelling and asked him what he meant.

'I mean, my boy, that as your mother has so sadly betrayed her Evangelical upbringing, not to mention my trust in her, that it is now for you to restore things. From now on you must so shape and live your life as to restore moral purpose to the name of Bunter.'

'How would you have me do that, Sir?'

'There is no higher calling, William, than that of the Ministry. There is nothing more laudable that a minister can do than work for the conversion of the heathen. So I would have you prepare, from this day, for Holy Orders. And when you have taken them I would have you go into the field in India. John Company has lifted its ban on missionaries now that we have convinced them that they do nothing to interfere with their trade. So we are daily adding to the number of our mission stations. Just think, boy, of the millions of heathens in Company territories whom you may be privileged to pluck as brands from the burning.'

'I ain't altogether sure,' said I, thinking suddenly of Harry, 'that your ordinary Indian wants to be plucked. And even if he does, I know I ain't qualified to do the plucking. All they teach us here is how to pluck some meaning out of Homer and Virgil.'

'I'm well aware, William, of the theological limitations of your present curriculum. But I'm also aware that, in the opinion of that good and wise man, the Reverend Boyer, you possess an aptitude for languages which your natural indolence cannot entirely conceal. And languages are what you'll need as a missionary.'

I was, by now, beginning to get thoroughly alarmed.

'I do assure you, Sir,' said I 'that my indolence don't conceal anything but more indolence. And I swear I've no aptitude for languages, or for anything else in the learning line for that matter.'

'Mr Boyer thinks otherwise. He has a high regard for what he calls your cunning but I prefer to think of as your sagacity. What's more, he's given me his undertaking that he will make you work a deal harder at your classics so that you can be sure, in a few years' time, of a sizarship at my old College of

St John the Evangelist at Cambridge, where you will, of course, read Divinity.'

This had begun to sound worse and worse.

'I ain't up to Cambridge and Divinity, Sir. Honestly I ain't.'

Mr Wilberforce, who might have been re-planning his own life from its beginnings, had a fanatical gleam in his eye and quite ignored me.

'For my part,' he continued, 'I shall see to it that from now on you are instructed in all the languages—Urdu, Hindi, Farsi and so on—that you will need in the mission field. You shall have extra lessons each day from such of our retired missionaries as are expert in those languages.'

'But it's dangerous business being a missionary. Missionaries generally die of fever or get captured and killed by pirates, or end up by being eaten by cannibals or . . .'

' "The blood of the martyrs", said Tertullian, "is the seed of the Church." '

'But that don't mean that I have to be a missionary. Why can't I be its seed here in England?'

'Whatever do you mean, boy?'

'I mean,' said I, hoping to at least mitigate his ardour, 'that I'd do a deal more good in a nice little country living in, say, Norfolk or Hampshire than I ever would on the banks of the Ganges. People would understand my sermons and I wouldn't have to go to the trouble of learning all those languages.'

As sometimes happened with me, the picture of what had only that moment come into my mind began to sharpen and to take on colour. So I cockily expanded the idea.

'Just picture it, Sir. The Reverend W. Bunter. Reasonable parish: goodish land: richish farmers: decent parsonage: enough of a glebe to keep me in milk, pork and spring lamb, not to mention October ale and cream for the strawberries: parishioners who won't grumble over their tithes: Squire who won't want much by way of a sermon but who'll give a Sunday dinner worth the eating: sow . . .'

'William!' thundered Mr Wilberforce. 'Cease your babbling.'

'Sow in the stye,' I went on, beginning to get desperate,

'hens in the yard: ducks on the pond: nice fat cob for riding round the parish: nice fat wife . . .'

'That,' roared Mr Wilberforce, redder in the face than I'd ever seen him, 'is more than enough of that nonsense. You owe it to your mother and myself to be a missionary, and so a missionary you shall be.'

He was, I'm sorry to say, as good as his word. From then on I was pushed and goaded and harried by Boyer during almost every hour of the school day. And when that day was over I still came under his supervision. For I had to go to Boyer's house every evening, there to be tutored in Oriental languages by that succession of retired missionaries Mr Wilberforce had promised me. Moreover if Mr Boyer did not come to the study to see to it that I was absorbing all that such tutors could cram into me, Mrs Boyer would.

Mrs Boyer was in many ways the very opposite of her husband. That is to say where he was large she was small, where he was old she was barely middle-aged, where he was disagreeable she was comparatively amiable, and where he was a tyrant she was a wheedler. What the two of them had most in common was an exaggerated respect for learning. Yet even in this they went their different ways. For where he was attracted to the past she was interested in the future, and where he was in love with theories she was only interested in facts. What's more, they had to be the sort of facts that could be expressed in statistical terms. I'm certain that if there were a Royal Statistical Society as there is a Royal Society of Arts Mrs Boyer would be their first choice as President.

My holidays were now spent with Mr Wilberforce, either at his gloomy London house or his even gloomier country one, and at neither of them could I look forward to getting an even half-decent dinner. It was not that my godfather and guardian was unkind or grudging. It was rather that, not being a hearty eater himself, he was quite unable to understand what I was suffering.

At school I now suffered from the absence of the Trotters and my consequent lack of grub for both eating and trading. Indeed the only break I had in my largely grubless existence came when, a year or two later, a portly, bewhiskered J.J. turned up at the school to invite me to spend the Christmas holidays at Coram Street. Mr Wilberforce took a deal of persuading for he thought I ought to be brushing up on my Sanskrit. In the end, however, he agreed, and I spent the happiest, jolliest, eatingest Christmas of my life in the generous bosom of the Jewkes family.

Apart from the fact that they were all a few years older, nothing seemed to have changed in that household, where food, drink and sporting conversation were still in unending supply. Maria had changed the most, for she was now thirteen, and had grown into as pleasant, buxom and plain a girl as you could hope to meet. What hadn't changed, however, was her enjoyment of food and her ability to put away great quantities of it. And where the rest of her family would talk sport to me, she would talk grub. Many and many an interesting conversation the two of us had on that endlessly interesting subject.

But on the whole my later school years were as miserable as my earliest ones had been. Even though I was eventually pushed by sheer weight of years into the Upper School I never could count on being free of the Boyers or the retired missionaries from the time I got up till the time I fell into my bed. Only on leave-days was I ever free of them for twelve hours at a stretch, for on these occasions even the Boyers and Mr Wilberforce thought I ought to be spared from any more cramming.

16   *Ad Pudendum*

Although dear Bessy had, ever since my mother's and the Trotters' flight, made it her duty to keep me informed of all that had happened to them, she never once referred to my mother's seducer. Indeed, until I was rising sixteen, I only knew that something shameful had happened to my mother.

Eventually, of course, I learnt what seduction was and what

women were like and for, and it was as well I did since shortly afterwards I was sent for once more by Reverend Boyer. Now, as on a previous occasion, I found him closeted with my mother, whom I had neither seen nor heard from for some five years.

She seemed to me, as I gawped at her from the doorway, to be cooler, calmer and handsomer than ever. But this time Boyer showed no desire to quote sweet-tongued Catullus at her. Instead he was at his scratch-wig worst. He growled at me to come in and departed forthwith, snarling that he'd leave the two of us to it.

My mother, having looked me up and down, offered me a cheek to kiss, which I, still resenting what I thought of as her desertion of me, ignored.

'Well, William,' said she. 'I can see that you've grown upwards a good deal, but I wish I could say that you've stopped growing outwards. You're fatter than ever.'

'If justice had anything to do with it,' said I bitterly, 'I would have grown into nothing more than a skeleton. I don't suppose it worries you, but I've had to rely on the school and Mr Wilberforce for my grub ever since you took Bessy off to France, and that means I've been on mighty short commons for the past five years.'

'Not too short to grow fat on,' said she.

I had almost forgotten how little regard she had always had for my adequate nourishment. So, being young, I waxed heavily sarcastic. 'I'm amazed,' said I, 'to see you here. From what Mr Wilberforce let drop from time to time I'd supposed you wouldn't dare show your face in London again.'

If that didn't quite bring her up standing, it at least brought a flush of anger to her face.

'Mr Wilberforce,' said she, 'has always been something too fond of letting things drop. It's the old woman in him. There's absolutely no reason why I shouldn't show my face in London whenever I want to. And I want to now. I've important business to attend to here.'

'I can't believe that I constitute part of that important business.'

'To be candid,' said my mother, 'I would always classify you as secondary business. I'm here to see a publisher.'

'I suppose you're trying to sell some more of Harriette's boring old Memoirs.'

'You know about them?'

'There's hardly a soul in London who doesn't know about them.'

'That's the first pleasing thing you've said.'

'Then you're easily pleased.'

'I'll be even more pleased when I've come to terms with that rogue Stockdale for Volume Two.'

'I suppose you're still acting as Harriette's literary agent then.'

'Ghost writer, business manager and literary agent all rolled into one. Negotiator as well, for I've got to see the Duke of Wellington and one or two others who are proving obdurate.'

'I have heard,' said I reflectively, 'that literary agents are even greater rogues than publishers.'

'That,' said my mother firmly, 'would be impossible. But I haven't come all the way here to Newgate in order to discuss the publishing business with you.'

'Then what have you come to discuss?'

'Family matters, William, family matters.'

'There ain't much family to discuss. If we leave Bessy and Trotter out of it, there's only you and me.'

'It may not always be so. I must tell you, William, that I have almost decided to get married again.'

One of Bessy's favourite phrases flashed across my mind.

'If that's the case,' said I, 'I wonder whether it will be to the mysterious gentleman who put that bun in your oven.'

'Don't be vulgar. Colonel Lutz may have been courting me for some time, but he's far too gentle a creature, for all that he's a famous soldier, to expect to put anything in my oven, as you phrase it, before we get married.'

'Lutz, heh? That ain't an English name. Don't tell me you're thinking of marrying a Frog after all that happened to Grandpa and the Honourable Fitz. It would be neither decent nor patriotic.'

'Antoine Lutz,' said my mother, 'was born an Alsatian. That means he can be either a German or a Frenchman, depending on circumstances. But circumstances at present have made him more than half an Englishman for he's now serving our own dear country in the King's German Legion. As he's served in more different armies than almost anyone else in Europe he's been put in charge of our garrison on Corfu which must be almost the only place one can think of where he would be in no danger of arrest as a deserter.'

'Corfu,' said I, 'is a deal farther from Christ's Hospital than Paris, so I don't suppose I'll see much of you.'

'Precisely,' said my mother, 'and that's why I'm here. I'm not a rich woman and the Colonel, for all the medals and stars that he's won, has nothing more than his pay for us to live on. Nevertheless I wouldn't like it to be thought that Dorothea Bunter has failed to make provision for her son.'

'I need provisions rather than provision,' said I, but my mother ignored this rather neat play upon words and placed what was either a very large handbag or a very small valise on the table. The first thing she pulled out of it was a large gold locket that hung from a long gold chain. It was a solid and imposing piece of trinketry which must have weighed close on half a pound. It had a cipher surmounted by a ducal coronet picked out in brilliants on the front, and when I opened it I found myself staring at a miniature of the Duke of York, whom I recognised because of his portrait that used to hang over our mantelpiece.

'This,' said my mother, 'was a christening present given to you by the Duke at a time when he still felt he owed the Bunters something. As you know, the Bunters now hold him in contempt, but that don't mean that the locket has no value. It's exactly the sort the Royal Family dishes out to minor foreign potentates, which must mean that it's worth at least fifty guineas. So if you ever need to raise the wind, it could come in handy. Meanwhile wear it around your neck and under your shirt.'

I took the locket and put it around my neck and under my shirt as she had ordered, and found it deucedly heavy and uncomfortable, though I have since grown so used to it that I would feel naked without it. My mother next drew a bulging little silk purse out of her bag and gave it to me.

'It may take you some time to sell the locket,' she said, 'and you may well have need of some ready money in a hurry. There are twenty guineas, seventeen gold Napoleons and twenty-three louis-d'or in this purse. Let it be your first refuge in an emergency.'

Since all my emergencies revolved around grub, and as I knew that sixty gold coins would translate into a great deal of grub, I took the purse with a deal more alacrity, and even said 'Thank you'. My mother then dipped into her bag again and brought out, to my great disappointment, a bundle of papers tied up with blue ribbon.

'What am I to do with these?' said I.

'You're not to look at them until I am dead,' said my mother. 'But by then they could be worth a deal of money.'

'They don't look as though they're worth very much.'

'Ah,' said my mother, 'that's because you don't know as much about publishers as I do.'

'Does that mean that they're more of Harriette's Memoirs?'

'Not at all. I sell Harriette's Memoirs just as soon as they come hot off my pen. These are letters and poems that a very famous person once wrote to me. If I know anything about men, he's the sort who must very shortly drink and fornicate his way into his grave. And when that happens anything written by him that has not already been published will be eagerly sought after. His own publisher, who's a rogue called John Murray, is only waiting for news of his decease in order to bring out a *Life and Letters* and a *Complete Poetical Works*. I'm sure he'd pay a great deal for these, if it's only in order to destroy them in case they queer his pitch. So put them away carefully and cash them in just as soon as I'm dead.'

I didn't much care for this, but I took the papers and my mother rose to depart.

'I must go now, dear boy,' she said. 'I am late for my appointment with the Duke of Wellington who's having one of his tantrums over the Memoirs.'

'Just a moment,' said I. 'What about that bun you had in your oven five years ago? If Bessy's to be believed, I must have a half-sister somewhere in France.'

'In Nonant, to be precise. I believe she's now called Marguerite Duplessis. I doubt the two of you will ever meet, but I wouldn't be surprised if you heard her talked about everywhere fifteen years from now.'

'What makes you say that?'

'Well, my dear, if she's inherited my looks and her father's morals she'll make a famous French whore, and the French, as you know, make a great deal of their whores.'

With that she departed, and I haven't seen her from that day to this.

Of course I examined that bundle of papers just as soon as I was alone, and it was through them that I learnt who my mother's seducer had been. He had, it seemed, been a client of Harriette Wilson's for so long that what started as a business relationship had long since ripened into a close and sedate friendship. So it had been to York Place that he had retreated when he was preparing to go into permanent exile. He himself, who had survived so many different scandals since leaving Harrow, had come to realise that he would never survive the new crop arising from his estrangement from his wife, his affair with Lady Caroline Lamb, and his at least equivocal entanglement with his half-sister. And it was at York Place, where she was a frequent visitor, that my mother first met Lord Byron.

Some of this was referred to in one of the letters, on the cover of which my mother had written: 'This was a letter addressed by Lord B. to Mr Thomas Moore, the poet. It was given to me by the latter gentleman when he was in Paris in 1819, he thinking the references to myself might amuse me. But by that time I had come to the conclusion that Lord B.'s private smut was more suited to schoolboys than to intelligent adults.'

As all the papers are now residing in a trunk in Calcutta, I can't quote from them verbatim. None the less, the gist of this particular letter was thus.

My Dearest Tom,

Here am I in York Place, holed-up for a month or two with our old and dear friend Harriette, whilst Lady B., Caroline L. and, for all I know, half the virtuous hags of London Society are all howling for my blood. I have business and publishing affairs to settle ere I depart, for ever I trust, from this land of bloodthirsty patriots, bloody roast beef and bloody old Castlereagh. But before I do so I have it in mind to dip my wick, once more, in an English setting. And I must tell you, Tom, that Harriette has a friend who visits her—a schoolmistress, no less—who, if you could only see her, would make you burst into more than merely *Irish Melodies*. I swear she has tits on her Tom that would do credit to Venus herself, and legs so long that they seem to run up well past her arse. None of your chubby English Misses, Tom, but something much closer to Arcadian Diana than I'd ever have expected to find in this land of Cockneys.

The other letters, the first of which bore the same date as that addressed to Mr Moore, were all written to my mother. The earlier ones were by no means as frank as those he had written to his fellow poet. But, from the first one of all, he made it plain that he proposed the shortest of courtships and the quickest of consummations. Nor, to judge by the quickly changing tone of his letters, did my mother differ from him in this regard. In the end, indeed, he had begun to doubt which of them was doing the seducing. He had never before, I assume, courted a liberated woman.

Be that as it may, Byron thought it appropriate, within a short while of their first meeting, to send her a series of highly erotic, not to say dirty verses. His smutty poems, written for private circulation, were, of course, much talked about by his cronies, though if they were no better than the ones he wrote for my mother, they can have done nothing to add to his reputation as a poet. There's better stuff to be found in any of the dirty-book shops in St Paul's Churchyard.

There's only one of those poems, and that probably the least smutty of 'em, that I can remember, and even then I won't swear that I've got the wording and scansion exactly right. He gave it, as a title, 'The Fair Nymph of Kensington', and it ran more or less thus:

> Keep, Fair Nymph, those Pheidian tits
> From the rude gaze of London cits.
> A Rowlandsonian bub or bum
> Is fine enough for Cockneydom.
> Those mounds marmoreal, my Sweet,
> Ain't meant for them: they're meant to meet
> A Byron's lips, a Poet's heat.

Allow me, then, I beg, to warm 'em,
And so from stone to flesh transform 'em.
Grant me next right to dote upon
The longest legs in Kensington.
And when, exploring them, I come,
As come I must, *ad pudendum*,
I'll storm the pass to Elysium.

I've worked it out that Byron had stormed his pass by
March and had abandoned his Elysian fields and fled to the
Continent before the end of April. My mother, as I've already
recorded, spent some of that summer with her nose in *Childe
Harold* and then, realising that she was unlikely to hear from
Byron again, went calmly about her business.

I have often wondered how someone as sensible and as
independent as my mother could have allowed herself to
be reduced to anything except laughter by such a doggerel
courtship. Yet, even though that courtship brought her some
passing inconveniences, laugh at it she did in the end, and I
admire her for it. The last paper in the bundle was a note
penned by my mother which ran:

I find it beyond believing now that such poor, smutty
verses as these should ever have laid me on my back and
caused me to open my legs. Yet what else, except perhaps
curiosity, could have brought me to such a position? Not
Lord B.'s pudgy looks to be sure, nor, I should add, his
performance. However clumsily it sometimes wagged, the
pen, I am certain, was ever Lord B.'s most persuasive
member. This may surprise all those scandal-mongers
whose tongues he kept so assiduously wagging. Nevertheless I owe it to posterity and Mary Wollstonecraft to put
down the truth, which is that Lord B. was far more forceful
on the page than he ever was between the sheets.

Merry, to my sorrow and Coker, to my delight, left Christ's Hospital in the summer of '22. By then I was growing so weary of being a schoolboy that I was almost looking forward to Cambridge and the Divinity Schools. The spring of '23 was, I remember, unusually dry and hot, so much so that, on a leave-day in late May, we all felt that there was nothing for it but to go down to the New River to swim, as we had so often done in those far-off happy days when we still had Trotter as our mentor.

I, strangely enough, was so eager to strip off and plunge in that I clean forgot that I always sank in river water. And that was what happened. I came as close to drowning as one can before anyone noticed. By the time they had dragged me out of the water and laid me unconscious on the river bank they were all certain I was dead. Fortunately a passer-by thought otherwise.

'What's wrong with him?' said he, pointing at my wet, naked and inanimate body with his cane.

'He's just got himself drowned,' said a boy called Nugent.

'Are you sure? He looks too fat to drown easily. Have you tried to get the water out of him?'

'No,' said Nugent, 'for we would never know how to do it.'

'Well, I do know,' said the passer-by, taking off his coat and rolling up his sleeves. 'And so, with your permission, I'll try to empty your fat friend.'

'Pray do,' said Nugent.

So the passer-by held me up by the heels, laid me down again, and then so banged, squeezed and pummelled me as to make me void the best part of a gallon of New River water. When I began to splutter, he put on his coat and looked at me for a while. I was, of course, too distressed to take any notice of what was happening, though I learnt all about it later from the others.

'Extraordinary,' said the passer-by. 'Quite astonishing.' And with that he took out a note book and wrote something down.

'I would judge,' he then said to Nugent, 'that your fat friend is not yet seventeen.'

'Sixteen last December.'

'Still at school?'

'Yes.'

'Day or boarding?'

'Boarding.'

'Do you all sleep in the same dormitory?'

'Some of us do.'

'And have you noticed anything unusual about our friend here?'

'Only that he's fatter than anyone else,' said one.

'And greedier,' said a second.

'And he's got a whopping great pecker,' said a third, at which the rest giggled.

'Is that so?' said the passer-by, putting his book back in his pocket.

'What do you think we ought to do with him now?' asked Nugent.

'My advice,' said the passer-by, 'is to get your friend back to school and into bed just as soon as you can. He'll need to be bled and given either a clyster or a calomel purge if he's to escape a congestion, so you'd best send for a doctor. And if that same doctor notices anything unusual about his patient, pray tell him to get in touch with me. Darwin's the name—Doctor Robert Waring Darwin. Tell him he can always get in touch with me through the Royal Society.'

Then he touched his hat to them, twirled his cane playfully in my direction, and was off.

Mrs Boyer, who was in charge of health matters, made something of a fuss over having to call in a doctor. However, once I'd been bled and purged I quickly recovered, and both she and I had forgotten the drowning until we were reminded of it two or three weeks later in a most unexpected manner.

It was an evening when my tutor, having congratulated me on my mastery of Urdu—I do, in fact, have a good ear for languages which I can pick up quicker than any parrot—had just departed and I was preparing to return to school.

Suddenly the study door was opened and Mrs Boyer burst into the room brandishing the latest copy of *The Philosophical Transactions of the Royal Society*. This was a journal she read assiduously on account of the large amount of statistical material contained in many of the articles.

'William,' she cried, thrusting the journal into my hand, 'you must read this article immediately.' Here she pointed to a dull-looking page headed *A Remarkable Case of Benign Hypertrophy*.

'But Ma'am,' I protested, 'I've been reading Latin and Greek all day and Urdu all evening. It's monstrous to require me to read English as well.'

'Don't argue with me boy! Read the article, tell me whether or not it refers to you, and then confirm to me that it is factually accurate. Sharp about it, now.'

'But it's a longish article, Ma'am.'

'Then the sooner you start the quicker you'll finish, and you'll not go from here till you do.'

So I read it. I ain't pompous enough to reproduce the editor's style, but I can give the gist of what was a long section of the editorial.

'We have recently received,' wrote the editor, putting himself into the plural as editors do, 'a communication from a Fellow of this Society whose work on comparative anatomy has justly earned him the reputation of being an expert in that particular branch of knowledge. What he had to say seems to us strange enough and important enough to be mentioned in these columns.

'Our learned correspondent, it seems, recently had occasion to revive a youth who had come close to drowning whilst swimming in the New River. Whilst engaged in this task his attention was drawn to the truly remarkable dimensions of that youth's *membrum virile*. There was no opportunity, we understand, for accurate measurements to be taken. Nevertheless our correspondent's reputation is such that we readily accept his estimate that the organ in question must have been some twenty per cent greater in length and some ten per cent greater in girth than the generality of such organs. It was, as he so justly remarked, considerably larger than any he had come across in an average mature adult.

'He found no symptoms of any morbidity such as dropsy or an elephantiasis to account for this hypertrophy. Indeed he judged the organ perfectly normal in all respects save size. If there was anything that could be described as an abnormality it was that the youth suffered from adiposity. This added to the interest of the case since it is commonly known that adiposity is seldom associated with a vigorous development of the generative organs. He was, moreover, under seventeen years of age, which suggests that further growth might still be possible.

'These observations, our correspondent points out, were made at a time when the youth's recent immersion in cold water must have ensured that the organ was in its most flaccid condition, which suggested to him that it would be of scientific interest to discover what its potential might be when it was otherwise.

'Our correspondent concluded with the suggestion that the subject, who came close in this one respect to being a *Lusus Naturae*, ought to be identified and subjected to a continuing series of scientific and statistical examinations.'

The editor then went on to discuss this suggestion in his own coyly ponderous fashion.

'We appreciate,' he wrote, 'the difficulty of identifying the subject, and the even greater difficulties that would attend such examinations. But no one, so far as we are aware, has ever before been presented with an opportunity to produce such important statistics as these. If there be one of our readers in a position to undertake this task, let him do so for, if we may sound the patriotic note over this, it would surely be a source of pride to every true Briton if we could publish to the world the statistics of an ordinary English schoolboy whose measurements must be a cause for wonder as much as for envy to the rest of the civilised world.'

As soon as I'd finished the article Mrs Boyer, who was by then in a high state of excitement, asked me whether I was the youth in question.

'I suppose I must be, Ma'am, although I was unconscious for most of the time. But I did go swimming and come close to drowning, and I was revived by a Doctor who said he was a Fellow of the Royal Society.'

'And,' she said anxiously, 'you are . . . better hung than other boys?'

'I'm afraid so, Ma'am. That's why I'm at Christ's Hospital.'

'In that case,' said she, 'we mustn't waste any more time. We don't want those German scientists to get at you first. This is precisely the opportunity I've been waiting for.'

'The opportunity for what, Ma'am?'

'Don't be wilfully stupid, boy! For me to get some vital and quite unusual statistical tables into print. Just think of it, Bunter! My name could go down to posterity. So would yours, even though I will have to refer to you as W.B.'

She stood for a minute staring into the distance and muttering something that sounded like 'Henrietta Boyer on Benign Hypertrophy of the *Membrum Virile*'. Then, recovering herself, she turned businesslike and brisk and said, 'Now, how's best to start? Tape measure may do. Note book for recording the figures. Two columns needed—one for statistics of length and t'other for those of girth. Oh . . .'

'What is it, Ma'am?'

'You are normally, I presume, in the flaccid condition.'

'Whatever you say, Ma'am.'

'But you can, when required, achieve an erection?'

'O yes, Ma'am, but only from time to time.'

'When you have amorous fantasies, I suppose.'

'No, Ma'am. When I have thoughts about puddings.'

'Puddings! How very strange. What sort of puddings?'

'Mainly beefsteak-and-oyster ones, Ma'am. But even treacle puddings will do.'

'Well, if puddings do the trick then puddings it will have to be. How much longer do you have at school, William?'

'Another few months, Ma'am.'

'Is that all? You may still be growing when you leave, which would be a pity. Still, we'll do the best we can with weekly measurements, starting now.'

'Now, Ma'am?'

'Certainly, we've no time to spare. Just let me get my tape measure and note book.'

She bustled around getting these things and then said:

'We shall have to duplicate our measurements, of course, on each separate occasion. That means splitting the statistics into two different sets to cover the flaccid and the erect states. We'll call the flaccid state "Condition A", and the pudding state "Condition B". But you must promise me, William, not to pass from Condition A to Condition B until I tell you.'

'I shall try not to, Ma'am. But puddings are often on my mind these days.'

'Well I tell you what,' said she, marking off a series of columns in her note book and brandishing her tape measure, 'I'll see to it that you get a pudding as a reward each time you provide me with a set of significant Condition B statistics.'

'Will it be a beefsteak-and-oyster one?'

'Don't start worrying about that now,' said she, suddenly snappish, 'or we'll never get to Condition A. So just drop your breeches and we'll make a start.'

'Drop me breeches, Ma'am?'

'How else do you think I can set about it?'

With that she dropped to her knees in front of me, pencil and note book in one hand and tape measure in the other and then, seeing that I still hesitated, she glared at me so fiercely that I swear my breeches came down of their own accord.

She spent some time over the measuring and a deal more over the entering of those measurements in her note book. She measured both length and girth at quarter-inch intervals and, for all I know, proceeded to calculate the quarter-girth of my pecker just as they do with timber trees. But by the time she had finished her first set of measurements I was beginning to feel remarkably cold. As a consequence I found it deucedly difficult to provide her with what she needed when she ordered me to think of puddings and proceed to Condition B.

'You must think harder,' said Mrs Boyer.

'I can't,' said I.

'What pudding are you thinking of?'

'Beefsteak-and-oyster.'

'Well if that won't do the trick think of another.'

I did as she asked but still nothing happened.

'Apple Pudding?' said she, hopefully. 'Plum? Yorkshire? Treacle? Rice? Batter Pudding?'

None of these were any use and soon Mrs Boyer grew impatient.

'You really are the most aggravating boy! Any other boy of your age would have managed it only too easily.'

'Perhaps,' said I, helpfully, 'I shouldn't think of puddings. I've almost forgotten what they're like. Perhaps I should think of something else.'

'Are you a patriot, boy?'

'Probably, Ma'am, but my mother don't think much of the Duke of York.'

'Never mind her. Just shut your eyes and think of England.'

I shut my eyes and thought as hard as I could, but all that happened was that I got goose pimples from the cold.

'Drat you, boy!' shouted Mrs Boyer, working herself into a frenzy of frustration. 'You're no true Englishman.'

I kept my eyes shut and began to sing 'God Save the King', but that didn't work either. Thereupon Mrs Boyer grew so impatient that she took hold of my pecker as if it were a pump-handle and gave it such a yank that I more than half-expected it to fly off.

'Oh!' cried I.

'Grow!' cried she.

And at that moment the door opened and the Reverend Boyer entered the room.

Mr Wilberforce sent his carriage to bring me away from the school the very next morning. But of Mr Wilberforce himself I saw nothing for the best part of a week, most of which I spent either in my bedroom or else trying to wheedle a little extra grub out of his cook.

When he did finally send for me I found him in a remarkably resigned yet determined mood.

'I don't want you to think,' said he, 'that I'm angry with you. It was wrong of me to expect that you could ever behave otherwise, given your parentage. The sins of the fathers . . . Aye, and of the mothers as well . . .'

'I know that appearances were against me,' said I, 'but I swear to you I weren't sinning. Leastways I weren't sinning the way you think I was. All I was doing was to help Mrs

Boyer compile statistics for *The Philosophical Transactions of the Royal Society* and so earn myself a pudding.'

'That,' said Mr Wilberforce, 'may or may not be so. But it is an explanation that has not as yet been accepted by anyone, not even by the lady's husband.'

'But I swear that's all it was.'

'Yet even if I accept your word others will not. Anyway, it makes no difference now. The manner of your leaving Christ's Hospital makes entry to either Cambridge or the Church impossible.'

For the first time since that awful moment when the Reverend Boyer had discovered his wife on her knees and me with my breeches down I began to feel a little more cheerful.

'You mustn't fret about that, Sir. I never cared for Cambridge, and between ourselves, I never thought I was really cut out for the Church. But I'm sure that, once we put our minds to it, we'll find something else that I can do.'

'I have already found it,' said Mr Wilberforce. 'Reginald Heber is an old friend of mine. He has just been made Bishop of Calcutta and All-India and you shall go out with him as his secretary. You sail from Ramsgate next Thursday.'

18   Passage to India

The next Thursday, which was 16 June 1823 (a date for ever fixed in my memory), Mr Wilberforce declared that he would have no rest until he had actually seen me shake the dust of Old England from my feet. So the two of us went in his carriage to Wapping Old Stairs and from there took the steam packet to Ramsgate. It was at that port that the East Indiaman, *Thomas Grenville*, Master, Captain Manning, was lying, waiting to take Bishop Heber and me to India.

Neither of us had travelled by steamboat before, but Mr Wilberforce took rather more interest in this novel form of transport than I did. As a politician he had, I suppose, to familiarise himself with anything to which his political opponents could apply the hated adjective 'progressive'. But machinery comes a long way down the list of things that interest me, and so I was free to decide that this was a damned dirty and noisy way in which to travel.

It also became apparent that there were those who liked steamboats even less than I did. For as we embarked we were sworn at and catcalled and pelted with lumps of coal by the crews of a couple of Newcastle colliers lying alongside. I wasn't hit, but Mr Wilberforce had his hat knocked into the water, at which all those ruffians cheered. When we had finally got away from them I asked Mr Wilberforce why we had been given such a hostile reception and why he was looking so cheerful over the loss of his hat. He answered that it was all because of the working class's deep-rooted and entirely wholesome opposition to change.

'But,' said I, 'this sort of change must be in those colliers' men's favour. These new steamboats surely increase the demand for their coals, which has to be to their long-term advantage.'

'You're still too young,' said he, 'to know anything about either politics or the labouring classes. Now I've been a Tory politician for better than forty years, and so I can assure you that every true Tory will be suspicious of change until it's been proved it will, in the long term you mention, work to his advantage.'

'And what about the labouring classes?'

'They will react in much the same way, but with this difference. They won't even consider your long-term benefits. In short, your working man's a true Tory for the first half of the argument and an out-and-out Ned Ludd for t'other half.'

'But what does that mean in terms of the colliers and the steamboat?'

'It means, my boy, that I'll never welcome anything new-fangled until it's become old-fangled, and that I'll have the support of the colliers in doing so. That's why I'm entirely happy to have lost a comparatively new hat to such a laudable demonstration of common sense and conservatism in action.

But mark this, William. There ain't a Progressive in Parliament who'd dare agree with me.'

He continued to warn me against Progressives all the way to Ramsgate where we found Bishop Heber and his party waiting for us on the quay. There were three in that party in addition to the Bishop. One was Mrs Heber. Another was the only Heber offspring, a small girl known to everybody, apparently, as Little Emily. The third was a squat, powerful, broad-spoken and plain-looking Scotswoman, well into her middle years, who had never, so far as I could ascertain, answered to any other name than that of Mistress MacPherson. I later learnt that she had been nursemaid to the infant Mrs Heber and was now going out to India to serve Little Emily in the same capacity but combining that lesser role with one of lady's maid and confidante to Mrs Heber.

The Bishop, we were soon told, was all impatience. The wind had turned favourable and Captain Manning was roaring to take advantage of it. It was to prove the last favourable wind we had, which was why our voyage to India took twice as long as it should have done. At that moment, however, the wind left us little time for protracted leave-takings. All Mr Wilberforce could do before we were rowed out to the *Thomas Grenville* was to shake me by the one hand, place a purse holding fifteen sovereigns in the other, and say:

'Much as I may desire it, William, it will not be easy for me to forget you. So I shall continue to pray for your material and moral advancement, even though that element of cowardice in your character bids me despair of the first and your readiness to succumb to temptation gives me few hopes for the second.'

'Come, Sir,' said I. 'I ain't such an entirely hopeless case, in spite of all that has happened.'

'What's bred in the bone, my boy, is bound to come out in the flesh. You inherit, I'm afraid, a whole catalogue of vice. And to these you have already added some of your own, such as gluttony, indolence and, I begin to fear, concupiscence.'

'It could be,' said I, hoping to cheer him for I was really quite fond of the old buffer, 'that my personal vices will crowd out the inherited ones. No sinner ever has room for everything.'

But he shook his head sadly, gave me his blessing, and went

back to the steam packet. I remember hoping that he would, in his hatless state, avoid catching cold and that the colliers' men would not, when he got back to Wapping, pelt him once more with coals.

This was my first sea journey. I imagine, however, that all long voyages are the same. That's to say that they're of little or no significance in a chap's life since they amount to nothing more than a few months taken out of it. But it took me several days to discover my sea legs. Until I did, my belly rose in rebellion against its food for the first time in its existence. As soon as I had found 'em, however, my appetite came roaring back and that was when I discovered how inadequate ship's fare can be. I had to give the ship's cook a couple of Mr Wilberforce's sovereigns before I could begin to keep abreast of my hunger.

That apart, it was a damned dull and ordinary sort of a voyage. We had the customary storms, during one of which the ship was struck by lightning which killed two of the passengers and caused one of the crew to fall out of the rigging and into the sea where he was promptly gobbled up by a shark. The usual number of sailors had to be triced up to the grating and flogged for petty misdemeanours, and the carpenter's mate had to be clapped into irons to save him from himself. He had developed religious mania and believed, in spite of all that the Bishop said to the contrary, that God had ordered him to go overboard and walk on the waters until the winds turned favourable. In short, if it hadn't been for my fellow passengers and the Bishop I'd have expired from tedium.

The Bishop kept me busy from the moment we boarded the *Thomas Grenville*. He was an experienced traveller who had brought his sea legs with him and, since he insisted that I should always keep him company, I had to remain active however queasy I felt. And active was the word, for he believed in activity. He was already skipping about the ship enquiring into everything before we had even weighed anchor. This was because he was a noted polymath, and as such felt he had to enquire into things a more ignorant man would have taken for granted, this being a preliminary to his theorising and philosophising about them.

It was all to be expected, I suppose, of such an intellectual man. He was, of course, a poet and had won the Craven at Oxford with that unreadable epic, *Jerusalem*. He had, almost from infancy, known and corresponded and argued with some of the most brilliant men of the day. He had discussed poetry and metaphysics with Coleridge, jurisprudence with Bentham, political economy with Ricardo, natural history with Sir Joseph Banks, and population problems with Malthus. Although he was not then much over forty, he was highly thought of in Church circles and, in addition to being poet, philosopher, naturalist, linguist and author all rolled into one, he had travelled widely in the civilised countries of Europe as well as in Muscovy, Tartary, and the lands of Asia Minor. And wherever he went in the civilised or barbarian places, he studied the languages of the regions and attempted to translate their literatures. For it was his firm belief that the best way of learning a language was to translate its poets. However, since he was, as poets go, a mere *petit maître*, this did little to reveal to the British the native worth of these poets.

Yet, although he was such an intellectual swell, he was one of the kindest of men, which is more than can be said for most of your brainy chaps. He called me William from the first, and ordered me to address him as Reggy whenever we were alone. He warned me, however, that I'd have to revert to 'my Lord' whenever Mrs Heber was present.

Although I was a green and untried youth of seventeen at that time he treated me as though I were his equal in years and experience. This often confused and sometimes embarrassed me since he was a guileless man and one who carried openness and candour well beyond the normal bounds of reticence. He would, for example, discuss the secrets of the marriage bed in exactly the same detailed way as he would discuss the structure of flying fishes and the constructions of Eastern poets.

Those poets, I soon realised, were his principal reason for taking me off Mr Wilberforce's hands. For although he knew a great deal more Greek, Latin, Hebrew, Aramaic, Russian and Serbo-Croat than I did, the tutelage I had had to endure at Christ's Hospital ensured that I knew rather more Urdu, Hindi, Sanskrit and Farsi. With that in mind he kept me at it for long hours each day helping him with his translations of the Vedas and the Ramayana, not to mention those Persian poets whose works are so popular in Indian intellectual circles. So we also had to try to put into English verse some of the poems of Firdausi, of Sa'adi of Shiraz, and of that other and greater Shiraz song-bird, Khwaja Shamsud-din-Muhammad, commonly known as Hafiz of the Sugar-Lip. Between the two of us we managed to English and butcher a good many of their most mellifluous poems. The Bishop, in his innocence, thought that all of these were concerned with the mystical joys of philosophy and religion. I, who knew more Farsi and was but recently away from my boarding school, soon realised that, as often as not, the joys referred to were those of buggery.

But if I recognised buggery when I came across it, I was all at sea whenever the Bishop began to discuss marriage and the procreation of children. This was a favourite topic with him and he never wearied of telling me how greatly, and in how many different ways, he loved Mrs Heber, she loved him, and they both loved Little Emily. Nor would he stop there. For he would then go on to describe all the efforts they had made to provide Little Emily with an infant brother or sister.

'But,' he would say at this stage, 'Little Emily is herself proof that our efforts must ere long be crowned with success. I'm convinced that this sea voyage will do the trick, and if it don't, then we'll soon have access to all the wisdom of the East and that will settle the matter. Our English physicians, you know, recommend sea air to women suffering from this temporary disability, and I've been told that the Indian physicians have remedies for it that we in the West have ignored.'

The Bishop, in short, was a thoroughly good man and, like most thoroughly good men, he was somewhat lacking in caution and common sense. Taking him all in all, with his cheerful, inquisitive, confident ways, he reminded me of nothing so much as a water wagtail hopping merrily along the river's bank and turning pebbles over for the mere joy of discovering what lay under 'em. But if he was a wagtail, his beloved wife it seemed to me had something in her of the heron.

By this I mean that she was, and still is for all I know, a tall, angular, long-nosed sort of woman who would not look entirely out of place perched on a tree looking down on that same river and wondering, in a supercilious sort of way, whether its small fry—elvers, minnows, fingerling trout and suchlike—were really worth fishing for. In spite of all that the Bishop had told me about their love for one another, I sometimes caught her looking at him as though she weren't altogether happy at having fished out that particular minnow. She was extremely haughty with me and with the other passengers. Indeed, the only person she was companionable with was Mistress MacPherson.

Those other passengers were, for the most part, a dull lot. There were old India hands returning from furlough, and new ones going out to take up their first appointments with John Company. There were three or four King's officers who kept themselves aloof from those who merely served in the Bengal Army, and a sprinkling of adventurers of various sorts who were in the service of different Indian rulers. There were half a dozen amiable and aged women returning to their mission stations but, these apart, there were only two younger females on board. One was Mrs Heber, if you could bring yourself to think of her as either young or female. The other I didn't set eyes on until we ran into calmer seas.

But I hadn't been on board for twenty-four hours before I encountered two old acquaintances among the new hands travelling to India for the first time. Both had spent their time since leaving school training for their future careers. One of them was Sam Merry, who was going out to join his father's old regiment, the 22nd Bengal Native Infantry. Meeting him again immediately raised my spirits until they were promptly lowered by my meeting the other. He was my old enemy Horace Augustus Coker, returning, though not as a missionary, to the land he had been born in. He, too, was destined for the 22nd, a regiment which was beginning to look as though it would, in the future, be entirely officered by old Bluecoats. He greeted me with forced amiability and said he was surprised that I wasn't still hanging on to Mrs Boyer's skirts—a remark I pointedly ignored.

Meanwhile the Bishop had made a discovery. He had found amongst the many books of Persian poetry he had brought with him the works of an older poet he claimed to be the greatest of 'em all. He was Omar Khayyam of Nishapur whose *Rubaiyat*, or Quatrains, he thought to be so full of spiritual delights that he declared we must immediately abandon Firdausi, Hafiz and all the others in order to concentrate on putting those same Quatrains into English verse. It was no good my arguing that Khayyam was no fit poet for a Bishop since my Bishop kept insisting that that old Persian voluptuary was not a voluptuary at all, but a Sufi mystic.

This eventually goaded me into making a most accurate and literal translation of the tenth Quatrain in order to disillusion the Bishop. So far as I can remember, that translation ran like this:

> Well Satan take them! What have we to do
> With Kaikobad and all his pervert crew?
> If Zil and Rustum bugger Hatim, still,
> 'Twill serve to turn their minds away from you.

The Bishop, for all his open-mindedness and candour, was deeply shocked by this, even after he had gone through the original word by word to check the accuracy of my translation. It served, however, to turn him away from the Persians for a time and, as he was quite incapable of passing a day without versifying, he went back to writing hymns and verses of his own. One of those hymns, I do believe, had its origins in a careless remark I made as we were pacing the deck together shivering in the icy blast of a Biscay gale.

'I shall be glad,' said I, 'to see the warm shores of India. This weather, as dear old Bessy would have put it, is cold enough to freeze the balls off a Greenland Eskimo.'

The Bishop looked at me strangely for a moment and, as he then left me abruptly, I feared I had offended him. The next morning, however, he rather diffidently showed me a new hymn he had just written which started:

> From Greenland's icy mountains
> From India's coral strand . . .

He never admitted that I may have given him the inspiration for this any more than he ever thanked me for putting him off Khayyam, a poet no Briton should ever seek to translate. None the less I still believe some gratitude was due to me on both accounts.

Once we had left Finisterre behind us we began to run into warmer weather and calmer seas. This brought out those of the passengers who had, until then, spent most of their days and nights in their bunks. And amongst those of them who now began to walk about on deck I discovered another old acquaintance or, to be more accurate, she discovered me. It happened like this.

I couldn't help noticing one couple who, on that first sunny day, were walking up and down the main deck. He was a grey-haired, sallow-faced, skinny sort of fellow who strode purposefully up and down. She was a remarkably plain and outstandingly plump young woman who hung on his arm and kept chattering away at him without extracting any greater response than an occasional grunt. But every time they passed, she stared at me in a way that I began to find embarrassing. After she had passed me and scrutinised me for the fourth or fifth time, she broke away from her partner, came up to me and said:

'I knew it! I knew it! You're Billy Bunter.'

I must have looked rather surprised at this blunt approach because she then went on:

'God bless my soul! Surely you remember me. I'm Maria Jewkes that was.'

I apologised for not recognising her, though as she was now half as old and half as large again as when I had last seen her, had her hair in ringlets, and was decked out in all manner of muslins, Indian shawls and brooches I could have been forgiven for not realising that here was my old Coram Street friend and fellow-gobbler.

She didn't take it amiss, however, but turned to her partner, who was looking at me with some suspicion, and said, 'This, dearest, is Mr William Bunter who was my brother's school chum and an old friend of my family. And this, Billy, is my husband, Colonel D'Arcy Huggins, once of the 54th of Foot, and now Commissary-General, no less, to His Highness the Maharajah of the Punjaub.'

The Commissary-General extended a languid hand and muttered ''Ow-de-do' in Cockney tones more fitting for a Huggins than a D'Arcy. I said 'Tolerably well' and went on to express my surprise at meeting Maria at such a distance from Coram Street and added something about wishing them well for their marriage. He nodded quite affably at that and then asked whether I was going all the way to Calcutta. When I said that I was he wanted to know whether I was about to enter one of the trading houses or was going out as a John Company writer.

'For,' said he, 'you don't look to me cut out for a soldier— not even in the Army of Bengal.'

I replied, quite civilly, that I was neither merchant, soldier, nor Company writer, but was travelling to India as secretary to Bishop Heber, at which he appeared to lose interest and said that he never had been much of a man for church-going and he must finish his constitutional. After which he went striding off leaving Maria to keep me company.

She immediately engulfed me in a sea of chatter. Once she had finished exclaiming 'Lor! Who'd ever have thought in the old days that we'd meet up like this and all bound for India' she went on to chat about her husband, her marriage, and her plans for the future.

'It was a whirlwind courtship,' she explained. 'And I do believe that we came together over food. D'Arcy's mighty interested in it, even though he's that thin you would think he lived on gruels and toast and water. Mark you, he don't talk about food quite as well as you used to in the old days, and he ain't even in the grocery trade like Papa. But he has to provision all the Maharajah's army, and that makes him a grocer of sorts, apart from which he's an absolute expert on Indian dishes. You might say that he courted and won me with his descriptions of curries and pilaus and meetai and mangoes and all the other delicious things I'll eat once we're safely established in his palace in Lahore. For he's enormously rich, you know, what with what he's paid by the Maharajah and makes out of the provisioning, and that's what persuaded Papa and Mama to agree to the marriage. Johnny was against it at first, but then he said that, since he was old and rich and none too healthy-looking I'd soon be a widow and so I could do a deal worse.'

Although I was, at this first meeting, dazed by this flow of chatter I found Maria, as the voyage progressed, as amiable as ever. I'd always had a soft spot for the Coram Street crowd and I've never found anyone other than Maria who enjoyed talking about food as much as I do. So, what with Sam Merry, and Maria, and the Bishop being off the old Persians, the voyage went happily enough until we came to the crossing of the Equator.

19 Crossing the Line

As we beat our painful way to the south and eventually got close to the Equator, some of the old India hands began to tease the new ones with alarming stories of the horseplay they would have to suffer whilst actually crossing the Line. Anything, they hinted, could happen to a chap during the initiation ceremony.

No mention of rituals or ceremonies or initiations could fail to interest my Bishop, for he was always eager to investigate such mysteries from various Anglican, œcumenical, historical, anthropological and philosophical viewpoints. But the descriptions he had of this crossing-the-Line ceremony differed so greatly from one old hand to the other that he decided to consult Captain Manning, who was a most amiable and garrulous mariner and very willing to be consulted.

'Sailors,' said he, 'have mighty little to look forward to here below—especially when they're aloft.' When he'd finished guffawing at this feeble witticism he went on:

'Whilst they're at sea it's all watch-keeping, sail-setting, deck-swabbing and hard tack. And when they're ashore the best most of them can expect is to be robbed in the grog-shops and poxed-up in the brothels. That's why they say that the service only survives on rum, the lash and sodomy.'

'Surely not,' said the Bishop.

'Perhaps not,' conceded the Captain. 'But it's a damned harsh and monotonous life none the less. So it's not surprising that sailors get as excited as children at Christmas time when it comes to something that will break that monotony, such as your crossing-the-Line ceremony.'

'And what,' asked the Bishop, 'is so wonderfully exciting about that?'

'It's the one day, my Lord, when all ship's discipline goes overboard. The lower deck takes control and has licence to do what it likes with those who have to be initiated.'

'It reminds me,' said the Bishop, predictably, 'of the old Roman festival of Saturnalia, when the slaves took over from their masters for the day.'

'It's odd, Sir, that you should have mentioned those Romans. Don't know much about them myself. But my bosun, a rough-spoken chap but of superior intellect for a sailor, is forever quoting 'em. Has an enormous respect for the classics, he has. And since he'll be in charge of the ceremony and will himself play Neptune, it's my guess that you'll see a crossing-the-Line ceremony that's altogether classier and more classical than usual. Most Neptunes are perfectly happy to have no more than a trumpeter, a barber and a couple of barber's assistants in attendance. Rumour has it that my Neptune plans to add an Amphitrite, a Mercury and two or three Tritons.'

'Neptune, Amphitrite, Tritons,' said the Bishop. 'How very interesting to come across these memories of pagan superstitions in the rude minds of our Jack Tars. How true it is, Captain Manning, that there's nothing new under the sun, and that we all carry the past with us. History, don't you agree, is never written on a blank sheet. Rather is it a palimpsest inscribed over things but partially erased.'

Such philosophising floored the Captain who was a plain-spoken man though a voluble one.

'I don't know about that palim-whatever-it-is,' said he. 'But I do know, my Lord, that King Neptune and the crossing-the-Line ceremony have always been important to mariners.'

'And of course they still are,' said the Bishop. 'These are things I might in due course look into. Some day, perhaps, I shall trace the histories of these ceremonies. I may even write a book about 'em. How would *Heber on the Pagan Origins of Maritime Ceremonies* strike you as a title?'

It didn't seem to strike the Captain at all, so I intervened to ask him why there had to be a barber and barber's assistants at the ceremony.

'I'm glad you asked that, Mr Bunter,' he replied, 'for that's something I do know about. The high point of all your crossing-the-Line ceremonies is the shaving of the neophytes.'

'The neophytes?' said the Bishop eagerly.

'I hope that's the right name for them, my Lord. I refer to those who haven't crossed the Equator before and so have to be initiated.'

'But why the barbers?' I insisted.

'Well, the head barber does the shaving with an old piece of hoop iron. Assistant Number One is in charge of the slush bucket, which provides the shaving soap, and Assistant Number Two does the lathering with a damned great brush made of spun yarn. Then all three of 'em see to it that the initiate has his face washed in bilge water. There's a large canvas bath rigged up for that purpose.'

'It all sounds,' said I, from the height of my seventeen-odd years, 'somewhat childish.'

'Childish or not, Mr Bunter, it's something you'll have to go through to mark your first crossing of the Line. And if you take my advice, you'll wear as few clothes as possible, and all of 'em old ones.'

'But what about me?' cried the Bishop. 'I've travelled a great deal but without once crossing the Line. Yet I can't help thinking it would be wrong of me to submit myself to such a ceremony. It's not that I mind a bit of fun. But I'm sure that Cantaur, and possibly Ebor as well, would maintain that no man of the cloth, and least of all a Bishop, ought to allow himself to be shaved in public with a piece of hoop iron.'

'I appreciate your problem, my Lord. But the ladies are, of course, excluded from a ceremony that is always rough and sometimes rude. So I don't see why, if you wear your surplice, you should not rank as one of the skirted.'

'I refuse,' said the Bishop stoutly, 'to wear such a Papish vestment, or to hide behind the ladies.'

'Then there's nothing for it, my Lord, but to exert my authority, which is something captains are reluctant to do on such occasions. I shall order the bosun to give you exemption *ex officio*, as they say, or *ex cathedra* if you think that more suitable.'

'*Ex officio* would cover it,' said the Bishop. 'But Mrs Heber and I shall watch the proceedings with interest.'

Those proceedings started, next morning, shortly after the close of the second dog-watch, with Neptune's Trumpeter, who was the ship's carpenter hidden inside an old sea-cloak and a great oakum beard, blowing a loud blast on an old brass bugle. Extra rum was then issued to all hands which did much to account for the enthusiasm with which they then joined in the ceremony. This began with the interrogatories. The Trumpeter, in his secondary role as Neptune's tipstaff, passed amongst the passengers picking out those of them who would qualify as neophytes. Neither Merry nor Coker so qualified. They had both been born in India and so must, by the mere logic of geography, have undergone infant initiation. Merry, indeed, had been enlisted as a Triton and was now equipped with a painted canvas breastplate and a helmet converted from a leather fire bucket to help him play the part. Coker aspired to a more important role, one in which he could satisfy his fondness for pushing people about and humiliating them. That is, he had persuaded the bosun to let him fill the position of Head Barber.

Those of us who were to be initiated were drawn up on the main deck some time soon after the second dog-watch. Thrones had been set up for King Neptune and Amphitrite, his spouse, facing an upturned half-barrel which would serve as a barber's chair and a large canvas bath full of bilge water. The ship's fiddler announced the arrival of King Neptune who emerged from the forrard hatch accompanied by his entourage and a strong smell of rum. The bosun, a bull of a man almost as broad as he was long, was imposing in a fish-skin corselet, a tin crown, a scarlet cloak, a long beard and a good deal of seaweed. He may have been, as the Captain had suggested, a superior sort of person, but I had from the first suspected that he was of that sodomitical persuasion which had also been mentioned. Certainly Amphitrite, who was the galley-boy lightly disguised with a gown, a spun-yarn wig and a couple of improbable boobs, still wore the hunted look which character-ised the other ship's boys whenever the bosun was around.

The ceremonies entailed a good deal of horseplay which varied somewhat from neophyte to neophyte depending on what Coker and his assistants thought appropriate. But, to treat of them as a whole, each victim was seized, hustled on to the barber's chair, lathered and shaved, and then presented to Neptune for acceptance before having his head ducked into the bath in a ritual purification.

I was the last to be dealt with and, even though I had removed my spectacles for safety's sake, I could see that Coker wore a gloating, relishing look as he and his assistants seized me. He was none too gentle with his hoop iron and, when he presented me to Neptune, he whispered something in his ear at which His Majesty's face lit up.

'Why,' roared he, ''ere's a fine, plump young chicken what's never been plucked naked before. Let's 'ave a look at 'im.'

With that, and before I had realised what was afoot, Coker and his assistants stripped me of the breeches and shirt I had thought sufficient for the occasion and, each of them taking either an arm or a leg, swung me in the air preparatory to throwing me neck and crop into the bath. I was terrified and, reaching out my one free hand to prevent this, managed to get a firm hold of Coker's ear.

'Leggo of me, you fat fool,' he shouted but this I refused to do. I continued to hang on to his ear even though I could feel it creaking under the strain. They swung me and shook me but, wherever I moved, Coker's ear went with me. The upshot of it all was that we both eventually went into the water, he in all his barber's finery and I as naked as the day I was born. The bath held no more than a couple of feet of bilge water, and as I spluttered to the surface I still had that ear in my grip and Coker was bellowing like a bull at a baiting. Eventually I released him, clambered out of the bath and stood dripping and naked on the deck demanding my breeches.

It was, now I look back on it, the New River situation all over again. But this time I was fully conscious, and the interest I aroused in the onlookers could not properly be described as scientific.

'Bugger me!' cried Neptune, 'what 'ave we 'ere?'

'That ain't no plump young chicken,' tittered Amphitrite sycophantically. 'That's as fine an old cock as ever I've seen.'

I looked up to the quarter deck for help from the Bishop, but he had turned away from the sorry spectacle, although Mrs Heber, looking more than ever like a hungry heron, continued to stare. I heard Mistress MacPherson say:

'Did you ever see the like of yon? It's fit for a Bishop!'

But then Mrs Heber dragged her away and Merry broke ranks from the Tritons and gave me my breeches. Coker, meanwhile, stood knee-deep in the bilge water nursing his ear and yelling for the ship's surgeon to examine it. By then, however, he was past medical help. The top half of the ear hung down for ever after, giving him, when viewed from that side, the sort of lop-eared appearance you sometimes see in fighting terriers.

Merry took me aside afterwards and warned me to look out for myself since Coker was not the man to forgive such an injury. I was not altogether surprised, therefore, to find a note on my bunk a couple of days later in which the following message was written in capital letters:

YOU HAVE ENEMIES ON THIS SHIP WHO PLAN TO DO YOU HARM. I WOULD PREVENT THIS. MEET ME IN THE PAINT LOCKER AN HOUR AFTER MIDNIGHT AND I WILL TELL YOU HOW TO AVERT THIS DANGER. TELL NO ONE OF THIS. ONE WHO WISHES YOU WELL

I was sufficiently alarmed by this to think of going immediately to either the Bishop or Captain Manning, but then I consulted Sam Merry and he dissuaded me.

'You must take it seriously, right enough,' he said, 'but first you've got to discover what it is you must be serious about. It's no good going to the Captain with a cock-and-bull story about who knows what sort of threats from devil knows which sources.'

'Well who do *you* think threatens me?'

'I have my suspicions, which is why I urge you to treat this seriously. I know that Coker's been going around swearing to get even with you for his lop ear. And then there's the bosun as well.'

'What on earth has the bosun to do with it?'

'The Captain had him up before him over that business of stripping you naked. He said it was no part of any crossing-the-Line ceremony he'd ever heard tell of and was nothing more than ruffianly behaviour. So he reprimanded the bosun and logged him, which is why he now has little love for you and has declared that he's only waiting to get you in some dark alley in Calcutta in order to demonstrate that fact. What's more he and Coker have become as thick as two thieves.'

This had begun to sound very dangerous indeed, and so I asked Sam Merry what I should do.

'First of all you must keep that appointment in the paint locker and find out who your mysterious well-wisher is. I've little doubt that it's one of the ship's boys, for all of them hate the bosun. Then, just as soon as you've learnt what he has to tell you, you can take him before Captain Manning and have Coker and the bosun dealt with.'

So that night I plucked up my courage and did as Sam had advised. It was devilish dark inside the paint locker, and it became darker still when the door slammed shut behind me. I could sense, however, that I was not alone, and so I crept forward hissing hopefully, 'It's Bunter here.'

No one responded until I was well inside the locker. Then, in a sudden rush of activity, I was pushed from the front and tripped up from behind, which caused me to go sprawling on my back. I had fallen so heavily that I came mighty close to stunning myself. Nevertheless I was conscious, as I lay there, of strong hands seizing me at either end. My coat was pulled up over my head, pinioning my arms, whilst at the same time my breeches were pulled down over my ankles. Someone extremely solid then sat on my chest, after which things were done to me which I later realised amounted to rape by female or females unknown.

It was a truly awful experience made even more awful

by the fact that I did not understand what was happening. Before it had all ended I had fainted clean away and so could not tell, with any degree of accuracy, how often I was assaulted; let alone who my assailants were. By the time I came to I was on my own, on my back, and in such a state of funk and exhaustion as I would not again experience until I had to embark on these enforced nightly gallops with the Begum.

I eventually managed to pull up my breeches and limp back to my bunk. The next morning I tried to console myself with the thought that, whatever it was that had been done to me, being beaten up by Coker and the bosun would have been worse. It didn't work. I may not have much manly vanity, but what I have of it had been hurt, and this made me most unusually angry.

'Bunter,' said I to myself, 'you must find out who did this to you.'

'And what,' said common sense, 'will you do to 'em when you find 'em?'

'That,' said I, 'is something I'll consider once I've discovered who I'm dealing with. Meanwhile I must concentrate on detecting the culprits.'

'And how,' said common sense, 'will you set about that? You can't go around complaining that you've been raped and demanding to know who's done it.'

'I'll consult Merry,' said I, which I did. He fell about laughing when I first told him what had happened to me. But then my evident distress must have touched his kind heart for he offered to help me with my detecting.

'It's a good thing they were women,' he said, 'for there ain't more than nine or ten of 'em on board, and that narrows the field. What we must discover is what each of them was doing between midnight and one o'clock or thereabouts this morning.'

'They'll all say they were asleep in their cabins, whether they were or not.'

'But that wouldn't establish what the lawyer fellows would call their alibis, and alibis are awfully important in detection work.'

Merry was being a little too theoretical for my liking, and

so I said, 'When none of them have alibis, all of them have alibis.'

'I see what you mean,' said Merry. 'Then we must set about it psychologically.'

'Whatever do you mean?'

'We must ask ourselves which of the females on board are most likely to indulge in rape. Now there are all those mission women. My father always said that anyone who'd done long service in an up-country station in India would be bound to turn queer.'

'I'm certain,' said I, 'that none of them is as queer as that. They're all too old, too frail, and too desiccated to go in for rape.'

'Well then, there's the Bishop's wife and that Scots biddy who serves her.'

'A bishop's wife is, by definition, too chaste even to be suspected of rape. And as for Mistress MacPherson, she's such a respectable body that she puts her nose in the air and sniffs whenever I have to speak to her.'

'Then, Billy, I'm afraid that only leaves your Maria.'

'What do you mean by "my Maria"?'

'I don't want to pry into your private affairs, but the two of you have been fairly thick ever since we left Ushant. No one could help noticing that. You spend hours together, chatting away to each other whilst that spurious old Colonel of hers takes his constitutionals. It wouldn't surprise me to learn that you've so enflamed her passions as to make her determined to have her way with you.'

'I'll have you know, Merry, that I've known Maria ever since she was four feet high and three feet wide and that the only thing that draws us together and that we ever talk about is grub. Besides, there were two of them in the paint locker.'

'She may have got her horrible husband to assist her.'

'I've already told you they were both women. Besides, there's the chitterlings.'

'The chitterlings? What have they got to do with it?'

'They provide Maria with the only alibi we've yet got. That's what they've got to do with it.'

'I can't for the life of me understand what you're talking about.'

'I'm talking about the ship's pig that was slaughtered last Thursday. We had chitterlings the next day, if you remember.'

'So we did. I'd quite forgotten.'

'You ain't sufficiently interested in grub. That's why you'll never understand someone like Maria. She's enormously fond of chitterlings, even though they're not the best things to tuck into when you're close to the Equator.'

'I wouldn't tuck into them anywhere.'

'Well, Maria did more tucking in than was wise, and that's why she's the only female on board with a cast-iron alibi.'

'I don't see the connection.'

'Colic's the connection. The flux is the connection. Vomiting and a belly-ache is the connection. By the Friday afternoon Maria had to take to her bunk and she's been there, on toast and water, ever since.'

'Are you sure of that?'

'Of course I'm sure. And if her colic don't constitute an alibi by itself, consider it in connection with her psychology. You said something about my enflaming her to rape. Let me tell you that no woman with colic would ever contemplate rape even if it was something she engaged in at other times. As for Maria, the only thing that ever enflames her is grub.'

'Well, that lets Maria out. But do you realise what you've now done?'

'What?'

'You've satisfied me that there ain't a single female on this ship who's capable of rape. And do you know what follows from that?'

'No.'

'Why, you fat idiot, it follows quite clearly that you never were raped. All that happened to you was that you were assaulted by a couple of ruffians who were, I suspect, Coker and the bosun. You went into a swoon and dreamed up the rest. My advice to you is to forget all about it and to avoid all such sexual fantasies in the future.'

I thought the bit about sexual fantasies was quite unfair. Nevertheless memories of the paint locker would, over the remaining nine or ten weeks, have begun to fade had I not been given reason to suspect that tales concerning those supposed fantasies were being told. The evidence I had for this was, perhaps, slight and consisted of no more than changes in Mrs Heber's and Mistress MacPherson's attitudes towards me. Each of them, it seemed to me, changed in a different way. Mrs Heber, who had always treated me rather haughtily, now ignored me entirely. Mistress MacPherson, on the other hand, stopped sniffing at me in her former disparaging fashion and began, instead, to show some solicitude for me. She even managed, from time to time, to provide me with extra food, saying that a 'puir laddie like you needs to keep his strength up'.

However, since no one else treated me any differently from before, I began to absolve Merry from any tittle-tattling. Time passed and, in spite of the head winds, we eventually got close enough to the Malabar coast to be able to smell India. As I leant over the rail trying to get a glimpse of land I decided that there was little enough of the Bishop's 'spicy breezes' in that particular smell. It was at that moment that the Bishop joined me in a high and most unusual state of elation.

I had put that elation down to the fact that we were finally approaching the last leg of our journey until the Bishop came out with something that put other and quite different thoughts into my mind.

'You'll remember, William,' said he, grinning like a jackanapes and hopping from one leg to another in a most unepiscopal and joyful manner, 'that I've frequently asserted that sea air would do the trick.'

'With reference to Mrs Heber, do you mean?'

'Undoubtedly with reference to Mrs Heber. But we need to refer to her no longer. The physicians were right, William, to recommend a sea voyage. Mrs Heber has just informed me that she is now with child.'

'Oh!' said I, and I've no doubt that my jaw dropped.

'And all because of the sea air, William. Just think of that.'

'I'm thinking of it, my Lord.'

'But,' said the Bishop, and here he put on a more serious face, 'there is a further development which owes quite as much to villainy and strong liquor as it does to sea air.'

'What development is that?'

'One I never would have expected seeing that she's well

past forty. But Mrs Heber has also just informed me that
Mistress MacPherson is with child as well.'

'You surprise me, my Lord,' said I, beginning to feel weak
about the knees.

'It's surprised us all, William, including Mistress MacPherson
herself who remembers nothing of what happened. There's a
scoundrel somewhere on this ship whose identity is unknown
but whose conscience, if he has one, must haunt him for
evermore. For William, on the night we crossed the Line,
Mistress MacPherson, I am informed, was most woefully
betrayed after having succumbed to the combined influences
of sea air and rum.'

20 *Joys of India and the Bishop*

As I sit here in Sumroo, sweating, scribbling and trying to
unravel the various causes of my present discontents, I have
had to ask myself when it was that I ceased to enjoy India.
The only honest answer must be—little more than a few
months ago. Until then, and for the best part of five years,
India was greatly more to my taste than Kensington or
Christ's Hospital had ever been.

Yet it was, as I now consider it, my sheer enjoyment of
India that helped bring me here. Mine is a nature that swings
easily between cowardice and cockiness, and it is when I am
most enjoying myself that I am at my cockiest. But cockiness
begets imprudence, and it was partly imprudence that
plunged me in this situation. That's why I must attempt to
decide which of the joys India brought me tempted me out of
my native prudence.

Some things I would have enjoyed whether I'd been in
India or not. One of them was just growing up, a process
which in its initial stages at least is generally enjoyable.
Another was being well away from Mr Wilberforce, the

Reverend Mr Boyer and Mr Boyer's statistically-minded wife. But what was more specific to my enjoyment was the fact that I was an Englishman in India. That is something which cannot but add to every Englishman's good opinion of himself. For, whatever he was in England, he automatically becomes a member of the ruling class the moment he sets foot on Indian soil. That is, of course, so long as he has not had to run from John Company and other assorted enemies, and has not had to place himself, as I have, in the power of an aged and randy Begum.

But I was not just any Briton when I arrived in India. Since I occupied the position I did, I was immediately assigned to the higher rather than the lower echelons of the current ruling class. For I was in India not as a mere military or John Company man, but as private secretary, confidant and presumptive adviser to the very first Bishop of All-India.

News of Bishop Heber's appointment had convinced most Indians and not a few old India hands that Britain's Imperial policy was about to change. The London government, they said to one another, is no longer content that Britons should do no more than trade with Indians, either peacefully or at the point of the bayonet. It has now concluded that Indians have to be both anglicised and civilised, the one necessarily flowing from the other. And, since this was a moral rather than a commercial imperative, it no longer mattered a scrap whether it was done at the bayonet point or not. The decision had been taken to turn all Indians into God-fearing, church-going, darker-skinned Englishmen.

That, according to the theory, was why the Bishop had been sent to India. And that was why my good, gentle, open-minded, philosophical Heber was so unwarrantably assumed to be a man of great authority; a sort of Grand Inquisitor invested with every kind of spiritual and temporal power.

It was not an anglicised India but India as it was that so suited the Bishop. No other spot on earth could have offered him so many strange races, languages, religions, cultures, fauna and flora on which to exercise his insatiable curiosity. Nor was there one which could so have engaged his speculative faculties.

He had begun to construct theories about India before he

had even set foot in it. Just as soon as the *Thomas Grenville* had made its way up the Hooghly and arrived at the mouth of the Ganges he declared that that great and muddy river was exactly like the Russian Don at the point where it flows into the Sea of Azov. When we got closer in, he had to retract slightly on account of the smells and the charred corpses floating down in the current. Not even the Muscovites, he admitted, could have endured or created such smells. Moreover those same Muscovites did at least bury their dear departeds instead of inadequately toasting them on a funeral pyre before throwing whatever was left into the river.

When we finally dropped anchor a few miles off Diamond Head we found that the Governor General had sent his own yacht to meet us and to carry us as far up-river and towards Calcutta as winds and current would permit. This meant that I had to take a hurried farewell of my old chums Sam and Maria. Sam, I knew, I would soon meet again. He was to be stationed at Barrackpoor, not many miles up the road from Calcutta. Maria, however, would be hundreds of miles away in Lahore. Nevertheless she made me promise to visit her as soon as I could.

Lord Amherst, the Governor General, had seen to it that the yacht should contain a reception party made up of every canon, dean, chaplain and missionary he could lay his hands on. Mrs Heber, I thought, was exceedingly *de-haut-en-bas* with every one of 'em. The Bishop, to my surprise, came close to ignoring 'em. But this was because he was much more interested in the score or so natives who were the yacht's crew. His very first remark to me made it clear that his speculative faculties were already at work.

'Have you noticed,' he said, 'by how much they vary in colour from one to the other?'

'I haven't had time to notice anything,' said I, still waving farewell to Maria.

'Well, my boy, if you look at 'em now, you'll see they're of every shade of complexion. There are some quite as black as Abyssinians or Hottentots, and there are others you could almost take for Sicilians, Neapolitans or Algerines. And betwixt and between these there are a good few who are just brown. Now I wonder why that is.'

He wondered aloud for the best part of an hour without being able to decide whether it was race, caste, climate or miscegenation which was the determining factor. What he did decide in the end, however, was that only brown was beautiful.

'Try as I might,' he said, 'I can't find a black complexion pleasing. As for those of the lightest complexion, they so remind me of some rascally Sicilians who once cheated me in Palermo that I find it difficult to admire them. But just look at that man . . .' And here he pointed at a crewman whose brownness no one could ignore, seeing that he wore no more to conceal it than a rag around his loins and another one around his head. 'Is he not attractive? And by the same token, William, must we not seem most unattractive to him?'

'I know I ain't especially attractive,' I replied. 'But I'll be jiggered if I can see why I should be more than usually unattractive to a heathen.'

'It's the pallor of our complexions, William. They must think of us as albino freaks, and unhealthy ones at that. And then we're more clumsily built. Not for us such delicate features and such lithe and slender forms.'

I'm not a vain man so far as physical appearances go, but this was going too far.

'And not for us,' said I, 'such savage nakedness. I'm sure Mrs Heber must find such nudity indelicate.'

Mrs Heber appeared to be doing no such thing, for she was looking at the crewmen with just as much interest as the Bishop, as he pointed out.

'My wife, William, is a person of the most refined sensibilities. But you will observe that she's not such a niminypiminy as to think brown nudity indelicate. Now if you or I were to go around in such a state of undress, it would most certainly offend her sense of delicacy, for we'd look like nothing more than a couple of blanched cabbage-stalks. But there's nothing either offensive or indelicate in these beautiful brown creatures. I would go so far as to say *"Angeli ferent, si essent Christiani"*.'

It was the only occasion he ever went so far. I never again heard him suggest that any Indian might be improved by the changing of his religion.

We soon had to transfer from the yacht, because of adverse currents and winds, to a twenty-oared bhotiah. And from that, after battling for some miles against the stream, we transferred to the land and to a carriage that was waiting for us. This was drawn by a pair of scrawny little switch-tailed horses, each with a tall and bewhiskered postillion on its back. They wore blue livery coats heavily decorated with tarnished gold lace, and these went strangely with their dhotis and skinny black legs. A saeece, similarly liveried, ran beside each horse. The Bishop, at first, thought that might be too arduous for them in the heat, but he soon discovered that the condition of the roads and of our horseflesh was such, that these saeeces never had to break into anything faster than an occasional jog. Half a score horsemen followed behind, completing our cortège. These were, we discovered, a few of the mace bearers, chaprassees, khitmutgars and bearers already assigned to the episcopal household.

We were, as distance goes, no more than a long day's journey away from Calcutta, but that didn't apply to the Bishop who insisted on stopping every time we passed anything that interested him. An elephant had to be studied and sketched in the first village we went through. There were strange trees such as banyans, mangoes and neems to be measured and botanised over. We met a band of gipsies or Kunja with whom he spent several hours. He was interested to discover that they spoke Hindoostanee whereas the same people in England spoke a mixture of Romany and English and in Russia spoke nothing but Russian. He was also much struck by the bold looks of the gipsy women, whom he thought much handsomer than the Bengalee women and well-enough shaped to serve as models for any sculptor.

A little later we passed some fishermen casting their nets in the river, and he straightway waded out to them so that he might attempt to classify what they caught. The huts the peasants lived in had to be examined and compared in terms of utility and neatness with the cottages of the farm labourers in England and the hovels of the serfs in Russia. We had, of course, to stop when we came to a pagoda for, although the Bishop was not allowed to enter it, he insisted on discussing its layout and architecture with the Brahmin in charge.

It was from that same Brahmin that he learnt of the existence of some ancient rock carvings in a nearby cave, to which we all had to trudge although the Bishop, who went in first, advised Mrs Heber to advance no further. When he came out he declared that some of the work would not have disgraced Donatello and much of it, viewed aesthetically, was not really indecent. All of this, together with frequent stops to examine the crops, birds, wild flowers and suchlike meant that we had to turn one day's journey into two, and so were obliged to spend the night in a *dak* or posting house.

Mrs Heber grumbled a good deal about this, and was far from satisfied with the skinny chicken the dak attendant served up for our evening meal. But before that meal had even been placed on the table our Bishop was outside and sitting at the cooking fire over which our followers were preparing their own evening meal. Like most economists, the Bishop was less interested in the food he put into his own belly than he was in the diets of others, and he could talk a great deal about economies of production, costs, ease of preparation, palatability and nutritional values without being able to tell you whether it was beef or mutton that he had just dined on.

He was naturally interested, therefore, in what our followers were cooking, which was no more out of the ordinary than their normal rice with a small amount of vegetable curry to give it some relish. The curry was split up into small portions which were placed on banyan leaves between every two men. The rice, however, was put on a tray for everyone to dip into communally. Before they could do so, however, the Bishop insisted on having the rice weighed, after which he said it was his opinion that the men would have done twice as well on half the quantity of boiled potatoes.

'Remind me, William,' he said, 'to raise the matter of potatoes with the Governor General when first we meet. I'm sure that useful root would serve India better than any amount of this rice.'

When we finally reached Kidapoor late on the following day we got our first view of Calcutta. The distant scene immediately reminded the Bishop of somewhere else. 'It looks,' he said, 'exactly like the neighbourhood around Connaught Place as seen from Hyde Park.'

When we reached the city, however, and were going through the quarter where the rich merchants and the more important officials had their mansions, he said it reminded him of nothing so much as the area around the Nevski Prospekt in Saint Petersburg.

Lord Amherst lived, for the most part, in his country house, which was a pretty place near Barrackpoor set in two or three hundred acres of parkland. He was able, therefore, to place the old Government House at the Bishop's disposal to serve him as a temporary Palace until a more suitable one had been built close to the new Cathedral. This Government House was a great barrack of a place set in the middle of the old Fort William which, as its name implies, had been built in King Billy's time when the Emperor Aurungzebe made a present of the village of Calcutta to the East India Company.

Large though it was, Mrs Heber had decided that I could not be housed there but should live in a bengaloo on the other side of the maidan. It was, like all such buildings in Bengal, a single-storey affair with a verandah running across its front and no more than three or four rooms, all of them unceilinged and open to the rafters. I was happy to settle there, however, since it got me away from Mrs Heber, even though both the Bishop and Mistress MacPherson complained at my being so exiled.

Exile it was not, so far as the Bishop was concerned. The first morning after our arrival he was knocking at my bedroom door before the dawn had properly broken to tell me to accompany him on his exploration of the fort. And so in no time at all we were clambering over crumbling ramparts and bastions and the Bishop was chatting away very knowledgeably about defilades, fields of fire, sally ports and other such matters of military architecture.

The Bishop's behaviour during this, our first journey together on Indian soil, proved typical of his behaviour in all those other journeys we made across the length and breadth of the sub-continent. He was seldom less than idiosyncratic and never less than enjoyable. So far as I was concerned, he was one of the great joys of India or of anywhere else.

21   *Calcutta Bluecoats*

I had not been long in Calcutta before Sam Merry and I were as intimate as we had been in Christ's Hospital. We were both, I suppose, maturing but, although he looked different sporting his new-grown whiskers and was more imposing in his regimentals than he had been in his blue gown, Sam was still the same calm, friendly and glum-faced companion I had always known. It was through him that I was introduced to the convivialities of Army life and the easy friendships of an officers' mess.

I was slightly surprised at being so readily accepted by military men. But there must have been something military in my blood for, when it came to such things as drills, retreats, parades, guard mountings, bugle calls, uniforms, decorations and turn-outs I soon found that I was as concerned with the minutiae of these as the most stick-in-the-mud and purple-faced of field officers.

Many of them, indeed, urged me to abandon my ecclesiastical connections and take up a military career. One wag suggested that I should enrol myself in the Fattepoor Lancers, and I did not entirely take that as a joke. However, I would never have abandoned my Bishop, besides which I ain't at my best in uniform and have never been able to cut much of a dash on a horse.

One consequence of my cordial reception in the mess was that Coker, who was also a member of it, was obliged to forget former animosities for the moment and play the *faux bonhomme*. He even referred to me as an old school chum, although I am sure that it stuck in his gullet.

Merry and Coker, however, were far from being the only former Bluecoats in the Bengal Presidency. There were generally at least a dozen of us, those who were taken off by cholera, fever, or the pox being replaced by new drafts of Bluecoats fresh out from England. It was not surprising that there should be so many of us in India. John Company, being a force in the City, could always contrive a nomination to Christ's Hospital. They made use of this whenever a junior, and therefore still impecunious, employee of theirs died, leaving an orphaned son to be educated. Christ's Hospital not only saved the Board of the Honourable East India Company the cost of that education. It also assured the Company of a steady succession of cadets. For, having been born in John Company territory, and having been educated through its good offices, what could be more natural than that some of them should return to their roots, which is to say to India and the East India Company's service?

The number of former Bluecoats stationed in and around Calcutta was first revealed to me by an early visitor to my bengaloo. He might, to judge by his get-up, have been visiting in Mayfair rather than in Fort William. He wore, under his beautifully-fitting, cut-away, pale lavender coat a frilled silk shirt and a double-breasted grey satin waistcoat across which a number of gold chains were hung. His neck was tightly enclosed by his carefully-tied neckcloth which was held in place by a sparkling diamond pin. He might have been poured in to his nankeen pantaloons which were strapped under the shiniest of patent-leather boots. His gloves were the whitest I'd ever seen, and he had a curly-brimmed, low-crowned hat on his head which he whipped off as he advanced on me with outstretched arms.

My first reaction was that he must be devilish hot in such a rig. My second was that, under the pomaded curls and whiskers, I could still recognise the dusky, smiling face of my old school friend, Hurree Ram Thukoor.

'Ah, my dear,' he said, once he had finished embracing me and drowning me in a cloud of *Fleur de Chypre*, 'how much good it does my panting heart to see your fat form once more. I was only now convivially foregathering with Merry and Coker when I learnt that you, also, were here. So I have naturally hurried and hastened to your abode to bid you two or even three times welcome to Calcutta.'

'That's very handsome of you, Harry.'

'Not at all, dear friend. Auld acquaintanceships must never be forgot, as our North British bard has it. Former school chums are ever best chums, even when circumstances have changed.'

'They must have changed for the better so far as you're concerned, for I've never seen anyone look quite so smart. I'm delighted to see you.'

'That delightfulness, my dear Bunter, is mutual, I assure you. As for the coat'—here he shot his cuffs, flicked an imaginary fleck of dust off his sleeve and jingled the charms attached to a massive gold fob—'it's well-enough built. I have my coats made by Snips of St James's, you know. So much better than any local durzi. But the same warm heart is beating under it. You must not be jumping at the idea that just because I am now senior partner in Thukoor, Baring and Company, bankers and bullion-brokers, bills discounted and exchanged, that I have become the least bit snobbish and would be ignoring my old Bluecoat chums. Oh dear me no, whatever some of my relations may be saying.'

'And what *are* they saying?'

'It is hardly worth noticing. They are saying that it is all jolly well having an English education, for that will be helping me in business. But they are also saying that now I am back in India and senior partner, it is quite infra-dig to mix with former school chums except in the way of business. I cannot agree with them.'

'I should hope not, indeed.'

'You see, my dear, I retain so much affection for our beloved old Alma Mater and for the dear old days.'

'I don't know that we thought of them in exactly that way when we were actually at our beloved Alma Mater.'

'But it is the being away from there that is, according to old proverb, making the hearts grow fonder for both of us. That is why you will be so very pleased to become member of ACBC.'

'What on earth is that?'

'The ACBC is Association of Calcutta Bluecoats, of which association I am now wishing to make you a member.'

'I don't know that my heart *has* grown fonder, Harry. So until I know what the Calcutta Bluecoats actually do, I ain't all that certain that I want to join 'em.'

'But you must, my dear. It's quite the best small club in the Presidency. We do so many, many enjoyable things and have such jolly evenings. Sometimes we play cricket or footballs. Sometimes we do horse racings. Sometimes we go shooting at ducks. And most often we have supper evenings, with very, very much merrymaking and a lot of whatever you fancies in the way of wine and women.'

As he threatened to nudge me in the ribs, I backed away, blinking at him through my glasses.

'I'm not all that keen on women, Harry, and I don't play cricket if I can help it because of my spectacles.'

'Then you can be the non-playing member on each occasion. As a three-times married man I fully understand. But I do enjoy cricket.'

That last bit was true enough. I remembered how successful he had been at school with his slow breaks. So, as I didn't want to argue about either women or cricket, I shifted my ground.

'Don't you think it would be better if I looked at your club before joining it?'

'That's quite exactly what I do think, my dear. What are you doing at this moment?'

'Nothing much: the Bishop's closeted with the Governor General, and he'll be lecturing him about potatoes all afternoon.'

That did it. Harry had me out of the door and in his waiting phaeton immediately. He was a fair whip and we were soon bowling along the Barrackpoor Road until we came to some iron gates which led to a large, rather run-down country house, built in what the Bishop would certainly have described as the Indo-Gothic style, which is to say it had a great many arches, pillars, spires and battlements built, not in the dark, heavy, unadorned stone of our own Northern Gothic, but in the white and fantastically fretted marble of Indian architecture.

The house was set in what must once have been a well-laid-out garden, and peacocks were still strutting across what was left of the lawns. These fled screaming into a nearby shrubbery as we drew up at the front door, which was opened for us by a khansaman wearing a rather unusual livery. His lofty turban was blue and yellow, his pelisse was blue and his pajamas yellow.

'You will observe,' said Harry, 'that we are sticking to the dear old school colours.'

The house had certainly seen better days, but it contained a good many large apartments, most of them furnished in an Indian version of the European style of the previous century. There was even a billiard room on whose walls there hung several indifferent copies of those Verrio portraits we had had to look at when we were schoolboys. Harry saw me looking at them.

'Another reminder of our Alma Mater, my dear. I had Mr Hume, who has painted many portraits for my family here in India, copy them when he was last on leave in London.'

'Wouldn't you have done better to have the house painted instead? It looks as if it needs it.'

'That, my dear, would be to spoil its antique charm. It is an old house as houses go in India. My late and revered pater had it built when he first began to study the strange character of the English, and that must have been in Warren Hastings's time. It is, of course, too old-fashioned now for me, which is why I have let it, at a very reasonable rent, to the ACBC. But you must not be thinking that I am a bad landlord. No, indeed: I have installed an English cooking range in the kitchen, even though coal is difficult to get, and I have also had a truly splendid thunder-box built in the shrubbery.'

'Very sensible of you, Harry. There's nothing in life half so important as the ins and outs of grub.'

Harry was so persuasive and friendly that, at the end of the day, I agreed to become a member of the ACBC, and I never regretted it. What I most enjoyed were our supper parties. I wasn't much of a one for the women Harry provided, who were generally nautch girls or other professionals from Calcutta. But the grub and wine were as good as Harry could ensure, and very much better than anything I could find in Calcutta. We could usually muster a dozen or so members for a supper night, so half a dozen women were more than sufficient. The strange thing was that I found myself actually enjoying the company of Bluecoats I had heartily disliked at school and still tried to avoid in Calcutta. Even including Coker.

The ACBC was such a successful and enjoyable club that

others in Calcutta sought to imitate it. Former school fellows began to form their own Associations, of which the one that came nearest to emulating us was COW—the Calcutta Old Wykehamists. The time soon came when COW challenged ACBC to a cricket match—one innings each, eleven-a-side.

We had some initial difficulty finding eleven playing members but happily an East Indiaman had just arrived with two more former Bluecoats on board, and Harry whisked them ashore and enrolled them in our eleven before they even realised what was happening to them. This saved me from playing and allowed me to perform my accustomed part as scorer.

The Governor General, who had himself been at Winchester and was largely responsible for the formation of COW, took a keen personal interest in the match. He not only offered to umpire, but also provided a large silver trophy which, he said, should be called the Calcutta Cup, to be played for every year by Bluecoats and Wykehamists of the Bengal Presidency. He even sent his head gardener to do what he could with the pitch Harry had selected as our venue. This was a kindly but futile gesture as Harry had chosen a pitch in the middle of the maidan in front of the Fort. The feet of drilling Sepoys and the pounding of passing traffic had reduced its dirt surface to a series of dusty bumps which made the bounce and movement of the ball almost impossible to predict. That, of course, was why Harry had chosen it. He had an extraordinarily supple wrist which would bend back so far that it sometimes seemed that the ball must come out backwards. These, together with what seemed like sextuple-jointed fingers, allowed him to flick the ball out of the front, sides or back of his hand in a way which had made his bowling difficult to read even on an English wicket.

The match was played on an exceedingly hot day, and this added to the unpredictability of the game. Players had to stop every twenty minutes or so for refreshments and by the time the tenth round of hock-and-seltzers, iced claret, bottled beer and brandy panees had been carried out and consumed, play began to look increasingly erratic.

As we won the toss we batted first and started sober, which could have been thought to our advantage. There was some argument over the action of one of the Wykehamist bowlers who seemed to be raising his bowling arm almost shoulder high and delivering the ball with an illegal round-arm action, but the Governor General decided in his favour, and he went on to take four wickets. None the less we notched up 78 increasingly uncertain runs which, considering everything, was a respectable total.

But when the other side came in our bowlers were beginning to feel the effects of the refreshments quite as much as their batsmen were. And their opening batsman, an up-country chaplain who never drank anything stronger than lemonade, was feeling nothing at all and threatened to win the match almost single-handed.

Harry, certainly the best of our bowlers, was still at the stage when batsmen could legitimately wonder whether it was drink or cunning that controlled his constant variation of pace, length and direction. This allowed him to go steadily through the drinking Wykehamists, although at a cost. He bowled so many wides, byes and leg-byes that, by the time the ninth man came in, the up-country chaplain still at the other end and facing Harry, their score stood at 76. Two to get and the last man yet to come. Then Harry, staggering slightly, bowled a short-pitched one which held up on a scrap of dried elephant dung no one had noticed, and that was the end of the chaplain.

Their last man was, for a Wykehamist, a very cheerful sort of fellow, and the drink he'd taken had done nothing to turn him serious. Harry looked at him, though I doubt whether he saw him very clearly, and then delivered what was plainly intended to be one of his most cunning balls, that is the one that comes out of the back of the hand. This time, however, he overdid the wrist-flexing business and the ball did fly out backwards, hitting the Governor General, who was umpiring at that end, smartly in the eye. The cheerful Wykehamist laughed so much at this that his straw hat fell off and broke his wicket, which left those who were still sober in something of a quandary.

The Governor General, who was nursing an incipient black eye, was not in the camp of the sober, and this allowed him to deliver an immediate judgment.

'Under the laws of cricket,' said he, 'a ball that hasn't reached beyond the bowling crease is not regarded as having been delivered. But, having regard to the fact that I decided earlier in favour of a Wykehamist bowler, I must now, in all fairness, decide in favour of a Bluecoat one. Out!'

And that was how we won the Calcutta Cup.

We were all of us, victors and vanquished, pretty elated by this time, and no one more so than Harry who had, if one counts the straw hat, taken six wickets. Bluecoats and Wykehamists, he insisted, must now go on to make a night of it, ending up with supper at our clubhouse out on the Barrackpoor Road.

All except the up-country chaplain, who was too sober, and the Governor General, who was too drunk, thought this a splendid idea. They also agreed to his next suggestion.

'But first,' he declared, 'we must all go to the theatre where, they tell me, there is an absolutely top-hole performance. Madame Assoluta's dramatic, operatic and balletic troupe, straight from the most famous opera houses of Europe in a programme of drama, songs, recitations and dancing.'

As all we normally had at our local theatre were amateur theatricals and an occasional reading from the works of William Shakespeare by the resident Dean, we thought this was a splendid idea. We all arrived, in the best of spirits, at the theatre where Harry, by some means unknown, had secured us the two stage boxes. Some of the corps de ballet, I have to admit, looked as though they were more accustomed to performing at the theatre in Goa rather than in La Scala or Covent Garden, but they were all very pretty and danced, to our minds, as well as Taglioni herself. We clapped them time and again and hallooed for encores.

It was then that Harry got his next idea.

'My dear Bunter,' he said to me, 'you are impartial in such matters and must, therefore, be giving sound judgment. I had arranged some nautch girls for tonight, but don't you think it would be a jolly sight better to have some of Madame Assoluta's enchanting corps de ballet instead?'

'They wouldn't come,' I said.

Harry looked sly and put an unsteady finger to his nose.

'You forget, dear friend, that I am a banker.'

'What's that got to do with it?'

'Aha,' said he, 'where do you think Madame Assoluta goes when she runs out of money, as she has done in Calcutta? She's booked to appear next month in Bombay, and she won't be able to get there unless I agree to a loan.'

And that was how a mixed assortment of Bluecoats, Wykehamists and ladies from the corps de ballet found themselves in our club-house and sitting down, some time after midnight, to the richest and most extensive supper Harry had ever contrived for us.

I concentrated on the food and drink until I reached the stage when I could positively eat and drink no more until I had taken sufficient exercise to allow me to return to the supper table. Some were, by now, underneath it. Others having satisfied one appetite, were now departing with one or other of the dancers to satisfy another. I stood up unsteadily, looked at those still around the table, and said:

'Who's for a game of billiards?'

I was joined by Sam Merry, as glum-faced as ever, by Coker who was showing visible signs of strain, and by the cheerful Wykehamist who wanted to show us a new game he was in the process of inventing. This involved a great number of billiard balls, some of which had to be pocketed before the others, and we had lengthy discussions about the Wykehamist's rules and kept offering him new ones of our own.

Suddenly Coker, who had been looking green about the face, let off a tremendous fart and then clapped his hand to the seat of his breeches and groaned.

'He's got the flux,' said the Wykehamist.

'It's all those mangoes he ate,' said Merry.

'You'd best go to the thunder-box,' said I.

Coker did just that, which finished our game and so we rejoined what was left of the party in the dining room. Suddenly, the door was flung open and a white-faced Coker rushed in screaming, 'A snake! A snake! I've been bitten by a snake!'

If we could have been sobered up, this would have done it for if there is one thing we take seriously in India, it's snake bites.

Merry, who may have been the soberest of us, shook him heartily and told him to stop babbling and show us where he was bitten.

'On my arse,' said Coker. 'I was sitting on the thunder-box.'

'Did you see the snake?' I asked.

'It was too damned dark to see anything. But I felt it right enough. It was like two hot needles being stuck into my behind.'

'That,' said Harry, who had joined us, 'sounds as though it may have been a cobra de capello. And that means unless we do something right away, the poor fellow will be as dead as a door hinge before you can say John Robertson.'

But what to do was a problem. Merry set off immediately to rouse out the surgeon at Barrackpoor, I made Coker drop his breeches so that we might inspect the bite. And there, sure enough, were two small, angry red spots on his left buttock. It was then that the Wykehamist, who was much the drunkest of any of us, told us what we must do.

'There's nothing for it,' he said, 'but to use the knife on him. Then we must fill him up with brandy and keep him awake. If he falls into a coma it's the end of him.'

We looked at one another.

'I can't use the knife,' said Harry. 'I always faint when I see blood.'

'I'm too drunk to see what I'm doing,' said the Wykehamist. They both looked at me.

'You don't mean I should do it,' I cried.

'I've got a razor upstairs,' said Harry. 'I'll get it for you.'

And so Coker, his breeches round his ankles, was bent over the dining-room table. The Wykehamist held him down and whilst Madame Assoluta's girls were all oohing and aahing and vowing they were about to faint, but crowding in all the while to watch me perform, I set to work on Coker with the razor. The only one who did faint at that point was Harry. But I, being full of Dutch courage, went boldly about it for once, and when I came away from the table, I had a wedge of Coker's arse in my hands that must have weighed the best part of half a pound.

Coker, for his part, was bleeding like a pig and roaring like a bull.

'Keep giving him brandy,' said the Wykehamist.

'Keep walking him round,' said I, 'for he's either going to have an apoplexy or fall into a coma.'

And so we went at it all three of us: Coker with a large part of one buttock missing and getting steadily more maudlin; myself holding him firmly by the arm and steering him round and round the table; and the Wykehamist stopping us at the end of each round to pour more brandy down my throat and Coker's. Goodness knows how long this bloody rogue's march went on before Merry returned from Barrackpoor bringing the Irish garrison surgeon with him. The surgeon, whose name was O'Shaughnessy, and who was none too sober himself, took one look at Coker and another at us.

'B'Jasus,' said he. 'It's a good thing that you're all of yez as drunk as fiddlers' bitches and that Oi'm more sober than a judge. If Oi were not, Oi'd never have been able to belayve me eyes. You've butchered the poor crayture more thoroughly than Oi could ivver have done it meself. Niver again will he sit intoirly level, whether he be drunk or sober. Whativer made yez do it?'

'He was,' said the Wykehamist, speaking slowly and with great dignity, 'bitten by a snake. I advised excision, exercise and alcohol. What would you have done, my good fellow?'

'Howiver can Oi tell until Oi know what sort of snake it was, and even when Oi do know, it's by no means certain that Oi can help the poor butchered crayture.'

We'd never thought of finding out what sort of snake it was, for we'd all concluded, along with Harry, that it had to be a cobra. Now, at O'Shaughnessy's urging, we organised a search party and went down to the thunder-box with lanterns and torches. I was beginning to sober up, which was why I didn't push myself forward when we entered the shrubbery and got close to the thunder-box. O'Shaughnessy snatched the lantern from me, flung open the door and, seeing nothing above ground, shone the light down the box itself. He was silent for a moment.

'Bedad,' he said in the end, 'it's a quarer sort of a sarpint than any holy St Patrick ivver chased out of ould Oireland.'

Then he turned to me and said, 'Since 'twas yourself did the cutting it's yourself should see what you were doing it for.'

I pulled myself together, advanced cautiously, and looked into the thunder-box. There, at the bottom, was an indignant looking pea-hen sitting on a clutch of eggs.

22   *Travels with my Bishop*

I do believe that there'll always be people, the most of 'em women, who hate to see others enjoying themselves. That's why the activities of the ACBC were so often discussed with much disapproval by the old biddies of Calcutta society. But it was not until the most distorted descriptions of what had happened at our cricket match supper had reached Mrs Heber that she sent for me.

Her summons threw me into something of a funk, for she is not the sort of woman who carries a child with grace and good humour. Pregnancy had made her ruder than ever to me, harsh with the Bishop and positively glacial with the Cathedral clergy. She had even begun to snap at Mistress MacPherson. That lady, however, was setting her an example, for she was bearing her pregnancy with a good deal more equanimity . . . The Bishop had accepted by now that it had been the bosun of the *Thomas Grenville* who had first filled her up with rum and then put a bun in her oven. Although everyone else thought this excusable I, and perhaps Mrs Heber, thought it improbable.

Some women, I'm told, look their best when *enceinte*. But pregnancy had done nothing to Mrs Heber beyond enlarging her belly. So, whilst she still looked like a hungry heron up aloft, she was all Michaelmas goose down below. She put the table between us as I came into the room and looked at me as though I was bringing in the sort of infection a Bishop's lady can't even refer to.

'Mr Bunter,' she said. 'I shall be plain with you. I have just finished speaking to the Bishop about you, and it is only right that you should know what I said.'

'And what was that, Ma'am?'

'I said that I had formed the opinion you were no fit person to be in the employ of any clergyman, let alone in that of a Bishop of All-India.'

'Good God, Ma'am!'

'Don't interrupt me Mr Bunter. I also told my husband that he would be better served both in his work and his reputation by an older and less dissolute person.'

'Dissolute, Ma'am? You can't think I'm dissolute.'

'Such is my information. The Dean's wife in particular was most explicit about it.'

'The Dean's wife, Ma'am, is well known to be a scandal-mongering old hag who's for ever making mischief.'

'Vulgar abuse of my friends, Mr Bunter, will get you nowhere. My own advice to you would be to tender your resignation to the Bishop. It seems to me you'd be better suited in a barracks, or, indeed, in a bagnio, than in a Bishop's Palace.'

I had feared trouble but I had never anticipated an attack such as this. And as is usual with me when attacked, I began to babble.

'I don't know what you mean, Ma'am. 'Pon my soul I don't. Great regard for your husband, as I believe he has for me. Always tried to be useful. Know spelling, grammar and handwriting ain't exactly up to scratch. But then there are the translations . . .'

'Translations are nothing to the point.'

'Oh but they are, Ma'am. There's still Firdausi . . . and Hafiz . . . and we haven't got very far with the Ramayana . . . and unless I stop him, the Bishop'll be back again trying to translate Omar Khayyam. And if I'm not there to do it, who'd look after his butterfly collection and all the pressed flowers and the appointments—I always remind him of his . . .'

'Mr Bunter,' she said, 'cease your chatter.'

'Just as you say, Ma'am. Silence itself. Lips sealed. But . . .'

'But what?'

'Why are you being so beastly to me?'

'The beastliness, Mr Bunter, lies in your behaviour and not in mine.'

'My behaviour? What behaviour, Ma'am? I'm sure I don't know what you refer to.'

'I refer to low company, Sir. I refer to drunken orgies and savage assaults. I refer to fornications and strumpets. I refer to the black eye inflicted on dear Lord Amherst.'

'If it's only the black eye, Ma'am, I swear I weren't responsible for it. How could I have been? I was scoring, not bowling.'

'Were you scoring when that young Mr Coker was so shamefully mutilated? That was a scoring indeed. And did you keep the score of all that was drunk, which I'm told was more in the one night than can be consumed in a Bishop's Palace in one year? And tell me this, Mr Bunter. What score did you notch up with Madame Assoluta's dancing girls?'

'I did no scoring with them, Ma'am, I assure you. Why, I wouldn't properly know how to score with a dancing girl, and even if I did, I'm sure I'd never enjoy it.'

'*Never enjoy it, Mr Bunter?* Don't compound your sins by lying to me. Everyone in Calcutta knows that you and your associates are all whore-mongers, and I have some reason to suspect that you, for your part, do not confine yourself to whores.'

I was so shocked by the injustice of this that I gaped at her open-mouthed, which seemed to make her even angrier.

'No gentlewoman,' she said, 'enjoys discussing such matters in mixed company. But I have to consider my duty to the Bishop, to my own conscience, and to society.'

'By telling the Bishop that I'm a whore-monger and a seducer?'

'I have too much regard for his sense of modesty and mine to mention such things. I merely told him that it was my firm opinion that you are not, and never can be, a fit companion for a Bishop. And there, Sir, I must leave it.'

'But,' I cried in desperation, 'it ain't true. Leastways only bits of it are.'

'That's for the Bishop to decide,' she snapped, looking angrier than ever. 'And the only other thing I have to say to you, Sir, is to look to your health. Dancing girls are never the healthiest of company, especially in hot weather.'

And with that she tossed her head at me and waddled out of the room muttering, if I heard her rightly, 'Never enjoyed it, indeed!'

I immediately went to look for the Bishop and found him in the dining room with a glass in his hand and a decanter at his elbow. He looked, if anything, even more confused than myself.

'My Lord,' said I just as soon as I was through the door.

'Reggy would be better on such an occasion. And don't say a word, my boy, until you've composed yourself. A drink may help you towards that end.'

He made me sit down, poured me a brimmer of brandy and refilled his own.

'But Mrs Heber just . . .'

'I know, I know. Mrs Heber had half an hour with me before ever she started on you.'

'I can explain it all, Reggy, I swear I can . . .'

'Come, come, William, there's nothing to explain, or if there is, it's I who must do it on my wife's behalf. All that you were involved in was a young man's jolly. I ain't so old that I can't remember what that means. Why, I recall that when I was at Brasenose and had just won the Craven . . . But there, *Tempus edax rerum*, and I must not reminisce. Besides which the Craven ain't exactly the same as your Calcutta Cup, even though it warrants a certain amount of celebrating.'

'Then you don't condemn me?'

'Condemn you? I come unclerically close to envying you.'

'But Mrs Heber was so beastly about it.'

'You must make allowances, William. She's pregnant, which is not something she's been used to of late. It makes her more than usually a bit . . . tetchy. But you must not let that worry you, my dear boy.'

And here the dear old fellow looked at me in such a kindly and encouraging way that I started to blub. We both needed more brandy before he could continue:

'It seems to me, William, that the time has come when we should embark on our travels around the diocese. That will remove you for a few months from your Bluecoat friends and from what Mrs Heber doubtless described as your orgies. It will also remove the both of us from Mrs Heber.'

And that was how the Bishop and I embarked on those travels which took us across so much of the length and breadth of India. He, being a literary man, kept a journal describing all that we did and saw and I hope that, one day, that journal will be published so that the public may know something of the sort of man he was. But I have already described how he used to conduct himself whilst travelling and will only add that it was a manner which never ceased to amaze and delight me.

It was not all enjoyment, of course. The travelling itself was arduous, and doubly so for me who didn't share the Bishop's love of horses, his enjoyment of walking, or his fondness for fording raging rivers and riding along goat tracks on the very edges of precipices. There were occasions when I insisted on being carried in a dhoolie, which is a sort of covered palanquin, and even then I would keep my eyes tight shut.

And there was also the question of the quality of the grub. The Bishop may not have minded what he put into his belly, but I did. Yet in spite of our train of servants, all that they could generally find for us when we camped for the night would be something like a greasy goat stew or a skinny chicken, neither made the more palatable by being accompanied by the inevitable boiled rice. The fact was that they were so busy looking after all the animals the Bishop had accumulated—a bear-cub here, a python there, an egret somewhere else, and monkeys nearly everywhere—that they had almost no time left to look after us.

But there were compensations. At the end of a stage, Rajahs, Nawabs and other local dignitaries would compete with each other to see who could feast us most lavishly. The Bishop, busy discussing religion, or poetry, or the state of the crops with his host could ignore such things as a roast peacock stuffed with dates and pistachios, or quails cooked in honey, but I certainly could not.

And then, whilst we were still on the road, there was the Bishop's travelling cellar to reconcile us to all those greasy goats and skinny chickens. For although he displayed an almost barbaric degree of indifference to what he ate, he was by no means indifferent to what he drank. In fact wine constituted by far the most important part of any and every meal he sat down to. That was why, wherever we travelled, the baggage train always included a camel whom we called Ganymede. He carried on either side of his back two large and well-padded cases of the Bishop's own designing, and these held everything that he might need from burgundies to beers and from usquebaughs to araks. I had learnt little or nothing about drink at Christ's Hospital or staying with Mr Wilberforce, but the Bishop soon put this to rights. He began to educate me in such things from the first moment we boarded the *Thomas Grenville*, and I took to 'em just as readily as I had taken to jam tarts in my infancy.

I doubt whether there has ever been, in the history of the Church of England, a bishop who was quite as eclectic but as open-minded, as argumentative yet as philosophical as mine was. He would argue his own case so eloquently that it always seemed that no one could stand against it, but then, just as his opponent was ready to cry 'Quits' he would turn around and argue the opposite equally well. It was a strange and joyful experience when, with a couple of bottles inside him, he set out to convince some Hindoo priest or fakir, or it might be a mollah or Sikh guru, of the irrefutable truths of Christianity. If they'd been able to understand even half of his arguments they would have been ready to convert if he had not by then changed to arguing oecumenically. Truth, he would then say, is no one's monopoly, and there is as much of it to be found in the Purana or the Qu'ran or the Adi Granth as could be discovered in the Gospels. He may not have made many new Christians, but he did make a good many new friends.

This weathercock method of arguing was particularly enjoyable to me when he suddenly remembered his political economy. There were two such disputations in particular which I shall always remember as perfect examples of his inspired dottiness.

The first revolved around the Hindoo custom of suttee, which was one of the few rites of any religion I ever heard him object to. He objected even more strongly when, soon after leaving Calcutta, we passed a funeral pyre on which a widow had just burnt herself to death. The sight and smell of her remains affected him greatly and he railed against the cruelty of the practice when, a little later, we met Doctor Marshman, who was a Baptist missionary long resident in Serampoor.

The Doctor tried to reassure him in relation to the cruelty. 'The widow,' he said, 'is always placed under her deceased husband, where she's nearer the flames. And the priests see to it that she's well-soaked in ghee. So you see, my Lord, she'll burn quite quickly. Nevertheless I do agree with you that it's a wicked and quite unnecessary practice.'

This was quite enough to send my Bishop weathercocking. 'Wicked, certainly, Doctor Marshman. But as to unnecessary I'm by no means so sure.'

'I don't follow you, my Lord.'

'Suttee, I'm told, is most commonly practised by the middle and upper-middle classes of Hindoo society. That is to say by those who most need to keep up appearances, and who can, as a consequence, least afford the expense of keeping a widowed mother or mother-in-law for the rest of her life. So there are sound economic reasons for burning her, as both Malthus and Adam Smith would have agreed.'

The other argument was with a young captain in the BNI called Sleeman. He had just completed an intensive study of the religious beliefs and practices of the Thugs. My Bishop, needless to say, wanted to learn all he could concerning a cult which was much whispered about but had never, till then, been studied. Sleeman spent the best part of an hour describing to him how members of this secret and greatly-feared society contrived to combine their worship of the goddess Kali with a reasonably profitable engagement in highway robbery and murder.

'It's a dreadful business,' said the Bishop at the end.

'It is, my Lord,' said Sleeman. 'And if it takes me the rest of my life I'll see to it that they're exterminated. For exterminated they have to be.'

'And yet,' said the Bishop, 'I can see some reason for allowing them to continue.'

'I can see none.'

'That, Captain Sleeman, is because you've never studied political economy and know little about the needs of governments.'

'With respect, my Lord, the perpetuation of Thuggee cannot be listed as one of those needs.'

'Consider the habits of these people. Indians would, if they could, be for ever travelling. The roads of this country are permanently crowded with people going from one place to another for no apparent reason. Now fear of falling victim to the Thugs must lessen this quite unreasonable craving of theirs for travel. And that cannot but help the government's finances.'

'How so, my Lord?'

'As you would know if you had studied the political economy of this country, the largest part of the government's revenues depends on a prompt and regular collection of the rents to which every piece of land is assessed. If those who cultivate that land and pay those rents are for ever travelling, collection becomes difficult. Ergo, anything that keeps 'em at home, even though it's a fear of being strangled and robbed by the Thugs, must be an aid to good government.'

I don't believe he convinced Captain Sleeman. But it was an enjoyable argument, made even more enjoyable by the couple of bottles of Chambertin that fuelled it.

It was when we were in Lucknow, where we were well received by the King of Oude, that I suddenly realised that Lahore was not too far distant and that Maria Huggins, née Jewkes, lived in that city. It was, however, independent Sikh territory and no part of the Bishop's diocese. It had not, therefore, been his intention to visit it. But I persuaded him that the Golden Temple at Umritsar, which was not very far from Lahore, was a place he must visit and I also reminded him that the Maharajah Runjeet Singh who had made himself master of the Sikh khalsa and was now the mightiest of all the independent princes, was the best friend the British had in India and so deserving of a visit.

And that was how we went to Lahore, where we were welcomed and fêted by the Maharajah and I was received in a most friendly manner by Maria and Colonel Huggins. Maria did not seem to me to be enjoying married life and India as much as she had assured me she would when we were on the *Thomas Grenville*.

When I got her alone and asked her what was amiss she

burst into tears, which wasn't at all like her. What I gathered, when she calmed down, was that she was homesick. Although she now lived in something close to a palace she longed to be back in Coram Street. Being a warm-hearted, friendly sort of girl, she missed her family and friends, and doubly so because her husband refused to allow her to visit unless he was there to chaperone her.

'I might as well,' she said, 'be one of those Indian women they keep in bananas or zenanas or whatever they call 'em. And all because I ain't skinny.'

'What on earth has that got to do with it?'

'D'Arcy keeps telling me that the Maharajah thinks fat is beautiful and that it would be dangerous for me to go flaunting myself around Lahore and tempting that monster. I think it's just a jealous man's excuse. The Maharajah does like 'em fat, but everyone knows he don't like 'em female.'

But even that was not the sum of her troubles. Her husband was away a good deal on Army matters, which meant that for long periods she had no one even to talk to apart from the servants. And things were no better when he returned.

'For,' she said, 'he's a deal healthier than we ever thought. So, far from making me a widow, he's for ever trying to make me a mother. And as you know, Billy, I've little taste for that sort of thing.'

'And I don't blame you,' said I. 'It's not half so interesting or satisfying as a good tuck-in. But you mustn't despair, my dear. Your D'Arcy looked distinctly groggy this morning, and what with the heat and the cholera you may be a wholesomely plump and desirably rich young widow sooner than you think.'

'But what if the heat and the cholera get to me first? Besides, he only looked groggy because he was closeted for most of last night with the Maharajah, and that always means that he's had to take a deal more bhang and arak than he likes, and he suffers for it the next morning.'

'I didn't know he was one of the Maharajah's boozing cronies.'

'Who knows,' said Maria grimly, 'what he is to that fat little monster.'

It was all very well for Maria to refer to Runjeet Singh as a fat little monster, but the Bishop was of an entirely opposite opinion.

'That man,' he said to me when he'd returned from his first audience with the Maharajah, 'is an intellectual and military genius: a veritable Indian Bonaparte.'

This was just about as far as the Bishop could go in praising a man. His engrained contrariness had caused him to start admiring Napoleon at just about the time almost everyone else in England had begun to think of him as a brigand, a murderer, a tyrant and a very vulgar, peacocking sort of upstart.

I suppose what the Bishop most liked about the Maharajah was the fact that he was used to Feringhis and was not in the least deferential when dealing with them. The fact was that Colonel Huggins was far from being the only European in his employ. He had Frenchmen running his artillery, Englishmen drilling his infantry, and Swiss in control of his finances, and he never allowed one of them to put on any airs but kept them all running around in a state of fear which, although it may have been wholesome for them, was quite unusual for Europeans in the service of other Indian princes. It was this lack of deference that allowed Runjeet Singh to argue with the Bishop on his own terms, which was something that he had not experienced since leaving Oxford.

It was clear from the first that the Maharajah enjoyed the Bishop's company just as much as the Bishop enjoyed his. We were, as a consequence, most magnificently entertained but I did rather resent the fact that I was largely ignored by the Maharajah, who treated me as a servant of little or no consequence. I was not even included in the nuzzur ceremony, when gifts are offered and returned by both sides. Indeed, the Maharajah was the first Indian potentate who had overlooked my presence and the part I ought to have played in those proceedings.

Besides I found him, in physical terms, exactly as Maria had described him—a fat little monster. For this Indian Napoleon was even less prepossessing than his Corsican counterpart, being one-eyed, pock-marked, and remarkably dissolute-looking. But then Napoleon wasn't the only ugly little man to have set his mark on a continent. Alexander, they say, was little larger than a Tom Thumb. Tom Thumb or not, the Bishop felt it was now time that we took a couple of days off in order to accept the pressing invitation of the Begum of Sumroo. The Maharajah made no objection. From small things, bigger things flow.

23   *The Outcome of a Tiger Hunt*

Towards the end of our stay in Lahore, a city which for no obvious reason reminded the Bishop of Dresden, the Maharajah organised a tiger hunt in our honour. This did something to lessen the Bishop's liking for him, the Bishop being one of those odd animal lovers who don't enjoy hunting and killing what they love. But he knew that a tiger hunt was a very special occasion and something that one Indian potentate would normally offer only to another. It was not, therefore, something he could abstain from without being discourteous to his host.

So when all the gaily-painted and caparisoned elephants were drawn up the next day to carry the guns to the hunt, he climbed, unprotestingly, into the howdah of the great beast allotted to him. He turned aside the offer of a rifle, however, saying that he was such a bad shot that he would be more dangerous to the hunters than the hunted. This made me insist that he should, at least, take his pistols with him, these being a toylike pocket pair Mrs Heber made him carry in case he should be attacked by dacoits whilst on the road.

But if the Bishop felt reluctant, I felt terrified. It wasn't that I had any moral objections to killing a tiger: it was rather that I objected to giving any tiger a chance to kill me. So, although it did little to restore my confidence, I accepted the rifle offered me and then looked for my elephant. When I found it I realised that, whether by intention or oversight, I was once more being slighted.

The animal that waited for me was quite the smallest, hairiest and dirtiest female elephant I had ever seen. She was no larger than a fair-sized Durham ox and as curly-coated as an Irish water poodle. Although she now carried a howdah on her back, there was much about her to suggest that her normal occupation was pulling the night-soil cart. Her mahout did nothing to upset this suggestion. He was ancient, dirty, smelly, and so seemingly senile that I wondered whether he'd realised that he was no longer engaged in sanitary duties but was responsible for conveying me to the tiger hunt, which was to start from a piece of jungle some two hours' travel at elephant pace from Lahore.

When we reached the edge of that jungle the guns were lined up on their elephants some thirty or forty paces distant from one another. My self-confidence was in no way increased when I realised that the gun on my right was the Maharajah and the one on my left was the Bishop. The first was so half-sighted I doubted his ability to hit anything he aimed at whilst the other was more accurately described as a reluctant pistol than a gun.

'Bunter, my boy,' I said to myself, 'pray that nothing larger than a pi-dog comes your way.'

But then the ancient mahout lifted my spirits for a moment by saying, 'This is all nonsense, Sahib. Until age weakened my sight and took the strength from my limbs I was head shikaree to the Maharajah. No one in the whole of the Punjaub knew more about tigers than I. And even now, when it is my fate to cart shit, I can still tell you that never in the experience of man has a tiger been found in this piece of jungle.'

A moment later, as the banging of drums by the beaters grew closer, an enormous tigress bounded out of the cover between the Maharajah and myself. The Maharajah's shot brought down a coconut from a tall palm ten yards to the left and rear of the tigress, who blinked and then turned her gaze towards me.

'Shoot, Sahib,' screamed the mahout.

I shut my eyes and shot. Another coconut fell. The tigress,

glaring at me, crouched for the spring and I knew that it would be no more than a matter of seconds before I found myself sharing my howdah with her. The mahout must have been of a similar frame of mind, for he slipped nimbly off the elephant's neck and retired to the rear at such a pace that it was a wonder that such an ancient and skinny pair of legs could still twinkle so fast.

I was, so far as I can remember, calling for Bessy and wondering which bit of me the tigress would chew first when two more shots rang out. The Bishop, very valiantly and quite against his principles, had opened up with both his batteries. At that range those pocket pistols might have damaged a rabbit, but all they did to the tigress was to sting her just as she was about to take off. Whether that gave additional impetus to her spring or whether she was accustomed to much taller elephants I cannot say. But the spring, when it came, carried her clean over me and my elephant and she landed swearing and spitting on the other side. The Maharajah, meanwhile, was trying to get his second gun to bear and, as the tigress loped back into the jungle, he sent a shot after her. The loud shriek that followed suggested that some unfortunate beater had got in the way of either the Maharajah's bullet or the tigress.

All of this had notably upset my little elephant. She raised her trunk, squealed, reared, whipped round and set off pretty sharply in the direction of Lahore, her mahout and the night-soil cart. The suddenness of this hurled me out of the howdah on to her back, whence I slid backwards over her tail and on to a surprisingly soft and wet piece of ground.

I don't know much about hunting, but there was one thing J.J. had told me in those far-off Bluecoat days that has always stuck in my mind:

'Once your quarry's been flushed,' he stated, 'then the very first thing it does, whether it's bird, hare, fox, or stag, is to dung. Some say they do it out of fright, others that it's because it makes flight easier, and others that it's just an automatic, unthinking reaction. But whatever the reason, the one thing a huntsman can always depend on finding is shit.'

My little curly-haired elephant proved that J.J. was, for once, being factual. And to judge by the size of the steaming elephant pat I fell into, little elephants are fully as productive as big-'uns in this respect, which was just as well since it meant my fall was fully cushioned.

After groaning a bit and moving each of my limbs to see if any of 'em were broken, I sat up and tried to wipe the stuff off my spectacles. I cleared them enough to be able to see the last of the other elephants disappearing into the jungle in hot pursuit of the tigress. Only the Bishop's elephant remained, and this was now collapsing so that its rider might dismount. When he had done so, the Bishop came hurrying towards me.

He was too dignified a man to do more than trot—I don't suppose he'd ever actually run since he was out of petticoats—but trot he did until he got within smelling distance of me. Then he hauled off and moved upwind.

'Dear me, William,' he said, 'in a mess once more.'

'And not a very nice mess,' said I.

'A man's mind, my boy, works in mysterious ways. Can you explain to me why, at this very moment, you've just reminded me of those very mellifluous lines by the poet Marvell?'

I groaned. Here was I up to my eyebrows in shit and my Bishop off weathercocking again.

'What mellifluous lines?' I grunted, trying to get to my feet.

> 'Stumbling on melons, as I pass,
> Ensnared with flowers, I fall on grass.'

'The connection's a simple one,' I said. 'I stumbled from elephants and fell in shit.'

'Yes, of course. What peculiar references and connections the mind can make. But what are you going to do now, my boy?'

'Get back to Lahore as quick as I can.'

'I shall do the same. I've had quite enough of tiger hunting. But how are you going to get there? It's quite a long walk.'

'I thought I might share your elephant.'

'Not without getting yourself cleaned up you can't.'

'And how,' said I, trying to wipe my face on my sleeve and doing no more than rearrange the shit on both. 'How do you propose I should do that?'

The Bishop pointed to a small bheel or mere not very far off.

'Get into that, my boy.'

'What! In my clothes?'

'First in your clothes and then without your clothes for so far as I can see everything about you stands in need of water. Your clothes will easily dry on you whilst we amble back to Lahore.'

So I did what the Bishop suggested. I was at the second stage of the proceedings and wallowing around happily enough in the buff when I suddenly realised that the other guns had returned and were sitting on their elephants at the water's edge looking down on me. It was soon apparent that they regarded me as the best and only sport of the day. One or two of them actually fell off their elephants they laughed so much.

'It is,' said one wag, 'a great white wart-hog.'

'Nay,' said another. 'Never was there a wart-hog with such full buttocks as those.'

'By my beard,' said a third, 'it is as though two conjoined full moons were floating in the bheel.'

'Would that my Afghan boy,' said the second, 'had such full moons as those.'

Almost the only one who didn't exercise his wit at my expense was the Maharajah. He looked at me in silence for a time and then rode his elephant away to where Colonel Huggins was. He said something to him and then, reminding his followers that there were still other tigers to be found, led them away leaving me to the Bishop and my nakedness.

The next night the Maharajah gave a farewell banquet for the Bishop. I was surprised to find that on this occasion I was placed on Runjeet's left, the Bishop, of course, being on his right. The two engaged in one of their arguments for most of the time but, when the music and the nautch girls had started, Runjeet turned to me and said:

'We shall miss you, Bunterjee, when you depart.'

'That we shall,' tittered the Treasurer, a lean and wizened whitebeard who should have been too old for tittering. 'Tiger hunting will have lost some of its charm when Bunter Sahib is no longer here to delight us.'

'Never again shall I go pig-sticking without thinking of Bunter Sahib,' said the conjoined moons man.

'He may not be a great shikaree,' said the wag, 'but did you observe, my brothers, how quickly he picked up the scent?'

I scowled through my spectacles at them. I never minded playing the clown at school, but I had no intention of encouraging a gaggle of drunken Sikhs to make fun of me. Runjeet Singh was quick to notice that I was annoyed. He put his hand over mine, squeezed it, and said:

'You must not mind our Sikh ways, Bunterjee. We are quick to fight, quick to laugh, and'—here he gave my hand another squeeze—'quick to love. Truly we must talk together again ere you leave.'

I withdrew my hand and said, 'With your Highness's permission, I would leave now. I still feel the effects of my fall from my elephant and stand in need of rest.'

Runjeet looked hurt, but he nodded his permission and turned his attention to the Bishop. And I was thankful to depart even though I had not eaten all that I otherwise would have tucked into.

The following morning I went to take my leave of Maria. She, to my embarrassment, started to blub, so I put my arms round her substantial form and was trying to soothe her when her husband burst in.

'Aha,' said he, 'at last I've caught you.'

'There's nothing to catch,' said I haughtily. 'Maria and I are just old friends.'

'I know that, and that ain't why I've been searching for you everywhere. I've got an offer from 'Is 'Ighness for you.'

'What sort of offer?' said Maria, taking him up mighty sharp.

'None of your business, my dear. This is man to man as between the Maharajah and 'im.'

'We all know what the Maharajah's man-to-man business is, and I suspect we know the part you usually play in it.'

This angered the Colonel so I intervened to prevent a quarrel. Nevertheless, remembering what Maria had said about Runjeet Singh liking 'em fat, and the way he'd looked at me when I was in the bheel and the manner in which he had squeezed my hand, a nasty suspicion was beginning to enter my mind.

'I think,' said I, 'that we should both hear what the Maharajah has ordered the Colonel to offer me.'

The Colonel, to give him his due, began to look embarrassed. ''E's prepared to offer you a post as 'is private secretary. That's what 'e's offering. And I'd think twice about it if I was you. There'd be plenty of pickings.'

'And what else would there be? What duties?'

'Oh, much the same as what you do for the Bishop . . . Letter-writing, translations . . . that sort of thing.'

'Anything else?'

'Nothing you could define. It would be an informal and friendly sort of relationship.'

'Don't you touch it, Billy,' cried Maria. 'The fat little monster's taken a fancy to you, and you know what that means.'

'I can guess, even though it surprises me. I spent seven years at boarding school without anyone ever taking a fancy to me. I wouldn't have thought I was the sort.'

'It's just as I told you,' said Maria. 'He likes 'em fat.'

'But what surprises me even more,' said I, ignoring Maria's last remark and turning to D'Arcy, 'is that Colonel Huggins, who is, after all, an Englishman, should see fit to play the pander.'

To my surprise the Colonel turned pale.

'I know it ain't British,' he said dolefully. 'But you've no idea of the things one 'as to put up with when you're in the service of one of these 'eathens. Why, when I was younger and in the service of the Nizam of 'Yderabad, I 'ad to hembrace Islam. And that cost me better than 'alf-an-inch of foreskin.'

'You ought to be ashamed of yourself,' said Maria.

He looked at her for some time, mopping at his eyes with a large red, white-spotted handkerchief.

'Well,' he said at last and in some surprise, 'I suppose that I am. But when you're in Rome you 'ave to do what the bloody 'eathens do.'

'That's as may be,' said I. 'But I'm no heathen, and what's more I'm a Bishop's secretary and propose to remain one. So you can return to the Maharajah and tell him that I've refused his offer.'

'I daren't do that. He'd see to it that something nasty, such as powdered glass in your grub, 'appened to you, and I, like as not, would suffer pro rata.'

'Then what would you have me do?' said I, beginning to feel decidedly alarmed.

'Get out of La'ore just as quick as you can. I'll tell Runjeet Singh that you'd left before I could deliver 'is message, and I'll try to hexplain things to your Bishop. Can you ride?'

'After a fashion.'

'Take one of my horses and get the hell out of here and out of the Punjaub immediate. And you might as well take this with you.'

With that he fished in his pocket and brought out a string of pearls and a ring with a large if not very good ruby.

'What on earth are these?'

'They're what I was supposed to give you as an earnest of 'is favour. They'll fetch 'alf a lakh in Calcutta, and I don't see why you shouldn't 'ave that.'

'You're a good fellow at heart, D'Arcy. I'll take your horse, but you take the pearls and the ruby in return. And tell the Bishop that I'll be waiting for him in Lucknow.'

With that I bade farewell to them both, took D'Arcy's horse, made my way, unchecked, through the gates of Lahore and set my nose towards Oude, whose boundaries I crossed after four days of riding which left me so saddle sore that I had, eventually, to limp into Lucknow on foot, leading the horse behind me.

The Bishop never referred to my flight from Lahore and I never tried to discuss it with him. We resumed our travels from mission to mission and from Raja to Raja and never again was I placed in such an awkward position unless, of course, I include what is happening to me here.

All in all, the Bishop and I were the best part of a year on the road, which meant that Mrs Heber and Mistress MacPherson had long been delivered of their babies by the time we returned to Calcutta. The Bishop was delighted with his new daughter, but there was considerable trouble with Mrs Heber when he suggested that it should be called Wilhelmina and that I should be asked to stand as its godfather. It took a long time for the rumblings of that quarrel to die away.

Mistress MacPherson insisted on calling her infant son Reginald, which the Bishop thought flattering until he learnt that the bosun of the *Thomas Grenville* had also been called Reginald. She often brought it down to my bengaloo for me to admire. I remember that the first time she did that, she asked me, rather coyly, if the babe reminded me of anyone.

'Why,' said I, 'all babies look alike to me. But if yours reminds me of anyone, it's the Duke of York.'

'The Duke of York?' she exclaimed.

'Yes,' I said firmly. 'All babies look alike and they all resemble the Duke of York.'

24   *A Cock and Cow Affair*

The Bishop's first tour of his diocese took, on and off, the best part of twelve months. In the course of it we pitched our tents in the shadow of Adam's Peak at one end of the sub-continent and of the Himalayas at t'other. Thereafter we found ourselves having to spend more and more of our time in Calcutta in the shadow of Mrs Heber.

That lady's second attack of motherhood had done nothing to sweeten her temper or to lessen her determination to get rid of me. I did not then, and cannot now account for her antipathy towards me. If, as I was forced to accept, she had been one of those who had assaulted me in the *Thomas Grenville*'s paint locker, then I certainly had, in both senses of the word, done her a service. And that, to my mind, gave her no sensible reason for being beastly to Bunter.

Yet there she was having, so to speak, had her way with me, trying to do *away* with me as the Bishop's secretary. And if the Bishop hadn't been firm with her, she'd have succeeded. In the end her unconcealed dislike of me and her overt intrigues against me became so difficult to stomach that I made up my mind to keep as far away from her as I could.

This, sadly enough, meant that in my off-duty hours the Bishop had less and less of my company whilst the ACBC and the officers' mess of the 22nd BNI had a good deal more. It also meant that I paid increasingly frequent visits to Harry at his family home. This was a luxurious, palace sort of a place he had recently had built a few miles out of Calcutta.

India is full of architectural follies, but this was one of the rummest of 'em. Harry, in his Bluecoat days, had been taken to see Hampton Court and had been so impressed by it that nothing would satisfy him but to have a slightly smaller version of it built on the banks of the Ganges. He brought an architect out to India for that purpose and, when he had done all that he could for Indian Tudor, Harry had got Doctor Wallich, the celebrated curator of the Botanical Gardens at Calcutta and Tittyghur, to lay out the grounds for him.

Trees, shrubberies, parterres, cascades, grottoes and vistas are quickly established in India where vegetation springs up overnight and labour is cheap. The grounds, therefore, already provided a handsome setting for Harry's Hampton Court. Its only drawbacks were practical ones. Red Tudor brick, Tudor lattice casements, and low Tudor ceilings ain't the best things for a Bengal summer. It took the best part of a battalion of punkah-wallahs to keep the rooms cool enough for human habitation, and even then the Hampton Court look had to be modified in the hot season, when a tatty was hung over every window and door. These mats of sweet-smelling kuskus grass would, when dampened, do something to keep out the heat, but I don't believe that any of the Tudors had ever got round to inventing anything half so ingenious.

But tatty or no tatty, Harry was devilish proud of his Hampton-Court-on-the-Ganges and *le tout de Calcutta* was frequently entertained there. At any other time, however, I had a standing invitation to dine there with him *en famille*.

'My dear old chum,' he said to me when he first issued the invitation. 'There's no one in Calcutta who enjoys a decent but simple dinner half as much as your excellent self. So, if you don't mind taking lucky pot, you'll always be gladly welcome to put your legs under my mahogany any evening we're not having to hold a swarry or a ball. I can at least promise you that there'll always be Madeira to go with your turtle soup, Lafitte to go with your simple Baron of Beef, and a drop of good, gob-stopping port wine to follow the puddings.'

Harry, in short, had been so anglicised by Christ's Hospital that he'd not only sent to London for his architect and all his furnishings, but had also sent there for all his menus. He had also, as I soon discovered, tried to anglicise his wives. He hadn't got very far with the two younger ones. They still giggled and tried to veil their faces whenever I dined there, and spent their time chattering between themselves in Bengalee. They were always plainly relieved when, before it came to the port, Harry dismissed them to the women's quarters.

But Mahtab Begum, who was his senior wife, was a different kettle of fish altogether. For one thing she always stayed with us for the port and the cheroots and the talk that accompanied it. For another, she generally dominated the conversation. She had, I must add, been pretty well anglicised before Harry had anything to do with her. Her parents, who must have been remarkably broad-minded Brahmins, had sent her as a small girl to be educated at the Native Female School run by the Church Missionary Society. There, under the formidable tutelage of Mrs Wilson, who was much admired by the Bishop, but whom I found only slightly less awesome than Mrs Heber, she had acquired most of the benefits of a British education. That is to say she had been taught English, plain sewing, the use of the globes, the capitals and rivers of Europe, selected pieces from Shakespeare, and the names and dates of all the Kings and Queens of England. She had also acquired, doubtless from Mrs Wilson herself, the odd habit of popping a Scriptural text into her conversation whether it was apropos or not.

She can't have been much more than thirteen when their respective parents arranged her marriage to Harry, who was then three years older, and he had sired two or three children on her before he departed to England to complete his education. She wasn't all that old by our standards when he returned. But she was by then quite old enough to establish who, in the Thukoor household, should wear the trousers. In short, she was a born matriarch of the type you seldom find outside India, and I must say that India's none the worse or the poorer for 'em.

That apart, she was not exactly what I had expected a well-born and well-brought-up Bengalee wife to be. Few such are at their ease in the company of strange men, especially if they are Feringhis. But whether it was because of the way Mahtab had been educated, or whether it was in her nature, she was at her ease with me from the moment we met.

She was, I rapidly discovered, an uninhibited, frank, outgoing, merry and remarkably broad-minded, not to say earthy sort of girl. There were times when, if I'd shut my eyes, I could have sworn that I was listening to a younger, better-educated, slightly less buxom and bawdy Bessy Trotter.

'Billee,' Mahtab had said when I was introduced. 'You shall not mind if I am calling you that. Hurree is always calling you Billee when he is telling me his so-long stories about his so-happy schooldays in Bilatee. "Let thy heart cheer thee in the days of thy youth." Ecclesiasticus, 10:9.'

'Exactly so, Ma'am,' I said. I was new to her style then, which is why I thought it a bit rum that, whilst I was in the Bishop's Palace, I should be assailed with texts from the Purana, the Ramayana and the Qu'ran, and that now I was in Harry's, I should be attacked by a Brahmin lady with texts from the Scriptures.

'Hurree,' she went on, leaning her plump and handsome bosom on the table, 'is also always telling me that his old chum Billee is fat. But you are fatter, and thus more beautiful, than he is telling me. "Thy navel is like a round goblet, which wanteth not liquor: thy belly is like an heap of wheat set about with lilies." Song of Solomon, 8:2.'

'I say, Ma'am, that's coming it a bit.'

'There is more that is coming,' she said, smiling at me in a very friendly sort of way. 'Is it true what Hurree is also telling me?'

'Depends on what he is telling you.'

'He is telling me that you were—how do you say?—best-hung schoolboy in the whole of Bilatee and that learned hakims are writing passages about you.'

That was, I admit, a bit of a facer, but Harry thought it was time for him to intervene.

'Mahtab,' he said firmly, 'you are not to be mentioning such things to our guest. In England we are not discussing these subjects with ladies, but only in boarding schools and in the top-notch clubs in St James's Street, London.'

'That I am completely not understanding,' she said. 'Well-hanging is important part of man's beauty. The longness and strongness of the linga'—here she turned to me—'linga is what you call, I think, cock—is most precious attribute of man. Also of gods. Is symbol, is it not, Hurree, of divine Siva to which we do puja in temple.'

'I suppose so,' said Harry sulkily.

'Then why should you not be talking about such precious thing with ladies, to whom size of cock is more important than to anyone else?'

She had, of course, the logic of it, which was probably why Harry started to bluster.

'That is quite enough chitter-chattering about this subject. We shall now be discussing cricket.'

Mahtab ignored him and turned to me, the expert. 'My husband, poor man, never is understanding the importance of size. But you, Billee, will certainly agree that while there are many, many small things that are beautiful, a small linga is not one of them.'

Harry was mortified by the quite un-English turn the conversation had taken. But Mahtab, having got to the point of her argument, was now smiling broadly.

'Why I am saying these things to you, Billee, even though my husband is not liking them, is very simple. I am wanting to make you welcome. You are Hurree's old school chum, which is nice. You are, as all can see, very fat, which is beautiful. But you are also, Hurree is telling me, highly well-hung, which is even more beautiful. And so I am very, very pleased to make your beautiful acquaintance.'

It was enough to shake any chap. Even Bessy, who'd always stuck up for me, never thought I was beautiful. So I blushed a bit and stammered when I said:

'Thank you indeed, Ma'am. Mighty kind of you, I'm sure. But your humble ain't really deserving of such praise.'

'"Let us now,"' she said, ' "praise famous men, and our fathers that begat us." Ecclesiasticus, 44:1.'

Our little dinner parties did not always end in such embarrassment for Harry and, so far as I was concerned, they were always enjoyable in spite of the heat engendered by the red brick and the turtle soup, and the confusion so often created by Mahtab's uninhibited prattle. So I fell into the habit of hiring a gharry and driving out to dine with them just about once every week.

But as the weeks became months I noticed that Harry was beginning to lose his appetite and look a worried man. So one evening, when we were enjoying our cheroots in the grounds, Mahtab having departed to bed, I asked him if anything was wrong.

'If I am confiding in you, Billee, you must be keeping it in your bosom.'

'Mum's the word.'

'It is the beastly, confounded, bloody old Barings.'

'What have they done to you?'

'You know that when I was returning to India they are sending one of their confidential clerks with me to be helping me with the banking?'

'I remember something of that sort.'

'The name of said clerk is Smith. Oh, very humble and ordinary name. But he is nephew of another banker, also Smith, who is now aristocrat and called Lord Carrington. I am not understanding the English in this. When bank clerk becomes rich he is made aristocrat, and when aristocrat becomes poor he is made bank clerk. With us, once a Brahmin always a Brahmin, unless you are being like my father and are losing your cord by mixing with Englishmen and other low-class peoples.'

'I know that it's puzzling, Harry. We can't even understand our class system ourselves, which is why we're always so obsessed by it. But where do the Barings come into it?'

'This Mr Algernon Smith I am telling you about was persuading me to go into partnership with them—Thukoor and Baring. He is doing the banking work and I am senior partner as you jolly well know.'

'It seems a convenient arrangement to me.'

'But then they are objecting to the way in which I am spending the bank's money, even though I am senior partner. This place was costing many lakhs of rupees to build, all of which, of course, I am taking from my bank. Now Baring and Sons of London is wanting to sue me for malfeasance, malversation, and maltreatment of depositors' funds.'

'I see why you've lost your appetite. Law suits are tricky things, especially when you've got so many mal-what-do-you-call-'ems against you. Where are they suing you?'

'In High Court of Chancery, London, Master of Rolls presiding.'

'Then you've nothing immediate to worry about. Chancery cases go on for years and years. How much are they claiming from you?'

'Fifteen lakh of rupees plus costs, fees, etcetera, etcetera.'

Entirely fresh ideas, as is so often the case with me, were forming in my mind.

'Fifteen lakhs,' I said, 'wouldn't come near to exhausting the funds of your bank?'

'Certainly not,' said Harry.

'And you still have control over the way in which the bank's funds are invested?'

'I am still,' he said proudly, 'senior partner.'

'Then,' I said firmly, 'you must speculate.'

'With the bank's monies?'

'Certainly.'

'And what should I speculate in and why?'

'You should speculate in'—here I thought for a while—'commodities. And the reason for doing so is to prove that you have been an enterprising guardian of the monies deposited with you.'

'That is very well-sounding in theory, Billee, but what commodity should I be speculating in to satisfy Baring and Company?'

I thought for a moment, and then, as usual, a brilliant solution to his problems flashed across my mind.

'Indigo.'

'Indigo?'

'Indigo. The Bengal indigo crop is what all the Manchester

and Bradford textile magnates depend upon. It's the best in the world. And yet, when the Bishop and I spoke to the indigo planters on our voyage up the Ganges, they all complained of being in debt to the Calcutta bankers and of having the price for their crop settled by the brokers in Tooley Street.'

'That is true. Thukoor and Baring are taking many notes of hand from indigo planters, not to mention arranging bills of lading and exchange and the discounting of bills.'

'Well,' said I, 'their troubles seem to arise from the fact that the indigo crop is marketed in penny numbers and there are far too many middlemen making a profit out of it.'

'Middlemen,' said Harry, 'are absolutely essential. You have to have buyers and storers and shippers and brokers before you can sell anything, and each of them must be having his profit or he wouldn't be brokering, shipping and so on. And above all you have to have bankers to provide the finance which keeps jolly old wheels of commerce turning.'

'But what,' said I, surprising even myself at the simplicity and genius of the plan then falling into place in my mind, 'what if the banker were the only one to set the price and to take the profits?'

It was quite irritating to see how little commercial understanding Harry had, even though he was a banker.

'I am not following that most cryptical remark.'

'It's dead simple,' said I, almost pitying him. 'All you have to do is to buy up the whole of the Bengal indigo crop before it ever comes on to the market. Then, instead of shipping it, you keep it in your godowns here in Calcutta. You must see what will happen as a result.'

'It is not, my dear, quite absolutely crystal-clear.'

'Why, you fathead, you'll have the whole of the Manchester and Bradford textile trade at your mercy. If the indigo crop don't get to England there'll be no blue cloth made or sold and half the world's population will have to go naked.'

'But that would be terrible.'

'No it won't, 'cos it won't happen. What will happen instead is that the price of indigo will double and then you can sell the crop direct to the factory chappies and make an immense amount of money for Thukoor, Baring and Company.'

'You really think so?'

'Absolutely certain of it, old chap. And I'm also certain that when the bloody old Barings learn what you've done they'll offer you a partnership in their London bank instead of trying to sue you in the Chancery Court.'

'Billee,' said Harry, 'you are really very dark horse. None of us Bluecoats were ever thinking you are a genius.'

'Oh, I ain't a genius, Harry. But I do believe'—and here memories of my venture into the gag trade came into my mind—'I do believe I've a bit of a gift for commerce.'

'That I cannot be doubting. No one in India has ever been thinking of cornering the indigo market before. How did you think of it?'

'Just one of my ideas,' said I modestly.

'Then you must be having many more of such ideas. I tell you Billee, you are wasting yourself on this Bishop business. Why don't you leave your Bishop and join me as partner—junior partner of course. You do the ideas and I do the cash.'

'Very decent of you, Harry, and if Mrs Heber don't mend her ways I might take you up on the offer. But I'm too fond of my Bishop to want to leave him to Mrs Heber unless I have to.'

'Then just as soon as I have made all this money from indigo-cornering I shall give you handsome present so that I can be thanking you for the idea.'

'Think nothing of it. But there are a few tailor's bills and mess bills you could settle for me.'

The mess bills were ones I'd run up at the 22nd BNI's officers' mess where, thanks to Merry and in spite of Coker, I was something of an honorary member. It was, like Harry's place, another refuge from Mrs Heber. And a very jolly refuge it was. The subalterns, or those of 'em who'd not yet been drained and debilitated by the Indian climate, were as jovial a lot as you could find anywhere, and once the senior members of the mess had withdrawn to nurse their gout and their dignities, the fun, as they say, tended to become furious.

I've never been much of a one for games that involve physical exertion but I was, because of my build, very popular when it came to one we called High Cockalorum, though in some other messes, I believe, it is called Weak Horses. It is a quite simple but more dangerous variant of the schoolboy's leapfrog, the intention being to make the frog—or rather frogs, for there are three of 'em—collapse rather than be leapt over. It works like this. The four who are to be frogs have one of their number stand with his back against the wall. The other three then form the frog by each tucking his head into the crutch of the man in front, so offering three backs for the other side to attack.

The leaping members then endeavour to land as heavily as they can, one on top of the other, on what is considered to be the weakest sector of back with a view to making it collapse which, if it does, constitutes victory. Quite large wagers can be laid on the various teams, and the one that included me was generally at odds-on. For I was always the last to leap and it was generally considered that few backs could withstand the impact.

'To see Bunter come thundering down at you,' an anchor man once said, 'is rather like watching Ney letting the Old Guard loose at Waterloo.'

Coker, who was as unpopular in the mess as he had been at Christ's Hospital, seldom engaged in these pranks although he did bet on 'em, which was another reason for his unpopularity. People thought he did rather too well out of his wagers. There came a night when he laid heavily against the highly fancied Cockalorum team I belonged to. As he seldom bet against favourites it was thought that his dislike of me, which he now never concealed, had, for once, clouded his judgment.

It had been a more than usually bibulous mess night and I know that I was feeling uncommonly elated and pot-valiant when, as the last of my team, I came to make my run and leap. I may even have been swaying a little as I came thundering down, but certainly no more than the opposing side who were already swaying so much under the weight of those who had gone before me that it seemed that they would collapse before ever I had taken off. Certainly no one watching doubted that I was about to administer the *coup-de-grâce*.

'Here comes the Heavy Brigade,' said one.

'Bunter looks in fine fettle,' said another. 'Lay anyone even money he settles their hash.'

'I'd want three to one on,' said a third. 'Bunter's certain to clinch it.'

And clinched it would have been had not a foot come out just as I was about to leap. The consequence was that instead of collapsing my opponents I collapsed myself, flat on my arse.

The fall, unfortunately, did nothing to help clear my head. Quite the contrary, it robbed me of all prudence. I picked myself up, looked for my spectacles and, when I had found them, put them on and rubbed my behind, I immediately began to protest in what was, for me, an unusually bellicose manner. I even put up my fists and pranced around in a way Trotter would have approved of.

'I was tripped,' I roared, 'and I know who did it. To trip a fellow in that way is cheating, and to cheat at High Cockalorum ain't the act of a gentleman, and I'm going to give him a black eye for his pains.'

There was a sudden silence and Merry tugged at my coat tails and whispered, 'Keep your mouth shut, you fat fool.' But I had too much champagne inside me for that and kept dancing around in front of Coker inviting him to put his dukes up. The senior subaltern, who was already more than half-way towards his gout and his dignity, intervened.

'We'll have no vulgar brawling in this mess, Mr Bunter. Do I understand that you are not only offering to black an officer's eye, but are also accusing him of ungentlemanly conduct?'

Where, at that moment, was my customary caution? Drowned, doubtless, in champagne and anger.

'Mr Coker,' I bellowed, 'laid a hundred chips against our winning, and everyone in this mess knows that he takes care never to lose a wager.'

If they had been silent before they were all like so many Egyptian mummies now. The senior subaltern turned to Coker and said, the solemnity of his utterance slightly marred by an attack of hiccups:

'Mr Coker . . . hic . . . you have heard Mr . . . hic . . . Bunter?'

Coker looked calmly at me, and I swear he was as pleased with himself as a cat that had got at the cream.

'If Mr Bunter, Sir, questions my conduct, I'm sure he'll

give me the satisfaction due to a gentleman. I shall communicate with him tomorrow. And now, with your permission, I shall leave it at that.'

He turned on his heel and left the room. The others, all suddenly looking as sober and as solemn as mutes at a wake, drew away from me and I began to realise that I might have gone a bit too far.

'I need a drink,' I said to Merry.

'Not a drop more,' he replied. 'You'll need a clear head and a steady hand for tomorrow. I will, of course, act for you.'

'Act for me in what?'

'In the duel, you dolt. Coker's going to call you out.'

'A duel? I don't want to duel. All I wanted to do was black Coker's eye, and now I've sobered up a bit I'm not even sure I want to do that.'

'It ain't a question of what you want. You'll have his challenge by breakfast time and you'll be facing him with sword or pistol by evening. Which are you going to choose?'

I shuddered. All my pot-valour had been replaced by my native cowardice.

'How would it be,' I suggested, 'if I offered to apologise to him? Told him I was drunk and didn't really know what I was saying?'

'If you did you'd never be able to show your face anywhere in Calcutta, or in the whole of the Presidency come to that. And it still wouldn't do you any good. Coker will never let you off the hook now he's managed to get you on it. He's never forgiven you for what you did to his ear and his arse.'

'It's all damned unfair,' said I.

'Well, don't blub about it. I recommend a pot of strong coffee followed by a cold bath and a couple of hours' sleep. I assume you'll want me to choose pistols. You can at least pull a trigger, and I doubt you'd know a lunge from a parry if it came to swords.'

'Pistols are devilish dangerous things.'

'Of course they are. But he might miss you. I don't know what Coker's like with a pistol, but I've been duck shooting with him and I must warn you that he's a dab hand with a fowling piece. Perhaps he'll be satisfied with winging you.'

'I doubt it,' said I bitterly.

'So do I,' said Merry.

But if Sam Merry took all this with a deal more composure than I did, Harry, who came round to see me next morning at cock crow, seemed almost as upset as I was. He moaned and wailed and wrung his hands and even offered to lend me a shirt of chain mail to wear under my coat, but then decided that I'd never be able to get into it, it having been made for a rather slender ancestor of his. Then, suddenly, he had a different idea.

'There is an Indian drug,' he said, 'which our women take when they want to make their eyes look large and beautiful.'

'I don't want to look beautiful, you chump. All I want is not to be shot.'

'You are not fully understanding. Because they make their eyes large, everything the women are looking at seems twice as big as it is. That is a good thing when you are making love. It is not a good thing when you are firing a pistol.'

This sounded rather more sensible.

'What have you got in mind, Harry?'

He looked at me and then put a finger to his lips. 'It is better I am not telling you. But Mr Bloody Coker's bearer is nephew of my cook's wife.'

He moved his finger from his lips to his nose, gave me a knowing sort of look and departed.

Whatever small hope Harry had given me rapidly evaporated when Merry turned up to tell me what had been arranged between himself and Coker's second. He was so businesslike about it all that I felt I was listening to the arrangements for my funeral.

'It'll be pistols at five o'clock this evening, in the clearing behind the mango tope t'other side of the maidan. O'Shaughnessy will act as surgeon. I've laid on a gharry to take us there and he'll wait to take us back.'

'Cart me back, you mean.'

'Come, no need to despair. Coker's second tells me his man don't intend to kill you if he can help it. I suppose you know what to do and can handle a pistol? It will look better for Coker if you actually manage to fire your piece.'

Merry was taking altogether too professional an interest in the affair for my liking.

'You must thank Coker for me,' I said, bitterly. 'And yes, I do know what to do and how to fire a pistol, though what good that's going to do me when that murdering blackguard gets to work I'm damned if I know.'

'We must hope for the best,' said Merry, 'and I'll call for you at four-thirty sharp.'

As I waited for four-thirty I desperately tried to remember all that Trotter had attempted to teach me in my boyhood days, but the only thing that came into my mind was the memory of my lack of any success with the candle ends. I did remember, however, that Trotter had told me never to wear anything white in a duel, so, hot though it was, I put on a black tail coat which I could button up to my neck.

Coker, ever the dandy, had taken no such precaution. When Merry and I arrived at the mango tope he was waiting there with his coat already off. He was wearing a white neckcloth, white ruffled shirt and an elegant, skin-tight pair of buckskin breeches of the palest yellow.

There were none of the formalities I had hoped for. Our seconds didn't even try to persuade us to call it off. They were too busy pushing back a Brahminy cow and a small bunch of Indians who had appeared, as if by magic, to enjoy the tomasha. Coker kept glaring at me out of eyes that looked as large as saucers, and O'Shaughnessy was whistling happily to himself as he laid out his instruments and bandages. Before I knew where I was I found myself back to back with Coker and setting off on my ten paces. And I couldn't remember one thing that Trotter had taught me except something about not raising my pistol till I'd turned.

But I forgot even that and stood there, square-on, with the pistol still dangling from my hand and pointing towards the ground as I looked at Coker and my imminent doom. He, of course, stood sideways on and I remember thinking how well-cut his breeches were and wishing he'd get on with it as I'd had all the fright I could stand. He grinned when he saw the condition I was in and took his time raising his pistol arm. I heard the shot and a bellow from the Brahminy cow but felt nothing. Coker looked, at first, vaguely puzzled, but this turned to consternation as, almost of its own accord, my own pistol arm began to come up. I suddenly remembered what

Trotter had said about squeezing the trigger once my pistol was knee-high. I don't know whether I did that or not, but there was a report, a loud shriek from Coker who fell writhing to the ground, and then O'Shaughnessy came bustling up and Sam Merry was shaking me by the hand and the group of Indians was muttering angrily.

'Damme if Coker didn't shoot the Brahminy cow,' said Merry. And he actually laughed.

'Damn the cow,' said I. 'I'm afraid I've killed Coker.'

'Not you,' said Merry. 'You came as near to a clean miss as is possible. I swear you've only nicked him.'

Nevertheless we both hurried over to where O'Shaughnessy was dealing with the writhing Coker. The beautiful buckskin breeches were blood-stained around the cod-piece.

'Aisy, now,' said O'Shaughnessy, 'whilst I cut these most aligant unmentionables off of yiz', which he proceeded to do very rapidly.

'I'm dying,' shrieked Coker.

'Divil a bit of ut,' said O'Shaughnessy, examining the damage. 'But our fat friend here has taken the tip off your pecker. It's as clean and nate a circumcision as iver I've witnessed.'

'Will it heal?' asked Merry, looking at the wound with considerable interest.

'In due course,' said O'Shaughnessy, winding a bandage round the bleeding member. 'But it'll be some time before he'll iver empty his bladder with any degree of comfort, and he'll not be plasing the fair sex one little bit for a dale longer than that.'

Coker's shrieks had now given way to groans. I bent over him: 'I'm truly sorry, Coker,' I said. 'I never meant to circumcise you.'

He stopped groaning for a moment and glared at me. 'I hate you, Bunter,' he said.

'You've no reason to,' I said.

'No reason!' he shrieked. 'No reason to hate you! It's because of you that I'm lop-eared, lop-arsed, and half-cocked. I'll see you pay for it if it's the last thing I do.'

A few days later the Bishop, looking more sorrowful than I had ever seen him, raised the matter of the duel with me.

'You should never have allowed that Brahminy cow to be shot,' he said. 'Anything else and I might have been able to stand out against Mrs Heber and the rest of 'em, but the Brahminy cow put paid to it.'

'I don't see where the cow comes into it. Besides, it was Coker who shot it.'

'It was shot, and that's all that matters. The Hindoo priests have complained to the Governor General, the Governor General has complained to the Dean and Chapter, and they have complained to Mrs Heber. And I've been forced to agree with 'em all.'

'Agree on what?'

'Agree that no Bishop *in partibus infidelium* can go on employing a duelling secretary who not only goes around shooting bits off chaps' peckers but goes on to enrage the natives by attacking their sacred cows. If we'd been in England I might have got away with it, although Mrs Heber would certainly have disapproved. But as we're in India, William, I'm afraid you'll have to go, or we'll be having a massacre of the missionaries out in the mofussil.'

'And all just because of a Brahminy cow,' said I bitterly.

'And Mrs Heber,' said the Bishop. 'You must never forget Mrs Heber, William.'

The next day I went to see Harry. 'Do you still want a junior partner in your indigo scheme?'

'I was thinking, my dear, that you would be asking that. Mrs Heber, I am hearing, is very, jolly angry. But I am very pleased. What shall we be calling our new firm?'

'What about Thukoor and Bunter, Commodity Brokers?'

'And no bloody old Barings?'

'No bloody old Barings.'

Harry, Mahtab and I made a merry trio that night at dinner, at the end of which Mahtab, looking particularly sly, presented me with a small silver phial containing a dark, evil-smelling liquid.

'What the devil's this?' I asked.

'It is some of the special drug I am sometimes using to make my eyes very, very big and beautiful.'

If all my scribbling has, over the past weeks, done something to put the harsh realities of my situation out of my mind, then Gurmakh Singh has, today, made me face them once more.

'I have heavy news for you,' he said when he brought me my midday meal.

'Is it,' said I, looking at my spinach and horse beans with distaste, 'that plump roast chickens will no longer nest in your turban?'

'It is good that the Sahib should be light-hearted in adversity, but this is no longer the time for him to jest.'

'I never jest about food, Gurmakh Singh. Nor am I light-hearted. No scribbler ever is. But what makes you heavy-hearted?'

'The state of Ismail Khan, Huzoor.'

'Yet it is not long since that you told me his was an exceedingly comfortable state.'

'That was before the Begum, may her name be accursed, succeeded in wearing him down, as she has done to so many before him, as Your Honour well knows. Ismail Khan is now close to physical and nervous collapse.'

This was, indeed, heavy news.

'Is the Begum aware of his condition?'

'Today she questioned me closely about your own condition, asking me whether you were now more vigorous and lustful.'

'And what did you answer?'

'What, for both our sakes, could I answer? I told her, of course, that you had grown strong and wilful in idleness, and were even now snorting with lust as the stallion does ere he is turned out in spring to the mares.'

'Was it wise of you thus to pollute the fountain of truth with the dung of deception? You know full well that I have become more like a gelding than a stallion.'

'If it was not wise, Bunter Sahib, it was at least prudent.'

'Yet if you had but spoken the truth she would surely have turned to some other man as a replacement for Ismail Khan, and so have left me to my spinach and my scribbling.'

'The Begum is an older woman than she was when she kept a full stud of lusty young men for her pleasuring, and the years have made her mean. She will not now readily stable and feed more than one stallion at a time.'

'But has she not, whilst Ismail Khan was pleasuring her, continued to stable and feed me?'

'Your member, Sahib, is still talked about in every zenana in Hindoostan. So long as the Begum believes that rest and diet will endow it with the activity she demands from it she will keep you, knowing that, at its best, it is unmatchable. But if it is not at its best, she can always dispose of you profitably to Runjeet Singh. Judge, then, what would have happened to each of us if I had told her that all my administering and all her spinach had done nothing to bring you up to full vigour and to make you pant for her embrace.'

'All I pant for, Gurmakh Singh, is to be away from here and safely back in my own country.'

'I also wish that for you, as do my sister's daughters-in-law, and if the Gods are willing we may yet bring that about. But meanwhile, if you have more scribbling to do, scribble with all the speed your hand and pen can command. Any night, now, the Begum may put you to the test which, if you fail, will make Runjeet Singh's offer for you attractive.'

26   *Thukoor and Bunter: Commodity Brokers*

Although I now was, as Harry kept pointing out to me, the junior partner in our new enterprise, he still dealt generously with me. He, or rather Thukoor and Baring, paid me a handsome salary considering how little I really knew about the indigo business. Moreover Harry, if I had allowed him, would have had me live with him as one of the family. It was only after I had argued him out of this that he had his bank purchase a small house, not fifty yards from the entrance to his grounds. This he assigned to me as my quarters after he had had it furnished in quasi-European style.

All that it lacked was kitchen furniture and the accommodation required for the train of servants considered necessary for the running of even a humble Indian establishment.

'If you refuse to live with us, my dear,' said Harry, 'you must at least eat with us. But I am understanding that this could, occasionally, be irksome. So whenever you are desiring to feed in solitary state rather than in our convivial company, food shall be brought to you from my kitchens. Now how could a bachelor such as yourself fare better? And, what is being more to the point, you will not be having to trouble yourself with servants, for I am having many dozens of them all eating their faces off and doing exactly bugger all.'

I didn't argue with him over this. I've never turned down good grub when it's on offer, and I would have been a fool not to prefer the products of Harry's kitchens and cellars to anything an uncontrolled Indian cook would have thought suitable for a bachelor. But when I offered to pay even a token sum for my bed and board Harry refused to accept a single rupee.

'Am I not, even now,' said he, 'spending many, many lakhs on buying up large part of indigo crop? And was it not your entirely ripping idea that we should go into this indigo-cornering business? And won't bloody old Barings derive great pecuniary benefits therefrom? Consequently, my dear old chum, it is jolly right that bank should disburse trifling sums for your upkeepings, even though you are not pukka member of Thukoor and Baring.'

Harry found an office for us in a shed in the Calcutta dock area which was attached to the godown in which the indigo crop would be stored. He furnished it with a couple of desks, a pile of ledgers, and a baboo to look after them. But he provided no accommodation for himself. His own office at the bank was a good deal more comfortable.

I drove down to my new office daily in the buggy Harry had

put at my disposal, even though there was little enough for me to do when I got there beyond trying to think up some more ripping ideas for commodity-cornering. The baboo, a remarkably taciturn chap, spent his time crouched over his still virginal ledgers and said nothing beyond 'Good Morning' and 'Good Night'. As there was seldom anyone else to talk to I tended to feel lonely.

Nor could I do much to lessen my loneliness by calling on my former gossips. I dared not visit the Bishop for fear of coming across Mrs Heber, or make frequent use of the 22nd's mess and the ACBC for fear of meeting Coker. Merry had warned me that Coker had sworn he'd call me out a second time just as soon as he could fix a quarrel on me.

'He keeps saying,' said Merry, 'that you may have half-cocked him but there'll be nothing half-cocked about what he'll do to you.'

All of this made me value the only company I could still rely on, which was that of Harry and Mahtab over the dinner table. It was seldom, in those early months, that I chose to dine alone. And quite jolly evenings the three of us would generally make of 'em, even though Mahtab frequently came close to ignoring Harry whilst she concentrated her attention on me.

She had, probably as a consequence of Mrs Wilson and the Native Female School, an unquenchable thirst for knowledge. This manifested itself, principally, in an intense curiosity about everything English. She would spend the whole of an evening plying me with questions about such things as the marital, sexual and domestic habits of the British, my answers to which always made her laugh. But when she was in a more serious mood she would want to know everything about such different things as Britain's principal exports and imports, or the names of the English county towns, or how the young Princess Alexandrina Victoria stood in the line of succession to George IV.

There came an evening when Harry finally objected to this continuous inquisition.

'Mahtab,' he said firmly, 'always you are asking Billee your stupid questions about England. He will soon get very jolly weary of answering them.'

She came back at him with one of her Scriptural quota-
tions which generally floored him: ' "If they will learn anything," ' said she, ' "let them ask their husbands at home."
1 Corinthians, 45.'

But this time Harry refused to be floored: 'Billee is not
being your husband. I am.'

'Of course you are, my dear,' said Mahtab dismissively.
'But Billee has become like second and English husband.'

That was when I first began to entertain doubts about the
wisdom of continuing our little *ménage à trois*. Harry, for all I
know, had anticipated me in this respect for he immediately
set out to quash this second-husband idea. It was unfortunate
that his voice was rather too high-pitched to be as authorita-
tive as it needed to be.

'In future, which is to say from now on, if you are wanting
to be knowing anything about England, you will only be
learning it from me. You are only knowing about England
from Mrs Wilson. I was brought up by a learned parent who
had made deep study of that particular subject. Also I was
instructed, from early days, by English nanny, Miss Fiona
Mackintosh, and by English tutor, the Reverend Malachi
O'Connor. Not to mention long period of schooling at
venerable and venerated Christ's Hospital in Newgate,
London.'

Mahtab, however, merely fell back on the Scriptures:
' "How can he get wisdom whose talk is of bullocks?"
Ecclesiasticus, 38:25.'

She was off target this time, for I'm sure no one had ever
heard Harry spend his time talking about cattle. But off target
or not, it floored him. And so he spent the rest of the evening
glaring at the two of us and muttering something about not
being a bloody peasant.

Eventually he said that he was going to bed. This left
Mahtab to do what Harry normally did, which was to stroll
down the drive with me until we came to the gates. I tried to
stop her, for that remark about second husbands had made
me uneasy, but she was quietly and politely insistent. My
unease increased as she took my arm and, slowing our stroll to
a crawl, chatted away to me in a most confident, not to say
confidential, manner.

'You must not be minding Harry. He is never understanding how important it is that we are learning from one another.'

'Quite,' said I, trying to brisken our pace.

'Why are you hurrying so, Billee, when we are having such interesting conversations? I am talking to you about the getting of wisdom, which the Bible says is very necessary. I have got much wisdom about Englishmen from you. Now I think you must be getting wisdom about Indian women from me.'

'I've already done that, thanks largely to you.'

'Why are you pretending? I am teaching you very little until now about Indian women, and I am only Indian woman you are meeting every day. I am certainly thinking you have never yet permitted one to—how do you say?—make love to you. Some Indian women are very good at that, most especially me.'

I felt that I was getting into the sort of stoat-and-rabbit situation that had done for me when I was dealing with other masterful women such as Mrs Boyer and Mrs Heber.

'Steady on, Mahtab,' I said. 'You're Harry's senior wife. You oughtn't to be talking to me about love.'

'Perhaps I was being too polite and too English. I am not really talking about love. I am talking about jigajig, which may or may not be having anything to do with love, although you English pretend the two should always be going together.'

This was worse than anything I had feared. I tried to disengage my arm from hers, but she merely took a firmer grip of me and went relentlessly on.

'I am thinking, Billee, that you know very little about jigajig, which is very interesting subject. From now on Mahtab will be teaching you.'

I was in a rare state of funk by then but we had, thank goodness, arrived at the gates. So I said:

'Jolly decent of you to offer, Mahtab, but I must say good-night now. Eight hours' sleep, you know . . .'

'But my dear,' she said firmly, 'I shall be sleeping with you, although I am not believing there will be much sleeping if you are good pupil.'

As is usual for me in moments of crisis, I could only babble at her. 'Know you mean well . . . would be quite instructive . . . but absolutely impossible . . . Harry old friend and business partner . . . certain to object . . .'

'Business is having nothing to do with it. And what partner is not knowing about partner is not worrying about.'

'Bound to suspect, though'—here memories of the Reverend Boyer flashed across my mind—'suspicious husbands absolute hell.'

'You,' said Mahtab firmly, 'are needing lessons about husbands as well as about jigajig. Now Harry is not needing to be taught about jigajig. He is Indian. Also he is not very highly well-hung. You are in opposite direction both ways, which is why it will be my pleasure as well as my duty to be teaching you.'

'Harry won't like it,' I said.

'Harry is having two other wives. Nice girls but ignorant. They are not knowing what very pleasing, artistic and complicated thing jigajig can be. So they are quite pleased and I am very pleased when Harry is doing his not very complicated or artistic jigajigs with them.'

'I always thought that what you refer to is a pretty simple business.'

'That shows how much I am having to teach you. You will study, as I have, the literature of the subject. I have read many times the *Kama Sutra* of Vatsyayana, the *Ananga Kanga* of Kalyana Malla, the *Perfumed Garden* of Shaykh Nefwazi, the *Book of Carnal Copulation* of Aziz al-Din al-Masihi, and many, many other learned works in Sanskrit, Farsi and Arabic.'

For a moment I thought I was saved. 'Hang on,' I said. 'I'll read all those, if that's what you want, even though I've never been one for learning from books.'

'Books will be coming later. We have a saying that a Seer of practice is worth a whole Maund of theory for beginners. I am only mentioning these works to show you I have enough theory to be excellent teacher. But also I have strong, round thighs, supple back, narrow waist, wide haunches, big bosoms, small mouth, and very fine crinkum-crankum. All of these, Billee, are highly enjoyable and very necessary for practical teachings.'

We had, by now, crept out of the gates and arrived at my quarters. If I could have done so I would have bolted, but she kept a firm hold of me and, steering me through the front door, she brought me, willy-nilly, into the bedroom. I must, by then, have been showing signs of alarm for she smiled at me and said:

'It will not in the least be hurting you.'

Her voice was so determined and her look so benevolent that I knew I was sunk. And that was how I came to be seduced—and kept on being seduced—by Mahtab Begum.

27 *Indigo and Other Monopolies*

Our indigo project, meanwhile, was well under way. We had started it with one unexpected piece of good fortune. Mr Algernon Smith, who might have objected to the use we were making of Thukoor and Baring's funds, suddenly succumbed to delirium tremens and a disease he had contracted in the most reputable of all the Calcutta brothels.

Harry designed Smith's headstone himself, and some would say that he overdid it. The top quarter was devoted to emblems of mortality, being full of skulls, hour glasses, and mourning angels tastefully arranged around the Great Reaper, complete with scythe. Underneath these Commerce, who was depicted as a plump lady in Grecian robes, held a laurel wreath over the inscription which took up all the rest of the stone.

Harry excelled himself with the inscription. It recorded the deceased's accomplishments as a banker. It spoke of his industry and probity as well as of the profits he had earned his employers. It listed his many virtues such as piety, charity, chastity and frugality. It mentioned his connections with the famous house of Smith and made much of his services to the great banking establishment of Thukoor, Baring and Company. All that was left out was the fact that Harry and the late Algernon Smith had heartily hated each other.

Our godown was half full of indigo before Harry thought it right to let the Barings know of his proposals for cornering the indigo market. It would be full before the letter arrived, by which time it would be too late for the Barings to forbid the venture.

They didn't even do that. When their reply arrived, several months later, it was difficult to decide what the Barings thought.

'We have,' they wrote, 'no intimate knowledge of the indigo trade, which we understood to be a speculative one. We have no objections in principle to cornering a market, so long as it returns a profit commensurate to the risk. We would consider any return in excess of two hundred per centum commensurate, and trust this will be achieved. We would remind you, however, that we are already conducting proceedings against you in the Chancery Court. In the event of your project involving Thukoor and Baring in any losses, we shall not hesitate to add these to the already substantial claims we have against you. We regret the death of our Mr Algernon Smith and must thank you for the sketch of the headstone you have had placed in Calcutta cemetery.'

'Typical of the bloody old Barings,' said Harry, when he had read this to me. 'They are squatting on the railings as usual.'

Very little of the Bengalee indigo crop arrived on the London market that year for most of it was lying in our godown. The London papers, when they reached us, spoke of distress and unemployment in the spinning and weaving regions, which pleased Harry a good deal. We were just preparing to ship a consignment of our own indigo to arrive at a time when we calculated prices could rise no higher, when we got another letter from the Barings.

'It now seems apparent that your ill-conceived plans for cornering the indigo market took no account of the existence of indigo substitutes. As soon as it was spread about that there would be a large shortfall in this year's Bengalee crop, our manufacturers turned elsewhere for their supplies. The Americans extract from the young shoots of *Amorpha cœrulea* an inferior but cheaper dye, and a supply of this has now arrived on the English market. A similar dye can be derived, in this country, from the plant *Isatis tinctoria* and our farmers have, for the first time in centuries, been planting large acreages of this. So, what with the American dye, known in the trade as *"Bastard Indigo"* and with the *Woad* which will be extracted from *Isatis tinctoria*, the market for Bengalee indigo has largely disappeared. The large supplies you hold could now, we gather, only be sold at a heavy discount. We would remind you that we shall sue you for the loss Thukoor and Baring will undoubtedly make as a consequence, and would only add that our suit against you in the Court of Chancery has this week been decided in our favour.'

The letter upset Harry a good deal more than it did me. Never, even in my most abject moments, have I howled, yowled and yarooed as loudly as he did even though no one was actually offering to do him physical violence. He was so distraught that, when he turned round to blame me, he cursed me, at first, in Hindi. It was only after he had finished calling me a dog's pizzle, a camel's turd, a snake's prick and so on that he lapsed into English and coherence.

'You and your so-ripping ideas,' he screamed, 'have brought me and mine to becoming beggars. Twice, now, will I be sued in Chancery Court, London, and I cannot even be paying once. I am being ruined.'

'It can't be as bad as that.'

'You are not knowing the bloody Barings. They shall take my bank and my beautiful house away from me and Mahtab and my other wives and all my children will have to beg for their bread in the streets of Calcutta. And it's all your fault.'

'That ain't fair, Harry. All I did was to give you an idea. It was you who decided that it was a ripping one. Anyway, the Barings haven't won yet. If you'd only stop screaming at me, I'm sure I could think of an idea for foiling 'em.'

'An idea! I am absolutely forbidding you to have even one more idea.'

'That's a great pity.'

'Why are you telling me that?'

'Because I've only just begun to think of one for getting you out of this mess.'

Whoever said Orientals were inscrutable was wrong. I've

never seen suspicion replace anger and hope replace suspicion so quickly.

'What is it that you are now saying to me?'

'Only that I've got half of an idea for getting rid of the indigo.'

'Then why aren't you telling me of it before instead of all this shally-shingling?'

'Because you've just forbidden me to have an idea.'

'Billee, my dear, are we not partners and ancient school chums? Always I have been trusting you just as I trust Mahtab. Never would I have expected you to oyster up on me.'

'Well, if you put it like that.'

'I will put it any way you jolly well like if you get me out of the terrible clutches of the bloody Barings.'

This put me on my mettle, and I began to flesh out the skeleton of a thought that had just entered my mind.

'You know, Harry,' I said, 'that I was still with the Bishop when I first gave you the idea for cornering the indigo market.'

'Would I forget the blackest day of my life?'

'Do you also know that the Bishop, who is a very learned man, has a very extensive library?'

'What is all this about bloody bishops? Bishops are having absolutely nothing to do with indigo.'

'I'll tell you what they have to do with it. When I threw out that idea about indigo and you jumped at it I thought I ought to find out a bit more about that miserable commodity. So I looked in all the Bishop's botanical, geographical and economic works of reference, and do you know what I discovered?'

'No, but you will now be telling me, instanter.'

'Do you know anything about China?'

'Thukoor and Baring are doing some financial transactions with Canton, but not with Chinese, who are too clever by three-quarters.'

'You don't need to deal directly with the Chinese when you are trading with China. There are now European merchants in Canton.'

'Of course there are. Are we not lending them money to finance the trade between here and Canton? But still I am not understanding what bishops and Chinese are having to do with the bloody indigo which we cannot sell and is now in our godown.'

'The Chinese, Harry, are great exporters of silks. The only blue dyes they use are extracted from trees. One is called, according to the Bishop's books, *Hom-bi* and the other *Pa-bi*, and both of them are so expensive that they make their blue and green silks too dear for the European market. Now, if only they had supplies of indigo . . .'

'I have been saying it before, Billee, and I am saying it now. When it comes to having an idea you are absolutely tip-top.'

'Hold on, it's not as simple as that. You'd have to have an agent in Canton who'd handle the indigo.'

'But I am having one already. He is what you call a North Briton.'

'You mean a Scot.'

'That is right, just like Walter Scott of Kenilworth. He is called, I think, Jardeen—Oh, a very rough sort of man who is even suspected of trying to break East India Company's monopoly by smuggling opium from here to China. But he is owing Thukoor and Baring money, and so would be glad to act as agent.'

'Hold on a minute. What was it you just said about the fellow?'

'I said he is very rough type. North Briton.'

'No, what was it you said about smuggling opium?'

'That is only rumouring. If it were more than rumouring Mr Jardeen would now be being in prison. Opium is East India Company monopoly and it is criminal offence for private individual to export it. So if Mr Jardeen is smuggling opium he is not talking about it.'

'You know, Harry, that's where we went wrong with the indigo. We tried to establish a monopoly, which is always a risky thing to do. What we ought to have done is to try to smash a monopoly, such as the Company's monopoly of the export of opium to China.'

'That is impossible, or only possible in very small quantities.'

'Indigo, when it's been processed, is cut up into dark little cubes, is it not?'

'Yes.'

'If a cake of opium was cut up into cubes what would they look like?'

'Dark little cubes.'

'Exactly, and it would be difficult to distinguish the one from t'other. Now we've got enough indigo to fill a ship. If we could put opium cubes at the bottom of one barrel in every ten, and we sent a couple of thousand barrels to Canton, we'd make our fortunes just by breaking a monopoly.'

'And what about the indigo?'

'Why, you chump, it wouldn't matter whether the Chinese bought it or not. One barrel of opium will pay for a hundred of indigo on the Canton market.'

'This is a very highly dangerous idea of yours. Much safer just trying to sell the Chinese indigo instead of *Hom-bi*.'

'That might not save you from the Barings. This would. You've already got an agent in Canton who does a bit of opium smuggling. All we've got to do is to come to terms with him. We can't lose.'

'We?' asked Harry.

'Of course. We're partners, ain't we? I provide the ideas, you provide the cash.'

It's always a bad sign when Harry starts to look cunning for he's the most un-cunning Indian I've ever come across.

'If we are partners in this opium smuggling I must be very sleeping partner. This can only be for Thukoor and Bunter: Commodity Brokers *sub-geranium*. Publicly it is having to be done by Billee Bunter: Exports and Imports.'

'Don't talk nonsense, Harry. I haven't the capital to set up for myself. Besides, it's not me who's in trouble with the Barings.'

'I shall, of course, be supplying the opium and paying all expenses. But already I am in great trouble with Chancery Court, London. I do not propose being in very much greater trouble with High Court, Calcutta. If anyone is being caught smuggling opium it is having to be you.'

'Partners are partners. If one goes to prison, both ought to.'

'I shall, of course, be paying you ten per centum—no, seven and a half per centum—of all profits. Also providing all capital and pay all expenses. Only fair that you provide the risk.'

I wish, now, that I'd dropped the whole scheme there and then. But after we'd argued a good deal, and after I'd beaten Harry back to ten per centum, I agreed to his conditions. The first of these was that I should immediately take ship to Canton in order to arrange the deal with the Cantonese agent. Harry resolutely refused to be involved beyond providing me with a letter of introduction.

I didn't much care for Canton, and I found the person Harry referred to as Mr Jardeen quite as rough as Harry had said he was. It took a week of haggling before we came to an agreement, largely because of the amount of Scotch whisky the two of us consumed, he being, as Harry had said, a North Briton. When we were finally sober enough to strike a bargain I produced the few cubes of indigo and opium I had brought with me, and showed him how to separate the one from the other by weighing.

I then took ship for Calcutta where, as soon as I arrived, I set about finding a ship on the China run that was prepared to take a large consignment of indigo to Canton. Most of the shippers and ship's captains laughed at me, for they assured me that the Chinese, being the traditionalists they are, would never take to indigo. But then I happened to bump into Captain Manning who insisted on taking me off to dine with him on the *Thomas Grenville*.

He had, he told me, just unloaded a cargo for Calcutta and was proceeding in ballast to China to pick up the first of that season's tea.

'I have,' he said, winking at me—we'd drunk a deal of claret by then—'a little chest o' something I've acquired here what'll fetch a fortune in Canton. The Company don't like us trading on our own account, and least of all in this sort of stuff. But we all do it when we're on the China run and, so long as it ain't more than a single chest, they'll shut their eyes to it, especially as I'll be sailing with nothing in my holds.'

'What would you say,' said I, 'if I found you a cargo of indigo?'

He looked at me in a fuddled, puzzled, but kindly manner.

'Come now, Mr Bunter. If you were a merchant you'd know that indigo's never shipped to Canton.'

'But I am a merchant.'

'Bless my soul! I knew Bishop Heber was an intelligent man, but I never knew that he was engaged in any other trade than the saving of souls.'

'I've left the Bishop and have set up in trade. And I've got an agent in Canton to handle the consignment.'

'He must be remarkably green to try selling indigo to the Chinee. What's his name?'

'Mr Jardine.'

'Well, *he's* certainly not green. But I do hope, Mr Bunter, that you know what you're doing.'

'If you'll take the cargo I'll be able to start loading within the week.'

'Well, if you're serious, it'll have to be done through the Company, though I don't suppose they'll grumble if I've found them a cargo. Usual rates of course.'

'Of course.'

And we left it at that.

28 *Goodbye Calcutta*

Whilst I was in China Harry, in a permanent state of funk, set about acquiring enough opium to repair our fortunes and keep the Barings at bay. This could not, of course, be done in British territory. Even in the up-country Native States, where the market was more or less free, Harry thought it necessary to buy in small packets and through intermediaries who never knew who their principal was.

Nevertheless by the time I got back almost two tons of the best opium was lying in our godown, packed in chests marked 'Best Quality Cinnamon'. What then had to be done could only be done by the two of us and in secret. Any one of our employees could, by informing on us to the authorities, have earned more by way of a reward than Harry was willing to pay him for a year's work.

It was only when we had the godown to ourselves that Harry and I could set about preparing the opium for secret shipment. What with cutting it up into indigo-sized cubes, packing it into the bottoms of certain barrels, refilling those barrels with indigo, and then hammering the tops back on, it was generally midnight before we could get to our beds. We could then sink back on them, however, happy in the knowledge that we had another honest night's toil behind us and were another day closer to dishing the Barings.

But if Harry could then sleep the sleep of the just, I still had to worry about Mahtab. I could never be certain that, somewhere between moonset and cockcrow, she wouldn't turn up hell-bent on another educational session.

It was with her much as it had been with the Reverend Boyer, both being possessed by the *furor docendi*. She was as determined to make me appreciate the finer points of jigajig as he had been to make me appreciate the finer points of Juvenal. I, never a willing pupil, disliked such pedantic complications. It's still my belief that copulation's a basically simple undertaking—any mechanic will agree that there ain't so many different ways in which a piston can move up and down in its cylinder.

I would frequently beg Mahtab to stick to basics, at which she would laugh and say that it was only the English who had fifty different puddings and but one method of copulating. She would add that this was why that method was known amongst Indians as the 'missionary jigajig'. So I continued to be taught out of her many books, even though most of what they recommended was so impracticable as to be of little use to any but acrobats, and of even less use to one of my build. In the end she had to agree to temper the wind to the shorn lamb, and to teach me only those positions that were possible for the portly.

The night Harry and I had nailed the last top on the last barrel had been a particularly fatiguing one. I went to bed praying to be left undisturbed. But I hadn't been asleep very long before I was briskly shaken, and there, sure enough, was

Mahtab. I groaned and hid my head under the pillow, but that was soon pulled away, after which the sheet was whisked off the bed.

'This time, my dear,' she said in the school-ma'amish voice she kept for such encounters, 'we shall be studying the position called The Two Wrestlers. So please to put on your spectacles and stand up.'

Figuratively speaking, I've never been able to stand up to any masterful woman, which was why I couldn't refuse to stand up for Mahtab. So I crawled out of my bed and stood there naked, groaning and scratching myself whilst she quickly ran through the theory of The Two Wrestlers. It sounded simple enough to me, involving, as it seemed, a mere coupling in the standing position.

I could not, however, have been following everything she said because I was astonished when she suddenly put her left foot on my right one and somehow or other contrived to hook her right leg around the back of my neck. To complete the manoeuvre she then leant backwards which had the effect of thrusting her groin into mine.

I may eventually have discovered how I was supposed to proceed from there if she hadn't suddenly gone into a spasm and let rip with the sort of scream you expect from a rape, though Heaven knows, if there was a rapist around, it wasn't Bunter.

'If you don't shut up,' I said, 'you'll wake everyone in the big house. They may even hear you in Calcutta. What's more, this is all devilish uncomfortable and I'm sure it leads nowhere.'

To my horror she screamed again, and kept on screaming until I clapped my hand over her mouth. I refused to remove it until she seemed capable of speech.

'Billee,' she then said, 'I cannot be staying like this and I cannot be moving from this and I am hurting exceedingly. Please to get my right leg down, but very carefully, or I shall be screaming some more.'

It was only then that I began to understand what had happened. I would never have dared mention it to her, but Mahtab was rather less lissom than she may once have been, and considerably less so than her favourite authors demanded of her. She had, in short, ricked her back, and the screaming wasn't an esoteric part of The Two Wrestlers.

It took some time and several screams to get her leg from behind my neck. At one stage I thought it must stay there for ever, and that we would have to go around like a pair of bizarrely conjoined Siamese Twins. But eventually I got her disentangled and managed to pull and push her on to the bed—she was too substantial for lifting. She lay there, legs apart, moaning and groaning and occasionally squealing like a stuck pig.

Her earlier screams may not have carried as far as Calcutta, but they must have carried as far as the big house, for there now came a loud knocking on the front door, after which the bedroom door burst open and Harry rushed in brandishing a rather rusty tulwar. It was the worst of all situations, and Harry couldn't have taken it all in at first.

'Billee, my dear, whatever . . .'

Then he stopped short and stood there gawping at us. My mind was busy trying to arrive at some explanation, but it wouldn't work as nimbly as it usually does in emergencies. The excuse I finally came out with sounded thin, even to myself.

'I'm glad you got here . . . Just going to get you . . . Heard screams, rushed outside and found Mahtab on ground writhing in pain . . . About to try some massage . . .'

My voice was dying away by then for it seemed obvious to me that Harry wasn't even listening. He took a deep breath and then wailed like a banshee. Next he blubbed a bit and tore at his hair. Then he just stood and glared at us. After that he didn't seem to know what he should do. Windy though I was, I couldn't help feeling deeply sorry for the chap for it was clear that his upbringing had done nothing to equip him for such a situation. Any other Indian would have said something about Izzat and have gone for the two of us with the tulwar. Harry had become too anglicised for that, but not anglicised enough to be able to accept a cuckolding with a good grace and laugh the whole thing off.

He stood there for what seemed like hours, looking angrier and sulkier than I'd ever seen him. Then he hurled the tulwar at me, missed, put up his fists, put them down again, turned on his heel and stormed out of the room yelling:

'Don't you be thinking, Bunter, that I shall be overlooking this. Not at all. I shall most certainly be having something to be saying to you later.'

Mahtab had stopped groaning, squealing and going into spasm by now, and we were both silent for a while.

'That's torn it,' I then said.

'I shall be having to speak to Hurree,' said Mahtab, 'about terrible condition of drive. It is full of pit-holes over which person taking innocent walk at night will trip.'

We looked at one another and knew in our hearts that even when our two explanations had been put together they couldn't amount to anything very plausible.

'I wouldn't even try it, Mahtab,' I said. 'I know Harry's under your thumb, but I doubt he'll wear that one.'

Harry didn't come near the godown that day or for several days after, which was just as well since, as the putative shipper, I was busy supervising the loading of the indigo on to the *Thomas Grenville*. By the time this had been completed I had come close to believing that Mahtab might have got away with it and that Harry wasn't going to have something to say to me after all.

But it was on that day, when my self-confidence was beginning to return, that I had a stream of visitors to the little office I occupied by the godown. The first was Merry.

'You haven't been seen at the ACBC much lately, so I thought I ought to tell you that there may be something rum afoot.'

'How do you mean rum?'

'You know how much Coker and Thukoor dislike each other?'

'They ain't exactly David and Jonathan.'

'Quite. But the other night they seemed as thick as thieves. They were gabbling away to each other, and I heard Thukoor mention your name. Then Coker laughed like a jackass, and he ain't much given to laughing as you know, and clapped Thukoor on the back and bought him a drink. I can't help thinking they were planning to do you a mischief even though Thukoor's supposed to be your partner.'

'I doubt there was anything in it,' I said, 'but it was good of you to tell me.'

'Well, treat it as you like. But I know what scrapes you can get into, you fat chump. So I thought it best to tip you the wink. Verb. Sap?'

That last scrap of Bluecoat slang brought back so many memories that, despite the uneasiness his news had caused me, I felt truly touched. So I smiled at him and said, 'Verb. Sap.'

He had barely left when I had another and altogether more surprising visitor, for Mistress MacPherson came waddling in through the door. She ignored my surprise, looked around, and then said, pointing at my baboo:

'Can ye no' rid yoursel' o' yon for a bittie?'

I thought up an errand that would get rid of him for a while, bade Mistress MacPherson be seated, said a few words about the weather and old times, and then asked her what I could do for her. She looked at me with as much compassion as she could get on to her stolid face and said:

'It's no' whit ye can dae for me, ma puir laddie. It's whit Maggie MacPherson can dae for yew, an' that's little enow, mair's the peety.'

'I'm sure I don't know what there is you could do for me, and if there is, I still don't know why you should want to do it.'

'As to that last, Mr Bunter, Ah've ne'er been yin for forgettin' auld acquaintances and auld times. But afore I treat with the forepart of your obsairvation, Ah've a pair of questions for ye, an' Ah'll be wanting honest answers to 'em.'

'What questions are those?'

She leant across my desk and fixed me with a particularly beady eye. 'Ha' ye been fornicating an' adulterating with yin o' thon Thukoor's wives?'

It was the sort of question that hits you bang between the eyes, so I stuttered a bit before answering, 'Well, sort of . . .'

'Ah'm no preecisely an idjeet, laddy. Ah ken fine that when it comes to fornicating, you're a domned sight more likely to have been druv than led.'

'It was something like that, Mistress MacPherson.'

'Ah'm domn sure it was, but 'twas fornication an' adulteration all the same.'

'I'm afraid it must have been.'

'Ah also want to know if it's true that you're trying to make a heap o'siller for yoursel' by smuggling opium.'

That was a knock-out blow, and it took me some time to recover sufficiently to ask, 'How on earth did you get to know about that?'

'Then it is true?'

'Not exactly. The siller . . . the money wasn't going to be for myself, or only a small part of it. The rest was going to save Mr Thukoor from bankruptcy.'

'He isna worth saving from the De'il himsel'. But it's as I thocht. Ye're no' such a bad laddie, for all that you're in such a deal o' trouble.'

'I wish,' I said desperately, for I was getting very alarmed by now, 'that you'd tell me what sort of trouble you think I'm in.'

'It's no' whit Maggie MacPherson's thinking. It's whit thon Reginald's thinking.'

'Do you mean the Bishop?'

'Ah dinna. If Ah'd ony occasion tae be fameeliar wi' ma employer, Ah'd address him as *Oor* Reginald. *Thon* Reginald's the yin wha's bosun on the *Thomas Grenville*.'

'But ain't he supposed to be the chap who got you drunk and did you wrong?'

'That's as mebbe. But Time's a gey fine healer. So he an' masel' are jist aboot to come to an understanding.'

'An understanding? What sort of an understanding?'

'A soort as wull deal wi' whit the Bishop calls *Legitimayteeo per subsequent Matrimonials* an' wi' ma little Wully.'

It took me some time to follow her rendering of legal dog Latin. It must have taken even more to understand what she had followed it with, for I blurted out:

'Hold on a bit. Even you can't have a Little Wi . . .'

She cut me short at that point, for which I was thankful.

'Ah'm refairing tae ma wee bairn, wha's like tae gang thro' life nae better nor a baistard if thon Reginald and masel' dinna come to that understanding. The Bishop, guid mon, inseests on yin. He's e'en promised Reginald a position as Assistant Harbour Maister here yince he's got back frae Chinee, swallowed the anchor, an' made honest folk oot o' ma bairn an' masel'. Whit's mair, Reginald's wulling, which only gaes tae show what unlikely things a body wull do in order tae better himsel'.'

'Well I must say I never thought thon Reginald was a marrying man, but I wish you both happy with all my heart. But you still haven't told me what Reginald has to do with your presence here.'

'The twae o' us were tae meet last night tae finalise certain heads o' agreement, an' instead o' meeting me, he sent me this.'

She handed me the bosun's letter. It was written in a fine Italian hand which reminded me that Captain Manning had spoken of his bosun as a superior sort of man with a weakness for the classics.

Honoured Mistress Maggie,
This to inform you that cruel Fate and the Calcutta Excise men will prevent me from coming ashore tonight. The said Excise men are at this moment swarming all over our holds searching for contraband opium, enough of which has already been discovered to make it necessary to unload our entire cargo. So, sweet Chloe, your Daphnis will be busy swaying out barrels instead of dallying, as he had hoped, with the sweetest and kindest of all shepherdesses. The cargo was consigned to us by Mr Bunter, who will, I fear, have much to answer for. I have little affection, myself, for Mr Bunter, but I know that Fate has fashioned a net in which he, you, your Willy and myself are bound. So if you would forewarn him and bid him scarper, do so now, for tomorrow may be too late. But ere you do, sweet Chloe, 'twere best to inform the Bishop, for I would not have you involved in a devilishly tricky situation with nothing at the end of it for Mr Bunter but flight or imprisonment. Your aspiring and ever-affectionate Reginald.
Post Scriptum. Tomorrow night, perhaps: same time, same place?

I read it three times with increasing horror before I could say anything. And then all I could get out was:
'And did you show this to the Bishop?'
'Ah did that. And sair vexit he was at first. But then he bade

me tak' it to yew an' to tell yew tae dae naught afore speaking
tae him.'

'I'll do that if Mrs Heber isn't about.'

'She's awa' the noo wi' the bairns at Barrackpoor. The
Dean's gudewife is having a garden pairty.'

'Your Reginald—I don't mean the Bishop—says nothing
about how the Excise got on to the fact that there was opium
on the *Thomas Grenville*. I wonder how they found out.'

'Ah wouldna be surprised if it were thon Thukoor payin' ye
oot for fornicating an' adulterating wi' his wife.'

'He wouldn't have done that. It was his opium, and it will
ruin him to have lost it.'

'Ye'll hae to ask the Bishop aboot it. He's been making
enquiries all this forenoon, an' nae doot he kens more aboot it
all by noo than masel'.'

She stood up, laid an almost gentle hand on my shoulder,
whispered something about 'Ma puir laddie', and departed.

I was sitting there with my head in my hands trying to
make sense of it all when my next and last visitor sailed into
the room. Although she was muffled in shawls and had a black
chudda concealing her face I never doubted that it was
Mahtab. She took off her shawls and veil, seated herself, and
said with the utmost cheerfulness:

'My poor Billee. Things are not going very top-hole for
you.'

Such cheerfulness was intolerable.

'They can't be going very top-hole for you either. I'm
surprised Harry hasn't sent you back to your parents, cut your
throat or beaten you within an inch of your life.'

'But he is doing none of those things. As you can see, I am
very well, except that my back is still hurting.'

'Then Harry ain't doing his duty as an Indian and a husband.'

'Oh Hurree! I am always being able to manage Hurree.'

'And how did you manage him after that other night?'

'I am simply explaining how I was taking cooling walk
when you are rushing out on me like hungry tiger. Then you
are knocking me down and hurting my back. After that you
are dragging me to your bed and tearing my clothes off. If
Hurree had not been hero and been galloping up in time,

he would not have been saving me from fate worse than death.'

'He believed that guff?'

'Certainly he is believing it. How can he be saving face if he is not? But because he is, it is meaning, my poor Billee, that he is having to be very beastly to you. That is why he is telling the authorities about the opium.'

'I don't believe you. Harry's too fond of money and too near to ruin to sacrifice all the opium he bought just for that.'

'I don't know how he is arranging it, but he is not losing very much money. Last night he is telling that Mr Coker about it at dinner, and they are both laughing and drinking toasts to your downfalling.'

I've had many hard knocks in my life, but I've never suffered such abominable treachery. I was furious.

'God damn all Thukoors,' I roared. 'You betray me to Harry and Harry betrays me to the authorities. I wish I'd never met either of you.'

'It is not good to be getting so angry. "He that is slow to anger is better than the mighty." Proverbs, 16:12.'

I stared at her despairingly. There may have been tears in my eyes as I contemplated what all this meant.

'You realise that this means prison for me?'

'But of course. For many, many years. And Calcutta chokey is not good place for anyone fond of his grub.'

'I'll take Harry there with me. I swear I will. When it comes to court it'll only be his word against mine.'

'How little you are knowing, my poor Billee. What witnesses will you be calling? Hurree will be having ten, twenty, maybe thirty. It is much better you are running away.'

'How can I? They'll have a warrant out for me already, and all the ports and highways will be watched. Besides, I haven't more than fifty rupees on me.'

'You must be disguising yourself as Indian. As Bocas-waller perhaps, and then be making your way north out of Company jurisdiction. As for money, Mahtab is thinking of that.'

Here she placed a small bundle on my desk, opened it, and shook out several pieces of jewellery and a purse.

'The ruby rings and nose studs,' she said, 'were belonging to second wife, gold anklets and bracelets to third. The purse, with many gold mohurs, I am taking from strong-box under Hurree's charpoy.'

I've suffered from masterful women ever since birth without once being able to resent them for long. Here was another who had most vilely betrayed me to save her own skin and was now trying to help me at the expense of everyone in the Thukoor family excepting herself, looking at me cheerfully as though it was all the most natural thing to do. How could I have reacted except to pocket the loot and thank her?

'It is nothing,' she said. 'Teacher always must be caring for pupil. You were not very good pupil, Billee. I am thinking you are either lazy or not very interested. But I shall be missing you.'

I came damned near at that moment to apologising for not having done better with The Two Wrestlers and all the other tedious exercises she had forced on me. Instead I merely said, 'I shall miss you too.'

She got up and said briskly, 'And now you must be skedaddling from Calcutta ack-dum. Do not be lingering. "O generation of vipers, who hath warned you to flee from the wrath to come." Matthew, 3:7.'

I thought as she went out, still looking mighty cheerful, that that was as close as I'd ever heard her come to an appropriate quotation.

The Bishop, when I went to see him, wasn't looking nearly as cheerful as Mahtab. But he wasted no time on lectures.

'You know, William,' he said, 'I never did like that Thukoor fellow. And look what he's done to you now.'

'That's what I don't understand. It was his opium, and the money from it was supposed to save him from bankruptcy. And I never thought he was the sort of chap who'd cut off his nose to spite his face.'

'Or to pay you out for cuckolding him, heh? But you don't need to worry about him. His nose is still more or less intact, and so is his money.'

'Well I don't know how he managed it.'

'Do you know the fellow who's Attorney General of the Presidency?'

'No.'

'He's called Money, which is a little inappropriate since it's the one commodity he's most in need of. Expensive wife and a whole parcel of brats to educate.'

'I'm sorry for him, but where does he come into it?'

'I had it in confidence from the Governor General's private secretary that Money has accepted your friend Thukoor's claim that the opium was his and that you stole it from him and tried to smuggle it out of the country.'

'But Thukoor ain't supposed to own any opium.'

'He's got documents and witnesses to prove that he bought it on behalf of the East India Company.'

'The Devil he has.'

'The Devil certainly had a deal to do with it. But you can see what happens?'

'Not exactly.'

'Why, the Company will have to pay Thukoor the full value of the opium plus a reward of ten per centum ad valorem for laying an information against you. So he'll get his money back, the impecunious Mr Money will probably pocket the ten per centum, and you'll go to prison. How could a cuckolded husband do better?'

'I only wish I'd wanted to cuckold him.'

'Come, my boy. I don't want to hear the details of your sordid amours. They ain't fit subjects for a Bishop's ears. What we must talk about is how to get you away from here.'

'Mahtab suggested . . .'

'Mahtab?'

'The sordid amour, my Lord.'

'Quite, quite. Well, get on with it. What did she suggest?'

'That I should try to get north and out of Company territory disguised as an Indian.'

'Intelligent woman. I've been thinking along those lines meself. But not as an Indian. You'd not get away with it.'

'Then as what? I'd not get very far as Billy Bunter. I ain't exactly what you'd call inconspicuous.'

'I realise that. I've been thinking all morning of Father Mecazinas. Do you remember him? It was during your time with me.'

I had to remember Father Jacob Mecazinas if only because he was the only person I ever came across who had caused the Bishop to lose his temper. It had happened like this.

I had come into the study one morning with a note for the Bishop which stated that this same Father Mecazinas, having recently arrived from Rome, would give himself the pleasure of calling on the Bishop of All-India that midday. The Bishop, who liked nothing better than a long oecumenical discussion, rubbed his hands and said:

'Fresh from Rome, heh? He's probably been sent by the Pope. We must lunch him well, William. I know these Vatican magnificoes. They never stint themselves. I think some of the Château Lafitte, don't you? Champagne first, perhaps, and some of the best port at the end. And tell Mrs Heber that I want the cooks to knock up two or three extra removes and something more in the way of puddings.'

The Father, when he arrived, turned out to be a fairly young but already portly sort of man wearing a cheerful expression, a triangular hat, and a long, rusty black cassock. He greeted the Bishop in such broken English that the Bishop, out of politeness, answered him in Italian. When this didn't go down very well he switched to French, but the Father's French proved to be even worse than his English. The Bishop next tried him in Latin and then in Greek, but I could see that his hopes of a long and interesting discussion of theological and philosophical problems were rapidly fading. It was then that he discovered that he was dealing, not with an Italian magnifico from the Vatican, but with an Armenian from Tiflis whose one and only visit to Rome had been undertaken fifteen years previously, as a youthful seminarist. After that they managed to sustain a conversation of sorts in a mixture of Russian, Turkish and dog-English.

It was hard work, and all three of us were thankful to break off for a meal. I'm a good trencherman myself, but it soon became clear that the language Father Mecazinas liked best was the language of guttling and guzzling. The Bishop watched him with amazement as he helped himself three times to every dish offered him. But what irritated him most, I think, was that each gobbled mouthful had to be washed down with a deep swig of the Château Lafitte. It was, he said to me after, like watching a bricklayer mix his mortar with wine rather than water.

The Bishop's temper finally broke when, after the port and

the brandy, Father Mecazinas produced a grubby note book and asked how much the Bishop would contribute to the fund for the support of indigent widowers in Tiflis.

'Sir,' roared the Bishop. 'You may, or may not, be a brother of the cloth. But I believe you to be no more than a mendicant charlatan. A mere beggar, Sir, who under the pretence of coming to me from the Bishop of Rome, has wasted my time, eaten my food, insulted my cellar, exhausted my patience, and now expects to be paid for it.'

The good Father was not in the least upset. He gave the Bishop to understand, in one and a half languages, that he had met with a similar reception from similar churchmen in half a dozen countries. This would not, however, prevent him from doing his duty by the indigent widowers of Tiflis, on whose behalf he had recently travelled from the Black Sea to the Indian Ocean and beyond. He then gave a profound belch, blessed us both, and departed.

Remembering all this, I was naturally surprised that the Bishop should have brought his name up. 'What,' I asked him, 'has Father Mecazinas to do with my escaping from Company territory?'

'I have,' said the Bishop, 'a three-cornered hat, with a calotte to go under it, a long black cassock, and a false beard I once used in amateur theatricals when I played Shylock in an undergraduate production of *The Merchant of Venice*. Now you are not altogether unlike Father Mecazinas in that you are portly and wear spectacles. If you also wore the hat, cassock and beard, you would look very like him indeed.'

'That may be, but I still don't see what good that would do me.'

'He's become a familiar figure on the roads of India, having cadged and begged his way along them for the best part of five years. If you became a deutero-Mecazinas, you would pass almost unnoticed wherever you went.'

'But I'd still have to go a long way before I'd be out of the clutches of John Company.'

'It so happens,' said the Bishop, 'that I have a young curate, freshly out from England, whom I am sending to Lucknow to act as chaplain and secretary to our Residency there. He will, of course, travel officially, and with an escort of sepoys provided by the government. But he knows little or nothing of the languages of this country, and so requires an interpreter. You, William, will, as Father Mecazinas, be that interpreter.'

It was, I had to admit, a brilliant idea, even if it entailed wearing a false beard and speaking only broken Russian and even more broken English with the curate.

'But,' I said, 'Oudh is still in the sphere of British influence, even if we have not yet annexed it. I can hardly believe that I would be altogether safe in Lucknow.'

'I'm inclined to agree with you,' said the Bishop. 'But Oudh borders on the Punjaub, and you have, I believe, a powerful friend at Lahore in the shape of Colonel Huggins.'

'But there is also the Maharajah living in Lahore. And, if you remember, I had to leave that city in haste to avoid his attentions.'

'Runjeet Singh will not be in Lahore. Soon there will be held a great Durbar at Ruper, on the banks of the Sutlej, which marks the boundary of his spheres of influence and our own. There he is to confer with the Governor General regarding the renewing of his treaty with the British. This is of such importance to the Maharajah that he will spend the next six months in the camp he has set up there, preparing to receive the Governor General as splendidly and as imposingly as he can. Impressions are important, William, when it comes to drawing up treaties. So you will be safe in Lahore until the rains come, and by that time you must have arranged to travel through Persia and Turkey so that you can arrive somewhere whence you can take ship to England.'

'There's nothing else for it, I suppose.'

'Nothing. The beard and the cassock are in my bedroom, and the curate and his escort leave tonight.'

I gave my good and dear friend the Bishop a look which, I hoped, expressed all the gratitude I felt and none of the doubts I entertained concerning the outcome of his plan. He, for his part, looked at me gravely and said:

'I have never, William, endeavoured either by example or precept to lead you to better things. You are, I know, indolent, greedy and lamentably weak. But you have helped me with my translations, you have saved me from Omar Khayyam, and you did, whilst you were with me, do something to divert Mrs Heber's attention from me to yourself.'

'I did what I could, and wish I could have done more.'

'I have,' he continued, 'taken it on myself to raid the Fund for Distressed Missionaries to the tune of one thousand rupees. Take this purse, put on your beard, and be on your way.'

29   *The Road to Lahore*

The Bishop's plan worked well in that it eventually got me as far as Lucknow, but I could not decide whether the two months we spent on the road were enjoyable ones or not. I found my beard and cassock devilish hot and uncomfortable, besides which being treated as some sort of inferior foreigner who could only communicate with the curate in a mixture of dog-English, dog-Latin and dumb crambo became tedious. On the other hand every day's journey took me farther from my enemies and I actually began to enjoy the part I was playing. As I worked myself into the role, I began to believe that not even Garrick himself could have played Father Mecazinas better; and amazingly enough everyone, Indian or otherwise, accepted me as a mendicant fakir of dubious origins working his way across India as interpreter to a raw young English curate.

Fortunately I never had a large audience to play to. The roads north were so crowded with convoys of military and civilians all moving towards the Sutlej and the great Durbar that no one took any notice of our small and not very distinguished party. And then, as luck would have it, I discovered when we got to Lucknow that another party, headed this time by an important government official, was just about to set off for Lahore. It is all very well, thought I, to travel hopefully, but it's always wiser, in India, to travel in convoy. And so I delivered my curate to the Residency and hurried off to attach myself to this Lahore convoy.

It was quite a large one, for no important British official can travel without his full complement of secretaries, moonshies, bearers, grooms, grass-cutters, water-carriers, cooks and so on, together with all the female camp-followers necessary to their comfort, not to mention the cavalry escort that will ensure the official's safety and bear testimony to his impor-tance. The escort of native lancers was commanded, in this case, by an apple-cheeked subaltern only recently out from England, and it was to him that I presented myself. He looked doubtfully at my beard and filthy cassock and listened patiently to my Anglo-Latin-Armenian babble and then said:

'I'm not sure I know what you're getting at, Your Reverence . . .'

'Ees Father . . . Father Mecazinas.'

'Well, Father Nicodemus, I gather you want to join the convoy.'

'Ees right, my son, for which Heaven will be blessing you.'

'Better not start any blessing business yet. If you want to travel with us you'll have to get permission from the Great Man himself. It's his convoy and he decides who travels in it.'

'Am understanding. When can I be seeing Great Man?'

'Best not call him that or he might think you're poking fun. He's Chief Protocol Secretary to the Governor General, and I'll find out if you can see him.'

It took some time to get an audience but I was eventually admitted to the great man's raotee, which was more of a lordly pavilion than a mere tent. He was bent over a travelling desk scribbling away and didn't even look up as a secretary ushered me in. After a while the secretary coughed and said:

'The . . . er . . . clerical person I told you about, Sir. So far as I can gather he wants permission to travel with us to Lahore, but he don't appear to speak much English.'

'Why,' asked the great man, still scribbling away, 'don't he travel there on his own?'

The secretary, however, had withdrawn, so I answered that question myself.

'Ees molto pericoloso, Excellency, to be travelling alone. Maybe dacoits is robbing and cutting throats.'

He looked up from his papers; and there, looking at me in a tetchy sort of way, was the cheerful Wykehamist who had lost his straw hat at the Calcutta Cup cricket match and then collaborated so happily in the lop-arsing of Coker. I even remembered his name, Ponsonby-Harris, and that he was reputed to be a very important man indeed in Government House circles.

I realised that if I gave way to panic I was lost, and that only Bunter impudence and Bunter acting skills could save me. I would have to out-Garrick Garrick. For this was no raw young curate or subaltern unable to tell the difference between an Armenian and an Eskimo. This was a man who knew the world, India, and possibly Bunter, only too well. So I executed several bows, each one of which allowed me to draw back a little from the lamplight, and then stood up straight, waved my arms about in a highly Armenian fashion, and said:

'I am humbly praying Excellency to save me from dacoits.'

He looked at me in a puzzled sort of way as though he were trying to remember whether he'd ever seen me before. 'Nonsense.'

No Armenian, thought I, could be expected to understand such a bluff, Anglo-Saxon attitude. Consequently I, also, reverted to monosyllables.

'Pliz?'

'I said "nonsense". No sane dacoit would think you were worth robbing, let alone murdering. And why, may I ask, are you so keen to get to Lahore if you're so windy about travelling?'

'Pliz?'

He sighed and repeated the question, speaking slowly and loudly as one has to when dealing with foreigners. 'Why . . . you . . . go . . . Lahore?'

'Ah, Excellence, now ees understanding. Ees collecting for charity.'

'You won't get much of that out of Runjeet Singh, or anyone else in Lahore.'

'Ees good mans everywhere, even in Lahore.'

'You take a more Christian view than I do,' said he, 'but then that's part of your job.'

He's swallowed it, thought I, and relaxed. Ponsonby-Harris continued to look at me and then said, quite innocently:

'What charity are you collecting for, Father?'

'Ees poor widow mans in Tiflis.'

'Sounds rum to me.'

And that was where I went wrong. I was so convinced that I had out-Garricked him that I grew cocky and played the buffoon.

'Ees giving rum?' said I, grinning at him. 'Ees very kind. I am accepting large glass—neat if you don't mind.'

The last bit had slipped out in pure English, besides which rum ain't the sort of drink Armenians are supposed to know about. Ponsonby-Harris's eyes narrowed. I could see that he'd suddenly got a distinct smell of rat in his nostrils.

'You did,' said he, 'mention Tiflis. Is that where you come from?'

'Ees beloved birthplace.'

'Then you must be a Russian.'

I didn't much like this. Ever since the Treaty of Tilsit when Boney agreed that the Tsar could have a free hand in India so long as he had a similar one in Turkey, our people in India had become mighty suspicious of any Russians found travelling in either British territory or one of the Native States. All were thought, not unreasonably, to be either spies or agents.

'No, no, no, not at all Russ. Am Armenian. Tiflis is being in . . .' here I couldn't remember where Tiflis actually was and so fell into an incoherence which Ponsonby-Harris smiled at.

'Tiflis, Reverend Father,' said he, 'is in Georgia, and Georgia's been part of Russia ever since 1805.'

'Pliz?' said I, falling back on monosyllables, which seemed to annoy Ponsonby-Harris for he now stuck his face close to mine and said:

'Tell you what, Reverend Father, I don't believe you're a Reverend Father at all. I believe you're a Russian spy trying to attach himself to my mission in order to stir up mischief between us and the Sikhs.'

'Ees absolutely not the case.'

'And as a spy,' he continued, 'I shall hand you over to the military with orders to shoot you.'

'You can't do that,' said I. 'We ain't on British territory and I haven't even been tried.'

'Hallo!' said he. 'So you've suddenly discovered you can talk proper English. I thought that accent of yours might be as false as that beard obviously is.'

And with that he stretched out a hand and gave my beard a tug. When it came away he stared into my face with a growing mixture of disappointment and incredulity.

'Upon my soul,' said he, 'I do believe you're Bunter.'

The game was up, Garrick was out, and I couldn't decide whether to be relieved or not. It was one thing to be hauled back to Calcutta and thrown into the chokey for opium smuggling, but quite another to be shot out of hand as a Russian spy.

'And what,' said I, 'if I am? If I'm Bunter I can't be a Russian spy. And since we're no longer on British territory I don't see what you can do about my being Bunter.'

He glared at me, for I do believe he'd greatly have preferred me to be a Russian. His disappointment revived my cockiness, so I then said:

'And now that we've sorted out who I am, what about that rum?'

I thought, for a moment, that he was going to strike me for, like all bureaucrats, he resented impudence. But to give him his due he was, as I'd always thought, a remarkably cheerful man for a Wykehamist. He now drew up a camp stool, plumped himself down on it, looked at my filthy cassock and the equally filthy beard he still held in his hand and burst into a loud and prolonged fit of laughter. And then, when he'd finally recovered himself, he clapped his hands and when a bearer appeared ordered 'two burra brandy-panee ack-dum'.

'You ain't a naval man,' he said, almost apologetically, though he was still giggling, 'so I don't suppose you really prefer rum to brandy.'

'What made you suspicious?' I asked, pulling up another camp stool, seating myself, and relieving him of my beard.

'Well, I was once Second Secretary in Constantinople, and I've met a good many more Armenians than you ever have. Besides which I didn't altogether trust your accent, and I could see where your beard was hooked over your ears.'

'And that made you think I was a Russian spy?'

'Not at first. You ain't really the make and shape for a spy. But I'd been warned that there were at least half a dozen of 'em in the Punjaub trying to persuade the Sikhs to make a treaty with the Tsar rather than with us, so it was natural to think that you were one of 'em.'

'And would you really have had me shot?'

'Of course, but not before I'd asked you a few questions.'

He looked at me and I suddenly realised with a shudder how cruel a thoroughly cheerful man could look.

'But that's enough of that,' he continued. 'Sadly enough you're not a spy but Bunter, and I suppose that you're on the run because of that opium affair.'

'I am,' said I in a dignified manner, 'trying to save the authorities from getting involved in a miscarriage of justice. I've been the victim of a conspiracy.'

'You mean that your old pal Thukoor shopped you?'

My jaw may or may not have dropped.

'How on earth did you know about that?'

'Had it from the Governor General himself, who had it originally, of course, from the late Bishop Heber.'

'Did you say the *late* Bishop Heber?'

'Didn't you know?'

'I've been Father Mecazinas and on the road for the past two months.'

'That explains it. The dear chap snuffed it less than a month ago. Only heard about it meself when I was in Lucknow. It seems he got over-heated climbing around the old fort in Trichinapalli, which he said reminded him strongly of Edinburgh Castle. Got back, jumped into a cold bath, and that was that . . . I say, don't give way, old chap', he went on, embarrassed. 'I had no idea that it would upset you so much.'

I don't know how long I just stood there and blubbed, but I do know that Ponsonby-Harris kept on talking to me, which was probably the least embarrassing thing he could do.

'It would not be wise,' he said, 'to return to Calcutta. Amongst other things you'd run into Thukoor and Coker. But so long as you keep away from British territory I don't think the authorities are going to chase after you.'

There was nothing he could have said better calculated to quieten my sobs.

'Does that mean there are no charges against me?'

'Hardly. After all, you were trying to smuggle opium, and John Company never likes that. Hits 'em in the pocket. But it hasn't hit them this time.'

'What do you mean?'

'Well, after the late Bishop, bless his cheerful soul, spoke to the Governor General, H.E. decided to take a personal interest in your case. One thing then led to another. That fellow Money got his fingers rapped after they'd had Thukoor up for fresh questioning. And the long and the short of it was that the opium was confiscated without a penny of compensation or reward being paid to anyone. And now, since it has cost the Company nothing and will sell for a tidy sum in Canton by and by, the Company ain't nearly so keen on putting you in chokey.'

'Thank God for that.'

'But it don't mean that your friends Thukoor and Coker ain't looking for you, and that Thukoor chap seems to know something about anyone who travels the roads of India. I have been told they've come north with half a dozen of the prettiest native cut-throats you've ever seen, asking everyone whether a fat party wearing spectacles has passed by lately. The last I heard was they were no more than a day's journey from Lucknow.'

'In that case you must save me from them.'

He looked at me for a while and then grinned. 'I'll help you as far as Lahore. Can't ever forget the night you and I cured Coker's snake bite. Most comical thing I've come across in years and I've never been able to refuse anything to a chap who's made me laugh.'

'God bless you,' said I.

He looked a bit more serious then. 'But mark you,' said he. 'You're on your own once we get to Lahore. There's only so much a Chief Secretary can do helping a fugitive from British justice. What's more, you'll have to go on being Father Mecazinas. It could save me from H.E.'s wrath and it might still save you from Thukoor and Coker. So if you have to address me at all whilst we're actually on the road, make sure you do so in that awful Armenian accent of yours.'

Ponsonby-Harris was as good as his word. When we set out the next morning for Lahore, Father Mecazinas was a lowly and unconsidered member of his entourage. Since I was no longer even an interpreter, I had to travel and camp with the grooms, grass-cutters and the rest of the camp followers which meant that I slept hard and fed sparsely.

But although Ponsonby-Harris ignored my very existence for most of the time we were on the road, he did, occasionally, send for me in secret after we had camped for the night and then, after he had dismissed his bearers and secretaries, the two of us would sit down together to enjoy a cold supper and a bottle or two. And enjoy was the word. After nearly three months of being Father Mecazinas I would have enjoyed the company of any Englishman, Wykehamist or not.

I'm not saying that Ponsonby-Harris wouldn't have been good company whatever school he'd gone to. But he was inclined, towards the end of a second bottle, to carry on at length about the intricacies of his job, the importance of his present mission, and the civilising value of all protocol. I listened to all this because I couldn't decently avoid it, and because these late suppers gave me a chance to get rid of my beard, which interfered with my eating, and to have something better to eat than the communal rice and curry and something considerably better to drink than doodh panee or, if I was lucky, sugar-water.

It was on the last of these occasions, when we were no more than two days' travel from Lahore, that Ponsonby-Harris insisted on demonstrating to me the importance of his role in the forthcoming Durbar.

'It will,' said he, 'settle the shape of India for the next forty years, and yet it can't even start until I give the off.'

'Really,' said I, helping myself to another glass.

'I don't think,' said he, 'that you appreciate the true importance of protocol. You can't have a treaty without a durbar, and you can't have a durbar without protocol. That's the only reason for this mission. Nothing can happen until I've arranged things with my Sikh opposite number.'

'But I thought that the Durbar's been arranged so that the Governor General and Runjeet Singh can sign a Treaty, and that the Treaty fixes the boundaries between ourselves and the Sikhs. I don't see what protocol's got to do with that.'

'Then you don't know anything about protocol. Let me,' said he, fixing me with a rather glassy eye, 'give you an example. Where do you think the Durbar should actually be held? North bank of the Sutlej in Sikh territory, or south bank in ours?'

'Is that important?'

'My dear fellow, of course it's important. Might even have to settle in the end for a raft in the middle of the river, just as that damned fellow Boney did when he met the Tsar at Tilsit in '07. Very hot on protocol, the Frogs.'

'I must confess,' said I, stifling a yawn, 'that I hadn't thought about it.'

'Of course you haven't. Not your pigeon. But have you considered the problem of military reviews? H.E. will have the best part of five thousand troops—horse, foot and artillery—with him. The Maharajah's bound to have three times that number. Now which of 'em, do you think, should review t'other's forces first? And what about the manoeuvres, heh? They're bound to want to show off to each other. But suppose you get those Sikh gunners putting on an artillery display. Some of 'em are bound to forget to load with blanks, and what happens then?'

'Tricky,' said I.

'Tricky! It could easily land us in a Sikh War which is the one thing we want to avoid. That's why my opposite number and I will have to deal with manoeuvres before ever they start. And then there's the whole question of reciprocal banquets.'

This sounded a bit more in my line, so I asked him where protocol came into banquets.

'It comes in,' said he, smashing his fist down on the table, 'in relation to precedence, and it's my job to see that we get in first.'

'I don't quite follow you.'

'Well, is it to be H.E for Maharajah or Maharajah for H.E? That will set the whole sequence of things since there will be Political Secretary for Grand Vizier, Grand Vizier for Political Secretary and so on right down to mere Generals and Third Secretaries. What's more, who of 'em gets invited to which?

I tell you, Bunter, drawing up the Treaty's going to be mere child's play compared with arranging the protocol.'

A surfeit of grub, drink and protocol was lulling me into a torpor when I was abruptly recalled to some of the dangers of my position by an altercation outside in the lines. This had started with the sound of a horse galloping up close to the raotee following which there was a challenge from the guard and a good deal of heated argument. Finally Ponsonby-Harris's secretary came scuttling in wearing nightdress and nightcap to whisper in his master's ear.

'Is he, by God,' said Ponsonby-Harris, darting a quick look at me. 'And what may Mr Coker be wanting of me at this time of night?'

If Ponsonby-Harris had lost his glassy look I had just acquired a terrified one. I shrank back into the shadows as I hastily put on my beard and returned to being Father Mecazinas. The secretary was given no time to reply for the sentry outside the entrance was brushed aside and a wild-looking, travel-stained and weary Coker lurched into the tent.

'And what,' enquired Ponsonby-Harris icily, 'does this intrusion mean, Mr Coker?'

Coker, who was in civilian clothes, started to salute, thought better of it, bowed instead and said, 'So you do remember me, Sir?'

'Couldn't ever forget you, seeing that we were once cheek by jowl so to speak. But that don't give you the right, young feller, to burst in on me like this well after midnight.'

'Your pardon, Sir, but I've been riding all day and am somewhat fatigued. May I sit down?'

Coker had seated himself on a camp stool and was reaching for one of the bottles on the table when he was blasted out of seat and bottle by a roar from Ponsonby-Harris who seemed determined to show Coker the sort of manners that makyth a Winchester man when he's annoyed.

'Indeed you may not sit down and you'll leave my claret alone however far you've ridden. And now, Sir, kindly explain this intrusion.'

Bullies seldom appreciate being bullied and Coker was so taken aback by this reception that he paid no attention to anyone except the red-faced man who was glaring and roaring at him from the other side of the table.

'I must declare, Sir,' said he, attempting to bluster, 'that I object to your tone.'

'And I,' said Ponsonby-Harris, 'object to your presence. Kindly explain yourself, Sir, before I have you thrown out.'

'That ain't the way,' said Coker, attempting now to wheedle, 'for one Briton to greet another when they meet in the middle of nowhere.'

'No true Briton ever intrudes on another Briton unless he's invited to.'

Coker flushed at this. 'You might at least let me sit down and wash some of the dust from my throat before I explain myself.'

'Jenkins,' Ponsonby-Harris growled at his secretary, 'give the man a stool and a glass of wine before throwing him out of here.'

The nightcapped Jenkins, who was half Coker's size, flutteringly did what he was told. From my place in the shadows I was delighted to see that Coker, tired though he was, took care to seat himself on no more than one buttock. He tossed off his glass of claret before he spoke, and then he clearly made a considerable effort to placate his reluctant and angry host.

'Sir,' said he, eventually. 'We both serve His Majesty and the cause of British justice in our different ways.'

'That's as may be.'

'I am, Sir, in hot pursuit of a fugitive from that justice and have a right to call on every loyal subject to assist me in that pursuit.'

'Don't know what you're talking about, and I don't believe you do either.'

'You'll have heard of that dangerous criminal Bunter, I suppose,' Coker went on. 'Well, my latest information, Sir, is that he's travelling in your convoy, Sir, and in disguise, Sir, and I propose to apprehend him and take him back to Calcutta.'

'Jenkins,' said Ponsonby-Harris. 'Have we a Bunter travelling with us?'

'Oh no, Sir,' said Jenkins.

'Well, Mr Coker, will you take Jenkins's word for it, or do

you wish to examine everyone, black, brown or white in this encampment? Perhaps you would like to start here where, as you see, there are only myself, Jenkins who's not big enough to be a criminal, and Father Mecazinas over there, who's a worthy Armenian priest and don't speak much English.'

Coker cast a quick glance at me and I wagged my beard at him, waved my arms a little and said, 'Pliz?'

That finished him. He stood up and said curtly, 'I shall, of course, take your word for it, Sir, even though I remember that you and that same Bunter were as thick as thieves the night you so wantonly assaulted me.'

'Mr Coker,' said Ponsonby-Harris. 'Would you prefer to walk out or be thrown out?'

'I shan't forget this,' said Coker. 'And don't think I'll abandon my search for Bunter, whether you're hiding him or not. I bid you good-night, Sir.'

'Good morning would be more appropriate. But sweet dreams, Mr Coker, none the less.'

I was panting and sweating so much by the time Coker departed that Ponsonby-Harris had to pour the best part of another bottle of claret down me before I was restored to any degree of equanimity. Two days later we reached Lahore. Ponsonby-Harris bustled off to embark on his protocolian duties. And I, still wearing my beard and cassock, set off to find D'Arcy Huggins.

30   *The Road to Sumroo*

The Huggins's place, when I reached it, seemed strangely deserted. There was no chuprassee at the gates, no malees or mehturs about the grounds, and when I knocked on the front door there was no khansaman to answer that knock. So I let myself in to what seemed, at first, a quite empty mansion. But then, hearing footsteps overhead, I went up the great marble staircase and into the large, over-furnished, crimson-and-gilt salon I remembered from my previous visit. There I found, wandering aimlessly about, an oddly apathetic and lethargic Maria.

Even after I'd convinced her that the beard and cassock concealed her old chum Billy Bunter she refused, to my chagrin, to show either interest or pleasure in my arrival. So, since my business was with her husband rather than herself, I came quickly to the point.

'Where on earth,' said I, 'is D'Arcy?'

She didn't answer, and so I went on:

'I suppose he's gone off with the pultuns to Ruper, preparing for the Durbar?'

This did get a reply from her, although not the one I expected.

'He's gone off, all right, but not with the Army. He's dead.'

If I thought more about my loss than hers at that moment, it was because it began to look as if all my efforts to get to Lahore had been wasted.

'That,' said I, 'is a bloody shame and deuced inconvenient.'

This seemed to surprise her for she said, 'I thought you didn't like him.'

'Nor I do . . . did. But I do . . . did badly need his help.'

'Well he can't help you or anyone else now.'

It seemed to me that she was unnerved and so deserving a little sympathy.

'It must have been a dreadful shock for you, my dear. When did it happen?'

'Last Thursday.'

'Fever, cholera, booze or old age?'

'Something a deal more sudden.'

'Well, you mustn't fret too much about it, even though it does leave me in a pickle. Just remember that you always wanted to be a rich young widow and think of the stir you'll make in Coram Street when you turn up there with half the wealth of the Punjaub in your bank account.'

'As I won't have even enough for a gharry,' she said bitterly, 'I don't see how I'll ever get to Coram Street, let alone make a stir.'

'But you always said that D'Arcy was as rich as Croesus. Don't tell me it's all been left away from you.'

'Not left away: taken away.'

'I don't understand you, Maria. You used to be such a jolly, open, candid sort of girl, and now you're being tiresomely cryptical.'

'Cryptical, Billy? There ain't anything very cryptical about being torn apart by wild elephants in front of the Maharajah and a large part of the population of Lahore.'

'Good God! Is that how D'Arcy snuffed it?'

'Yes.'

'Do you really mean torn apart? By wild elephants?'

'Well, they weren't tame ones.'

'At Runjeet Singh's orders?'

'The fat little monster sat there just to see that they were carried out.'

'Typical of him,' said I. 'Anyone less ostentatious would have been content to do the job with wild horses.'

'Horses or elephants—it would have come to the same. The only blessing was that he'd always been notably weak in the joints.'

I twitched my shoulders uneasily and became more determined than ever not to renew my acquaintance with Runjeet Singh.

'Poor Maria,' I said. 'And, of course, poor D'Arcy. Whatever had he done to deserve such a fate?'

'I'm not altogether certain he did deserve it. But you'll remember that he'd always done a certain amount of private dealing as a sideline?'

'Now you mention it, I do.'

'If there was one thing poor D'Arcy hated, it was to lose money, and he'd lost a deal of it last year speculating in indigo.'

'Indigo!'

'Yes. It seems some scoundrelly Calcutta merchant had rigged the market against him. So he thought he'd recoup by doing something he'd sworn he'd never do.'

'What was that?'

'He began to shave bits off, here and there, from the soldiers' pay and ration allowances which he controlled as

Commissary General. The sepoys began to grumble and complained, in the end, to the Maharajah, who was furious. And that's why D'Arcy was given to the elephants.'

'Given to the elephants just for dipping his fingers into public funds? I can't believe it. The whole of India, British and Native, is run by chaps who dip their fingers into public funds. How do you think the Nabobs make enough to retire on and to buy their titles, estates and seats in Parliament? I'm damned if I can see why Runjeet Singh should object to that.'

'Oh he doesn't object to it in general. He does a deal of dipping himself, and he's perfectly prepared to let others shave what they can off the taxes, rents and charities under their control. But the one thing he won't let anyone do is shave anything off the troops. That's why he's the only ruler in India who's never had an Army mutiny.'

'I suppose that's why my old friend the Bishop always referred to him as the Punjaubi Napoleon. All the same, it was a bit hard to throw poor old D'Arcy to the elephants. Where does that leave you, now?'

There was something of the old Maria Jewkes in her reply.

'In the shit, I fear. They've clapped a confiscation order on everything D'Arcy ever owned, and that old goat, the Maharajah's Treasurer, has been charged with taking an inventory of everything the servants haven't already pinched. They departed en masse just as soon as D'Arcy had been fragmented.'

'I do hope you've managed to salt something away.'

'The only things of any value they don't already know about are the ruby ring and pearls you gave back to D'Arcy. They think you took them with you to Calcutta. But I've got them here, sewn into my bodice.'

That, of course, accounted for her burgeoning and more than usually lumpy appearance.

'But what,' I now asked, 'is going to happen to you?'

'What do you think can happen to an Englishwoman who's been widowed, stripped down to her bones, and left at the mercy of a ruffian like Runjeet Singh?'

She looked so brave and yet so vulnerable as she courageously faced her future, that something which is seldom touched in Bunter, a certain altruism, was gently fingered if not violently poked. I almost forgot my concern for my own skin in worrying about Maria's.

'Maria,' I said firmly. 'There are two things you must now do. You must appeal for help to a chap called Ponsonby-Harris. He's in camp just outside Lahore at this very moment. You must tell him that you're a British subject and a widow, that you are, through no fault of your own, in distressed and distressing circumstances, and that you require to be repatriated. He can't, as a servant of the Crown, refuse to help you, and Runjeet Singh wouldn't dare imperil the Treaty by interfering.'

'If I can get to your Ponsonby-Harris,' said Maria, 'I will. And what's the second thing I must do?'

It was improvident and reckless of me, but I'm still proud of having risen to the occasion. I fished inside my cassock and brought out the trinkets and the purse of gold mohurs Mahtab had stolen for me.

'You must add these,' said I, 'to the ruby and the pearls. And if there ain't room for them inside your bodice, you must find room for them inside something else.'

'And what,' asked Maria, 'do you want me to do with them?'

'Spend what you need to pay for your passage to England and for your upkeep once you get there. If there's anything left when I get back—which I hope to do by some means or other—then we'll go into partnership over it.'

For the first time since my arrival she smiled.

'What sort of partnership,' she whispered, 'do you contemplate?'

I don't know how I'd have got out of that difficulty if there hadn't been a sudden clatter of horsemen in the grounds. I went to the window and saw that a troop of Sikh cavalry was dismounting outside the house, and that whilst one section was deploying around it, another was entering it.

We heard a trampling on the stairs, and I was just about to ask Maria what it all meant when the door was flung open. The troopers marched in and arranged themselves around the walls. They were followed by a fat, bespectacled baboo wearing a dirty dhoti, and he was followed by that tittering, tottering old horror, the Maharajah's Treasurer.

This threw me into a great funk, for the last thing I wanted was to be recognised. Maria, however, was less put out. She drew herself up to as great a height as her dumpiness would permit and said:

'And what the hell are you doing here?'

That, I thought, is just how John Bull himself would have looked if he'd been a female, or Joan of Arc, if she hadn't been a Frog. But I, being neither, clapped on my hat, fluffed out my beard, and, turning my back on them all, examined one of the Persian court paintings that hung on the wall.

The Treasurer said nothing, but waved the baboo forward. That gentleman, having wiped his spectacles and cleared his throat, began to read from a document he held in his hand. What it had to say, shorn of its legal jargon, boiled down to this.

It was a warrant issued by the Maharajah Runjeet Singh, Lion of the Punjaub, Light of the Sikhs, Ruler of the Land of the Five Rivers and so on, ordering the discovery and confiscation of all monies, articles, properties real and personal, chattels, hereditaments, and so on and so on, belonging to or once in the possession of the late Colonel D'Arcy Huggins Sahib, once Commissary General to the Armies of the Punjaub. It was therefore ordered, required and demanded that Maria Huggins, widow of the aforesaid Colonel D'Arcy Huggins, should forthwith and at once surrender control of all such articles, monies etcetera to the herewith designated authority: viz the Treasurer to his Royal Highness the Maharajah Runjeet Singh Lion of and so on and so on.

When the baboo had finished this rigmarole he nodded to the havildar who sent his men off in pairs to occupy every room whilst the baboo, producing a taper, sealing wax and ribbon, proceeded to go round every item of furniture fixing a damned great seal on everything from pictures to armchairs. In due course he came to the Persian court painting and, thrusting himself between me and it, forced me to turn round and move away. This attracted the Treasurer's attention to me for the first time.

'Who,' he said, his white beard wagging with suspicion, 'is this?'

I thought it best to say nothing, so Maria answered.

'A man of religion who has come to pray with me and comfort me in my grief.'

The trouble was that she didn't look very grief-stricken. The Treasurer looked first at her and then at me, after which he came up to me and said:

'We allow few men of your religion into the holy lands of the Sikhs, and I have long known every missionary who has come here. You I do not know. How got you here?'

I bowed and joined my hands together in the Indian gesture of greeting and respect known as namaste. That seemed only to make him suspicious.

'It is not thus that missionaries hold their hands when they pray. Would you mock us because we are Indians?'

With that he whipped off my hat in order, I suppose, to get a look at my face. Unfortunately he did this so briskly that he brought away my beard with it. He stared for a moment, and then a smile came across his face.

'Why,' said he, 'it is Bunter Sahib. The great white warthog. He whose buttocks are like unto two white and conjoined moons.'

I blinked at him and said, 'Hang on. There's a lady present.' He took no notice of that. 'What a pity it is that His Highness is not now in Lahore. How it would gladden his heart to see, once again, one towards whom he entertained such warm and friendly emotions. But never matter. He will soon return for he must prepare himself for the Durbar, and how great will be his joy when I tell him that Bunter Sahib is to be found in the house of the late and lamented Colonel Huggins.' Here he suddenly changed his bantering tone to something a deal more businesslike. 'For, Bunter Sahib, you will, of course, remain in this house awaiting his return. Should you wish, however, to take the dawn or evening air, my sowars, who will be at every entrance, and exit, will escort you.'

The Calcutta chokey, or even Thukoor and Coker, would have been better than having to wait for Runjeet Singh. I can put up with a deal of maltreatment, but the thought of a series of tête-à-tête with him made me shudder. The Treasurer saw this, smiled, took my arm and said gently:

'Meanwhile, my dear, you and I must discuss the problem

of a certain pearl necklace and ruby ring. You will remember
that you forgot to return them to His Highness when you so
suddenly terminated your last stay in Lahore.'

I looked over his shoulder and was relieved to see Maria
whip the trinkets and purse into a placket in her petticoat.
That having been done I rose, I'm glad to say, to the
occasion.

'Those tokens of His Highness's esteem, O Nana Singh, I
still treasure.'

He looked disappointed. 'Could it not be, Bunter Sahib,
that you have discovered you no longer have those pearls? The
ruby is no great matter, but I, who have ever been a lover of
such things, greatly admired the pearls.'

'Then you shall admire them once again when I pay my
respects to Runjeet Singh.'

'Doubtless,' said he, 'you now regret not having done so
when you first received them.'

'That will lie between His Highness and myself.'

'And that,' he snapped, 'is why you will stay here until he
returns. And Huggins Begum will stay with you until everything in this house has been inventoried and handed over to
the Maharajah's Treasurer who is, of course, myself.'

Maria bristled at this. 'Those who are plundered by
dacoits,' she said, almost spitting in her anger, 'have no choice
but to wait until the plundering is completed. But when your
dacoits have done their work, Nana Singh, what happens to
me?'

I thought she was being needlessly defiant. But something
resembling a glint of admiration crept into Nana Singh's
rheumy old eyes.

'Truly,' he said, 'you are a tigress amongst women and
deserving of a more tigerish mate than the late Colonel
Huggins. Ah, were I but younger . . .'

'But you ain't, for which I'm thankful.'

'Were I but younger,' he went on, quite ignoring the inter-
ruption, 'I would claim you for myself. His Highness would
not deny me. But, alas, my household is already full of women
I can no longer service, so it will be left to His Highness to
decide which of his followers is most worthy of so much fire,
courage and solid beauty in his zenana.'

'That's as may be,' said Maria. 'But until then, and bananas or no bananas, just you bugger off out of this house and take your fat tipstaff and your tatty soldiers with you.'

I shuddered, but he came mighty close to crowing his admiration.

'When I was younger and more virile,' he said, tugging at his straggly white beard, 'there were three things I prized above all others. The first was a fast and willing horse, the second a docile and plump-cheeked boy, and the third a spirited woman such as you, Huggins Begum. But now, alas, I mount only the first of these. How I wish I were young again. Do not forget, O moon of vain desiring, that there will be men at every door to this house.'

He motioned to the baboo and went out, calling to the sowars to follow him.

Maria and I were left looking at each other.

'I'll kill myself,' she said stoutly, 'before I go into one of their bananas.'

'And I,' I said, though rather less stoutly, 'will kill myself also before I let myself become the Maharajah's bum-boy.'

'Quite right,' said Maria. 'Spoken like a true Briton. Do you realise, Billy, that we now stand as representatives of our race before these bloody heathens?'

Statements like that put a bit of backbone into a chap. For the first time in my life I felt terrified but still vaguely heroic. It may have been the influence of Garrick, but I took up a posture seldom bettered in Drury Lane.

'It's only you I worry about Maria. If only I'd been able to place you under the protection of Ponsonby-Harris—but there! 'Tis but a vain imagining. I cannot get you out of this vile imprisonment.'

'You're talking very oddly, Billy. In fact there's a very easy way out which no one is guarding. D'Arcy may have been too cunning for his own good. That was why he was given to the elephants. But he was still cunning enough to provide an emergency exit in case of need. It's a tunnel that leads from the cellar to a well in the bottom of the garden, and I'm sure they won't have put a sentry over an old, disused well.'

'In that case you must put on Indian clothes, escape out of

that emergency exit, and make your way to Ponsonby-Harris. He's just outside the South Gate.'

'But what about you?'

The Garrick mood was still upon me. 'You must not worry about me, Maria. Ponsonby-Harris can give you protection. But he cannot do anything for me without angering the Maharajah and endangering the Durbar. I shall know what to do, when the moment comes.'

'Don't be silly. You can get away from here without having to go to Ponsonby-Harris, if you don't think he could help.'

'How? As Billy Bunter? As Father Mecazinas? How far from here do you think I'd get?'

'You really are being very stupid. You don't need to escape as either.'

'Then what do you suggest I escape as?'

'Did you notice the baboo-fellow who read out the warrant?'

'A very nasty-looking, dirty, half-naked sort of chap, I thought.'

'If you were stained brown, and wore nothing but a dhoti, a turban and your spectacles, you would look not unlike him. He has a similar belly to yours.'

I abandoned Garrick and heroism immediately.

'Do you really think I'd get away with it?'

'It's worth a try. Anything's better than waiting here. What you've got to think about is where you'll go to once you've got out of here.'

The Bunter brain was now working furiously, and I'd got the answer to that before she'd even posed the problem.

'The Bishop and I, when we were on tour, were most kindly received at Sumroo. At least it's not ruled by a sodomitical Raja, but by a very learned and thoroughly pious Begum. I'm sure she'd give me shelter.'

'Then I shall find a sari and a chuddha for myself and a dhoti for you. It's fortunate that we made a lot of walnut chutney this year. It will make an ideal stain.'

'Do you think you could find me one of those striped cotton waistcoats as well? I haven't really got the figure for going around dressed only in a dhoti. Besides, I'd need a deal of walnut chutney if I had to be stained all over.'

'The servants all fled in such a hurry after the elephant business, grabbing what they could of our goods, that I'm sure they left enough of their own behind to provide us with all the clothes we will need.'

And so they had. We waited until it began to grow dark before Maria and I put on our Indian clothes, she first having daubed me liberally with walnut chutney. Then—she in her sari and chuddha and I in my dhoti and striped vest—crept down to the cellar.

Romantic novelists seem to think it's a simple matter for their heroes to break out of prisons through tunnels they've dug out with a bent spoon and their fingernails. But getting through tunnels, even properly built ones, ain't at all like that. Leastways not for the people built like Maria and myself, especially as D'Arcy, a skinny and fundamentally selfish man, hadn't even considered Maria when he'd had his tunnel made.

It was, so far as we were concerned, a slow and often painful business wriggling along that dark, hot, and excessively skimpy hole and long before we'd got to the end of it, I was very conscious of the strong smell of vinegar and spices that was rising from me. And to judge from the grunts and wheezes arising from Maria, who was close at my heels, so was she. And all the time I was cursing myself for not having enquired from Maria whether there was any water left in the well.

Fortunately there was none. But the well shaft stretched a full twenty feet above the floor, and the only way up was by means of a few slabs of stone the masons had left projecting to form a sort of ladder to the outer world. I couldn't turn round to talk to Maria, so I gave her a good kick to indicate that she should stop where she was until I'd reconnoitred, and I then wriggled my way into the shaft until I was able to stand upright and begin my ascent.

I made good progress until I was standing on the last of the slabs and was head and shoulders above the well-coping. But Indian workmen, being thin little men, seldom build for those of my weight. Most of the slab I stood on suddenly collapsed just as I was putting on my spectacles in order to look around.

It was only by clinging to the coping that I avoided falling back down on top of Maria who had already given a hearty howl as part of the falling slab hit her.

So there I was, with only my fingertips holding me up, whilst the rest of me was scrabbling inside the well to find something that would support me and stones were clattering down. Maria was howling and I was wondering what would happen to her if I let go. It was then that I heard footsteps and chatter and saw, just over the edge of the coping to which I clung, the tops of two pairs of red-leather riding boots such as sowars wear.

I've often read that, when men are thoroughly frightened, their bowels turn to water. That ain't true. What actually happens is that their bellies rumble. My rumbles added grace notes to Maria's howls and the clatter of stones.

'Aiee, brother,' said one of the pairs of boots. 'Those are strange noises that rise from the ground. Think you the spirit of he who was torn apart by the elephants has come here to haunt us?'

The other pair of boots sniggered at this.

'The only spirit, you drunken fool, is that which you drank when we were searching the cursed Feringhi's house by order of Nana Singh. The only noises I hear are such as would be made by a mongoose down a snake-hole.'

'Never, brother, have I heard a mongoose that sounded like a woman wailing.'

'You have women on the brain, which is why every sound you hear reminds you of them, O lecherous one.'

The lecherous one laughed at this.

'What can there be better to think of on sentry duty than women? Did you not, my brother, feel your pizzle stir at the sight of the Feringhi woman we guard? There, indeed, was a handful of fine pink flesh more exciting than anything that can be found in the brothels of Lahore. Think you we shall, in due course, be permitted to pleasure her?'

'That Feringhi drink has addled your brains. We are but sowars. The naik comes before us, the havildar before the naik, and the jemadar before the havildar. And think you that Nana Singh, or even his baboo, would allow such delights to pass down to them, let alone to such as you and me?'

'You are right, my brother. The poor bloody trooper comes last to the pickings.'

If I had not found with one foot a crevice in the masonry that could take part of my weight I would, before this, have fallen. As it was my fingers were slipping from the coping, they not being designed to take the rest of my not inconsiderable weight for long. But then, to my relief, I heard the second pair of boots say:

'Come, I have hidden that bottle of Feringhi brandee from which you drank under the bushes where the naik cannot discover it. More if it will take your mind off the plump pink woman you dribble about. And when we come off guard, you can take that pizzle of yours to the whores in the bazaar and so work off your fantasies.'

As I eased myself on to the coping, after much scrabbling, I could see the two of them, in the darkening distance, walking away, hand in hand, towards the solace of that stolen brandy bottle. Then, to my horror, my rumbling belly vented itself in a fart of truly mammoth sonority. One of them stopped and looked round, and I froze into the coping as a lizard does into a rock. They argued for a moment, but the one who wished to turn back was chided by the other for still imagining that he heard a woman's voice issuing from the ground, although it would indeed have been a bull-voiced woman who could have produced such a note. In the end they went off again, arguing companionably with one another, and I lay panting and sweating and full of a strange elation. I had never, until then, thought of myself as a man of action, but that, oddly enough, was what I was having to be.

Part of that action now had to consist of getting Maria out of the well, and how I managed to do that I can still scarcely explain, though I do remember making a rope of sorts out of my dhoti and turban knotted together. Eventually Maria rose up like a substantial ghost from out of the ground, and the two of us lay there, in the shadow of the well, until we had recovered. And a damned odd sight we must have been, for Maria was panting like a grampus and I, until I dressed myself again, must have looked, what with the stained and the unstained parts of me, very like an Essex saddleback pig.

It seemed as though we had spent hours in that tunnel and

well, but the South Gate of the city was still open and the market people were still returning through it to their villages when we, mingling with them, passed through unnoticed. Once we were clear, I drew Maria into the shelter of a mango tope, pointed out where Ponsonby-Harris's encampment lay, and took my farewell of her. She was, by now, completely recovered and a good deal less jittery than I was. She gave me a quick, bearlike hug, said, 'See you in Coram Street, partner,' and went shuffling off down the road.

I waited until she had disappeared from sight and then followed her, for the road didn't branch off towards Sumroo until well past Ponsonby-Harris's camp. Like a fool, I took the crown of the road and was nearly ridden down by a band of horsemen who passed me, riding hell-for-leather. The leader snarled at me to get out of the way, and it was only then that I realised he was Hurree Ram Thukoor, who was indeed followed by half a dozen of the most villainous-looking cut-throats that India could produce. Riding some way behind them and hallooing to them to stop came Coker.

I drew into the shade at the side of the road, but they took no notice of me as Hurree and his cut-throats pulled up and waited for Coker.

'It ain't any good chasing down this road,' said he. 'If Bunter's anywhere in this area he'll still be in Lahore. At any rate, my horse is foundering, so we'd best turn back and spend the night in the city.'

After a little arguing, turn back they did. It was then I noticed that Coker rode lop-sided in the saddle. As they disappeared towards Lahore I said to myself:

'There ain't a horse in the whole of India that won't be given a sore back by that lop-arsed ruffian.'

And with that cheering thought I trudged off towards the road that led to Sumroo.

Now that Gurmakh Singh has departed I have decided that this must be the last of my scribblings. They have occupied many days and nights that would otherwise have been devoted to funk and frustration, but they still have not revealed to me the first cause of my former and present miseries. All that I have been able to fasten on is that the size of my pecker has contributed to every one of my misfortunes.

Be that as it may, I am no longer concerned to discover how and why I got here. What worries me is how I am to get *out* of here.

When Gurmakh Singh came in with my food a couple of hours ago there was something unusual about both the meal and his demeanour. The first was hidden, for the first time, under a great dish cover. But his manner was one of nervous excitement.

'Ismail Khan,' he said, 'has at last been paid for his horses and departed. Yet he is no more than a shadow of the man who came to Sumroo only two moons ago.'

'I can guess what the poor man endured, and wonder that he endured it so long.'

'Poor man indeed, yet not so poor as he might have been. He lasted longer than most, and for that reason alone the Begum had less reason to quarrel with him. So she gave him an almost fair price for his remounts and bade him return with more of the same breed after he himself had summered on his native uplands, as his stallions do, and had like those same stallions, recovered condition.'

This was sad news, for I knew that even stallions took many months to recuperate. So I said:

'The Begum, Gurmakh Singh, is no mare to take eleven months between services. Whom will she send for as a bed-mate whilst Ismail Khan is getting back into condition?'

'Who—and how many—will be sent for before then no one

can foretell. But it is said that for tomorrow night it will be Bunter Sahib who will undergo trial gallops.'

'Trial gallops! I would be hard put to it to break into more than a few trots in my present debilitated state.'

'If that be so, then they could be your last trots on earth. Yet it need not be so if you have a few gallops left in you.'

'A few gallops? How would they serve her who demands night after night of split-arse galloping?'

'I speak only of one night, my Lord. That could suffice.'

'Do not go round and ever round the subject like a blindfold ass harnessed to a water-wheel. What are you trying to say to me?'

'When lives are at risk wise men proceed prudently. They do not let their thoughts come hot off their tongues. There are plans to be made, precautions to be taken, and . . . bargains to be struck.'

'Bargains? What bargains?'

'You have often spoken to me, Excellency, of your longing to return to your own country.'

'What of that?'

'If your servant—and others—were to help you achieve what you long for, what would you say to them?'

'I would say it is impossible. The country outside swarms with those who want either to kill me or bugger me. The ports from which ships sail to my country are many hundreds of cos from here and are watched by those who, if they caught me, would throw me into prison. And I cannot move one step from this room without being followed by a guard.'

'Yet there is always a long way home as well as a short one. Again I ask you. What would you say to your servant if he put you on it?'

'I would say that he had earned Bunter Sahib's undying gratitude.'

'Gratitude, Sahib, is like the mist over the mountain-tops. It comes and it goes.'

'I'm penniless and a fugitive, Gurmakh Singh. I have no money to offer.'

'I ask not for money, though money will be needed. That is something we will have to consider. What I do ask, ere we go one word further, is that you accept our conditions.'

'I'll accept anything—within reason of course—if it will
get me away from here and back to Bilatee. What are your
conditions?'

'I am not alone in this. My sister's daughters-in-law are
involved. You will understand what dangers we risk in even
making these plans. Nowhere in India would be safe for us
should the Begum discover the part we would play.'

'Then what would you have me do?'

'I have heard, Sahib, that England is a fine, rich country,
and one in which industrious Sikhs may prosper. Will you
swear that, if we bring you to a ship that can take you home,
you will take us with you to England?'

'If there be such a place and such a ship, and if there be
money for the fares, then I do swear. But England, Gurmakh
Singh, is a cold and wet place, and not everyone there
prospers.'

'We Sikhs, Sahib, would prosper even in the middle of a
desert.'

'You are indeed a brave and energetic people. But you
spoke, I believe, of conditions, and have mentioned but one.'

'I, my Lord, desire only your safety and happiness. My
sister's daughters-in-law, not having enjoyed the delights of
your company, are not moved, as I am, by love for your
Honour. What they want is to be avenged on her who had
their husband boiled in oil. Will you swear to help them to
their revenge?'

'Not if it means murdering the Begum, I won't. For one
thing I ain't much good at murder. And for another I'd be cut
into little pieces just as soon as I'd done it.'

'Murder, Bunter Sahib, is not the only or the sweetest
revenge.'

'Glad to hear it. What then is it that your sister's daughters-
in-law have in mind?'

'The Begum's randiness, as you know, has brought misery
and mourning to many. They would cure her of that randiness.'

'Then they plan the impossible. The Begum will go randy
to her grave, and if, as the Prophet has said, there is fornicating in Paradise, she will weary the best part of its male
inhabitants.'

'There are those, most of them Baluchis, whose work it is to lead camel caravans across the deserts. If the journey be one of many months, they will have difficulties with the she-camels.'

'What is this talk of camels? We were speaking but now of a cure for randiness.'

'Let my Lord have patience with his servant and allow him, for a moment, to talk of she-camels. They come on heat but once in a twelvemonth, but when they do they are, for a time, unfit either to ride or as beasts of burden. They also upset all the male camels. It is, your Honour will agree, something to be avoided when in the middle of the desert.'

'This talk of camels would be interesting to men talking around the cooking fire in a serai, but it does not seem what we should be talking about now.'

'The Baluchis, who know more about camels, Bunter Sahib, than any other people, being almost camels themselves, have a drug prepared according to a secret formula. This they sometimes sell, for it is worth its weight in silver, and is of inestimable value to those who have to travel with camels.'

I began to get interested. I remembered how Mahtab's eye-drug had once saved my skin. If one of these Indian concoctions had worked for me, why should not another?

'Tell me, Gurmakh Singh, the purpose of this drug.'

'If it is given in the correct quantities to a she-camel at the start of a long journey you can be sure that she will not come on heat for the next twenty-four months. What is more, should a male camel approach her with a view of mounting her, she will savage and tear him and chase him away. It is truly a terrible sight for any man to witness.'

'And what,' said I, beginning to see what he was at, 'what if some of that drug be given to a woman?'

'Lightning itself is not quicker than your Honour's mind. There are those, it is said, who have indeed tried it on their wives in order to ensure that they do not look lasciviously at other men whilst the husband is away for such long periods as will test a woman's chastity.'

'And does it work with such women?'

'Alas! Such is the power of the drug that there is no certainty about it when it is given to humans.'

This was not what I had expected.

'Then it does not prevent randiness in women? Surely, if it works to that effect with a she-camel . . .'

'Now you go too fast, Bunter Sahib. It does indeed work with women but, whatever the dose there is no certainty that it will work for no more than twenty-four months.'

'It lasts longer?'

'Sometimes it works for the whole of a woman's breeding life. The Baluchis speak of travellers who, after long months from their homes, return to embraces they have dreamt of whilst crossing the deserts, only to find every form of marital bliss denied them for ever.'

'They must be faint-hearted husbands who accept that.'

'Those who have tried to force the issue have carried, they say, the scars of that encounter to their graves.'

No one should describe me as a devotee of jigajig. Nor did I owe the Begum anything, having already paid dearly for my house and board. Nevertheless this seemed a rather beastly thing to do to her. But, since it was, apparently, the price the daughters-in-law demanded for their collaboration, it had to be paid. So I said:

'If I guessed that the daughters-in-law have acquired some of that camel drug from the Baluchis, would I be wrong?'

'Yesterday you would have been right. But today you are indeed wrong, for I have the drug with me.'

He felt inside his cummerbund and extracted a small phial which he handed to me. I took it reluctantly.

'What would you and the daughters-in-law have me do with this?'

'The nights are warm at this time of year. Tomorrow night, when the Begum sends for you, your Honour must summon up so much ardour, gallop her so long and so often, that the two of you will, in the end, suffer from thirst. It is known that she always has a pitcher of wine cooling in a bowl of snow by her bedside to meet such occasions.'

'That at least is true, Gurmakh Singh. Often have I had to pour from that pitcher for her.'

'This time, when you have reduced her to panting for wine and you rise to pour it, you will see that the Begum's goblet holds the contents of this phial.'

'That's all very well. But will she not then turn on me and savage me as the she-camel does the male?'

'As soon as the drug is given to the she-camel, she becomes unconscious for at least three hours. This is a camel-sized dose and the Begum is not one-fifth the size of even the smallest camel. She should sleep peacefully for ten times three hours.'

That, it seemed, dealt with the daughters-in-law's revenge, but it did nothing to deal with Bunter's escape. And so, for the next hour, Gurmakh Singh outlined his plans for that, whilst I kept raising objections and he kept countering them. Plan, objection and counter-objection ran roughly as follows:

My first task, once I had successfully drugged the Begum, would be to pocket the jewellery she always took off and placed on a table before going to bed.

'For,' said Gurmakh Singh, 'your Honour knows that she will wear nothing but a nose-stud in bed for fear of her bangles and anklets and necklaces rattling during the jigajig. It is necessary that we acquire those trinkets to help pay for our flight.'

'What flight?' said I. 'All you have arranged is that I should drug and rob the Begum, for which I shall pay dear when she wakes up . . .'

He bade me be patient and listen.

'Once she is asleep and dreaming, I trust, of camels and once you have pocketed the jewellery you will, for the benefit of the guards outside, bid her good night in tones they can hear. Then you shall return here, where I shall be waiting for you.'

'And will you be waiting thirty hours later when she has awoken and has already ordered the oil to be heated?'

'Not at all,' he said and went into procedure. The sentry who guarded my quarters would be sleeping, having had something slipped into a flask of wine which Gurmakh Singh, in a comradely spirit, would have shared with him. This would allow the two of us to creep to the kitchens which had a gate leading to a lane outside the palace walls. That gate was never guarded because it was kept locked to prevent the cooks smuggling out food. On this occasion, however, it would be unlocked, and outside in the lane there would be a tilted hackery and the bullocks to pull it. Gurmakh Singh would act as driver, and I would be inside the cart, along with the daughters-in-law, all three of us concealed from sight by the tilt.

Now a bullock cart is a mighty slow form of transport and, although Sumroo is a pocket handkerchief sort of State, the Punjaub is vast and the rest of India even vaster. All of this I pointed out to Gurmakh Singh, to which he replied that two days' journey, along jungle tracks would take us out of Sumroo, after which we would be just another of the thousands of bullock carts plodding slowly along the roads of India.

'And soon,' he said, 'we shall be in those parts of the Punjaub which are inhabited by Muslims, may they and their Prophet be for ever accursed.'

'How will that benefit us?'

'To get to Bilatee, Sahib, I, Gurmakh Singh, will do what few Sikhs would do. I shall travel as a Muslim. And, what is more, I shall wear a green turban.'

'Will that act as a protection?'

'The green turban will show that I am a Hadji and have already made the pilgrimage to Mecca. If I am asked why I travel now, I shall explain that I would undertake that pilgrimage again, but this time with my three wives, and every Muslim knows that to molest those who undertake the Hadj is to condemn oneself to Gehenna in the hereafter.'

'You mention three wives, Gurmakh Singh?'

He whipped off the dish cover to reveal a bundle of black clothes. These, when I examined them, constituted a complete set of garments, from pantaloons to the veil and the all-enshrouding chaddoor, such as a lower-class Muslim woman of stoutish build might wear. He waved at them and said:

'My Lord must, for the purposes of the plan, become my Lady.'

I'd already done a bit of masquerading since I'd fled from Calcutta, but I was very dubious about being a woman and said so.

'I have already dressed up as an Armenian priest and down as a Bengalee baboo, but never yet have I played the transvestite. Think you, Gurmakh Singh, that I could pass as a woman?'

'As a Muslim woman, certainly, so long as the Sahib remembers to squat when he should and takes care, as I shall, to show nothing that is uncircumcised. For what is a Muslim woman, when she travels abroad, but a bundle of clothing?'

'Yet even a bundle of clothing in a bullock cart will be exposed to dangers during the months that will be spent on the road. How can an aged Sikh posing as a Hadji, Bunter posing as a woman and the two daughters-in-law prevent our being stopped, robbed, and murdered by dacoits, Thugs, Pindaris, and all the other cut-throats who look for such easy prey?'

'That, Bunter Sahib, is where the Begum's jewellery comes into it.'

'It merely makes us the better worth robbing.'

'Not so. Three of my brethren who serve, as I once served, in the forces of John Company, are even now on long furlough in my village. They have, as is the custom, brought their arms with them, and I still possess the Brown Bessy I carried in my day. That makes four armed men, and such are seldom attacked.'

'Do those brethren also wish to go to Bilatee? Soon there will be more Sikhs there than natives.'

'They are simple men with no desire to leave India. But, in return for the Begum's jewellery, they are willing to accompany us until we reach the banks of the Indus.'

'Why there?'

However improbable it seemed that we should ever reach the Indus his reasons for travelling half-way across India in order to get there seemed, and seem, logical enough. That river runs, for much of its navigable length, through Sinde, which is Muslim territory whose rulers have little liking for the East India Company. I would not, therefore, be handed over to the authorities in Calcutta even if I was revealed as Bunter the runaway. There are several ports in the great delta known as The Mouths of the Indus and of these Kurachee is the one from which pilgrims normally take ship for Jiddah on their way to Mecca. Consequently there would be nothing suspicious if we, as ostensible pilgrims, hired a river craft that would take us to Kurachee, one with covered accommodation suitable for Muslim women in purdah.

But the chief advantage of Kurachee was that the East India Company's monopoly over shipping and trade did not operate in Sinde, and such British vessels as touched there would not be East Indiamen. The captains of these could be persuaded to provide passage for Bunter, Gurmakh Singh and the daughters-in-law if adequately rewarded, whereas the captain of an East Indiaman would promptly have me thrown into chokey.

The question of paying for our passage, however, still worried me.

'You have dreamed dreams, Gurmakh Singh,' I said, 'and they may even come true and all four of us may reach Kurachee. But have you thought of the money we shall need to get there and the even greater sums needed if we are to take passage to Bilatee? It will take months to get from here to the Indus. We must eat, as must the bullocks. We cannot hire a river boat for nothing, and the Begum's jewellery, you remember, pays for your brethren the sepoys.'

'Ours is a poor family, Huzoor, but I have put some small sums of money by. To these I have recently added larger sums paid to me by your enemies.'

'What mean you by that?'

'Both the Maharajah and the bunniah Thukoor have offered rewards for information as to your whereabouts. I received two hundred rupees from the one for telling him that you had joined a caravan bound for Kabul, and seventy rupees from the other—those bunniahs are always mean in such matters—for telling him that you had disguised yourself as an Armenian fakir and were even now on your way to Khatmandu. Besides this, the daughters-in-law have turned such jewellery as they possess into cash. These sums you will, of course, repay us when we reach Bilatee, for they will have been expended in Your Honour's service.'

I didn't much like this for, if he had sold me false to the Maharajah and Thukoor, what was to prevent him from selling me true? But he looked so pleased with himself whilst he told me this that I dared not raise the subject. Instead I removed the Duke's miniature from around my neck and gave it to him.

'This also is worth money.'

Like most Indians, Gurmakh Singh knew a good deal about trinkets, and so he examined it closely.

'The gold weighs well,' he said, 'but the diamonds are of little value and the portrait within is marvellously ugly. Is it of some English Lord?'

'It is of the brother to King Georgey himself.'

'I have ever thought, Bunter Sahib, that one as well-hung, as fat, and as ugly as you must be of the blood of kings, and this portrait proves it.'

'Maybe it does and maybe it doesn't. But if the painting offends you because of its ugliness, you may remove it and sell only the case.'

He handed it back to me and said, 'Ugly though it is, the picture of such a great man will surely prove better to us than money when we come to persuading a ship's captain to carry us to Bilatee. He who carries such a portrait round his neck must himself be a person of note. So keep it, Bunter Sahib, as our passport to Bilatee.'

By this time we had discussed the whole wildly impossible scheme exhaustively, and Gurmakh Singh had come close to persuading me that it was improbable rather than impossible. And whether it was the one or the other, it was still, as he pointed out, better than the alternative I was facing. For if I did not escape from Sumroo within twenty-four hours it was very probable that I'd be galloped to exhaustion by the Begum prior to being handed over to Runjeet Singh to be galloped by him in a different manner.

Once he had got me to agree that this was, unfortunately, the case, he made me rehearse for my role as a Muslim woman of the lower class. He had me put on the garments he had brought and made me waddle around in them until I could do so without tripping over myself. He looked at me whilst I was doing this and suddenly smote his forehead in near despair and said:

'Something is missing.'

'What is missing?'

'Breasts. You slope too gradually to your belly, and surely a woman with a belly such as yours would have breasts of a similar amplitude.'

His eyes then fell on the heap of papers on which so many

weeks of scribbling have been recorded. He went to a closet and returned with a pair of the stockings I wear with my riding boots and a pugree. He divided the heap in two, put one half in each sock, tied the socks to the pugree with string, and so produced a pair of false boobs of truly impressive proportions. Once they had been attached to my chest by means of the pugree and my robe had been pulled down over this superstructure, I rustled a bit when I breathed, but the overall effect seemed to satisfy him. He stood in the door to look at me before departing and chuckled in his beard.

'Wallahi—which is how we Muslims swear—a woman as well-endowed as any of the houris we Muslims dream of.'

Since he departed I have expanded a little the boobs he so admired, for these last pages have been added to all that had been scribbled before. On this final page I want to record the fact that I tremble, now, between hope and funk. Funk keeps telling me that my situation is a hopeless one. I shall not even be able to raise a gallop for the Begum when she sends for me, let alone rattle her into a thirst. She will see me drugging her drink or fail to succumb to it, or turn round and savage me. The guard on my quarters will fail to fall asleep and I shall still be there, dressed as a woman, when the Begum awakes. If Gurmakh Singh does get me out, it will only be in order to sell me to either Runjeet Singh or Thukoor. If we get away from Sumroo we shall have our throats cut by dacoits. If we get to the Indus our bhotiah will sink. If we get to Kurachee it will be discovered that I'm a man, and an uncircumcised one at that. If we get on an English boat it will be attacked by pirates and I will be made to walk the plank.

And yet, what I am really saying to myself at this moment is 'In for a penny, in for a pound'. For there is also the luck of the Bunters, and we must trust to it.

EPILOGUE

I have, since my release from the Fleet prison, been arranging my affairs, for it is possible that I must, once again, travel abroad. Whilst doing so I came across this pile of stained and crumpled papers. It is some three years, now, since I sat scribbling them in Sumroo and then carried them in my bosom across the breadth of India. Heaven knows what author's vanity then led me to carry them back to England despite my determination never again to place myself in a position where I would once more have to resort to scribbling.

Yet they may still have a purpose. I seldom think of myself as the descendant of my ancestors, whoever they might have been. But it is perhaps right that I should begin to think of myself as the ancestor of my descendants, of whom there are now several. Besides those I left behind me in India there are those Maria has borne me each year in addition to the two coffee-coloured Bunters born to the daughters-in-law of Gurmakh Singh's sister. For what two sturdy Sikh widows demanded of Bunter in the back of a covered hackery during the months when we made our slow way to Kurachee produced results which, although inevitable, were far from being desired by their victim.

In short, as I am now beginning to accumulate descendants, I feel a duty to leave them some record of my Indian adventures. They could, in due course, be of as much interest to them as my grandfather's Notes about the Waterloo Pie were to me. But, as I feel no temptation to go scribbling again, I shall deal with the rest of that story as I deal with a business letter.

a) Improbable as it seemed at the time, the four of us arrived eventually in Kurachee whence we took ship for England. Six of us landed.

b) Those six ended up in Coram Street, for I no longer had any family in England and I thought Mr Wilberforce too old by now for the daughters-in-law and the coffee-coloured Bunters.

c) Maria did not greatly approve of them either. But after she had recovered from the initial shock, she took me into the front parlour and proudly placed on the table all Mahtab's stolen jewellery, Runjeet Singh's pearls, and Harry's golden mohurs. The dear girl had sold no more than the ruby ring to pay for her passage to England, and had, in the intervening years, steadfastly refused to dissipate what she at once referred to as partnership property. What could I do in the face of such fidelity but marry her, which was, of course, exactly what she expected me to do?

d) With the proceeds from the sale of that jewellery I set myself up in my first business venture. What it should be was already decided for me as I had Gurmakh Singh and the daughters-in-law to provide for besides myself and Maria. So, remembering how industrious all Sikhs were, and remembering also how, in India, customers could buy and carry away from almost any roadside stall a portion of rice and curry wrapped in a banyan leaf, I opened the first carry-away curry stall seen in London. This went so well—my compatriots seemed more than ready for such a convenient method of feeding themselves—that I soon embarked on a whole string of such stalls. It was my brother-in-law and old school chum, J.J., who eventually secured my release from the Fleet prison where I had been most unfairly incarcerated by my creditors.

e) My descendants must not expect more from me in the way of scribbling as I now set about repairing the Bunter fortunes.